Praise for the novels of Naima Simone

"Simone balances crackling, electric love scenes with exquisitely rendered characters."
—*Entertainment Weekly*

"Passion, heat and deep emotion—Naima Simone is a gem!"
—*New York Times* bestselling author Maisey Yates

"Simone never falters in mining the complexity of two people who grow and heal and eventually love together."
—*New York Times* bestselling author Sarah MacLean

"Small-town charm, a colorful cast, and a hero to root for give this romance its legs as it moves toward a hard-earned happily ever after. [This] slow-burning romance is well worth the wait."
—*Publishers Weekly* on *The Road to Rose Bend*

"I am a huge Naima Simone fan. With her stories, she has the ability to transport you to places you can only dream of, with characters who have a realness to them."
—*Read Your Writes*

"[Naima Simone] excels at creating drama and emotional scenes as well as strong heroines who are resilient survivors."
—*Harleq...*

NAIMA SIMONE

Christmas in Rose Bend

HQN

ISBN-13: 978-1-335-62099-6

Christmas in Rose Bend
Copyright © 2021 by Harlequin Books S.A.

Christmas in Rose Bend
Copyright © 2021 by Naima Simone

A Kiss to Remember
Copyright © 2021 by Naima Simone

Recycling programs for this product may not exist in your area.

This edition published by arrangement with Harlequin Books S.A.

For questions and comments about the quality of this book, please contact us at CustomerService@Harlequin.com.

HQN
22 Adelaide St. West, 40th Floor
Toronto, Ontario M5H 4E3, Canada
www.Harlequin.com

Printed and bound in Barcelona, Spain by CPI Black Print

CONTENTS

Christmas in
Rose Bend

To Gary. 143. Forever.

To Connie Marie Butts.
I think it's appropriate that I'm dedicating this
Christmas book to you. From the time I can remember,
you made this holiday magical. A child's joy-filled
fantasy. So much that I strived to give my own children
the same, but I still don't think I ever matched what
you gave us. You set an impossibly high bar. Even to
the last one. It's still hard to believe that I'll never have
another Christmas with you. Another day. Another moment
where I hear your voice, your laughter, your words of
wisdom or even your patient silence that
said just as much. I'll miss you every day of my life,
and I'll love you even more. This book, and every book,
I dedicate to you, who always believed in me,
supported me, was so proud of me and loved me.
No daughter could've asked for a better mother,
best friend, champion, counselor...my everything.
I love you, Connie.

CHAPTER ONE

NESSA HUNT DIDN'T do Christmas.

As an ER nurse, she'd seen the worst humanity had to offer during the holiday season. Electrocution injuries from plugging one too many Christmas lights into a single outlet. Shoppers with broken noses and blackened eyes from Black Friday fights that erupted over the newest must-have toy. Dads with busted backs from attempting to mount inflatable Frosties and reindeer-drawn sleighs on porch roofs.

And then there'd been that one memorable sex toy mishap—Santa had boldly gone where no Santa had gone before.

So, no, she was not a fan of Christmas.

Which meant the town of Rose Bend, Massachusetts, was her own personal version of hell.

"It looks like Santa Claus just threw up all over this place!" her sister, Ivy, whispered from the passenger seat.

Now, there was a nice visual. But slowing to a halt at a stoplight, Nessa had to admit the twelve-year-old had a point. Who knew that three hours north of Boston and tucked in the southern Berkshires existed a town straight out of a Thomas Kinkade painting? It seemed almost... unreal. If any place had that everybody-knows-your-name vibe, it was Rose Bend. Brick buildings housing drugstores, boutiques, a candy store, an ice cream parlor and diners lined the road. The long white steeple of a church towered in the distance. A colonial-style building stood in the center of town, the words Town Hall emblazoned above four columns. And everything was decorated with lights, garland, poinsettias, candy canes and big red bows. Even the stoplights sported huge wreaths decked out with miniature toys and elves—and the biggest pine cones she'd ever seen in her life.

Mom would've lost her mind over all this.

The thought snuck out of the steel door in her mind where she'd locked away all wayward, crippling memories of Evelyn Reed. A blazing pain stabbed Nessa in the chest, and she sucked in a breath. Briefly, she closed her eyes, blocking out the winter wonderland beyond her windshield.

It had been eight long, lonely, bitter months since she'd lost her mother to uterine cancer. Since she'd last heard her mother's pragmatic but affectionate voice that still held a faint Southern accent, even though she'd lived in Boston for over thirty years. Since she'd inhaled her mother's comforting roses-and-fresh-laundry scent.

Since her mother had rasped a devastating secret in a whisper thick with regret, edged with pain and slurred from morphine.

Maybe the well-meaning friends who'd advised Nessa to see a grief counselor could also counsel her on how to stop being so goddamn *angry* with her mother for lying to Nessa for twenty-eight years. Maybe then Nessa could start to heal.

'Til then, she had patients to care for. Now she had a sister to raise.

And secrets to keep.

"Oh wow!" Ivy squealed, jabbing the window with a finger. "There's a real town square and over there is the biggest Christmas tree I've ever seen! Can we get out and walk around? Please?"

Nessa glanced in the direction Ivy pointed, taking in the square, and in the distance, a massive tree. The idea of strolling around in the freezing weather to stare at a Douglas fir wasn't exactly her idea of fun. But when she'd agreed to make this trip with Ivy, Nessa had told herself to make an effort to connect. This was supposed to be about bonding with the sister she barely knew.

Emptiness spread through her and the greasy slide of guilt and pain flooded into the hole. She glanced at Ivy, Nessa's gaze lingering over the features they shared…but didn't. The high cheekbones that dominated a face Ivy hadn't yet grown into. The thin shoulders that had become even thinner in the last six weeks, since her father had died.

A scream welled up inside Nessa, scraping her throat raw. Ivy's father—Isaac Hunt—was the man who had raised Nessa until he and her mother divorced when she'd been about Ivy's age, and then he'd been more out of her life than in it. He had named Nessa as his daughter's guardian. He had trusted Nessa to care for Ivy, because she was his oldest daughter and Ivy's half sister. And though she and Isaac hadn't shared a close relationship when he'd been alive, she couldn't let him down. And Ivy…

Ivy had lost her mother as a baby, and now her father. Nessa knew what it was like to be alone. She couldn't take Ivy's sister away, too.

Even if Ivy resented the hell out of Nessa and begrudged her guardianship with every breath she took.

But God… Months of bearing a secret weighed on Nessa's shoulders. And they ached. These last six weeks had been a special kind of hell.

She was so damn tired.

Inhaling a deep breath, Nessa forced herself to push past the soul-deep ache.

She could do this.

One of the first things she'd had to learn when entering the nursing field was how to compartmentalize hurt, grief and anger. Not allowing herself to be sucked down in a morass of emotion. If she hadn't acquired that skill, she wouldn't have been any good to her patients, their families, the doctors or herself. So what if some people called her Nurse Freeze behind her back? She got the job done. Besides, as she'd learned—first, when her father left the family; second, when her ex had traded their relationship for a job in Miami; and third, when her parents died—loving someone, caring for them, was a liability. Feelings were unreliable, untrustworthy. Parents, lovers, friends, patients—everyone always left. Only fools didn't protect themselves.

And her mother hadn't raised a fool.

"Let's wait on that," she said, answering Ivy. "We need to find Kinsale Inn first and get settled. Then maybe later we can come back and do the tourist thing."

"Right." Ivy dropped against the passenger seat, arms crossed over her chest. The glance the preteen slid Nessa's way could only be described as side-eye. Paired with the curl to the corner of her mouth, Ivy's expression had gone from wide-eyed excitement to *Eff you, big sister* in three-point-five seconds flat. "In other words, no."

"Did I say no?" Nessa asked, striving for patience. *She's a grieving preteen. You can't bounce her out of your car. CPS frowns on that.* With the mantra running through her head, she tried again. "Check-in at the inn was at twelve, and it's now one thirty." She hadn't expected to hit so much traffic leaving Boston. Or to take the wrong exit halfway to the Berkshires and have to retrace her route. "We need to make sure they still know we're arriving. The square and the tree will be there in a few hours."

"Uh-huh." Ivy snorted. "And as soon as we get to the inn, you'll find another excuse not to do anything. Especially with me. It's not like you wanted to come here anyway."

"First off, kid, I'm not the kind of person who does anything she doesn't want to do. Second, if I give you my word, I mean it. And third, what does 'especially with me' mean? Who else would I be up here with?"

"Whatever," Ivy muttered.

Nessa breathed deep. Held it. Counted to ten. Released it. Then tried again. "Is this how the next month is going to be? You angry and me taking the brunt of it? Because I have to tell you, we could've done this dance back in Boston without carolers and hot chocolate stands."

"Don't pretend like you did this for me. You don't even *like* me. This is all for your guilt over Dad's letter. Fine with me if we go back to Boston. I don't care."

Nessa tightened her fingers around the steering wheel, not replying. Anything she said to Ivy at this moment would only end up in an argument. That's all she and Ivy had seemed to do since the funeral. Nothing Nessa did could make Ivy happy.

And as much as Nessa hated to admit it, there was some truth to Ivy's accusation. Because a part of her—Jesus, she hated admitting it even to herself—didn't like Ivy. Was jealous of her. For having more of Isaac's love. For having him when Nessa hadn't, even when she'd needed him.

Even though Nessa had called Isaac Hunt Dad all her life, he was more or less a stranger to her…just like the silent, stiff twelve-year-old hunched on the seat next to her. He'd been an absentee parent since his divorce from her mother sixteen years ago, and Nessa had met her half sister maybe five times before their father died from pancreatic cancer. Hell, she hadn't even known he'd been ill until the final time he'd ended up in the hospital. She hadn't even had a chance to say…what? Goodbye? Where the hell have you been as a father for sixteen years? Why didn't you love me as much as you loved your other daughter?

I love you.

Dammit. *Damn damn damn.*

She fisted her fingers to keep from pounding the steering wheel.

So yes, guilt had pushed her into taking a previously unheard-of short-term leave from the hospital. It'd goaded her into going up to Ivy's school and letting them know the girl would be missing the last two weeks before Christmas break to take an extended vacation.

She swallowed a sigh, and as the light changed, pressed on the gas pedal. A tense, edgy silence filled the car. Nothing new there either. Nessa snuck another look at the girl, noting the sullen expression turning down Ivy's mouth and creasing her eyebrows into a petulant frown.

Maybe their time in Rose Bend would give Ivy her smile back. Or at least rid Ivy's lovely dark brown eyes of the sadness lurking there.

And maybe Santa really did fly around the world.

Yeah, Nessa had stopped believing in miracles and fairy tales years ago. Better Ivy learn now that life dealt shitty hands, and you either folded or played to recoup your losses.

Soon, they left the downtown area and approached a fork in the road. As she turned her Durango left onto a paved road bordered by trees…

"Oh wow," Ivy breathed.

"Good God," Nessa murmured at the same time, bringing her vehicle to a halt in the driveway that circled in front of the huge white inn.

Oh, Mom. You would've so loved this.

A short set of stairs led up to a spacious porch that, according to the brochure, encircled the building. The wide lower level angled out to the side, with the equally long second floor following suit. The third, slightly smaller story graced the building with its dormer window, and a slanted roof topped it like a red cap. A broad red front door with glass panes along the top and dark green shutters at every window—and, damn, there were a lot of windows—and large bushes bordering the front and sides completed the image of a beautiful country inn. But it was the wreaths and bows hung on the door and walls, and the lights that twinkled along every surface, that transformed the building into a fairyland. A Christmas fairyland.

Shaking her head, Nessa thrust the gear into Park. There she went. Being silly and whimsical. It was a place that masterfully catered to the tourists who visited just to be wowed by the holiday splendor. That's it. Nothing magical waited for them on the other side of that door other than a hot meal and maybe cookies for Ivy and coffee for Nessa in front of a fireplace.

"Let's go sign in," she said, exiting the truck. "We can come back for our bags once we're done."

"Okay."

They hurried through the cold to the steps and onto the front porch. Nessa pushed the door open, stepping into warmth and peppermint-scented air. Absently closing the door behind Ivy, Nessa scanned the lobby and the wide, spacious living room that opened off the entry. Flames leaped and crackled in the huge fireplace, and she ordered herself not to stride over there and sink down into one of the chairs bracketing it. More bows, garland and pine cones decorated the mantel and walls. A gigantic Christmas tree stood in one corner before the windows, its lights reflecting off the glass.

"This place is amazing. Like Santa's workshop," Ivy whispered beside her.

Nessa blinked, emerging from her Christmas-induced stupor, and glanced down at Ivy. Her brown eyes glowed, and for the first time since they'd come back into each other's lives, wonder and pleasure momentarily replaced the sadness in her gaze.

Nessa's chest tightened, a combination of relief and sorrow swirling behind her sternum. Relief because in this moment, she glimpsed the girl Ivy had been before her father's death. Sadness for the same reason. No twelve-year-old should be touched by so much tragedy and loss. Losing both parents and being stuck with a sister she barely knew.

Shoving aside the thoughts and emotions, Nessa cleared her throat and walked toward the small desk tucked next to a curving wooden staircase. A sign-in book and pen sat on the top, but no one manned it. She tapped the bell perched on the corner and waited, but still, no sign of anyone.

"Does this mean we have to go back home?" Ivy asked, disappointment darkening her voice.

"No, of course not." Nessa shook her head. "Maybe they just had to sneak out for a moment. We are late for the twelve-o'clock sign-in." She summoned up a smile, although from the arch of Ivy's eyebrow, maybe Nessa fell short of the reassurance she'd aimed for. "I'll go back out and get our bags. Then we'll just sit by the fire and wait for whoever to return. It probably won't be that long."

Ivy nodded. "Yeah, fine," she said, the moody half sister returning. Shrugging a shoulder, she turned and headed into the common area, plopping down on the couch and removing her headphones from her coat pocket.

Nessa stared after her. For a second there, she'd almost believed... Well, it didn't matter. They were here for Ivy to get away from the house and city that were haunted with memories of her father. And also, to fulfill Isaac's dying wish. That his daughters be together for the holiday. In this moment, that seemed the most daunting of the hurdles to leap. If she and Ivy got through this holiday without stabbing holly through each other's hearts, well, Merry Christmas.

Note to proprietor: "Please remove all holly from room."

Pivoting on her boot heel, Nessa retraced her steps to the front entrance and grabbed the knob, pulling the door open. The sooner they got settled—

"Oof."

Blindsided by what felt like a truck, she stumbled backward several steps, arms pinwheeling before her ass smacked the floor. The impact sent jarring waves up her tailbone and spine, propelling the breath from her lungs.

Ouch. And... "What the...?" She gingerly touched the prickly object that had landed on top of her head.

A wreath?

"I'm sorry. I didn't see you there."

She tipped her head back, the wreath staying firmly in place like a crown, to meet a...stack of *more wreaths*? The stack shifted, lowering to the floor in front of her feet.

God, that face.

A masterpiece full of sharp angles, a pair of almond-shaped emerald eyes, a blade of nose, a mouth that was a puzzling dichotomy of firm and pillow soft, golden, sands-kissed-by-the-sun skin...and a beard. A neat full one that had her hands itching with the need to stroke...and tug.

She curled her fingers into her palms, trying to contain the prickling sensation as heat surged up her chest, throat and poured into her cheeks. Thick, wavy, dark brown hair tumbled around his face, the ends falling a couple of inches below his chin.

Her rapt gaze dropped, skimming over the wide, wide shoulders draped in a chocolate cable-knit sweater, down to powerful denim-covered thighs and even lower to large feet encased in well-worn work boots. Slowly, she followed the same path back up his body, meeting his green gaze.

Wow.

"Here." He stretched his hand out to her, palm up. "Let me help you."

For a long moment, she stared at his hand. An instinctual sense of self-preservation screamed at her not to do it. That whatever she did, she should. Not. Touch. To do so would set in motion something she wouldn't be able to stop. As if her body heeded that warning, she scooted back a little, pulling her arms in closer to her thighs. His eyes narrowed, sharpening.

Mistake on her part. Revealing weakness to a complete stranger.

"Thanks." Setting her jaw, she disregarded her body's blaring objection and laid her palm over his much bigger one. Strong fingers wrapped around hers, and he stood, drawing her to her feet in a show of negligent strength that had her breath lodging in her throat—that strength and his height. Tall didn't cover it. Big didn't cover it.

She'd always had a weakness for big men. Jeremy Havers, the surgeon she'd been in love with before he'd decided he loved Miami and his career more, had been tall with shoulders that would've made a linebacker pout in jealousy.

Even more reason to avoid this guy and touching his hands.

"Can I get that back?" He dipped his head toward the wreath still perched on her hair, a smile playing with his full lips.

Showing weakness be damned, she shuffled a step backward, planting space between them. And noticed he still held her hand.

Dammit. So much for her resolution of *just seconds ago*.

Uttering a sound that was somewhere between a mortified groan and a cough, she released him, taking yet another step back. She jerked the Christmas decoration off her head, wincing when the stiff leaves tugged on her hair.

"Wait. Let me help." He shifted closer, and his scent enveloped her. Cold air, wintergreen, mint and…and beneath, a trace of an unidentifiable fragrance.

Him.

His huge chest blocked out the rest of the room—hell, the world—as he lifted his arms and carefully, gently, untangled strands of her hair from the wreath. Mortification burned inside her, debunking the myth that Black people didn't blush. When he finally freed her, she ran her fingers over her hair, the gesture jumpy and unprecedented. She hadn't even had this attack of…of…nerves with Jeremy on their first date at L'Espalier, where she'd been terrified of sending escargot sailing across the room à la Julia Roberts in *Pretty Woman*.

Who *was* this guy?

Trouble. That's all she needed to know. And with so much on her plate already, she didn't have any room for trouble. Bearded and big or otherwise.

"Well, that was awkward." Ivy appeared at Nessa's elbow. She pinched the bridge of her nose while Ivy crossed her arms over her chest. "Who're you?" her sister demanded.

"Sorry," he said, the hint of a smile blooming into a full one. And *whoa*. That thing was the very definition of unfair practices. Or if it wasn't, it should be. He extended his hand to Ivy. "Wolf Dennison. My parents own Kinsale Inn."

"Wolf?" Ivy tilted her head to the side. "Like what? The animal?"

"No, like Wolfgang Amadeus Mozart, the composer."

"You're kidding," Nessa blurted out. His gaze swung to her, and she winced. "Sorry." Pause. "But you're *not* kidding."

"'Fraid not. My parents named all their kids after musicians and composers," he said, shaking his head. Then that killer grin returned with an arch of a dark eyebrow. God, so much trouble. "You think my name is bad, you should hear my brothers' and sisters' names. I got off easy."

"I don't think your name is bad," Ivy chimed in. "We learned about Mozart in school. He was awesome and a genius. He wrote over six hundred pieces of music before he died at thirty-five."

"Thanks, kid. 'Bout time someone recognized the coolness of it." He held his fist out, and Ivy bumped it, both doing the exploding hand and sound effect afterward.

Still smiling, the corners of his eyes crinkling, he returned his focus to Nessa. And she almost asked him to switch it back to Ivy. Those eyes *and* the smile? Shouldn't there be a squadron of sighing women following him everywhere he went?

"You're checking in?" he asked. Nessa nodded. "Great. Follow me. Sorry I wasn't here when you arrived. Since we were a little slow, I ran out back to grab more wreaths for the house."

"More?" Ivy asked, drawing the word out until it stretched to about three syllables. "To put where?"

Wolf chuckled, and the low, rumbling sound reminded her of the purring engine of a muscle car. Masculine. Sexy. Ready for anything.

"You'd be surprised," he teased, slipping past them and heading toward the desk.

Don't look down. Don't look down.

Dammit. Now the image of stressed denim hanging off his lean hips and cupping his firm ass was permanently emblazoned on her brain.

"I saw that," Ivy half whispered, half snapped. "You so checked out his ass."

"Language," Nessa half whispered, half snapped back. "And I did not."

Ivy snorted, clearly not believing her. Smart girl. Too nosy for her own good, but smart.

"All right." Wolf flipped open a book and scanned it. "You're either Mr. and Mrs. Calder or Nessa and Ivy Hunt. I'm going with Nessa and Ivy."

"I'm Ivy," her half sister volunteered. "She's Nessa. We're half sisters."

Wolf nodded, studying them. His gaze drifted over her face like fingertips skimming her forehead, cheekbones, nose…lips. There went that fanciful notion again, because she could've sworn, she could feel his visual touch. It stirred a simmering heat deep inside her.

A heat she hadn't experienced in five months.

She hated that heat. She'd once allowed it to convince her that men stayed. That her man, the one she'd permitted herself to imagine a future with, would be the one to stick. But while she'd been falling in love, he hadn't. Heart versus heat. Both had sucked in the end.

So, yeah, she *despised* heat.

"So you're spending the holidays together. That's good. Family's important." Wolf dragged her from her admittedly bitter thoughts and turned the book around, pushing it toward Nessa. "If sometimes a pain in the ass."

"Language," Ivy singsonged.

For the love of… "Thanks," Nessa said to Wolf from between clenched teeth and signed the book.

Wolf withdrew a key from a drawer and handed it over to her. "Room 2. It's the first room right at the top of the stairs. And before I forget. Breakfast is from seven to nine every morning, you're on your own for lunch and a buffet-style dinner is served at six. The kitchen closes at nine, but there's always some snacks left out in case you wake up with a sweet tooth." He rounded the desk and gestured for them to follow him up the steps. *Don't freaking look.* This time she forced herself to obey. "As you might have noticed on the way into town, Rose Bend really loves Christmas."

"You don't say," Ivy muttered.

"Really, Mozart? And here I thought we'd bonded over the fist bump."

He glanced over his shoulder at the preteen. And Ivy—broody, sullen, cantankerous Ivy—grinned at Wolf's nickname. Warmth unexpectedly blossomed in Nessa's belly, creeping its way into her chest. Had she ever seen her half sister look like that? Not even the few times they'd seen each other before her father's death. In this instant, Ivy was a normal, carefree girl.

"There's a pamphlet listing all the town's holiday activities. There's at least one thing every night, even if it's just a chocolate tasting at the candy store or caroling in the town square."

"I saw the Yulefest sign on the way in," Nessa said. "Not that we could miss it. Is that some kind of festival?"

"More than a festival," Wolf replied, glancing at her with that penetrating stare. "It's a Rose Bend tradition. Thirty days of holiday events to celebrate Christmas. The whole town participates."

Sounded...wholesome. "There are thirty-one days in December," she pointed out.

A small smile curved the corner of his soft-looking mouth, making it appear even fuller. "Christmas Day is for spending time with family."

"Oh. Right," she murmured.

For years, she'd had a small but loving family with her mother. But now, she'd never see her mother's smile or hear her laughter at their traditional gag gifts. She'd never have those Christmases again.

She blinked, dispelling the memory.

Nothing could bring back those times. Bring back her mother.

"We saw the square," Ivy said, passing Nessa on the stairs so she climbed them beside Wolf. "And the Christmas tree. It was huge. As big as the one in Boston Common."

"Every year, the committee finds the perfect tree at one of the farms outside of town. It's tradition. Speaking of tradition, the lighting is tonight. It officially kicks off the Christmas season. There will be food at Town Hall afterward. You should both go."

"I haven't been to a tree lighting in forever! The last one was about three years ago with my da—" Ivy's voice broke off as she froze on the top step, her fingers curling into fists by her sides.

Oh God. Nessa's heart flew to the base of her throat. Nessa almost went to her, almost wrapped an arm around those thin shoulders. But the fear of rejection quelled the impulse. Ivy didn't want her comfort...or Nessa.

"I'm cool. We're probably going to be too busy unpacking and everything," Ivy said quietly with a shrug.

Wolf peered over his shoulder at Nessa again as they cleared the second floor. And that look, as dark and mysterious as a forest and yet as sharp and incisive as a scalpel, had her nearly cringing from the intensity. She had to be careful around him. This man didn't miss much. And seemed to sense *too* much, saw too deep. He had her battling the urge to splay her palms over her chest and prevent him from peering beneath skin and bone to her secrets.

She turned from him, caving to a need for self-preservation. Emotional survival. That was her number one priority.

"We don't have to decide now," she said to Ivy. "It kind of sounds like fun."

Lie. It sounded like the very opposite of fun. Standing in the cold and freezing her ass off, surrounded by a bunch of strangers to watch the lighting of a tree. Give her a night of *Frontier* on Netflix, a glass of wine and Lisa Gardner's latest thriller. *That* was fun.

But to erase that flat, hopeless tone from Ivy's voice...to see the little girl who'd grinned up at Wolf again...

Wolf's chin dipped in a small nod. "Are your bags in your car?"

"Yes," Nessa said, removing the keys from her coat pocket. "I was just about to get—"

"I got it covered." He held out his hand, palm up. "If you'll give me your keys, I'll bring them up."

"That's not necessary. I can—"

"Nessa," he interrupted again, tone soft but firm. Too stunned by the way his deep, warm voice wrapped around her name and slid through her veins like sun-warmed molasses, she handed the keys over without a fuss. "I'll be right back," he murmured.

He turned and disappeared down the steps at a light jog.

"That man is hot," Ivy muttered.

"Ivy." Nessa glared at her.

She shrugged, totally unrepentant. "What? He is. And you're a liar if you tell me you don't think so, too."

With that, Ivy grabbed the doorknob to their room, turned and entered. Leaving Nessa to stare after her.

Well, what was one more lie added on top of everything else?

She muttered a curse under her breath, pinching the bridge of her nose.

Why did she suddenly feel like this month was going to pass by in Narnia time?

CHAPTER TWO

Now, there's a lot there to unload. And I don't mean the luggage.

Wolfgang Theodore Dennison—Wolf to most people— stared at the closed door of the Cobh Room after delivering the suitcases to Nessa and Ivy Hunt.

It was his favorite of all the suites named after towns in County Cork, Ireland. Huge bay windows provided an un- encumbered view of the barn, the oak and hickory trees that guarded their property like silent sentinels and the small frozen lake beyond. Framed photographs of Cork Harbor with its colorful houses, the historic St. Colman's Cathe- dral and Roche's Point Lighthouse decorated the walls. The window seat that he'd built for a cozy reading nook invited a guest to climb up and unwind with a good book. Every- thing from the heavy drapes that helped keep out the cold Berkshires winds to the bedspread to the throw rugs on the hardwood floor reflected the bright reds, yellows and blues that made Cobh such an inviting town.

Yet Wolf sensed the view, photos and warm, welcoming decor would be wasted on the duo behind the closed door.

"We're half sisters," the young girl had announced.

Wolf shook his head. That statement alone contained... a ton. A complicated, murky, most likely pain-filled ton.

He had six brothers and sisters and four of them were adopted. But never had Wolf referred to them as anything other than family. They were just his brothers and sisters. Love, trust, security, protection and acceptance trumped blood every time.

Nessa and Ivy Hunt might share blood and even love… but the rest of those things needed to form a tight, unshakeable bond?

Yeah, there was definitely a hell of a lot there to unload. But not his concern. Or his responsibility.

As he'd proved in the past, he didn't do well with responsibility. Especially when it came to other people's hearts… or lives.

Giving the closed, heavy wood door another long glance, he rubbed a hand over his beard and lumbered down the steps. Glancing at the clock on the entryway wall, he noted the time. Two o'clock. The Calders had yet to arrive, and with his mother still MIA, he had to hang around the inn until then. Hopefully, she wouldn't be too much longer. The to-do list he needed to get done before the tree lighting grew even though the hours required to accomplish the tasks remained the same. And that just included jobs around the inn, not counting the gazebo in the town square that needed to be finished by Christmas Eve. Because Coltrane, his brother and Rose Bend's mayor, had asked him to head the project, Wolf had put aside a couple of projects Dennison Carpentry already had lined up to tackle it.

He wouldn't betray the trust Cole placed in him for the gazebo project. Not when Cole depended on him. Not when he finally, *finally* now saw joy in his brother's eyes instead of grief. It'd been two years since Cole's wife and son had died in childbirth. And it'd been five months since Sydney Collins, now Dennison, the prodigal daughter of Rose Bend, had returned home and Cole had fallen in love and had become a father to her newborn daughter. For a time, the whole Dennison clan had believed Cole was lost to them. But now, thanks to Sydney and her love, he'd returned to them. And there wasn't anything Wolf wouldn't do for his brother, nor would he allow anything to throw a wrench in the task Cole had given him.

Not that he'd tell Cole that. He had to keep the guy humble.

Unbidden, he slid another glance in the direction of the staircase and the sisters at the top of it.

Those two—especially the older one with her espresso eyes and warrior queen features—were the very definition of *wrench*.

Shaking his head, he paused next to the front desk and hauled the wreaths up in his arms and headed toward the kitchen. Christmas was one of Kinsale Inn's busiest seasons. And that meant a seemingly endless list of tasks filled his and his family's days. Along with Wolf's own carpentry business, his time was rarely his own. So as much as the inn's newest guests might prick his curiosity, they were...complicated. He'd done complicated before. And complicated had led to failure that had left others scarred, traumatized...gone.

So no, he didn't do complicated. Not anymore. And never again.

Unbidden, an image of thick, brown, wavy hair with a closely shaved undercut and a fathomless but guarded dark gaze wavered in front of his eyes. A flicker of heat ignited low in Wolf's belly, the flame licking at him. This woman with her Madonna face and Lolita mouth sent lust weaving through him like a fucked-up frat boy on a pub crawl. An inconvenient and unwanted lust.

Yeah. He *especially* didn't need the kind of complication Nessa Hunt brought with her.

Clenching his jaw, he settled the stack of greenery near the back door. As he reached for the handle, the door swung open, permitting the cold and his mother inside.

"Good Lord," she gasped, kicking the panel shut behind her and plopping her oversize purse down on the small table just inside the entrance. Grasping the ends of her yellow-and-black-striped Hufflepuff scarf, she unwrapped the woolen length from around her neck. "It's getting colder than a witch's tit out there. I know better than to wear a dress outside this time of year." She tsked, hanging the scarf on the wall hook and shrugging out of her coat. "I swear, that wind slid up my skirt and touched places only your father and my ob-gyn have touched."

Christ. T-M-fucking-I. Wolf tipped his head back, wincing as he attempted to scrub that particular piece of information from his brain. But Billie Thomasina Dennison was on a roll, and thirty-one years of experience taught him to keep his mouth shut until she ran out of steam. And she would, eventually. Just what damage she'd inflict until then was anyone's guess.

"God, Moe," he groaned. When Cole had been a toddler, he couldn't pronounce *Mother*, so it'd been *Moe*. Eventually, it'd stuck, and now, everyone called her by the nickname, even the townspeople. For all of her kids, though, it was synonymous with *Mom*. "Really? What did I ever do to you to deserve that disturbing visual?"

"Oh grow up. You passed through these lady parts, so I don't know what you're so squeamish about. Anyway, as I was saying, I blame that Caroline Jacobs," his mother continued to grumble, mentioning the owner of the local ballet studio and member of Rose Bend's town council as he threw up a little in his mouth. Snorting, Moe hung her coat next to her scarf, then strode over to the pantry and threw open the door. "Not for the weather. That's on God, not her. But Jesus be a muzzle, that woman can *talk*. I could've delivered the muffins for the lighting tonight at the café and been home thirty minutes ago if not for her holding me hostage next to my car with her blabbering about... Shoot, I don't even know. I tuned her out after the first two minutes. Although I did manage to organize dinner in my head."

She turned from the cupboard with her arms full of potatoes, onions, flour and some cans. "Shepherd's pie. With four guests, it's not going to be a huge dinner, but shepherd's pie would be perfect on a day like this and before the tree lighting. Everyone will go with full, warm bellies. Speaking of guests," she said, switching topics with lightning-fast speed as she settled the food on the butcher block island in the middle of the spacious kitchen, "has anyone arrived yet? I noticed an SUV out front. Does it belong to the Calders or the Hunts? And have you seen your sisters? I told Leo and Sinead to make sure the bathrooms were well stocked with toiletries and the gift baskets were in the rooms before the guests arrived."

Wolf squinted at her.

"Well, son?" She tilted her head, jamming her fists on her narrow hips. "Are you spacing out on me again?"

"No." He shook his head. "I was making sure you were finished and not just taking a breath."

"Brat." The quirk of her lips ruined the irritation in her voice. As did her snicker. "Where's the respect due me as your mother? I suffered thirteen hours of labor for you. And that big head of yours was no walk in the park," she muttered.

Wolf laughed, rounding the island to wrap his mother in a hug, lifting her petite frame off the floor. She shrieked, but encircled her strong arms around his back, squeezing hard and damn near choking off his air. He closed his eyes as his mother's familiar baby-powder-and-lavender scent enveloped him as securely as her embrace. Relief coursed through him. At an even five feet, she'd always been a small woman. But the last two years had been rough on her as she grieved the loss of her son's family and worried about Cole. And Wolf had been helpless and felt like a failure that he couldn't ease that burden for her. For any of his family.

But now, with his brother in love, healed and whole again, Moe was more at peace than he'd seen her in a long time. He hugged her extra tight before smacking a loud kiss to her cheek and placing her back on her feet. He moved away from her swatting hands faster than most people believed a man his size could.

He'd learned that growing up in a loud, often chaotic house of nine, too.

"To answer your question, Leo and Sinead came through earlier and took care of the rooms. They're over at the cottages now, making sure they're ready for the guests coming in tomorrow," he said, leaning a hip against the edge of the island. "Flo is at Six Ways to Sundae for her shift and the twins are hanging with Sydney and baby Patience while Cole is handling last-minute festival details downtown," he said, explaining the whereabouts of the rest of her children. "And the Hunts have arrived, but not the Calders."

"Huh. Maybe they hit some traffic since they're coming down from New Hampshire. I'm glad the other two made it, though. I'll go up and introduce myself later and apologize for not meeting them." She turned to the industrial-size refrigerator and opened one of the doors. Seconds later, she bumped the door closed and moved back to the counter with a large package of ground beef. "So." She walked over to the sink and twisted the faucets. Sticking her hands under the gushing water, she glanced at him over her shoulder, eyebrow hiked high. "What were they like? What was your first impression?"

Wolf parted his lips, the "They're fine" hovering on his tongue. But he couldn't utter the lie. Frowning, he crossed his arms over his chest and bowed his head, staring at—but not seeing—the blue-and-white tile of the kitchen floor.

Instead, he saw an almost-too-slender, pretty young preteen girl with a chip on her shoulder the size of her own body weight and the loveliest, most haunted eyes he'd ever seen. He unfolded one of his arms, absently rubbing a hand over his chest, as if he could soothe the sharp ping that echoed there. All that anguish and pain contained in that small body... He shook his head. His twin sister and brother were about Ivy Hunt's age, and the impulse to gather her in his arms and hold her close as he would with his siblings had beat at him like fists. Maybe that's what he was trying to massage away right now—the bruises from resisting that urge.

But if he'd wanted to comfort Ivy, her older sister, Nessa, stirred a radically different and highly inappropriate need within him, considering she was a guest of the inn. From the moment he'd bumped into her, literally, she'd been the one to knock him on his ass. Even with that silly wreath sitting on top of her head like a crown, she was...beautiful. Frustration twisted inside him. He worked with his hands, creating and building furniture from wood, but he wasn't a man of flowery words. Yet *beautiful* seemed wholly insufficient to describe the interesting and fascinating face that was a jigsaw puzzle of strength and vulnerability.

Long, dark brown waves tumbled to one side, brushing a shoulder and falling down her back, and on the other an edgy, close-shaved undercut. High, razor-sharp cheekbones that would fit right in on a catwalk...or on a warrior queen of old. Oval-shaped, coffee-colored eyes with thoughts—secrets—she guarded closely. An elegantly slanted nose with wide, flared nostrils. Luminous skin that made him want to trek out to his workshop to see if a board of mahogany captured the beauty of her complexion. And then there was that mouth.

Fuck. He bowed his head deeper, turning to grip the edge of the island. If her cheekbones were regal and her nose elegant, that mouth was downright rude. A shade too big, bold and unapologetically carnal. A man looked at those full, lush lips and wondered how they would feel dragging over his bare skin...

He inhaled a ragged breath, forcing himself to shift away from thoughts he had no business thinking in front of his mother. Besides, that walking wet dream of a body had been clothed in a black puffy coat that smelled of cold weather and colder attitude, a soft-looking black sweater that molded to the high thrust of small breasts, dark blue jeans that encased sweet, thick thighs, and sexy-as-hell knee-length black boots. Real leather boots, if he wasn't mistaken.

All of it added up to Big City.

And Big City looked down on small towns like Rose Bend. Big City felt strangled by the faces that never changed, people who were always in their business, the lack of entertainment other than festivals, picnics and movies at the local two-screen movie theater, the limited opportunities...

The stagnation.

Big City slowly died in small towns. In Rose Bend.

He clenched his jaw, forcibly beating back the words, the memories they conjured.

Yeah, it didn't matter how gorgeous Nessa Hunt might be, or that his first instinct had been to kick in the walls guarding those eyes. Not only was she a guest—which dropped her firmly in the "don't shit where you eat" category—but she was only in Rose Bend for a matter of weeks before she returned home. He, more than anyone, understood the havoc a woman seeking a one-way ticket out of his hometown could wreak. He'd passed that class with honors, and he had zero intention of being teacher's pet again.

"Wolf?" His mother laid a hand over the fingers curled around the edge of the island. "What's wrong, honey?"

He lifted his head, and the warmth and comfort that had always been a mainstay in his life reached him, shoving back the dark ghosts of the past. "I'm good, Moe," he said, summoning up a smile. He flipped his hand and encircled hers with his. "No worries. Just thinking of the work I still have to get done today."

"I'm excited to see what the gazebo is going to look like. I'm sure it's going to be beautiful just like everything you do," she said, then cleared her throat. "I saw Regina Allen while I was in town."

A twinge spasmed in his chest at the name, but he shut it down. Schooling his features, he replied, "Yeah? How is she doing?"

"Fine." She studied him with the green gaze he'd inherited from her. "She told me Olivia might be coming home for Christmas."

He hated the sympathy that crept into his mother's voice. Hated more that she believed he needed it.

When Olivia Allen had broken off their engagement and left Rose Bend three years ago, she'd not only shattered his heart; she'd shattered *him*. Olivia had longed for more than what Rose Bend offered her—a job in a city with a population over five thousand; people who hadn't known her since she'd been in diapers; more entertainment than a two-screen theater and a motorcycle rally. She'd wanted that more than him, more than a future with him.

Olivia had been his best friend, the woman he'd loved, his fiancée. Then she'd been gone, leaving him an emotional amputee. He'd learned to live without that limb, and no way in hell would he give her—or anyone—the opportunity to take more from him.

"I'm glad for Regina. I know her and Gerald will be thrilled to finally have Olivia back home for a while," he said, careful to keep his voice neutral. To snuff out the embers of anger that kindled in his chest.

After several seconds, his mother arched a dark eyebrow. "I should put you out of my kitchen for trying to bullshit me," she drawled. "Just 'cause you got some hair on your chin and balls doesn't mean I can't pop those knuckles with my wooden spoon." And to prove her point, she waltzed over to the sink, snagged the large Spoon of Mass Destruction—Wolf and Cole had engraved the title on it for Mother's Day several years ago—off the hook and slapped it against her palm.

He laughed, holding up his hands. If he had a quarter for every time she'd threatened to rap one of them with that goddamn spoon, he'd hire Jay-Z's butler. Moe had yet to follow through with the warning, but that didn't mean he'd tempt her.

"First, can we agree to never discuss the state of my balls ever again?" He barked out another crack of laughter when she lifted the spoon in the air. "Moe, seriously, I'm good." He was, dammit. "Actually, I was thinking of

Nessa and Ivy Hunt," he said, the humor ebbing. Propping his crossed arms on the island, he couldn't decide where to begin. Finally, he shook his head and went with the thing that bothered him most. "When I met them, the youngest one, Ivy, introduced them as half sisters."

Surprise and then sympathy flashed across his mother's expressive face. She set the spoon on the counter and glanced toward the kitchen entrance as if the pair stood there. "Well, that says a lot, doesn't it?" she said, more to herself than to him. Her eyes softened further, and she whispered, "Those poor girls."

"Poor girls?" he echoed on a snort, drawing her attention back to him. "One of those 'girls' is a grown woman."

"Like age matters when your heart's been bruised and left to scar."

"Moe, how could you possibly decide that when you haven't even met them yet?" Wolf gently teased. His mother's heart had always been big, soft and as open as 7-Eleven.

"If you asked Flo how many brothers and sisters she had, what would she say?" she demanded, narrowing her eyes on him.

"Six," he answered without hesitation.

"How many adopted brothers and sisters would she claim to have?" Moe volleyed back.

"None," he said, voice soft.

"Because she's a Dennison as much as you are, maybe not by birth but definitely by love."

"I know," he murmured. "But they're not Flo. Or the twins. They're guests who are just here for the holidays, not kids for you to adopt. Or try and heal."

"See, that's where you're wrong," she scoffed, moving to the sink to grab her chopping board that hung over it.

Turning back to him, she spread her hands wide, the board almost smacking the refrigerator door handle. "It's Christmas, honey. What better time to find healing and family than now? It's the season of miracles, after all."

Amusement tugged the corner of his mouth. "Right, I'm sure—"

"Um, excuse me."

He and Moe jerked toward the kitchen doorway to find Nessa Hunt hovering there.

Well, hell.

How much had she overheard?

CHAPTER THREE

"YOU MUST BE Nessa Hunt." The petite older woman with gray-sprinkled dark hair and Wolf's eyes circled the island and approached Nessa, arms outstretched.

Nessa braced herself for the imminent hug; she read it all over this woman. From the wide, welcoming smile to the warm sparkle in her green eyes to the long bohemian skirt of her dress, everything about this woman screamed *hugger*. But she drew to a halt in front of Nessa and cupped Nessa's hands, giving them a friendly squeeze. Nessa smothered a sigh of relief. Not that she had a thing against getting close to people—as an ER nurse, she couldn't. But that was her job. Off the clock, she preferred her personal space.

Does it really matter that I'm leaving, Nessa? You've never let me in anyway.0

Her ex's accusation rang in her head like an indictment. An image of him throwing that allegation at her as he'd announced his decision to take a job offer at another hospital over a thousand miles away wavered in her head. It'd been five months since his defection, and those careless, cold words still stung like ice shards to her heart.

Because they hadn't been true.

She'd let Jeremy in as much as she'd allowed anyone else. *More* than anyone else, other than her mom.

So for him to still pack up and leave her must've meant he hadn't liked who he'd seen once she'd lowered her guard.

Hadn't seen that person worthy of his love...worthy of staying.

And that had almost destroyed her.

It had definitely reinforced those shields to titanium strength.

Unbidden, she slid a glance at the man who'd been trying to convince his mother that Nessa and Ivy were guests and not in need of any Christmas miracles when she'd interrupted their conversation.

She'd only spent minutes in Wolfgang Dennison's company, yet she sensed he wouldn't stand for a woman setting intentional distance between them. She imagined he would use those big bare hands to tear down those barriers and forge ahead, leaving no part of her untouched, unclaimed. Her scrutiny dipped to that beard.

Leaving no part of her unabraded.

Heat licked at the underside of her belly, even as her brain reminded her that one, her tastes in men ran toward the clean-shaven, Gucci-loafers-and-slick-Armani-suits-when-not-in-scrubs type, and two, Wolf's mother stood right there.

Totally inappropriate.

Nessa's gaze flicked upward and snagged on his. A dark brow arched high, and for the second time in an afternoon, warmth stained her cheeks. This from a woman who hadn't blinked an eye when a naked couple had been wheeled in on a gurney, his Prince Albert penis piercing snagged on her IUD birth control. But there was something about the... familiarity in those eyes. A familiarity that whispered of knowing, of *seeing*.

Yeah, Wolf Dennison might be hot as hell in his I-launch-axes-at-trees-for-fun way, but she didn't like him and his intrusive, rude stares.

"Yes, I'm Nessa Hunt," she replied to his mother, belatedly shaking the other woman's hand. "It's nice to meet you…"

"Billie Dennison, though most everyone calls me Moe. Don't ask. Long story." She held up a hand, shaking her head on a laugh. "My family and I own and run Kinsale Inn, and I'm thrilled you've decided to stay with us through the holidays. You couldn't have chosen a more fun and beautiful time of year to visit Rose Bend, although each season in the Berkshires holds its own special beauty. C'mon," she chattered on, cupping Nessa's elbow in a surprisingly strong grip for such a slim woman.

Billie Dennison led Nessa over to the big breakfast table next to a bank of windows that almost reached to the ceiling. Nessa glanced through the delicate white curtains to glimpse a broad porch, a couple of rockers, an old-fashioned swing and beyond, a field and trees. Sooo many trees.

A Starbucks. Was it bad form to offer up a perennially cranky preteen for just one Starbucks latte macchiato? Yeah, probably.

Dammit.

"You sit here and let me get you something to eat. You must be starved after your drive from…Boston, right?" Billie continued, dragging out a chair from the table and guiding Nessa into it with the efficiency of a mother who'd no doubt performed the same action many times before.

"Please, you don't have to go to any trouble, Mrs. Dennison—"

"Moe," the other woman corrected, patting Nessa's shoulder. "And it's no trouble at all, believe me."

"Wolf already explained that we're on our own for lunch—"

"Which is normally true," she interrupted again, but with

such a warm smile, Nessa, who usually hated the shit out of that, couldn't take offense. "But since this is your first day with us and you're our only guests so far, I'll make an exception. It won't be anything fancy, of course. But it'll be filling." With another smile and pat, she strode to her son to cup his face. "Good to know you haven't forgotten everything I taught you about front-of-the-house service," she teased, and Wolf grunted in response.

"I think what you meant to say was thank you," he replied, and though he was talking to his mother, his low rumble vibrated through Nessa. A spark of resentment flashed through her. She wanted no part of him rumbling or vibrating anywhere near her.

"Now, Nessa—do you mind me calling you Nessa?" Moe asked, tugging open the refrigerator door.

Normally, yes, she would've. Informality, casualness. She didn't do that. Hell, most of her coworkers called her by her last name. Her closest friend had been her mom. For years, Evelyn Reed had been Nessa's rock, her security... Nessa hadn't needed anyone else. Hadn't trusted anyone else. Especially after Isaac left. But for some reason, telling this gregarious, kind woman that no, she couldn't be that familiar with her seemed—she didn't know—ogre-ish. And, hell, part of her wasn't ashamed to admit that Billie "Moe" Dennison kind of scared her. All that damn...cheer.

"No, Nessa is fine," Nessa said.

Moe grinned at her before the upper half of her body disappeared behind the steel fridge door. "Now, it seems like my Wolf gave you a rundown of the schedule, but did he give you a tour?"

"No, we didn't do that yet."

"Well, no worries. If you'd like, we can do that after lunch." She reappeared, arms full of clear containers and produce. "How do you feel about homemade roast beef sandwiches?" She cocked her head, her eyes narrowing on Nessa. "I don't remember any dietary specifications on your reservation."

"No, Ivy and I are both carnivores and eat all the gluten," she said, earning a chuckle from Moe and another cavemanlike grunt from her son. A grunt that did *nothing* to her nipples or belly, thank you very much. "But really, you don't have to bother."

"It's no bother, and you aren't either." She started popping lids, then turned to the stove. Pans rattled. In moments, the mouthwatering aroma of warming meat and simmering gravy filled the air, and Nessa's stomach rumbled its approval. "As I was saying earlier, you've chosen a wonderful time to visit with us. The Yulefest is one of our most loved traditions. We've celebrated it since I married and moved here, so like ten years ago." Moe glanced up from her stirring to shoot a pointed look in Nessa's direction that dared her to dispute the statement.

Biting her lip, Nessa valiantly maintained a deadpan expression. "Wow, that long, huh?"

From his lean on the wall, Wolf snorted, crossing his arms across his massive chest. "That in dog years?"

"The spoon, boy," she said. No, threatened. Yep, definitely a threat.

But from the grin that flashed in Wolf's beard, he didn't appear particularly frightened.

"Uh, hi."

Nessa twisted around in her chair, facing the kitchen entrance. Ivy stood in the doorway, her small frame stiff, shoulders a little hunched, and her usual sullen expression firmly in place. After Wolf had dropped off their luggage, they'd retreated to their "corners." Ivy had claimed the window seat, plopped in her earphones and glued her eyes to her phone. Nessa had settled on the huge sleigh bed, picked up the remote and switched on the television.

But soon, the warmth from both the central heating and the fireplace that someone had thoughtfully lit in preparation for their arrival couldn't combat the icy chill from the cold war that waged between her and Ivy. At least back home, or back at Isaac's home, where she'd moved in after his death so Ivy wouldn't be uprooted, Nessa could go to her room or the living room while Ivy holed up in hers. But here, in this inn permeated with everything that she and Ivy were not—happy, loving, peaceful *family*—the loneliness seeped into Nessa's bones like the rain they'd run into on the outskirts of Boston.

With shame dogging her like one of those yippy purse-sized dogs, she'd escaped the room. And something, maybe the low voices—or maybe something more nebulous that her analytical mind objected to—led her to the kitchen. And now it seemed Ivy had found her way here, too.

Moe twisted the knobs on the stove, then crossed the room toward the preteen, wearing the same delighted smile she'd so selflessly given Nessa. Only, she didn't pump the hug-giving brakes with Ivy.

Worry for the girl trickled through, and Nessa half rose from her chair. Ivy had lost her mother when she'd been way too young, and it'd been her and Isaac for most of her life. God knows Nessa hadn't been much of a mother figure in the six weeks she'd been in Ivy's life on a daily basis. Should she go over there? Save her?

"What's wrong?" Wolf's cotton-over-gravel voice murmured in her ear, low enough so only she caught it. "Nessa?"

A hand, warm and huge, settled on her back and she

jerked, shocked by the…impact of it. An electrical current sizzled through her, penetrating through her black sweater and the thin tank top to her skin underneath. Like a live wire, it crackled over her.

A heavy sense of foreboding settled on her chest, and she struggled to draw in a deep breath. She'd known. In that hallway, she'd *known* that touching him would mean trouble. And the bolt of lust that left her staring at him like he was her next biggest mistake had alarm bells clanging in her head.

This man might not cradle her cheek with his huge palm or cup her breast with those long, elegant fingers if she ordered him not to touch, but he wouldn't be as courteous with keeping those stunning green eyes off her.

Wouldn't be as polite with her heart.

If she let him have access to any part of her.

And now, gazing into the unshielded concern in his eyes and sidestepping the disconcerting warmth of his hand, there was no way in hell she'd be stupid enough to grant that to him.

Not any man again for a long while.

But especially not him. Because something—call it instinct, ESP or the bad coffee from the last stop at that 7-Eleven—whispered he would finish the job Jeremy had started. And where her ex had left wreckage, Wolfgang Dennison wouldn't even leave ashes in his wake.

"Nessa?" He didn't try to touch her again, but his scrutiny and roughened-silk voice were almost a physical caress. She forced herself to refocus on Ivy.

Dammit. What kind of big sister did that make her? Well, if she were truly her big sister, instead of a sad impostor. She stepped forward, intent on rescuing the girl, but the older woman released Ivy from her embrace and shifted backward.

Slipping an arm around Ivy, Moe led her to the table. "I can definitely tell you two are sisters. You're both gorgeous," Moe continued, unaware of the gut punch she delivered to Nessa. "Now, like I was telling Nessa, you must be starving after traveling all the way from Boston, and with probably nothing more than junk food from convenience stores. I was about to fix her some lunch, and you can join her."

With the grace of a really nice bulldozer, Moe settled Ivy across from Nessa. The girl wore the same dazed expression Nessa no doubt had minutes earlier.

"Just go with it, Mozart," Wolf said, smirking. When Ivy glanced at him, he shook his head. "That's my mother, by the way. She forgot to introduce herself before she smothered you against her bosom. And my advice? It's easier if you don't fight it. We just smile, nod and agree around here."

"Um, okay." Ivy nodded. "Thank you."

"Good job, Mozart," Wolf praised with a low snort. "Now, don't look her in the eye."

"The. Spoon." Moe scowled, jabbing a finger in his huge chest. Turning back to Ivy, she shrugged, a sheepish smile warming her face. "My son is a pain in the—well, never mind, but he does have a point. My name is Billie Dennison, but everyone calls me Moe. I did fail to introduce myself...although this isn't the first time we've met. Which is why I was excited to see you again. Why, you couldn't have been older than three when you, your father and mom last stayed here. I was so delighted when I realized he'd made another reservation with us."

Even as Ivy gaped at Moe, shock pummeled into Nessa.

Isaac? Here, with Ivy and her mother? Why? And was his visit to the inn—his memories with the family he'd replaced Nessa and Evelyn with—why he'd sent them here? So his daughter—his favorite, his *loved* daughter—could have one last Christmas in a place where they'd been happy together? This trip wasn't about Ivy and Nessa bonding. This trip wasn't about Nessa *at all*.

As usual, she'd been an afterthought.

No, no. She'd been forgotten. By the only father she'd ever known.

Pain, anger, grief… Jesus. She blinked against the emotion that threatened to sweep her under its deluge. Instead, she focused on Ivy's elfin face and the brown eyes that lit up with wonder as Moe's words sank in. A desperate and heartbreaking hunger to hear more about her father burned in the girl's gaze.

"My dad," she whispered, voice thick before clearing it. "My dad was here. With my mom? And me?"

"Yes." Moe lifted an arm, her hand hovering over Ivy's shoulder. Then, as if she couldn't help herself, she gently squeezed it, then released her. "Like I said, years ago. You were a little thing, but I remember you and your parents. It was summer, during the motorcycle rally—"

"Motorcycle rally?" Ivy interrupted, her lips parted in a perfect O.

Moe chuckled. "Yep. We host one of the biggest in the country. And the best, in my opinion," she added, just a hint of smugness in her tone. Still smiling, she glanced at Nessa. "He mentioned he had an older daughter who he would've loved to have brought along…"

"Right," Nessa drawled, tasting the bitterness on her tongue, hearing it in her voice.

Ivy's head swung toward her, dark eyes wide with surprise and then a flash of anger. And underneath, betrayal. Betrayal that Nessa had dared malign her precious father. The apology razed a path up her throat, burning a trail onto her tongue. But she didn't deliver it. Couldn't. Because though Isaac had claimed to be her father, when he'd walked out on her and her mother, he'd failed to behave like it. So she had the right to be angry with him. The right to call bullshit on the lies he'd uttered so he appeared loving when he'd been an absentee father at best, a neglectful one at worst.

To Nessa.

Never to Ivy.

And dammit, here she was being a bitch again. A jealous, childish bitch.

A hand curved around her shoulder. Squeezed. She didn't need to glance down to confirm its owner.

Part of her had the urge to shrug off the clasp that struck her as too familiar, too tender, just...*too*. But the other part... The other part wanted to beg him not to remove his touch. It grounded her. Made her feel solid, real. And God, that made no sense even in her own head.

So she shifted out from under it. Because she *did* want it.

"Can you tell me more about my dad and mom when they came here? Do you have any pictures? Did he send anything when he made the reservation? Did he leave a message for me?" Ivy's questions nearly tripped over themselves as they tumbled out of her, her voice rising with unmistakable hope.

Moe's green eyes softened, and she shook her head. "I'm sorry, sweetie. I don't have any pictures, and he didn't leave any additional messages when he made the reservation." She glanced up at Nessa, a helplessness in her gaze.

Yeah, I know the feeling well.

"I'll be glad to tell you all that I remember about your parents' visit here, though," Moe continued when Ivy's shoulders slumped. "Just come find—" The peal of a phone cut her off and she held up a finger, reaching into a pocket and withdrawing a cell phone. "Excuse me a moment. Hey... All right...Behave yourselves. I'll see you two later. Love you." She ended the call and slipped the phone back into her pocket, smiling at Ivy. "Sorry. That was my twins, Sonny and Cher, checking in."

Sonny and Cher? Nessa jerked around and stared at Wolf, just managing to prevent her jaw from dropping and the "You're fucking kidding me" from falling out. But she couldn't do a damn thing about her face.

Wolf mouthed, "I told you so." And winked.

The man shouldn't wink. On other men, it was douchey. On him, her ovaries transformed into shameless hussies, throwing their panties at him. Bras, too.

No, he definitely shouldn't wink.

"Seriously? Sonny? Cher?" Ivy blinked. After a moment, a smile curled her lips. "That's so *cool*."

Moe grinned. "I think so, too." She headed over to the stove and back to the food she'd been preparing. "They're headed to the Christmas tree lighting later on this evening. You should go. I can tell them to keep an eye out for you. I think you three would get along famously."

"More like notoriously," Wolf muttered.

"Anyway..." Moe shot Wolf a narrow-eyed look as she returned to the table with two plates laden down with bread and thick slices of roast beef covered in steaming gravy. She set one down in front of Nessa and the other before Ivy. "It's okay if you're too tired to go tonight, Ivy," she said, voice gentle. "The town holds events every day for the whole month of December. There will be plenty of things for you to attend."

"Okay." Ivy shrugged her shoulders. "I'll think about it."

Nessa should leave it alone. After all, the last time Ivy'd been to a lighting had been with Isaac. Hell, maybe she should just let the girl heal on her own time in her own way...

"Not to push and get out my lane, Mozart," Wolf said, drawing Ivy's attention. "But from what Moe said, this must've been some of the reason your father sent you here, right? So you could enjoy yourself in a town that you and your parents once visited? Maybe the best way to do that is to jump in feetfirst. Christmas isn't something you ease into."

Ivy studied Wolf, then nodded and picked up her fork, but not before Nessa caught the glance Ivy slid her from under her lashes. And she caught the yearning in those dark eyes that the preteen would've probably sacrificed her precious phone to hide. Especially from Nessa.

But Nessa saw it. And couldn't ignore it.

Smothering a sigh and mentally whispering an apology to her toes, Nessa propped her crossed arms on the table. "Actually, I've never been to a tree lighting, and I'm looking forward to seeing one. If you want to go to it, I'm game."

"Nessa." Ivy fiddled with her fork, her gaze on the sandwich in front of her. "You're serious? You'll go?"

"Not in the habit of saying things I don't mean," Nessa reminded her, and unlike how that had irritated her earlier in the car, now it seemed to assure her.

When Ivy nodded, and softly said, "Okay, I'm in," relief rushed through Nessa.

"Wonderful." Moe clapped her hands once and strode back over to the kitchen island. "Let me get back to this shepherd's pie. No one's leaving this house tonight without full bellies. You're all going to need it out in that cold. No hot chocolate can do what my cooking can," she muttered.

Wolf snorted, and Nessa glanced at him. His green eyes glimmered with amusement, but when they connected with hers, the humor dimmed, softening with a warmth she didn't quite understand.

She also didn't grasp the meaning of the jolt of crackling electricity in her chest at the sight of it.

Inappropriate. That's what it was. Because she had no business feeling anything for a complete stranger. *You're here to fulfill your absentee father's dying wish.* That's what she needed to focus on. Well, that and making it through the next month with a moody preteen without inciting the next world war.

She sighed, picking up her fork and digging into the delicious sandwich on her plate.

If she were going to survive this, she was going to need a lot of hot chocolate.

A lot of hot chocolate laced with a shit ton of whiskey.

CHAPTER FOUR

SHE'D SAID IT BEFORE, and she'd say it again...

"Damn, you guys really take Christmas serious around here."

Beside her, Wolf's deep chuckle stroked over her chilled cheeks, reached beneath the collar of her coat and caressed the skin of her throat and farther down. She fidgeted, as if that could displace some of that heat. But nope. No hope there. Just as there'd been no hope of eluding him when she and Ivy had arrived fifteen minutes earlier in downtown Rose Bend for the Christmas tree lighting.

Nessa surveyed the huge open field that a street sign had identified as The Glen. It sat at the end of Main Street, hard to miss. Especially with the ginormous tree sitting smack in the middle of it. Wooden posts lined the field, with garland and festive multicolored lights wound around them. More lights adorned an array of booths crowded onto the left side of The Glen and were strung along the top of a huge tent on the far right side.

The illumination enabled her to easily locate Ivy. Unbidden, a smile tugged at the corner of Nessa's mouth. Her sister might be reserved—*shit*, would her heart ever not fucking seize with guilt when she looked at Ivy?—but Cher Dennison, one half of the twins, didn't seem to know the meaning of the word. Moe had been right about her kids and Ivy. As if Cher and Ivy had been besties all their lives, as soon as Wolf had introduced them, the beautiful teen with mahogany skin and light brown curls had hooked her arm through Ivy's and dragged her off. Now, Ivy stood near the stage with Cher, Sonny and a few more kids. She wasn't laughing and talking as animatedly as the others, but she did wear a smile, and she appeared...

"She's fine," Wolf said.

Apparently, mind reader was a talent of his along with professional wreath hauler and grower of beards. Nessa shot him a glance, which she sincerely prayed contained all the disgruntlement in her soul at his unwelcome intrusiveness. And too-keen observation skills.

"And to answer your question, yes, we do take Christmas seriously. Because it's serious business. Peace on earth and goodwill toward men is not something you half-ass, Nessa Hunt. You use your whole ass."

The bark of laughter erupted from her, taking her by surprise. She slapped a hand over her mouth. A big, warm hand wrapped around her wrist and gently lowered her arm.

"It's okay, Nessa," Wolf simultaneously admonished and assured her with a small shake of his head. "No one's going to cross the street, or the field, just because you indulge in a bit of inappropriate, loud laughter. Which, by the way, isn't inappropriate at all." He arched an eyebrow. "That's one of the pros about living in a small town as opposed to a big city. We embrace our crazy."

She didn't laugh again. Couldn't. Not with his touch branding her wrist through her coat and glove. The sensual, solid weight of it had evaporated every last drop of amusement like the sun soaking up a summer rain. Exerting every ounce of control learned on the battlefield of an emergency room, she didn't lift her other hand to rub the tingling skin. Didn't shift away from him when her instincts screeched at her to do just that.

"Well, my mother used to say all the time that she'd rather be crazy than care what people think about her," Nessa murmured, then mentally slapped a palm to her forehead. *Dammit.* Why had she mentioned her mother? This was what the lingering effect of his touch did to her. Had her slipping up and letting loose personal information.

Next thing you know, she would be telling him about...

No. Nope. Not going there.

She was here tonight—this whole damn month of December—so Ivy could apparently bond with the place her father and mother had brought her all those years ago. Not to bond with *her*, as Isaac's letter had led Nessa to believe. Which was fine. Nessa had come here to rest, regroup, heal and return to her job better than ever.

Preferably without panic attacks.

"Used to?" he murmured. Of course he would pick up on those telltale words, but she wasn't tugging on the bait. She hadn't spoken about her mother or her death with a therapist; no way was she doing it with a stranger.

"So when is this supposed to start?" She rubbed her gloved hands together, not replying to his question. Tilting her head back, she stared up at the tree that could rival the white spruce from Nova Scotia that would stand tall in Boston Common in just a few days. A gorgeous red-and-gold skirt with hand-sewn presents, a sleigh, a jolly Santa and an elegantly scrolled *Merry Christmas* circled the bottom of the trunk. "Good Lord, this is one huge tree. Did someone venture up into one of those mountains to cut it down?" She squinted at his beard. "I don't want to stereotype, but..."

He snorted. "Snark duly noted. I hate to disappoint you,

but no, I don't throw around axes or chop down trees in my spare time. A family the next town over owns a Christmas tree farm. Why the eye roll?" He spread his hands, palms up. "You asked."

"I just… Really? A Christmas tree farm?" She shook her head, half amused, half what-the-fuck-Hallmark-movie-have-I-catapulted-into. "I feel like I'm in some wholesome holiday film. Any minute I'm expecting an announcement about the start of the gingerbread house competition."

"Don't be silly."

"I'm just saying—"

"That's not until next week."

"That's not…" She gaped at him. "You're shittin' me."

"See?" He dipped his chin. "If you were actually in a wholesome film, 'shittin' me' would never be allowed." Lowering his head, he murmured next to her ear, "They're about to start. And if my brother catches me talking to a beautiful woman instead of paying attention to his opening speech, I'll never hear the end of it."

She stared at him, momentarily stunned. Beautiful woman? A shiver step-danced down her spine, followed by a shimmy of—what? Trepidation? Excitement? Pleasure? Those last two were bad. Very bad.

"Don't flirt with me," she ordered, voice flat.

The corner of his mouth quirked. "Is that what I'm doing?"

"You damn well know it is. And stop it."

He studied her, a glint entering his eyes that had her silently groaning. She didn't want this man curious about her. Didn't want him thinking about her at all.

Liar.

Oh shut up.

Dammit. Now she was arguing with herself.

"Tell me, Nessa," he said softly. "Is it me in particular that has those hackles up or men in general? Is there something I need to specifically apologize for or do I need to issue a blanket apology for my gender?"

"Hello, everyone," a deep, smooth voice boomed through the crisp night air. "As your mayor, Cole Dennison, I'd like to welcome you to Rose Bend's thirty-fifth annual Yulefest and the opening Christmas tree lighting."

Dragging her attention from Wolf, Nessa focused on the tall, well-built man on stage clothed in a long, caramel-colored wool coat and thick scarf. His honey-brown skin gleamed under the stage's lights, his dark curls framing his sculpted cheekbones.

Wait. Cole...Dennison?

She glanced from the imposing figure to the man beside her. "Wait. The *mayor* is your *brother*?"

Wolf winced. "I know. Such an overachiever, that one," he tsked. But no one could mistake the dry note in his voice for anything but pride. She certainly didn't.

Shaking her head, she turned back to the stage just as a pretty blonde woman strolled onto the stage carrying a vibrantly wrapped box with a large handle.

"Thanks, Caroline." Cole Dennison smiled, accepting the present, then returning his gaze to the crowd. "The lighting of the Christmas tree dates back hundreds of years, where the green of the trees symbolized the renewal and continuance of life in dark times. And the lights—first candles and later bulbs—first represented the light of the sun after the solstice. And later, Jesus Christ being the light of the world. The beauty of our community and this world is that we are all made up of different religions and faiths. Though Christmas may mean various things for us, for most, we can agree, it's a time of peace, love, joy and family. A time when the world is a little bit softer, kinder and yes, more beautiful. The Christmas tree represents that beauty. When the innate kindness of the human spirit shines bright and lights the world."

Applause swelled and thundered for a couple of minutes, and even Nessa clapped, because man, as far as sentimental speeches went, Wolf's brother had nailed it.

Y'know, if she went for that sort of thing. Which she didn't.

"Can I have Lee Mills come up here, please?" Cole smiled as an adorable boy of about six or seven years old climbed the steps and crossed the stage. When the child grinned up at the mayor, the lights clearly caught the missing two front teeth, and Cole settled a hand on the boy's hat-covered head. "Lee here, and the other children at the This Is Home youth home, handmade ornaments for our tree. As thanks, proceeds from several of our events this season will benefit the home, and tonight Lee will be lighting our Christmas tree. Give him a hand!"

The boy beamed as the townspeople chanted his name and cheered, and even Nessa, self-admitted grinch, couldn't help but grin as his little chest puffed out beneath his coat.

"Ready?" Cole knelt down next to Lee, holding out the bow-wrapped box to him.

"Ready!" Lee yelled, earning more chuckles from the crowd.

"Great. Now, we're going to count down from ten, and when we get to one, you press down the handle, okay?" When Lee nodded, Cole held up his free hand, five fingers splayed wide. "Let's go! Ten. Nine. Eight..."

The townspeople joined in, and the night air echoed with the countdown. Nessa couldn't say exactly when she joined in, but before "Four" reverberated around her, she yelled it along with everyone else. Wolf's deep voice rose above the others, vibrating through her, and she tried not to stare. Tried. And failed.

She reasoned that the man was a veritable giant, so she had no choice but to look at him. But she did have a choice whether or not to trace the razor-sharp blades of his cheekbones. Or the arrogant slope of his nose. She could've chosen to glance away from the almost-too-lush curves of his wide mouth. She could've opted not to wonder if his beard would tickle her skin or lightly abrade it...

Mouth suddenly dry, she swallowed hard, throat closing tight over "Two." Not caring how he perceived her action, she erred on the side of caution and edged a couple of inches away from him. Bad enough she still battled the urge to rub her ear in an attempt to erase the phantom warmth of his breath against her skin. And that she couldn't purge his quietly taunting question from her mind.

Tell me, Nessa. Is it me in particular that has those hackles up or men in general? Is there something I need to specifically apologize for or do I need to issue a blanket apology for my gender?

Oh yes, bad enough she couldn't decide on the answer to that question. Because, okay, she might have a chip on her shoulder toward the male gender at large. It seemed the ones she'd loved—from Isaac to Jeremy—who were supposed to unconditionally love her in return, all lied and abandoned her.

But Wolf... She'd met him hours ago. And yet the man should apologize for...what? Stirring a desire inside her that she'd believed Jeremy had extinguished? Making her reevaluate a vow to swear off men? Especially handsome men? Breathing?

She shifted over another inch.

Just 'cause.

"One!"

The shout broke through her thoughts, jerking her out of her head and back to the imminent lighting. As soon as the countdown reached its culmination, Lee slammed down the handle on the box. Logically, Nessa figured someone stood backstage with a switch that flipped the lights on. Yet the awe and joy on Lee's face as the tree lit up had delight ballooning inside her chest.

And as she tilted her head back and gazed up at the magnificent sight of the Christmas tree, its dense branches decorated with not just the homemade ornaments Cole mentioned, but with gorgeous glass balls, multicolored bulbs and red-and-silver tinsel, Nessa was glad she'd risked her nearly frostbitten toes and come tonight.

No, she didn't buy into all this Christmas frenzy, but for her first Christmas tree lighting? Not bad. Not bad at all.

"Let's give Lee a round of applause, folks," Cole said. The little boy bowed so deeply, his head nearly brushed the stage. Nessa shook her head, and Cole chuckled. "Let me be the first to wish all of you a Merry Christmas. Now, we have hot chocolate, cider and several stalls open for shopping. Enjoy yourselves. And remember, tomorrow night on Main Street is the Santa Run. Six o'clock. Good night!"

"You survived your first Christmas tree lighting, Nessa Hunt. How did you like it?" Wolf asked, stuffing his hands inside his coat pockets and arching a dark eyebrow. "And before you reply, let me warn you. Anything other than 'It was great' would be the wrong answer."

"How about it was all right?" She mimicked his pose.

He snorted. "How about you enjoyed yourself?"

"I could've been putting on a brave front to cover the

fact that I was losing feeling in my face," she said, only half joking.

"Oh, Nessa." He heaved a dramatic-as-hell sigh. "You can try and adopt that big-city ennui if you like, but the delight I saw on your face when that tree lit up can't be faked. You enjoyed yourself."

Heart thumping in her chest, she forced a frown. Forced herself not to focus on the fact that he'd been watching her close enough to glimpse her expression. "Ennui?" She wrinkled her nose, loosing a slightly strained laugh. "Really?"

"What can I say? I'm a worldly, learned man."

"Worldly, huh? What part of the globe is that beard from? Or what century?" She narrowed her eyes on him, tapping a gloved fingertip against her lip.

"You're going there?" Wolf crossed his arms over his chest, his sensual lips curling into a smile. "Between my beard and your haircut, we have a full Viking."

"Ouch." Nessa winced, patting the close-shaved side of her head. "That's fucking brutal."

They stared at one another. Then snickered.

Then laughed.

"So, truth time, Nessa the Proud," he murmured, and part of her longed to roll her eyes at his off-the-cuff Viking moniker. And the other part? Well, that part needed to grab ahold of the pride he accused her of having and stop preening under his compliments. "Admit it. You like my beard."

By *like* did he mean she had an itch to run her fingers through it and tug on the bristly strands? Because if so, then yes, maybe she did.

But damn if she'd confess that aloud.

"It's aiight."

"Tough crowd." With a smirk, he jerked his chin. "C'mon, let me get some hot chocolate in you. My treat."

"Oh no," she objected, her hands slamming up, palms out. She shook her head for added emphasis. "You don't have to do that. As a matter of fact, I insist you don't." One thing she'd learned early from her mother: always do for yourself. No handouts. Call it pride, call it stubbornness, whatever. But it was a cardinal rule of hers. As long as she provided for herself, she didn't have to depend on anyone else. Definitely didn't have to worry about them disappointing her, failing her or taking away what she'd come to treasure. "Actually, I probably need to find Ivy and get back to the inn."

She pulled her phone free of her pocket, and glanced at the time, pretending his gaze wasn't branding the side of her face.

"Nessa?"

"Yes?"

"Could you look at me?"

Stifling a sigh, she lifted her head and met his emerald gaze.

"It's a hot chocolate," he said softly. Gently.

Resentment flared bright and hot in her chest at the tone. No, it wasn't *just* hot chocolate. It was so much more than that. Not that she needed to explain *it* or *her* to him. Not him, with his huge house, doting mother, loving family and Thomas Kinkade–painting town. He couldn't possibly understand loss, abandonment and only having yourself to depend on. He couldn't understand a fear of failure and not having a safety net.

Or having parents one day, having a career, a whole identity, and having none of that the next.

So no, it wasn't *just* hot chocolate.

"I said no, thank you," she replied, injecting a steel in her voice he could either respect or not. And if he didn't, well, that would tell her more than she needed to know about Wolf Dennison.

"Okay," he murmured, nodding, surprising her by letting it go so easily. In her experience—namely with Jeremy—most people would've pressed her into explaining or tried to shame her into accepting. "Why don't you try and call Ivy and see where she's at. Tell her to meet us by the hot chocolate stand, and you can buy one for her while we wait."

Good idea. And it meant granting her several more moments where she could avoid speaking or looking directly at this man who she so desperately tried to paint with one brush but who insisted on covering himself in a completely different coat.

She pulled up her Favorites list and tapped on Ivy's name. After three rings, the girl's breathless voice echoed down the line. "Hey, Nessa."

"Hey, what's your location?"

"I'm with Sonny and Cher over at the food tent. We're getting cookies and then plan on heading over to the shopping booths to see what they have."

"I was thinking we should head back to the inn—" Nessa said.

"Can't we stay just a little longer? It's not even eight thirty yet, and what're we going to do back there anyway?" Ivy demanded.

A dull ache started at the back of Nessa's head, one that usually coincided with Ivy's *tone*. The tone that warned, *I'm about to go into a full-out preteen hellish mood that all the berserkers and centurions in Fortnite won't be able to save you from.* Usually, Nessa had no problem going head-to-head with Ivy, but another lesson she'd learned in life—especially since becoming the girl's guardian—was to pick your battles.

And just because Nessa had the desperate urge to escape Wolf's unsettling, too-perceptive gaze and the equally disconcerting shadow of his sexy, too-big body didn't mean she should cut short the first amount of fun Ivy was experiencing since her father's death.

Dammit. Sometimes she hated adulting.

"Okay," she conceded. "Call me when you're finished." But before Ivy could fully get out her reply, Nessa continued in the no-nonsense tone that got her the nickname Nurse Freeze. "And hey, no longer than a half hour. It's been a long day."

"Fine." Ivy ended the call before Nessa could point out that *fine* only had one syllable not three, and that a half hour could become fifteen minutes real quick.

"There is no way in hell I was that mouthy and moody at twelve. My mother wouldn't have allowed me to live if I'd been," she muttered, stuffing her phone back in her pocket.

Wolf laughed, moving forward, and she fell into step beside him. "You don't want to know how many times my mother told us she understood why some animals ate their young."

Nessa huffed out a chuckle, liking Moe more and more.

"I guarantee you, though, we were little shits, too. They're just more tech-savvy, better-dressed little shits."

"I'll give you the tech-savvy, but I beg to differ on the better dressed," she grumbled as they approached the wooden booth decked out in red-and-silver tinsel along with a crazy amount of cutout gingerbread men and women. Whoever decorated this stall must've added a little something with "proof" to their hot chocolate.

"Hey, Wolfgang!" called a lovely woman with long, dark brown hair pulled up into a high ponytail. Nessa snorted at Wolf's growl. And if the shape of her mouth and the elegant, sharp slant of her cheekbones hadn't announced her as his sister, that teasing note in her voice and his answer, an irritated rumble, certainly would've. "Come on over here and give your baby sister some love!"

Oh yeah. I want whatever she's having, Nessa snickered.

Scowling, Wolf marched over to his sister and nabbed her paper cup out of her hand. Holding it up to his nose, he sniffed. "What've you been up to, Leo?"

"Oh calm your tits." Grabbing the beverage back, she leveled a matching glare back at him. For a moment, the resemblance between them went from passing to uncanny. "There's nothing in there but hot cider. Can't a girl just be high on having a night off?" She poked a feeling in his massive chest. "Now look what you're doing. Giving your friend a bad first impression of your beautiful, engaging and brilliant sister." The brunette grinned, wriggling her fingers at Nessa. "Hi there. I'm Leontyne. Leo for short."

"Hi," Nessa said. She knew this one—Leontyne for Leontyne Price, the famous opera singer. "Nessa Hunt."

"Oh our guest at the inn? The nurse from Boston?" Not waiting for her reply, Leontyne shifted around Wolf and strode to her, arm outstretched. "It's so nice to meet you. Welcome to Rose Bend."

Accepting her hand, Nessa shook it, the other woman's grip strong, confident. "Thanks. Your family's inn is beautiful."

"We try." She grinned. "And we're so glad to have you. Even if it means you've been stuck with him—" she jerked a thumb over her shoulder toward Wolf "—this evening."

Wolf sighed. "Me. Standing right here."

Leontyne slid him a glance. "I know. While this lady waits for her hot chocolate. Go. Be useful." She flicked a hand at him.

Biting into her cheek to keep from smirking at their by-play, Nessa opened the bag slung sideways across her body and removed a five-dollar bill from her wallet. She passed it to Wolf, and said, "You can just donate the change."

He took the money, and relief trickled through her that their gloved fingertips didn't touch.

"While he does man things, let me introduce you." Leontyne didn't wait for acquiescence but hooked her free arm through Nessa's and guided her over to the woman she'd been standing with.

Okay, well then. Apparently, Leo was touchy-feely like her mother. They were what Evelyn Reed would've called people who knew no strangers. Or personal space.

"Nessa, I'd like to introduce you to my best friend, sister-in-love, also our illustrious mayor's wife, Sydney Dennison. Syd," Leontyne continued and smiled at her friend, "this is Nessa Hunt, a guest for the next month at the inn."

"Ooh I recognize that particular look in your eyes." Sydney laughed, and snuck in an embrace. What was it about this town and its people? Did they export pine cones, apple cider and beauty? Petite and gorgeous with dark brown eyes, a face that belonged on a movie screen and natural curls that gave Nessa a serious case of hair envy, Sydney also had a smirk that only added to her loveliness, didn't detract from it. "So what're you really thinking? I'm getting the hell out of here before they turn me into a Christmas pod person, or it's too late and I'm glad to be here at the end of all things."

Nessa snickered. "I'm about fifty-fifty." She paused. Returned the smirk. "And bonus points for the *Return of the King* reference."

"Meh." Sydney shrugged a shoulder. "Leo is a *Lord*

of the Rings fanatic. It's either pick up things or…" She frowned. "Well, yeah, I'm just afraid not to pick up things."

More hilarity bubbled up in Nessa's chest, and, damn. When was the last time she'd laughed this much? Definitely not since her mother had died. But even before then… God, it was sad that she couldn't pinpoint an exact memory.

"Here you go." Wolf appeared at her elbow, and her thank-you was almost a little too fervent for a hot beverage. But if he noticed, he let it go, instead passing her the paper cup. "I've been gone exactly three minutes. Have you let them conscript you into their brood yet, Nessa?"

"Brood, Wolf? That's implying that we're hens. And that's sexist," Sydney tsked. "Besides…we're a coven," she added, sipping from her own cup.

"Oh that's much better," he drawled, then directed a scowl at Leontyne. "What vile influence are you having on my sweet sister-in-law?"

Leontyne widened her eyes in feigned innocence. "I have no idea what you're talking about. Why, I was just talking to her about agency, equality and sexual autonomy."

"Shit," he grumbled, scrubbing a hand down his face. "All I heard was sex."

Nessa stared at them, head going back and forth as if watching a tennis match, fascinated by their familial interaction. And the glee they took in ribbing one another. But also their obvious affection for one another. Both cast a bright, glaring spotlight on her relationship with Ivy. They hadn't been raised as sisters and didn't behave like them.

But the truth was, they weren't sisters. Not by connection and not by…

She shivered.

From the cold that whispered over her skin. From the

secrets that settled in her bones like a sickness. But that's what lies did. They ate away at a person.

And standing here, in the light of this loving family, she'd never felt her lies more.

"You're cold." Before she could refute the claim, Wolf handed his cup over to Leontyne, yanked his black hat off his head and tugged it down over hers. "With that Viking hair, the wind is probably chillier," he teased.

"Thanks," she murmured, tipping her head back and meeting his gaze. He didn't move away, didn't release his hold on the cap. For a moment, his gaze dipped to her mouth, and her breath caught in her throat. The look was almost physical, and she barely stopped herself from lifting her fingertips to brush her lips.

His big body blocked out the wintry weather, and his mint scent enveloped her, taunted her. Or more specifically, the bit of strong, golden throat right above his coat collar and scarf taunted her. Enticed her with the promise of a warm, safe place to burrow her nose and inhale him, to maybe even sample that elusive flavor beneath the wintergreen that she suspected belonged solely to him.

Enticed her to…hide.

Because that temptation pulled too strong, she stepped back.

And met two wide and very curious stares.

Leontyne glanced from Nessa to Wolf, then back to her. "Huh."

The urge to take another step back—big enough to carry her out of The Glen and back to the car—vibrated through her, and only a hand pressed to the middle of her shoulder blades prevented her from retreating.

"Careful," Wolf warned, and a swift look over her shoulder revealed he'd saved her from knocking over a garbage can.

Great. In the space of time since she'd met him, she'd plowed into him, been dumped on her ass, sported a wreath crown and now almost two-stepped with a trash can.

What was it about Wolf Dennison that set her on edge? That had her so weirdly attuned to him but out of step with herself?

"Wolf," Leontyne whispered, stepping up to them and placing a hand on his arm. No smile curved her mouth, and the dimming of her gray-blue eyes reflected the taut note in her voice. "Incoming."

Reluctant curiosity crept through Nessa at the switch in Leontyne's demeanor. Wolf stiffened next to Nessa, his big frame going as still as one of the statues in Boston Public Garden. And a glance at his face...

She shivered again, despite wearing his hat.

Since meeting him, she'd glimpsed his warm, teasing smile. His amused grin. His wry smirk. Even his mock scowl.

But not this.

Not this...nothing. This blank sheet of expression with no emotion written on it. No, that wasn't accurate. One look into his eyes belied that remote mask. Green ice chips so hard, so painfully sharp, she had to glance away.

Up until now, she hadn't seen this version of Wolf Dennison.

And she didn't like it. Not at all.

"Hi, everyone," a new, sultry, feminine voice said, and as Wolf went impossibly stiffer, Nessa had her answer. Not *what* could cause this change in him—who.

But which woman did the honor belong to? Nessa studied the two newcomers. Was it the tall, willowy redhead and the owner of the pageant-princess voice? Or the shorter, slender woman with the black hair and violet eyes that stared at Wolf like he might disappear into a puff of smoke if she dared take her gaze off him?

Yep. She'd bet her prized letter from New Kids on the Block's Donnie Wahlberg that it was the former.

Who was she?

Better yet, who was she *to him*?

"Jenna," Leontyne replied, and Nessa noted how Wolf's sister's cool reception of the redhead lacked that Dennison cheer.

Not that Jenna seemed to notice or let it bother her. Jenna moved closer, giving Leontyne and Wolf—who still didn't move—quick hugs and air kisses. Then she paused in front of Sydney, and what could only be described as a sneer faintly twisted her poppy-red mouth.

"Sydney."

"Jenna," Sydney said, bland. "It's good—well, hey."

Nessa couldn't control the jacking of her eyebrow. *Whoa.* That didn't sound friendly. At all.

"Jenna, I'd like you to meet Nessa Hunt. She and her sister, Ivy, are guests at the inn for the holidays. Nessa," Leontyne said as she turned to her, smile as fake as the ID Nessa'd had in high school, "this is Jenna Landon."

"Nice to meet you. I hope you're enjoying our small corner of the world. We're like one big family here in Rose Bend."

The other woman smiled widely, showing all her teeth, and even if the rest of the group hadn't reacted as if this woman carried the strain for the next zombie plague, that smile would've had Nessa leery. Shark smiles—from people who grinned so huge you could count every tooth in their mouth—could rarely be trusted. In her experience, those wide grins overcompensated for the secrets they were hiding.

So what was it that Jenna Landon didn't want anyone to know?

"This is my friend Olivia Allen. She's in town for the holidays, as well, although she grew up here. Leo, you remember Olivia. Wolf, I know you do," Jenna added with a coy tone that didn't match the avaricious glitter in her blue eyes.

"Nice to meet you. Both of you," Nessa murmured.

"You, too." Olivia's gaze finally shifted from Wolf to meet hers. But it didn't last long, and the yearning in that one, brief glimpse had Nessa's throat tightening. "Wolf," the other woman whispered, "it's wonderful to see you again. You look great."

"Olivia."

The greeting was polite. The nod, equally so. And from the flinch Olivia didn't quite manage to conceal, painful.

God, only a dinner party with Kanye West and Taylor Swift could *possibly* have been more awkward.

"So, Olivia," Nessa said, once more drawing the attention of the woman with black hair. "Jenna mentioned you're in town for the holidays, too. Where are you visiting from?"

Jesus, small talk ranked right under a rusty spork in the eye, but one must do what one must do.

"I moved to Boston three years ago."

"Really? I'm from Boston, too," Nessa said. Then she lamely added, "Great city."

"I'm sure." The only thing missing from Jenna's saccharine smile was a pat on the head. "But Olivia isn't just visiting." The redhead paused, then announced with dramatic flair, "She's moving back to Rose Bend. Isn't that wonderful?"

"You're kidding me," Leontyne snapped.

"No, I'm not kidding," Jenna replied through gritted teeth, but still maintaining that pageant smile. Wow. That was a talent. The redhead swung her attention to Wolf. "Obviously, Olivia has missed Rose Bend and the people here. And I think it's great that she's returned home. Don't you think so, Wolf?"

"Jenna, please," Olivia murmured, pink staining her cheekbones. "Wolf." She edged closer, her violet eyes delivering a silent plea. "Can we go somewhere and talk?"

Glancing at the still-silent Wolf and then at Olivia, Nessa could practically feel the tension snap in the air. And it didn't just emanate from Wolf and Olivia, but from Leontyne and Sydney, as well. Nessa didn't understand it, didn't grasp the nuances and undercurrents, and frankly, didn't desire to. Because it didn't require a master's in history to realize Wolf and Olivia had plenty of it.

Didn't matter.

Another of her rules: mind your own damn business if you don't want people digging in yours.

Wolf flinched.

No one else caught the almost imperceptible jerk of his body; at least, Nessa didn't think anyone else did. She stood closest to him, and the small recoil vibrated through her.

Damn.

"Actually," she piped up with a cheer that only came from alcohol and, well…more alcohol, "I need to go find my sister, and Wolf already promised to take me over to her." She wrapped her fingers around his thick wrist. "Do you mind if we leave now? It's getting late, and I'd like to head back to the inn."

Jenna frowned, her mouth flattening into a line so thin her full lips almost disappeared. "Really? You don't need

Wolf for that. I'm sure Leo or Sydney would be glad to help you find your sister."

"Nope," Leontyne chimed in, once again cheerful, throwing Nessa a blinding smile. "No can do. I was just on my way over to Cherrie Moore's booth to shop for Moe's Christmas gift."

When Jenna shifted her glare to Sydney, the other woman just shrugged a shoulder. "No excuse. I'm just not going to do it." Giving Nessa a wink, she turned to Leontyne, crooking her elbow. "I'll walk you over to the stalls. You know I'm a sucker for Cherrie's jewelry. And drooling over her man."

"Maddox *is* fine." Leontyne sighed, hooking an arm through Sydney's.

"It's the tattoos." Sydney fanned herself, then with a lascivious cackle, the two walked away without a backward glance, leaving their unholy foursome.

God help her.

"Wolf?" Nessa squeezed his wrist, and for the first time since Jenna and Olivia approached them, he moved. His head dipped, and that fathomless green gaze met hers, and if she'd had doubts about butting in where she didn't belong—and yes, she had—then the shadows in those eyes hushed them. "Ready?"

"Yeah," he said.

That's it. But that's all she needed.

Tightening her grip on him, she forced another smile. Hopefully her last one for the night, because good Lord, her bullshit-o-meter could only take so much.

"It was nice meeting you both. If you'll excuse us, I really need to find my sister. Preteens, right?" With that parting comment, she led Wolf away toward the tents, and even the delicious aroma of cookies, funnel cakes and roasted peanuts couldn't distract her from her mission—to put as much distance between Wolf and Jenna and Olivia as possible.

Where was Ivy anyway? Pulling her phone from her pocket, she shot the girl a text to meet by the stage.

"Preteens, right?" Wolf rumbled, just as Nessa slipped the cell back in her pocket.

"Oh so you *can* talk?" She arched an eyebrow. "And whatever. I panicked. That Jenna had me feeling like if I didn't make a move, she was seconds from giving me a swirly in that pot of hot chocolate. The mean-girl force is strong with that one."

"You're not wrong." He tunneled his fingers over his hair, nearly dislodging the stubby ponytail that held his hair back from his face.

Several heartbeats of silence passed between them as he stared at the empty stage and she studied him.

"Just to make sure—we're going to pretend that didn't just happen back there, right?"

"Yes."

His scrutiny shifted back to her, and she easily read the flinty resolve there and in the grim set of his mouth. She sighed.

"Fine." Nessa narrowed her eyes on him. "But so you know, I'm not used to dodging the big-ass pink elephant in the room. So if we're not going to talk about that one, can we address another one?"

His head cocked to the side. "Yeah."

"Okay." She tucked her hands in her coat pockets and mimicked his pose, tilting her head. "I don't know how to ask this with any kind of political correctness, so please forgive me if I offend. But you do know your family's like

Rose Bend's clapback to the Pearsons from *This Is Us*, right?"

Wolf stared at her. Blinked. Blinked again.

Then threw back his head and howled.

By the time his laughter abated to low chuckles, she couldn't suppress the smile that curved her lips. The abominable snowman had disappeared, and the gently teasing giant she'd become familiar with the past few hours returned. Relief rushed through her, and no, she didn't bother questioning its intensity.

"We've had several names thrown our way over the years, but we definitely haven't heard the Pearsons. Which, can we just agree, is one hell of a family? Well, without the whole father-dying-and-leaving-me-curled-up-in-a-fetal-position-for-two-weeks-after-the-fire thing."

"Did you just...?" Nessa gaped at him. "Did you...?" She leaned forward, her voice lowering to a whisper. "Did you actually admit that Jack dying left you weeping and traumatized and calling for your mama?"

"You heard nothing, woman." His brows jacked down over his nose in a dark scowl. "Nothing."

"Oh sure." She held up her hands, palms out. And snickered. "Kevin."

He growled at her, but a second later, he shook his head. "Come here."

Inside her, something sweet, hot and achy pulled taut in response to his command. Her breath snagged in her lungs, and she froze, the proverbial deer caught in the headlights. Only instead of a car bearing down on her, it was the force of Wolf Dennison's innate sexuality and charisma. And though every self-protective instinctive screamed at her to run, she did just the opposite.

She went to him.

Because she trusted him not to harm her? Maybe physically. But there were other ways a man could hurt a woman, and as certain as she was that the holidays meant an influx of traffic into the emergency room, she knew, given a chance, Wolf could devastate her in all those ways. Yet she stood still as he cupped one of her hips through her coat, lifted his free hand and trailed his fingertips over the closely cut side of her head. The caress tingled in her breasts, tightening her nipples, rippling lower in her belly... and lower still...

What did that say about her?

Masochist. Starved for affection. Needed to stop watching *Aquaman* every time it came on HBO.

D—all of the above.

And all sad.

"Why do you keep touching me?" As soon as the words echoed in the air between them, she mentally cringed, flames of mortification dancing over her skin. God, she hadn't meant to say that. To let him know his nearness bothered her. That *he* bothered her.

"Do I?" he asked mildly, yet that soft tone belied the sharpness of his gaze, the firmness of his hold. The devastating sensuality of his touch as he dragged his fingers over her temple and traced her jaw.

Several strands of hair had made a break from the tie he'd had them in and teased the corner of his mouth, catching on the bristles of his beard. She focused on those rebellious strands, rather than on the riotous sensations wreaking havoc on her body.

And her common sense.

"Yes," she said, feeling foolish. Why, she couldn't explain to her own self. Because she needed him to acknowledge it? Or more specifically the *why* of it? "Earlier in the kitchen. Tonight at the hot chocolate stand. Now. Is that a Dennison thing, like the hugging?"

Or is it a me thing?

The question flew through her head, there and gone before she could banish it to the bowels of whatever hell it'd crawled from. She didn't want it to be about her.

Just as she didn't want to notice how faint lines radiated from the corners of his eyes. Laugh lines. Or how those same eyes weren't just simple emerald. Striations of black and dark blue melded to form a gorgeous hue that defied the simple description of green. Or how a faint dip dented the middle of his full bottom lip.

She curled her fingers into the sides of her thighs. It wasn't enough that her mother had charged her with keeping a secret and turned her into a liar by omission. Now Nessa was lying to herself. It was a bad habit.

"I'll be the first to admit my family is an affectionate bunch, and to the unsuspecting, we can be a little overwhelming. But, Nessa..." He leaned forward, his voice lowering to a rough rumble that had liquid desire winding a treacherous path south. She fought not to squirm under his watchful gaze and reveal how his nearness threatened her equilibrium—and the dry state of her panties. "Your decision. Which one do you really want to discuss? Why I called you closer or why I can't seem to keep my hands to myself? Fair warning. One is going to be a short conversation and the other is going to be peppered with four-letter words."

Holy. Fuck.

And good God, would that be one of the words?

Staring into his eyes that had darkened with... Whew. She was too much of a coward to put a name to that. But staring into those eyes, her sex practically shouted.

But then her mind intruded, reminding her of Wolf's

behavior around Olivia Allen. Those two had a past, and it'd been clear Olivia wasn't over it. And from Wolf's stoicism and refusal to barely speak to the other woman, he might not be either.

Get involved with a man when she would be leaving in a matter of weeks?

Get involved with a man *who was hung up on another woman* when she would be leaving in a matter of weeks?

One was a terrible idea. The other was a terrible idea on roid rage.

"I'd like to talk about why you called me over here," she whispered.

He nodded, although... Was that a flicker of disappointment in his eyes? No, she was obviously projecting.

"Good choice." He nodded again, but then paused. "One thing, Nessa. My family, me—we tend to communicate with our hands as much as our words. But that doesn't mean it's okay and you just have to accept it, if that makes you uncomfortable. Your space is your space, and none of us will violate that. Understood?"

Here was her opportunity to tell him to back off, to not touch her. Right here. She was going to do it...

"Understood."

He lowered his hand from her face and cradled her other hip, and the touch seemed to brand her through her coat and clothes.

"Thank you."

Her head snapped back as if he'd clipped her on the chin. "For what?"

He didn't immediately answer but studied her so closely she fought not to squirm. Fully grown women did *not* squirm. At least, that's what she told herself. But those eyes...

Turn away. Don't look at me. She bit the inside of her

cheek to keep from embarrassing herself by letting that damning statement loose.

"For not pretending there wasn't a story," he murmured. "And for coming to my rescue."

Nessa parted her lips, a glib, dismissive reply hovering on her tongue. But it didn't emerge. Instead, she met his steady, piercing gaze, and slowly dipped her head.

"Believe me, I'm no knight in shining armor. Or knightess. Whatever the female equivalent is." Guilt propelled that confession out of her. As if, since she couldn't admit to one secret, she needed to confess this fault.

"I think *knight* is gender neutral. What do you do for a living when you're not visiting random Massachusetts small towns, Nessa?"

"I'm a nurse. In the ER."

"So a natural-born caretaker. A problem solver. A healer." He hummed. "Makes sense now."

"What does?" Why did she ask? She shouldn't have asked. She didn't want to know what he thought.

This lying thing was really getting out of hand.

"How you instinctively protect people. Seek to put them at ease. I saw it back at the inn with Ivy. You tried to do it again with that obviously tense…scene back there. And once more with me."

His voice dropped, and his lids lowered, momentarily hiding his eyes from her. When his lashes lifted, she clenched her fists at her sides to stop herself from comforting him. Touching him. Anything to erase those dark shadows from his eyes.

"You can't help who you are, and though I've never seen you in action, I bet you're damn good at your job."

His praise sliced through her chest, and in pure reflex, her hands flew to that invisible injury.

He couldn't know. Couldn't understand how his compliments made her feel like a fraud...a failure.

Made her tremble in fear.

When her mother had died, Nessa had thrown herself into work, finding solace in the hectic pace and organized chaos that had allowed her to think and operate on autopilot. But after Isaac's death and the burden of caring for a bitter and grieving preteen, work had ceased to be that panacea. It'd stopped being her escape and had become something she'd longed to escape from. Her coworkers accused her of being an iceberg, but like that floating mountain of ice, above the water, she appeared stalwart, strong, unshakeable. But underneath... Underneath, the murky darkness hid a thick mess of weariness, fury, pain and sorrow.

Was it any surprise she'd eventually crashed into herself like her own personal *Titanic*?

Yeah, it had been.

One minute she'd been starting an IV and in the next, she'd been crouched against the wall, clutching her chest, terrified she was having her own coronary episode. Panic attack, the doctor had later informed her. Years in the ER, cool under pressure, and she'd suffered a panic attack. The next day, her supervisor and friend had "suggested" Nessa accept the bereavement time she'd refused after her mother's death, as well as put in for the vacation days she never took. With little choice, she'd made the decision to take a break.

No one wanted an emergency room nurse who couldn't remain reliable under pressure. She'd already lost her parents and her man. Losing her job might prove to be her tipping point. And if she lost nursing, what would she have then?

Who would she *be* then?

"Nessa?" Big hands cupped a shoulder and the back of her head. "You okay?"

She blinked, the delicious warmth seeping from him jerking her out of her dark memories. A panic of a different kind stirred in her chest, her belly. "I'm fine." She stepped back and out of his hold. She couldn't *think* with his hands on her. And around him, she needed every sense, every working brain cell. "And because I didn't say it before, you're welcome."

He didn't reply but scrubbed a hand down his beard. Then his attention shifted over her shoulder.

"Here comes your sister," he said as she turned and spotted the trio of kids walking slowly in their direction.

Sonny and Cher linked arms with Ivy, their heads bent together. Even in the distance and shadows, Nessa caught the flash of Ivy's smile. Gratitude and…envy…flickered in her chest. Warming her and leaving a filthy grime. What kind of person was jealous of preteens? Jealous over a smile?

She shook her head, wishing she could do the same with her heart and dislodge the emotions that had squatted there without her permission.

"Your mom called it with them." She dipped her chin in their direction. "They already seem tight. I don't know if that's a good thing or a bad thing."

"Friends can never be a bad thing, Nessa."

They are when you have to leave them, or they leave you. And make no mistake—someone inevitably leaves.

She sank her teeth into her bottom lip, trapping that bit of truth. Wolf of Rose Bend, Massachusetts, with his big, gorgeous family in a fairy-tale inn and Christmas-frenzied town wouldn't understand.

So she didn't comment at all but instead frowned as another thought struck her. "Earlier you said several names have been thrown your family's way over the years." She stared at the stunning, grinning twins as they neared. Pictured Cole on the stage behind them, handsome and so distinguished. "Like what?"

A dark, fierce expression crossed his face, leaving only sadness and quiet rage. "You don't want to know. And I don't want to repeat them."

She nodded. No, she didn't want to know. But as a Black woman who lived in the diverse but historically not so racially tolerant city of Boston, she could easily imagine. Too easily.

God, sometimes people—this fucking world—sucked.

"Just to make sure," Wolf said, his gaze still focused on Ivy and the twins, "but we're going to pretend there isn't a story there between you two, right?" he asked, mimicking her earlier question to him.

"Yes."

He didn't throw her reply to him back at her, but it was there between them, deafening in its hypocrisy.

I'm not used to dodging the big-ass pink elephant in the room.

"Fair enough." A heavy beat of silence. "And, Nessa?"

"Yes?" she rasped.

He shifted forward.

Lowered his head next to hers.

"Welcome to Rose Bend, Nessa Hunt," he said, his lips grazing the shell of her ear, the soft strands of his hair brushing her cheek.

Right. Welcome.

She'd just arrived in town to fulfill her absentee father's dying wish.

But she'd never felt more like running away in her life.

CHAPTER FIVE

"Trevor, we're going to get ready to set the posts," Wolf said to the teenager who worked for him part-time. Squinting at the wooden base that they'd already prepped and built in the middle of the town square, he pointed to a tool next to the sawhorse. It looked like two skinny shovels tied together with a flat collar where the heads met the handles. "You get the posthole digger and start digging. I'll get on cutting the posts to length. If we knock this out in the next couple of hours, we can set the posts before we call it quits for the day."

Trevor Haynes nodded, his blond hair flopping over his forehead. "Sounds good."

They didn't indulge in small talk as they got to work. Not because Trevor was the average moody sixteen-year-old. Well, to be fair, he had been when he'd initially started working with Wolf five months ago. But then again, he'd been ordered to do so by Cole, who was his lawyer. When the choices presented to a person were work at the town inn or take your ass to juvie, that kind of ultimatum tended to shrivel up the warm-and-tinglies. Trevor wasn't a bad kid; he'd just fallen in with a fast crowd and had got caught up. Cole believed in him, though, and so Wolf had taken the kid on, too.

Yeah, Trevor had more or less been blackmailed into working with him, but they'd soon found their rhythm. The teen had taken to carpentry like a natural. Wolf only had to demonstrate a process or task a couple of times, and Trevor had it down. It was…exciting for Wolf to watch Trevor discover this new side of himself, this gift. Because that's what it was. An artistic gift for crafting. And for Wolf, it was an honor to be his mentor.

Like today. It was Saturday, and Trevor should be hanging out with his friends. Instead, he'd shown up at Wolf's cottage this morning, ready to ride down to the square and work on the gazebo. Yeah, he was a good, hard worker.

Now, if Wolf could just get Cher to stop turning into a real-life hearts-for-eyes emoji around him.

Wolf sighed as he tugged on his gloves, pulled on his safety goggles and picked up the circular saw. He'd really hate to have to take the kid out. Especially when he liked him so much.

"Hey, Wolf."

Setting the saw back down, he tugged the goggles up on top of his head and grinned at the girl standing in front of the sawhorse. Today, Ivy Hunt had her thick curls down in a cloud around her thin shoulders, several multicolored bobby pins holding the hair back from her pretty face. Like yesterday, she wore the same puffy winter coat, jeans and her ever-present earbuds. But unlike the first time he'd met her, she donned a smile.

"Morning, Mozart. What're you doing here?"

Ivy jerked a thumb over her shoulder. "I caught a ride with your sister Florence since she was coming downtown. I wanted to walk around and do some exploring."

"By yourself?" He frowned. Yes, Rose Bend was pretty safe, but it was still a town in twenty-first-century America. And she was just a young girl alone. He wouldn't even be comfortable with Cher walking aimlessly around, and she'd grown up here. "Where's your sister?"

A cloud whispered across her face, sweeping away her smile and leaving behind a sulky pout and brown eyes darker with shadows. Just as Trevor's surly demeanor hadn't put off Wolf, neither did Ivy's. Maybe because he could see behind the sneer to the hurt and the sadness. No, he didn't know her and Nessa's story—and he'd promised not to ask—but whatever it was, that tale contained a lot of grief and pain.

Since he was acquainted with both grief and pain, bed partners in the most fucked-up of ménages, he recognized them well.

"I don't know." Ivy shrugged a shoulder. "I left her at the inn. We didn't come here to be in each other's back pockets. She doesn't even want to be here," she muttered under her breath, but Wolf caught it.

Why? Why doesn't she want to be here? What happened between you two? What can I do to help?

Fuck. And that right there. That ever-present need to help, to jump in and rescue, summed up quite nicely why he needed to back far away from Ivy and her prickly, goddamn sexy sister.

Complications.

Tangled complications. He'd proved time and time again he couldn't save anyone. Quite the opposite. He failed them. Sometimes with consequences no one came back from. Including himself. So no, he wasn't anyone's savior.

He couldn't even help himself.

These two sisters. Even knowing the best thing he could do for either one of them was keep his distance and let them work their own shit out, it didn't stop him from wondering what had happened to make them circle each other like wary cats...or cage fighters searching for weakness.

Didn't stop him from wanting to protect them from whatever ghosts had pursued them all the way from Boston.

Didn't stop him from just...wanting.

Jesus. If he could shove his size-fourteen shoe up his own ass, he would. He'd deserve it for staring down one of his biggest mistakes last night and still standing here in the bright light of day and considering a repeat.

Olivia had been his first love. And though she'd claimed to return that love, she'd left Rose Bend—*left him*—because small-town life had been suffocating for her. He hadn't been enough to compete with the sophisticated lure of the big city.

Watching her drive away had done more than break him. It'd *shattered* him in a way that only returning stateside from Iraq without his best friend Raylon Brandt had done. He'd failed someone he'd loved, again.

He'd failed to protect Raylon in that small village in the desert.

And he'd failed to be enough for the woman he loved.

On the steps of his cottage, watching her car fade into the distance, he'd vowed never again to be a failure. To never disappoint another person...disappoint himself.

Nessa Hunt had his failure scrawled in permanent marker all over her.

Nothing good could come from getting involved with her. Not for either of them.

Yet, as he peered down at Ivy's defiant scowl—the angry glare that couldn't conceal the flickers of insecurity, of pain—he called himself about fifty-six different kinds of fool.

Shit.

And he was stepping right in it.

"Listen, Mozart, I don't know what that means," he said, cocking his head and crossing his arms over his chest. "But I do know that if Sonny or Cher up and disappeared on me, I would be losing my shit."

"Language," she grumbled.

"Right. Sorry." He paused, struggling to hold back his smile, seeing how this was definitely not a smile situation. But damn, she was making it difficult. "Anyway, I won't get into you and your sister's business, but even if you two aren't 'in each other's back pockets,' she still deserves to know when you've gone MIA so she doesn't worry."

"She's not worried. Relieved, maybe. Not worried," Ivy insisted, stubbornly, her mouth twisting down at the corners. When Wolf just stared at her, not budging, she rolled her eyes and pulled her phone out of her coat pocket. "How about a deal? If I call Nessa and let her know where I'm at, you let me stay here and help you."

Surprise whistled through him, and he arched his eyebrows. "You interested in carpentry?"

She shrugged a shoulder, what he was becoming to recognize as her tell—the I-care-but-damn-if-I-let-you-know tell. "My dad used to do work on home projects like bookshelves and tables for our neighbors. He'd let me help."

Used to.

Oh, sweetheart, I'm so sorry. Wolf's arms physically twinged with the need to pull this prickly girl into a hug and hold her just as he would one of the twins.

When Moe had mentioned Ivy's parents in the kitchen yesterday, he'd sensed something—a tense undercurrent between Nessa and Ivy about their father. But Wolf hadn't guessed their father was gone. He slowly lowered his arms, involuntarily taking a step toward Ivy. What about her mother? Was she dead, too? As soon as the question ghosted through his mind, the answer struck him with certainty.

Oh Jesus, this little girl.

She was going to break his heart.

Swallowing hard, he used the excuse of turning to his toolbox, opening the lid and removing an extra pair of gloves to get a grip on the emotion that shoved its way into his chest and throat. His family had known death. Flo and the twins had all been touched by it. He'd been scarred by it. Still bore the wounds…

And then more recently, Cole had lost his wife and baby during childbirth. Losing someone you loved… It irrevocably changed you, and sometimes not for the better. So, yeah, he got how death could alter a person.

He just… He just hated that Ivy knew it, too.

And as pointless as it was, he longed to protect her from the knowledge. But he couldn't.

He could give her just a little of the memories with her father, though.

"Call your sister. No negotiating on that," he said, injecting the same steel in his voice that he used when reminding the twins of the chores-first, video-games-YouTube-videos-second rule.

Dismay flashed over her face before she schooled it into a carefully constructed mask of *You suck anyway.* "So, you're saying I can't stay and help?"

"No." He extended the pair of gloves to her. "I'm saying that's not a deal I'm willing to make. We don't have to bargain in order for you to hang out and give me an extra pair of hands. If you want to stay, then I want you to. That's it. No strings." He sent a pointed look toward her cell phone. "Now call your sister."

Shock widened her eyes and parted her lips, erasing all

evidence of preteen sneering. "Really?" she breathed. "I can stay?"

"Really," he said, softly. "Make the call and let me show you where I need you."

At the words "I need you," her face lit up like that damn Christmas tree in The Glen, and Wolf had to turn away again and quickly heft up one of the posts he'd prepared for cutting. Either that or snatch that girl up in a hug she might not appreciate.

The Hunts.

His next failure. Permanent marker.

Damn.

CHAPTER SIX

ONE OF EVELYN REED's favorite books had been *Alice's Adventures in Wonderland*, and she'd often read it to Nessa at bedtime. Back then, Nessa hadn't wanted to hurt her mother's feelings, but she'd hated the book. Her feelings hadn't changed over the years. Seriously, who followed a strange rabbit *anywhere*? Ever heard of stranger danger? Stay home where it's safe and people don't threaten to chop off any body parts, chick!

But now, as Nessa strolled down Main Street's sidewalks crowded with morning shoppers and tourists, she silently apologized to Alice. She got it. While a letter in a will had sent her down the rabbit hole that was Rose Bend, MA, she now understood Wonderland's appeal to Alice. No, this pretty, quaint town didn't have talking, tea-drinking animals or homicidal playing cards. But it did have an old-fashioned pharmacy with a sign for an honest-to-God soda fountain inside. And a brick-and-mortar bookstore with a Christmas tree made of books in the display window, as well as an adorable ice cream shop called Six Ways to Sundae.

Not a fantasyland, but a foreign wonderland just the same.

My bad, Alice.

Nessa paused in front of a coffee shop with Mimi's Café scrawled in elegant script across its black-and-gold aw-ning. Though the door was closed, she still caught a whiff of freshly brewed coffee, and her taste buds kicked up a massive protest, crying out for a daily dose of caffeine. Her morning routine of sitting and savoring her first cup of coffee had been replaced by a heaping serving of panic due to Ivy's disappearing act. Her belly rolled, clenching tight in phantom pangs.

She'd been so *scared* when she hadn't been able to find Ivy.

And as she'd started her second search around the outbuilding behind the inn, all she'd been able to think was that she'd lost someone else. This was what happened when she let people in her life. They left. They never stayed. They di—

Then her phone had rung.

It'd been Ivy, telling her she'd caught a ride downtown and was hanging out with Wolf at the square.

Nessa's knees had buckled. And she'd been grateful no one had been around to witness them hitting the cold, hard ground. But then, like a swollen flash flood, the anger had rushed in, streaming through her, and she embraced it. Let it power her to her feet and back to the inn. Pissed off was preferable to being weak.

Preferable to letting someone else become so important, so vital, that just the thought of their disappearance nearly wrecked her.

Needless to say, coffee hadn't been a priority that morning.

But it was now.

Grasping the handle, she pulled the entrance door and entered. Freshly ground coffee beans, fried dough, sugar and the Jackson 5's "Give Love on Christmas Day" welcomed her. Yearning, hot and strong like the coffee she'd longed for so badly, spread through her chest, swirling before surging for her throat. It clogged there, a thick ball of grief, wistfulness and threads of faded joy.

Only minutes ago, she'd thought of her mother's favorite book. And now, hearing this song bombarded her with memories of Evelyn playing the Jackson 5 Christmas CD over and over every holiday season. Without fail.

Nessa blinked against the sting of sudden tears. God, this needed to stop. She wasn't this person. This sentimental, weepy, touchy-feely person. And she damn sure wasn't going to get back into the ER if she was the emotional equivalent of a tangled string of Christmas lights.

Pragmatic. Rational. Cool.

Nurse Freeze, dammit.

See? This was why she didn't do Christmas.

"Hey, Nessa!"

Nessa jumped on the distraction of that bright greeting. Almost desperately, she wheeled around and met Sydney Dennison's warm smile.

"Morning, Syd— Oh wow, a baby," Nessa said, noticing the tiny infant bundled against the other woman's chest in a carrier. A white blanket with pink flowers folded back at the corner revealed the sweet face of a sleeping baby with the plumpest cheeks, longest lashes and thickest head of dark curls. "She's beautiful," she whispered, mindful not to wake her even though they were in a crowded café.

"Oh don't bother whispering." Sydney chuckled. "It amazes me how once she's asleep, it would take a bomb to wake her up. It's just the getting her to sleep that's the act of God," she drawled. "And thank you. I think she's absolutely gorgeous, but I figure I might be a tad biased. So, it's nice to receive objective confirmation from others." A smile infused with so much love it seemed to light up her face with an internal glow softly curved her mouth. "You're downtown pretty early this morning. Doing some shopping?"

"No." Nessa moved toward the line that led to the counter and Sydney joined her, though she held a to-go cup of coffee and a small white paper bag in her hand. "Ivy's over at the square with Wolf, so I decided to stop in for coffee before heading over there."

"Gotcha. You've picked the best place. There are several cafés in town, and they're all great, but Mimi's is the best. And the doughnuts here." She rolled her eyes and let out a groan. "The glazed ones are the best, and I admit—I have an addiction. It started when I moved back to town this summer, and it's only worsened since then." Sydney leaned forward, her voice lowering to a pseudowhisper. "One time, I asked Autumn Bryant, the owner, if she laced the glaze with crack. She denied it, but seriously, would she admit it? I think not."

Nessa snickered. "Okay, you've convinced me to try the doughnuts." Then, because she couldn't resist and curiosity niggled at her, she asked, "You said you moved back to Rose Bend. I thought you were from here."

"Born and raised," Sydney said, shifting forward in the line. "But I left after I graduated high school and returned home after almost ten years in June, freshly divorced and pregnant with this one." She gently smoothed a hand over her infant's head.

Uh, okay. That sounded like a story.

Sydney glanced up and laughed. "TMI? Well, this is a small town, and there's no such thing. I give it by the end of today before you've heard about it anyway. Funny." She laughed again, and it carried a rueful but fond note. "That everybody-in-everybody-else's-business thing used to drive me nuts about this place. Now, it's still annoying,

but kind of…comforting. Maybe because I'm a mother."
She shrugged. "But yep, I returned home, the black sheep,
snagged the mayor, married him and we became a ready-
made family. And it was the best decision I ever made."

From the love that brightened her brown eyes, Nessa believed *she* believed that. But what did Nessa know about
happily-ever-afters?

"So, Cole…"

"No, Cole isn't Patience's biological father, but he is
her father in every other way that counts. This little girl's
lucky enough to have two men who love and claim her,"
Sydney said. "My ex-husband and his wife recently moved
from North Carolina to Boston to be closer for visitations."
She huffed out a breath, her lips twisting into a wry smile.
"Now, to understand how that's a minor miracle, you'd need
to know our whole story. And we're going to need something a little stronger than coffee for that," she teased as
they approached the counter. Turning to the woman standing behind the register, Sydney grinned. "Bet you didn't expect to see me again so soon. Autumn, I'd like to introduce
you to one of our newest visitors, Nessa Hunt. Nessa, this
is Autumn Bryant, owner of this amazing café and home
of the doughnuts that may or may not be the subject of a
possible DEA investigation."

The pretty young woman, with her petite frame, wealth
of shoulder-length brown curls and sprinkle of chocolate
freckles on her cinnamon skin, didn't appear old enough to
own and run a successful business. She narrowed her hazel
eyes on Sydney, but they gleamed with humor. "That is a
rumor. A rumor I won't confirm or deny. Nice to meet you,
Nessa, and welcome to Rose Bend. What can I get you?"

Minutes later, Nessa exited the café with Sydney beside
her, a coffee and hot chocolate in her hands, and a dough-

nut already in her stomach. Sydney hadn't been wrong. If loving a baked good was wrong, she didn't want to be right.

"We're kind of in the same boat," Sydney said as they made their way down the sidewalk toward the square.

Since they'd left the coffee shop, several people had stopped and called out greetings to her and introduced themselves to Nessa. Sydney took it all in stride, but for Nessa, she again commiserated with Alice. In Boston, people weren't mean, but usually the most a stranger received was a nod and maybe a brief, polite smile. Maybe. Definitely not this friendliness that had the city-born, suspicious part of her doling out side-eye.

"In what way?"

"I've been gone so long, this will almost be like my first Christmas in Rose Bend. But I remember them. And, Nessa, my friend, you are in for a treat. Or shell shock." She snorted. "If you haven't guessed yet, they go all out here. The Christmas tree lighting is just the start of it. There's a pageant, caroling, a movie night, parade, tree decorating contests... It's a crazy, magnificent time."

"Sounds like you missed it," Nessa murmured.

Sydney nodded, and she lifted her hands, cradling her baby through the carrier. The gesture struck Nessa as instinctive, as if the other woman weren't aware she'd done it. "I did. If you'd asked me all the years I was in North Carolina whether I did, I probably would've denied it. But I did. I'm looking forward to the insanity. To introducing Patience to it."

Nessa didn't reply as they crossed the street and neared the walk that bordered the town square. It fit the name: short, neatly trimmed hedges decorated with bright red poinsettias, pine cones and greenery bordered a wide space set in the heart of town. Benches, little patches of winter grass and big stone pots that would probably boast beautiful, vibrant flowers in the spring and summer dotted the paved area. And right in the middle, bent over a couple of long lengths of wood laid across two triangular platforms, worked Wolf and Ivy. The loud buzzing sound of a saw whirred in the air, and Wolf stood behind Ivy, his arms bracketing her as he carefully guided her in cutting the wood. Absently, Nessa also noted a boy off to the side, digging into the ground with a long tool, but almost immediately, the man and the little girl recaptured her attention.

Even with goggles covering nearly half her face, Nessa spied the concentration creasing Ivy's expression, but it's what she didn't glimpse that caused her to stutter to a halt.

Anger. Resentment. Even sorrow. The emotions she was so used to seeing on Ivy's face were missing. For a moment, the vise that had seemed to become a permanent fixture around her chest since she received the call about Isaac loosened just a fraction.

Because for just a moment, she caught sight of the girl who'd once been a regular moody but happy preteen. A preteen with an attentive, protective father.

But as quick as that band relaxed, it tightened again. Constricting and leaving that desperate, hollow ache because that carefree girl was forever gone. Ivy no longer had an adoring father.

She only had Nessa.

The shittiest substitute ever.

"Your sister seems to be getting along well with Wolf," Sydney said, sipping from her own cup of coffee. "I'm not surprised, though. He has a way with kids. There's this core of…I don't know…no-bullshitness and strength in him that gives them a sense of stability. Of safety. See Trevor over there?" She dipped her head in the direction of the tall boy

Nessa had briefly noted. "He's one of Cole's clients. On his way down a rough road with a bad crowd. But working with Wolf has helped keep him straight. Trevor respects him when he doesn't respect many people."

Nessa remained quiet, but she could see that. From the instant they'd met, Wolf had managed to sneak past those heavy walls Ivy had erected around herself. Ivy had taken to Wolf. Hell, so had Nessa.

"Nessa, please feel free to tell me to mind my own business," Sydney murmured.

Well, she definitely had her attention with that opening. Nessa glanced at Sydney, who stared at her, brown gaze steady but with an understanding that both warmed Nessa and set her on edge. Nothing good ever came from a conversation that started like that.

"Last night, when I was leaving the lighting, I noticed you and your sister ahead of me. You two didn't seem… close. And let me apologize now for eavesdropping, but I overheard a little of your conversation, and your sister…" Sydney glanced at Ivy and Wolf again, and silence echoed between them for a moment. "Your sister reminds me of myself at her age. Angry. Hurt. A little lost. Not to give you my life story, but my sister died when I was younger, and for the longest time it created this wedge between me and my parents. Hell, between me and almost everyone."

"I'm sorry," Nessa whispered, hating those two words. They were ineffective, but at the moment, they were all she had. Because telling this almost stranger *I understand how it is to feel empty and full of rage at the same time. I get it* didn't seem appropriate, even if she could force it past her tight throat.

So she left it at the two most helpless words in the human language.

Sydney smiled, and it carried a hint of old sadness.

"Thank you. But I'm telling you all this to say, I know where you are. It's not easy trying to hold on to someone so determined to push you away. My parents and I were estranged for a lot of years because we were so afraid of being hurt by each other. But even underneath the misunderstandings and the pain and grief, we always had love. And that brought us to one another. That and Rose Bend."

When Sydney smiled this time, none of the sadness remained. Her face shone with an inner peace that was almost hard to look at—or maybe it was the kernel of envy buried deep inside Nessa that made it difficult.

"I just want to encourage you not to give up on reaching out to her, Nessa. Or just reaching her. It may seem impossible, but it's not. That bond of family, the security of it, is so worth it. And you've chosen the right town to start. This place…" She inhaled a deep breath and surveyed the square, gently cupping her child's bottom through the carrier. "Not to sound all mystical and woo-woo, but it has magic. It doesn't come from any kind of spell or enchanted book—I watch a ton of *Charmed* reruns if you can't tell." Sydney grinned. "It comes from the community, the sense of family and safety. It's why I moved back here to raise her after an almost-ten-year absence and a vow never to return."

Sydney bowed her head over her daughter's and pressed a kiss to the dark curls. Lifting her head, she squinted at Nessa, shrugging a shoulder.

"Anyway, enough of my getting in your business," she said, flashing a wry grin. "That's my quota for the day. C'mon, let's see how the gazebo is shaping up."

Nessa followed Sydney, the exchange whirling in her head. The part of her who was a toughened Bostonian who'd been raised on reality not Hallmark movies curled her lip at the conversation. The other woman knew nothing about her and Ivy's situation. Or about the messy resentment and pain that were the only things holding them together.

Or about the lies that dangled over their heads like the world's crappiest piñata—one strike and the untruths would rain down on them.

Or about the secret Nessa's mother had confessed on her deathbed.

That the man Nessa had believed to be her father all her life wasn't.

Hallmark didn't make a movie telling her how to handle being not only orphaned, but also left a liar.

God, Mom. Why couldn't you have just taken that one to your grave? Why did you have to tell me? I didn't want to know!

Isaac had entrusted Ivy into her care because he'd believed Nessa was his daughter. But it was a lie. And every day Nessa woke up and kept that secret, she made the choice to continue living in deceit. But what else could she do? Though Isaac Hunt wasn't truly her biological father, she couldn't abandon Ivy, whether they were blood or not. Ivy believed they were. Ivy might hate Nessa, but they were the only family they had. And Nessa refused to abandon her. To steal away all that Ivy had left, as Nessa's parents had done to her.

No, Sydney, as well-meaning as she was, couldn't be more wrong.

Rose Bend couldn't fix this.

"HEY, GUYS." Sydney stopped a small distance away from Wolf and Ivy, mindful not to startle them. Wolf glanced up and smiled at his sister-in-law. Carefully, he lifted the saw, turned it off and set it down. "Hey, Trevor."

The teen boy lifted his head from where he bent over a long tool that resembled a shovel. "Hi, Sydney." Giving her a chin lift that seemed to be a universal thing for males between the ages of thirteen and death, he said, "That Patience you got hiding in there?"

"It is." Sydney rolled her eyes as Trevor laid down his tool and tugged off his gloves as he headed toward her. "I swear, Trevor, you're worse than this guy right here." She cocked her head toward Wolf, who already had his goggles off and was moving around the sawhorses. "She's asleep," she whisper-yelled.

But she might as well as have saved that warning because Wolf already had the carrier straps removed from her shoulders and the baby in his large hands.

Well, Nessa didn't need her ovaries anyway.

Grinning, Sydney stretched her arm out to Ivy. "Hi, I'm Sydney, Wolf's sister-in-law. You must be Ivy. I've heard a lot about you."

"Yeah?" Ivy said, slipping off her safety glasses and sliding a look at Nessa. "Well, nice to meet you anyway." She shook the other woman's hand.

Sydney laughed. "I see you're busy here, but once I wrestle my baby back, I was headed over to city hall to meet my husband. The twins are there helping set up for the reception after the Santa Run tonight. Want to head over with me?"

"Cool!" Ivy's face brightened at the mention of the twins. Turning to Wolf, she asked, "Are you okay with me going, Wolf? I can stay if you still need me."

Handing the infant over to Trevor, Wolf tugged on one of Ivy's curls. "I got it covered here, Mozart. Go on. You were a great help, though, so anytime you want to come back and lend a hand, I have a pair of gloves with your name on them."

Ivy didn't smile, but her dark eyes brightened with his praise. Nodding, she removed her gloves and laid them on the wood they'd been cutting and rounded it to stand by Nessa.

"I'll walk you two over," Trevor offered, slipping the carrier straps on. "Be back in about twenty, Wolf," he called over his shoulder.

"Take your time. Here." Wolf freed his wallet from the back pocket of his jeans and pulled out a few bills. "Pick us up some lunch from Sunnyside Grille on your way back."

"Got it." Trevor tucked the money into his pocket, but before the trio could leave, Nessa spoke for the first time since they'd arrived.

"Ivy," she called.

The preteen stopped, then slowly turned, a scowl furrowing her eyebrows. Probably assuming Nessa would call a halt to her mission. Which, considering she hadn't asked permission, maybe she should. *Pick your battles.* That had become Nessa's mantra in the last six weeks since Isaac's death. And while they would have a discussion about her pulling Houdini acts, this wasn't a skirmish she intended to wage.

"Yeah?"

"Here." Nessa held out the hot chocolate that she'd bought for her at Mimi's Café.

The scowl didn't totally disappear, but it did lessen in intensity as Ivy crossed over and accepted the to-go cup. "Thanks," she muttered.

"You're welcome. And listen to Sydney, okay?"

Ivy gave her a sharp nod before wheeling around and

hurrying back to Sydney and Trevor. The three of them walked down another path that led in the opposite direction from where she and Sydney had approached the square.

"She'll be fine." Wolf's quiet assurance from behind her set her nerves tap-dancing, but for an entirely different reason.

Though she'd just met Sydney the night before, she trusted the other woman to watch over Ivy—mainly because Wolf trusted her. No, her skin tingled like it'd been kissed by sandpaper because wintergreen wrapped around her. Her belly tumbled because that voice invited her to cuddle against that wide chest at her back and sink her teeth into its dense muscle—both were cardinal sins in her book.

Oh God. She shivered, the tremble vibrating through her belly, culminating in her pulsing, suddenly damp feminine flesh.

Sex.

That was the problem. It'd been months since she'd had sex. Jeremy might have complained about her emotional competence, but he'd had no grievances about their love life. Where Nessa lacked in sharing her feelings, she more than made up for with her generosity in the bedroom. So much so that toward the end, he'd even accused her of using sex to avoid being close to him, talking to him. And that was utter bullshit. She was a woman who enjoyed sex. Nothing more to the story. Nothing to be ashamed of or apologize for.

But the deprivation explained her reaction to Wolf. Had to. Because the alternative—that there was something special about him, something different from the other men in her life—just didn't bear dwelling on.

Frankly, the thought scared the hell out of her.

Now that she understood the problem, though, she could handle the solution. Literally. The only tricky part was finding private, kid-free time. Relief trickled through her, and she closed her eyes, buying herself a few extra moments by sipping from her coffee.

Yeah, she would be finding that kid-free time *soon*.

"Santa Run?" she asked, pouring a healthy amount of skepticism into the question. Only then did she find it safe to turn around and face him.

But she might've been a bit premature when he smirked, cocking a dark eyebrow. "Town tradition."

"Do I want to know the details?" she asked. "Because I have to tell you, anything with *run* in the title usually has me avoiding it like Justin Bieber and toilets."

He laughed. "One time. The man uses a bucket one time, and he can never live it down." At her snort, he shook his head. "I think 'run' is pretty much a misnomer. The distance is from the top of Main past The Glen. Not a big distance. People dress up as Santa Claus, partner up with someone and they walk, skip, hop, whatever it takes to get to the finish line. It's a fundraiser, with everyone gathering at city hall afterward for food. Boston has them, right?"

She shrugged. "Probably. We have so many things during the holidays, but I wouldn't know. I'm usually working and don't get into all that."

"Yeah?" A beat of silence passed between them where his green gaze roamed her face, and she ordered herself not to duck her head and avoid it. "That's a shame. Well, you and Ivy should join in. I think she would really enjoy it. And you might surprise yourself and have fun, too."

Don't pity me. I don't need or want it. The hot rebuke burned her tongue, but she doused it, afraid of what he would infer from it if she let that loose. And she knew he would *infer*.

"Pass." She raised her cup for another sip. "Besides, if

Ivy and I partnered up for anything one of us might pull a *Lord of the Flies* and not come back alive."

Hell, she was only half joking.

"I didn't want to mention it, but I was contemplating diving in front of you and sacrificing my body to protect you from that death glare."

She squinted at him. "The fact that my sister and I would rather hide each other's bodies in the nearest snowbank than spend time with each other amuses you?"

"No." Pause. "Maybe." When she shot him a narrowed look, he held up his hands, shoulders hunched. "Woman, I have six brothers and sisters. *Six.* We've all wanted to off each other at one time or another." He sighed softly and rubbed a hand down his beard. For a moment, he glanced to the side, and she almost blurted out a demand to know what he was thinking. But thank God she squelched that urge. "All teasing aside, I get there's more between you and Ivy. She... she mentioned that she *used* to help her father with his carpentry. I'm guessing that's because he's not here anymore. Your father's dead, isn't he?"

He's not my father. The confession scrabbled up the back of her throat but found no purchase. Her secret. Her burden. Ivy had already lost both her parents. And as much as Ivy didn't want Nessa, she couldn't take away her sister, too.

And selfishly, Nessa couldn't admit aloud that she was so fucking alone and needed Ivy, the only family she had left. Even if she wasn't blood.

So she nodded, giving Wolf the only answer she could.

"What happened?" Wolf murmured, shifting closer to her.

"Pancreatic cancer," she said. "He died six weeks ago and left me as her guardian."

Why?

That question still rang in her head all these weeks later.

He hadn't even thought enough of Nessa to keep in any kind of meaningful contact for sixteen years. So why had she been his choice to raise his daughter? Unless she received a celestial visitation, she would never know. And that bothered her like a pebble stuck in her shoe.

"He must've trusted you to leave his daughter in your care," Wolf said softly. Gently. Too gently, as if he suspected she might be fragile when it came to Isaac Hunt. "Trusted and believed in you."

She barely contained her snort of disbelief. More like he probably didn't have anyone else. Because *anyone* else other than his estranged daughter-who-wasn't-his-daughter would've been a better candidate than her.

"Whatever his reasons were, he took them to the grave with him."

Jesus, that sounded callous. Cold. No wonder they called her Nurse Freeze. If she could snatch the words back out of the air, she'd have grabby hands right now. Not because they weren't true. No, she'd rescind them so Wolf wasn't looking at her with that awful sympathy in his emerald gaze.

"What did he do to hurt you so badly, Nessa?" He cocked his head and shifted closer. "Yesterday in the kitchen, you obviously didn't know he'd brought Ivy and her mother here—"

"What're you working on?" she interrupted, crossing over to the wood beam propped up on the sawhorses.

"Nessa—" He grasped her elbow, but she felt that grip in the sudden beading of her nipples, the dipping of her belly, the dampening of her sex. The breathlessness of her lungs.

The yearning in her chest.

Panic clawed at her.

"You're doing the touching thing again," she said, fighting dirty, and when his hold disappeared as if her skin seared him, guilt speared her right through the rib cage. She'd weaponized his sense of honor, but she didn't apologize. Didn't acknowledge her wrongdoing.

Desperation did that to a person.

"Well played," he murmured, stepping next to her, but leaving a careful distance between them. "But next time, if you want me to mind my own business, just say so. I told you last night, all you had to do was let me know if you needed space. I'd never put my hands on a woman if she didn't want them there, and I think you know that. So there's no need to use that against me. Understood?" he asked, and threading through his voice was a vein of steel that she hadn't heard until now.

"Yes." The guilt thickened. And underneath it… Jesus, what did it say about her that underneath a tiny thrill of excitement sparked inside her like flint struck against stone?

Layers.

There were layers to Wolf Dennison. And part of her wanted to peel back the laid-back, wreath-toting carpenter to explore the person who existed beneath. The person who'd issued that warning with the expectation of being obeyed.

And the other part of her—the wiser part—just desired to leave him alone and back off slowly, palms up, with no sudden movement.

Sighing, she looked away from him, an apology pressing against her throat, but she couldn't utter it. Because then she would have to explain why she'd thrown that grenade between them. And to tell him that she'd panicked at his touch—at her reaction to his touch—wasn't even an option. Inhaling, she tipped her chin toward the beginnings of the structure behind them.

"Can you tell me about what you're working on?" she asked, offering what she could. What she was capable of.

Maybe what they said about her at work was true. What Jeremy had lobbed at her as he left was true. Was this why people walked away from her?

Why Ivy couldn't trust her?

Couldn't...love her?

Wolf stared at her, his eyes shards of jade, but then he sharply nodded, and a sliver of relief slid between her ribs.

"Better if I show you."

He turned and retrieved a roll from a bag next to a big toolbox. Unfurling it, he pinned the sides with the saw and a wrench. She glanced down at the large blueprint and a detailed drawing of a gazebo with a domed roof. Beautiful latticework decorated the sides, shallow steps bordered the main structure and a dainty cupola crested the top. Though a technical design, the building's beauty shone through.

"Did you draw this?" She trailed a finger over the trellis at the front of the gazebo.

He nodded. "About twenty years ago, another gazebo stood here. It was one of the town's original structures. But we had a hurricane come through, and it was one of the casualties. There's been talk over the years about rebuilding it, but nothing's ever happened. When Cole approached me about doing the job for this year's festival, I said yes."

"That's a job." She peered behind her at the foundation that had already been laid and the holes that Trevor had been in the middle of digging when she and Sydney had approached. "When is it supposed to be done?"

"By Christmas Eve."

"Christmas Eve," she repeated, peering up into his face. "As in twenty-two days."

"The same."

"Not that I'm doubting your skills, but—" she waved a hand over the post and toward the wood foundation "—is that possible?"

"Don't know," he said, peering down at the blueprint, and surprise whipped through her at his honesty. When she shot him a look over her shoulder, he shrugged. "I don't. But that doesn't matter. What does is that I'll make it possible."

He crossed his arms over his chest, and she shot a glance up at him. His expression didn't change, yet…it did. The skin over his cheekbones tautened and his full, sensual mouth firmed just the slightest bit. And his eyes. Dark as the trees that surrounded the square.

There was something here. Something much more than a gazebo.

"This is Cole's first year as mayor, and he would never admit it to me, but he feels the pressure of the position and the responsibilities it brings."

"Why wouldn't he admit that?" She hadn't been around the Dennisons long, but just that limited amount of time had been enough to see how tight they were.

Though hair covered his jaw, Nessa couldn't miss the flex of it or the jump in his cheek. "Rose Bend is a good town with even better people. But like any place, we have those assholes who see others who aren't the same race, gender, religion or sexual identity as them as inferior or subhuman. We're not immune to that kind of rot just because we're a small town. And as Rose Bend's first non-white mayor, Cole has faced some opposition and pushback simply because he's Puerto Rican. You remember meeting Jenna last night?"

Nessa nodded, a soul-deep sadness and weariness weighing her down. A sadness born of knowing even in this day and age there were people who still clung to that harmful, racist mentality. A weariness that originated from fighting in the same trenches Cole battled in. As a nurse, she witnessed it every day. Experienced it more often than she should.

"Her father is the town's former mayor. Cole actually beat him in the last election, and he's one of the main instigators. The fact that the man's on the town council only makes it worse. Cole doesn't think I understand—and to be fair, I probably can only to a certain extent—but he doesn't just carry the weight of being Rose Bend's first mayor of color on his shoulders. He carries the burden of expectations for every nonwhite person who comes behind him who wants to be mayor. If he fails in any way, then people will look at him and say, see, we gave them a chance and they blew it. This is why they shouldn't be in positions of leadership. They can't handle it. He feels that weight. And though we're brothers, I *am* white. No matter how much I sympathize with him and want to fight on his behalf, I can't fully grasp what it is to live as a man of color in the United States. In this town. In a position of power. And though me and my brother are close, he doesn't share that with me because he believes I can't understand. And the truth is, I can't."

Silence fell between them, and words crowded into her mind in a jumbled mess that she struggled to parcel out. Give her medical terms to decipher or orders she needed to carry out, and she was in her element. But with emotions? Her tongue might as well be quicksand.

Staring at the stark lines of his face, the harsh set of his full mouth and the almost self-protective crossing of his arms, she pushed past her personal hang-ups and insecurities.

"Or," she slowly said, "maybe you, Moe, your father,

your family—you're all his haven. The one place where he doesn't have to face the world with his guard up. Having to explain and justify your—" she frowned, twirling her hand as she scrambled for the appropriate word "—personhood is exhausting. And often, it seems like that's what we have to do day in and day out—defend why we exist, why our lives are just as valuable and valid as others. But when he's with you, he doesn't have to. He's safe. He knows he's valued. He's *seen*. So what you take as him not believing you capable of understanding him—maybe he sees as you being his place to be understood. To simply *be*."

The three quick beeps of a horn, the festive melody of "Jingle Bells" playing from the PA system from the Christmas tree lot at the far corner of Main and the chatter of pedestrian voices floated around them. Heat flooded her stomach before scaling her chest and streaming into her face. This awkward-as-hell silence was why she didn't give in to emotions. They were messy, sticky bogs that left her floundering, with no control.

She hated having no control.

An image of her huddled against that hospital wall, shaking, terrified and gasping for breath, wavered in front of her face and disgust spilled through her.

So did fear.

"Thank you."

The raspy note in that deep sin-and-sex voice was overkill. And it cut through the thick self-recrimination. It slid beneath her layers of clothing and caressed her like calloused fingertips over bare skin. But even more alarming, it reached inside, grasped her heart and squeezed so hard, she barely managed to smother a gasp. She lifted her coffee cup to her mouth, her arm hiding the hand that rubbed at the ache behind her chest bone.

"You're welcome." She sipped from the cooling brew, bending her head to blindly peer at the blueprint again. "So all this for your brother, huh?"

"Pretty much."

"It's amazing the things we'll do for them, isn't it?"

"Yeah," he agreed.

She paused. Sipped again. "We're such suckers."

"Yeah."

CHAPTER SEVEN

WOLF STEPPED OUT of the post office's front entrance into the cold afternoon air. Smiling and nodding at a passerby, he headed down the sidewalk to his truck, the envelope with the money order inside, a leaden weight in his hand. That weight echoed in his chest and he curled the fingers of his other hand hard around his keys, the ridges biting into his palm through the gloves. He relished the dull pressure that carried the faintest hint of pain. As a matter of fact, he focused on that promise of pain, because it helped him focus. Helped him switch his brain to something other than what the next few minutes would hold.

As soon as he reached his truck, he unlocked it, stretched across the bucket seats to the glove compartment and retrieved a pen. Almost on autopilot, he fished the money order out of the envelope, leaned over the truck's hood and started filling out the fields.

Carol Brandt
33 Willow Bark Ln, Rose Bend, MA 01236

His hand hovered over the memo line. As it did every month when he filled out a money order to Raylon's mother. The most accurate description would be "Recompense for your son's life." Or "Meager absolution for my unforgiveable sin." Instead, he quickly jotted down "Monthly payment" on the line, tucked the money order for just under three thousand dollars in the envelope and sealed it. Poor restitution for a life and a shattered promise, but it was all he had to give.

Blood money.

The accusation whispered through his head as shame sloshed in his gut like sour liquor. He stalked to a nearby mailbox and slipped the envelope into the slot. Standing there for several seconds, head bowed, he rested his fist on the top of it.

The monthly routine should've been cathartic, like slipping into the confessional with a priest. But instead of emerging unburdened by his sins, he always left heavier, guiltier. Like a man chipping away at a mountain of pain and regret.

Eight years. It'd been eight years since he'd returned home from the military hospital, his knee a mess, his head even more of one. And his heart? There'd been a hollow hole where it'd once existed. A hole the size of the best friend who'd died in that village in the desert. The best friend he'd failed to protect.

It'd been Wolf who'd convinced Raylon to enlist in the army.

It'd been Wolf who promised Carol, his mother, that he'd protect her son.

It'd been Wolf who failed both mother and son.

So that monthly combat-disability check he received because he'd lived and Raylon hadn't was the very least he could give Carol Brandt. Because in the end, it didn't come even close to what she desired most—her son.

A howl of old pain clawed at his chest. Out of habit, he rubbed at the inside of his right forearm, directly over the spot where he'd had a tattoo inked several years ago. The same ache that bloomed in his chest pulsed there. Past experience had taught him the uselessness of trying to knead the pain away. Didn't stop him, though.

"Wolf?"

Dammit.

He lifted his head, deliberately straightened his fist and lowered his arm to his side. Of all the people… Just…damn.

Turning, he met the concerned gazes of Olivia and her mother, Regina. Not today. Not when he was so raw. That envelope was a reminder of how he'd failed one of the most important people in his life when he'd needed him most.

And as if the universe wasn't through with him, here stood the other example of how he hadn't measured up. How he hadn't been enough for the person he'd loved.

How he'd disappointed yet again.

With a force of will that deserved some kind of blue ribbon, he smiled at the women. Though from the deepening worry in their identical violet eyes, he must've failed in the endeavor.

Sighing, he nodded. "Olivia. Mrs. Allen. It's good to see you."

"Why so formal, Wolf? I know it's been a while, but I'll always be Regina to you." She smiled at him, and hers was a hell of a lot more genuine than his. "And it's wonderful to see you, too. I hope your mother told you I asked about you when I saw her the other day."

"She did. And thank you."

"Wolf." Olivia tilted her head to the side, peering up at him from under the bill of her pageboy cap. She was still beautiful. And at one time, that familiar gesture had been endearing and adorable. But now, it just left him… Fuck if he knew. "Are you okay?"

"I'm good."

She didn't look convinced, her glance clearly skeptical. Well, she'd always been a smart woman. He smothered a sigh. Too smart.

"Mom." She laid a hand on her mother's arm. "Would you mind if I met you at Mimi's?"

"Not at all, honey. I'll order your usual." Kissing her daughter's cheek, Regina wiggled her fingers at him. "Bye, Wolf. Please don't be a stranger. You're always welcome at our home." She gave him one last smile as she strolled away.

Jesus Christ. "Look, Olivia—"

"What's going on?" She stepped closer to him. So close her familiar lavender scent teased his nose. "And don't try to tell me nothing or you're good. You looked like you were in pain a couple of minutes ago. I know you too well."

Anger shot through him like a struck match, hot and quick. "Olivia, I don't want to disrespect you when I say this. But you forfeited the right to ask me that three years ago. And suddenly showing up back in town doesn't mean you get to reclaim it."

"Forfeited the right to ask if you're okay?" she demanded.

"No, the right to expect answers."

Silence crystallized between them like diamonds, bright, unbreakable and sharp.

Finally, he dragged a hand over his hair, not bothering to swallow this sigh. He hadn't wanted to do this right now, and definitely not right here on goddamn Main Street. Already, they were receiving looks from several people. And if he weren't mistaken, that was Wanda Mason's nose pressed to the window of Price's Pharmacy right between the greeting cards and the bifocals rack. *Fuck.* That meant this little confrontation would hit the Rose Bend grapevine by dinner.

"This might sound horrible," Olivia said softly. "But part

of me doesn't care if you yelled at me. That part of me says go right ahead and do it. Because then it would mean you at least feel something for me. I can deal with hate or spite as long as it's *something*, Wolf. It's when you look at me and I don't see anything in your eyes that I worry."

He stared at her. An emotion should beat in his chest at this moment. Elation. Rage. Disgust. Sorrow.

Anything.

But all that climbed up his throat from the empty husk that was his rib cage was the inane urge to laugh. And when it escaped him, he suspected it would sound faintly hysterical. And he still retained enough pride to know that wouldn't be a good look.

Well, that confirmed it.

He didn't have the emotional or mental bandwidth for this.

"Olivia, I don't know what you expected when you came back here. Especially from me. But I can't give it to you."

You broke that in me when you left. That piece that trusts, that loves without reservation. I can't give it to you. I can't give it to anyone.

He kept that gem to himself.

"Wolf."

She placed her hand on his forearm. It used to be one little brush of those delicate fingers and he'd melt. He'd do anything for her. Now the steel forged over his heart by her rejection didn't bend. Still, he shifted out from under her hand. And he pretended not to see the hurt that shadowed her eyes.

Just like she'd pretended not to see him three years ago, standing there at the end of his driveway, willing her to come back.

"You didn't mind that woman from last night touching you," she murmured. "What was her name? Nessa?"

If even the barest hint of accusation had colored her voice, he might've given in to the need to snap at her, to *hurt* her. But only sadness weighed down her tone, darkened her gaze.

He didn't have any responsibility for her feelings. They stopped being his concern the second his ceased being hers. But... Hell, what was he doing here?

"Like Leo said last night, Nessa Hunt and her sister are guests at the inn."

"So you two aren't...?"

She didn't finish the question, and he didn't answer it. Maybe she figured that she'd gone too far because she nodded, and another tense silence descended between them.

And again, she was the one who broke it.

"I'm sorry, Wolf. I'm sorry for leaving the way I did. I—"

"No." He cut her off, his voice harsh, sharper than her gasp at his interruption. "Look at me, Olivia. Really look at me. If you claim to know me as well as you do."

He paused, the air rasping out of his nose, his chest rising and falling. This...this *apology* in the middle of a busy sidewalk struck him as wrong. And selfish.

Because in the end this *I'm sorry* was about her, not him. What she needed.

Just as her leaving had been about her, what she needed, and fuck him.

It was like déjà vu all over again only with Christmas carols on the PA system and Willy Wonka–size candy canes aligning the sidewalks nearby.

No, thanks.

"I am looking at you, Wolf," she whispered. "It's all I've ever wanted to do."

He laughed, and the bitterness scraped his throat like sandpaper. "Then you would see I can't do this right now. What am I standing next to, Olivia?" He thumped a fist on top of the mailbox. And as her eyes widened, understanding dawning in them, another hard chuckle escaped him. "Yeah. Not today. Not now. Maybe not ever. And you know what? You'll have to be good with that because those are the consequences of the choices you made."

He turned, ignoring her calling his name, and strode back toward his truck. Jerking the door open, he slid inside. A glance through the windshield revealed Olivia hadn't moved from where he'd left her. But this time, it was him driving away.

And he took no joy in doing it.

In this moment, he took no joy in anything.

CHAPTER EIGHT

Nessa blinked.

Blinked again.

Slowly closed her eyes. Counted to five. Opened them.

Nope. Still a shit ton of Santas crowded onto Main Street like shoppers at Walmart on Black Friday during an early bird sale. Like, a *lot* of Santas.

Good God. She shook her head, more than a little awe winding through her. Boston had its own Santa Run, so she wasn't a stranger to the event. And even when Wolf had explained Rose Bend's version to her earlier that day on the town square, she hadn't imagined *this*.

Aside from what appeared to be most of the town packed onto the sidewalks and street and dressed in varying degrees of Santa Claus costumes, the top of Main Street had been cordoned off. About halfway down, the avenue had been transformed into an honest-to-God obstacle course. Oh yes. Complete with tires, a huge bouncy castle with balls, a mini-climbing wall and that's just what she could see. Another thing Wolf had neglected to mention.

She said it before, and she'd say it again. These people took Christmas seriously.

"Nessa!"

She glanced up and spotted Leo waving at her with the arm not bound to a younger woman with gorgeous, shoulder-length sister locs—Florence, Leo's sister, who Nessa had met earlier.

"You joining in or what?" Leo yelled, her voice somehow booming over the din on the crowded street.

Nessa shook her head, pointing to her hot chocolate as an excuse for why she was abstaining from getting sweaty in a St. Nick suit and possibly dying somewhere between the tire course and balance beam. A half hour on the treadmill at Gold's Gym did not prepare her for *that*.

Leo gave her an exaggerated pout but was distracted from Nessa's lack of team spirit by Sinead, another sister, and Cher. Next to them, Ivy and Sonny laughed together, pulling at their wrists, apparently testing the limits of the tie that held them together.

Ducking her head, Nessa glanced away from them. Hating the tightening in her chest, she lifted her cup to her mouth again and sipped the hot chocolate. As if that could wash away the bitter taste of envy in her mouth.

This was why Isaac had sent them here, after all. So Ivy could have this experience. The fun and happiness he'd had here with her and her mother those years ago.

This isn't about you.

It never was.

The more she reminded herself of that, the less she would feel these ridiculous feelings of petty, *useless* jealousy.

"Hey, you're missing something." A hat plopped down on her head, the brim falling over her eyes and momentarily blinding her. She shoved faux fur out of her face and met Wolf's emerald gaze and wide smile. "There. That's much better." He clapped his big hands together. "Now for the rest of your costume…"

"Whoa, whoa there, Jack Skellington," she drawled. "Slow your roll. Sorry, but hard pass on the holiday calisthenics. I'm good over here with my hot chocolate and below-average lung capacity, thank you very much."

"Seriously?"

He propped his fists on hips that still managed to look lean underneath an absurdly big red-and-white St. Nick coat. Jesus Christ, it was unfair to humans everywhere that in baggy red pants and black boots, he still managed to look sexy as hell. He'd forgone the white beard, sticking with his own, and any moment now, she was going to tear her gaze away from how the thickness of it highlighted the lush curves of his mouth.

Lumbersexual Santa.

He could make it a thing and sell millions of calendars.

"Yes, seriously," she grumbled, waving a hand and focusing on how the plastic lid so neatly met the cardboard cup. Safer than staring at him. At least the cup didn't have her belly twisting in ways that meant nothing good for her moratorium on men. Nor did the seam of the lid entice her to lick it like the seam of his lips did.

Hell.

She needed to pull it together.

"Nessa." Just her name in that deep, patient tone. She resisted it for all of point-zero-three seconds before lifting her gaze from the cup to him. His gaze narrowed on her.

"What?"

"I've been meaning to ask you. Is Nessa short for another name? Vanessa? Anastasia?" He leaned closer and lowered his voice. "Agnes?"

"Have you been drinking?"

He barked out a laugh, that though it held humor, also contained the faintest hint of an edge. She frowned, but he shook his head, smiling.

"Unfortunately, no. So give. What is it? What name do I get to call you that no one else does?"

"Sorry to disappoint, but I'm just Nessa. My mother's favorite place in the world was Loch Ness, Scotland, although she never did get to visit. So she named me after it." First money, then a child, work and responsibilities had prevented her mother from taking the trip. And then, finally, cancer. Nessa promised herself one day she would make the trip for her mother. She dipped her head on the pretext of sipping her beverage, hoping the chocolate would dislodge the thick ball of emotion in her throat.

"Disappoint? No, I don't think so, Nessie."

She stared at him, her pulse loud in her ears at his soft tone and gentle words. "Nessie?" She pulled a face, attempting to downplay how the nickname tugged at her belly.

"Yes. The name I get to call you that no one else does. It's mine."

Oh God. He had no right to say things like that to her. Men like him—pretty, smooth-talking, charming—possessed an innate talent for fooling people, especially women, into believing they were special. Isaac had been that man with her mother. Nessa had dated a man like that. Had fallen for him.

Had been left by him.

So no, she wouldn't be stupid enough to swoon like a human heart emoji just because he uttered pretty, *meaningless* words.

"C'mon. Don't leave me hanging." He flicked the ball on the hat she'd yet to yank off her head. "I need a partner in the Santa Run, and I nominate you."

Her eyes widened, and she held up the hand not wrapped around her coffee cup. "Oh no. That's not going to happen."

Why didn't these people get that she was the resident

Scrooge? Give her a cold, dark bedroom, a bowl of gruel and three spirits and she was good to go.

"Nessie." He still wore that same smile, but his eyes... Something there was off. "Don't be a Christmas snatcher. You're here to experience all there is about the holidays in Rose Bend, right? You can't do it from the sidelines. And I need a partner." He held up his arm as if to drive home the point that no one was attached to it. "You wouldn't really leave me alone, would you? I don't do well alone. God knows all the trouble I could get into..."

His tone was teasing, and she almost fell for it. Almost. If only she could ignore that glint in his eyes. She recognized it. Had glimpsed it in the mirror after Jeremy had packed up and left her.

Desperation.

She frowned. "Well, who do you usually partner up with? Get that sucker, I mean person, to join you."

He closed his eyes, and the unease that had been crawling around in her chest scratched its way to the surface and roared. Her grip on her cup threatened to spill the contents all over her hand. And when his dense lashes lifted, she shifted closer to him, forgetting the crowd, forgetting the run. Forgetting everything but the man before her with ghosts in his gaze.

"Wolf," she breathed.

"The person I loved doing this with most isn't here." A muscle flexed in his jaw. "He hasn't been in a long time, and I—I'm missing him tonight. I need to be with someone who is going to make me..."

"Forget?"

"No." He shook his head, lifted a hand toward her face but at the last minute dropped it back to his side. "Not forget. Make me remember why I loved it in the first place."

Well…damn.

"Fine," she huffed, tossing her drink into a trash can. And though she called herself foolish in about five different languages—including Elvish—when he smiled, and it reached his eyes, she didn't change her mind. Even though this thing would leave her looking like a hot mess.

Heading toward the rapidly dwindling pile of Santa costumes, she convinced herself this was for a good cause. It wouldn't kill her. One event. That's it. Reaching the box, she picked through the offerings until she found a coat. Her jeans and boots would have to do. And she already had the hat Wolf had dropped on her head.

"This can't possibly be sanitary," she grumbled under her breath, slipping on the red-and-white coat and buttoning it up. "I'm just not going to think about the last time it was washed."

"Good. Don't. I'm told they wash all of the costumes every year." Wolf appeared next to her, holding a tie. "But it's also Cole's secretary's job to do it. And everyone knows Marion Lowe makes Scrooge look like Oprah with her favorite things." He bent his head over hers and whispered in her ear, his warm breath sending goose bumps cascading over her skin. She shivered.

If she turned her head just the barest inch, his full lips would graze the curve of her ear, and she would finally know the texture of his mouth. Firm? Soft? A paradoxical and sensually delightful combination of both? As if her body cast its vote for the last option, her nipples beaded.

God, if she wasn't careful, she could become obsessed with Wolf Dennison's mouth.

And never was she so happy for this damn costume.

Clearing her throat, she bent her head and focused on finishing buttoning up the coat. "So what you're telling me is there's a fifty-fifty chance I'm wearing someone's sweat from last year."

He shrugged, wrapping the binding around her right and his left arms. "But it's Christmas sweat, so I think there's magic in it."

Nessa snickered. "Like Christmas snow?"

The corner of his mouth quirked up in a knowing smirk. "Exactly." He quickly knotted the tie and pulled on it, testing its tautness. "Now you can't escape me," he murmured.

Her foolish stomach plummeted south, culminating in a throb between her legs. And her even more foolish heart pounded against her rib cage.

Exercise. That's what she needed to work out this inconvenient lust. Fortunately, she had a whole obstacle course waiting on her. Like a flame couldn't burn without oxygen, if she couldn't breathe, this annoying need couldn't pour through her veins.

"Let's get this started," she said, striding toward his family. Since their arms were connected, he had little choice but to fall in beside her.

"Easy there." He chuckled, and it sounded too dark, too wicked to her overly sensitive ears. "You sound like you're headed to an execution instead of a *fun* holiday fundraiser."

She could debate his definition of *fun* but that would require looking at him again. More specifically, looking at the chiseled planes and flawless angles that made up the masculine perfection of his face. The carnal mouth that she'd bet her best pair of sneakers could deliver on the promises it hinted at. The wide, wide shoulders that looked like they could take a denting from fingernails...

Yeah, no looking at him again.

"Yes!" Leontyne held up her free hand high when they

neared his family's group. "You got her to join in. Good job, Wolf!"

Wolf slapped his palm to hers.

"Nessa?" Ivy frowned at her. "I thought you weren't going to do the Santa Run. Why'd you change your mind?"

"Because I'm that good, Mozart," Wolf bragged, polishing his knuckles over his chest. Then he shrugged. "That, and I bet Sydney and Cole that if they beat us, they could shave my beard and the other side of your sister's head."

Nessa gasped. "You. Did. Not." She whipped around to face his brother and sister-in-law, who had joined them. "He. Did. Not."

Cole grinned. "A bet's a bet. And we take them seriously in this family."

"And what happens if we win?" she demanded.

"They have to attend the next town council meeting as Mr. and Mrs. Claus," Wolf said, the smile he shot back at Cole positively evil.

That didn't seem like even odds. Tugging on their bound arms, she growled at him, "We better win this damn thing."

"Language," Ivy singsonged behind them.

"Good evening, everyone," a feminine voice boomed. Nessa glanced to her left, and a pretty blonde woman stood on a short makeshift platform on the sidewalk, a bullhorn in hand. "Welcome to our annual Santa Run!" The crowd cheered and whistled, and once it died down, she continued. "Thank you all for participating in our fundraiser. This year, the proceeds will benefit This Is Home, our own youth home, and Hope from the Heart, an organization that supports local hospitals in giving children and their families a wonderful Christmas. So, on behalf of the organizers and myself, thank you for your pledges and your generosity."

Nessa shook her head, moved in spite of herself, as once

more thunderous applause filled the air. As someone who worked in the hospital during the holidays, she understood how sad it could be for kids to be there instead of at home, with their own tree and gifts, surrounded by not just their parents and siblings but extended family. To bring cheer to them and the knowledge that they weren't forgotten was priceless.

"Now, let's get this year's Santa Run started!" the woman announced. "Here are the rules. The run starts at the yellow line or Sunnyside Grille. You're competing to beat your pledge time. You must complete the entire obstacle course—no skipping—and cross the finish line at The Glen, where your time will be recorded by the official timekeeper. Good luck, and may the odds be ever in your favor."

With a cheeky grin to cap off her *Hunger Games* salute, she climbed down off the platform.

"Is there something you're not telling me? Am I volunteering as tribute with this?" Nessa asked Wolf as everyone started counting down from five.

"Of course not." Wolf patted her hand. "Now, stay focused and watch out for Cher. She looks like she's above getting her hands dirty but she'll push her own brothers off the balance beam to get ahead."

"Taught her well, have you?" Nessa muttered.

"Damn right I have."

Just as she snickered, the crowd shouted, "One!" and the mass of Santas raced for the beginning of the obstacle course. Nessa might've been ambivalent about participating in the event, but once it started, her competitive spirit kicked in and she sprinted forward along with everyone else.

Her height and long legs allowed her to keep stride with

Wolf's even longer stride, and they hit the bouncy castle at the same time. She had every intention of stepping into the pool of balls. And with a sane partner, that might've happened. But she was bound to Wolf Dennison. Wrapping an arm around her waist, he launched them into the castle with a loud whoop. A shriek she would've never thought herself capable of emitting escaped her as her ass hit the balls.

Cackling like a maniac, he pulled her up for air, and they hustled for the other side.

"Get the lead out, Hunt," Wolf barked. "Cole and Sydney are gaining on us."

She glanced to her right, and seeing his brother and sister-in-law neck and neck with them lit a fire under her ball-stung ass. That and she could practically feel the buzz of the clippers over her scalp.

Clambering up the other side of the castle, she and Wolf broke for the next obstacle—the balance beam.

"You go first." He waited just long enough for the person in front of her to start across before hoisting her up onto the narrow, padded plank of wood. "Hold your arm out, and I'll be right beside you."

Slowly—and awkwardly—they shuffled across the beam, side by side.

"Your face and Patience's butt are going to be a matching pair once that thing you call a beard comes off, Wolfgang!" Cole heckled.

Wolf rocked on the beam, and Nessa stopped, quickly balancing them both before they tumbled off and would have to start over.

She slid a glance at him out of the corner of her eyes. "If you fall, I will make sure everyone knows you cried when Jack died."

Wolf glared at her. "You wouldn't."

"In. A. Fucking. Heartbeat."

A menacing rumble rolled out of him. "Get moving, Hunt." She did as ordered, and as soon as she cleared the beam and he jumped down behind her, he jabbed a finger at her. "I take back what I said about Cher. *You* fight dirty."

"Growl at me later. When I still have all my hair."

They ran for the next obstacle, where they accepted a spoon and a red plastic ball. It took them three attempts and a ton more curses before they made it across the line with the ball in the spoon. The only silver lining? It took Cole and Sydney four.

"We got 'em!" Wolf crowed as they charged toward the tire course.

Nessa laughed, but it ended on another undignified scream as he bent, put his shoulder to her stomach and hiked her over his shoulder in one smooth motion. Jesus, had he been a fireman in another life? He didn't even break stride as he sped through the tires, knees nearly jacking up to his stomach, some weird but hot combination of linebacker and ballerina.

Breathless with laughter and lust, she blinked up at him as he gently set her back on her feet and tugged her forward. Shaking her head, she raced after him, The Glen in view. A glance behind her revealed Cole and Sydney were finishing up on the tire course.

"They're gaining on us," she rasped to Wolf. And dammit, she had a stitch in her side. This was what she got for skipping the elliptical.

"Don't you give up now, Nessa. Mohawk, woman. *Mohawk.*"

"Dammit," she muttered. And pouring her last bit of energy into it, she made a mad dash for the mini-climbing wall and the finish line.

With a *lot* of help from Wolf, she scrambled over the wall and they charged across the finish line. Seconds later, Sydney and Cole dashed behind them. Wolf whooped loud and long. And if she'd had any breath left, she would've cheered, too.

"We did it!" Wolf swiftly untied their arms, then picked her up and swung her around as if she weighed six pounds instead of one hundred and sixty. He placed a loud, smacking kiss on her cheek. "My heroine. You saved my beard."

Shock pummeled her, and when he set her down on her feet and moved off to tease his brother, she couldn't move. Could only stand there, trembling fingers brushing the tingling spot where his mouth had pressed to her skin. Just a simple kiss on the cheek and yet, she *burned*. Flames licked the underside of her skin, and she wondered how no one noticed she was on fire.

A hard, low breath shuddered out of her.

At least she had an answer to her question.

Firm and soft.

His mouth was a sexy and dangerous combination of both.

And God, how she wished she didn't know.

CHAPTER NINE

NESSA DESCENDED THE stairs of the inn the next morning, already craving that first hit of coffee. Her stomach emitted an annoyed grumble, but she ignored it. Soon enough she would be grabbing a muffin or whatever baked good Moe Dennison always seemed to have out for guests. It would have to do, as she'd missed breakfast.

Deliberately.

After last night, the Santa Run and the kiss on the cheek, she'd fallen on the side of prudence and returned to Kinsale Inn instead of going to the reception with everyone else.

Okay, fine.

She'd run.

She'd pulled one of the oldest tricks in the books, claimed a headache, asked Leontyne if Ivy could ride back to the inn with her and the twins and drove back. All the while avoiding Wolf. Because at that moment, avoiding him hadn't been a choice; it'd been self-preservation. Last night, lured by that flash of pain in his eyes, she'd made the colossal mistake of letting her guard down.

Jesus. Had she learned nothing?

Let yourself be vulnerable—even the slightest bit—and people took advantage. They hurt you. They abandoned you. Isaac. Jeremy.

Even her mother.

Evelyn probably believed she'd been doing Nessa a favor

by telling her the truth about her biological father. But she'd only stripped Nessa of her identity, of the only father figure she'd known, even as unreliable in her life as he'd been. Leaving her more alone and adrift than she'd been before.

Yes, she'd only known Wolf a matter of days—hours really—but the fact that she'd already slipped in her personal vow not to allow him too close... It didn't speak well of her control around him. Which meant she'd just have to stay out of his way until the reasons why she'd come to this town were firmly entrenched in her head and soul.

Isaac's last wish for his daughter to spend the holiday here.

And for Nessa to regroup so she could return to her job stronger, more centered. Less fucking fragile. The old her. Nurse Fucking Freeze.

Nowhere on that agenda did she have the time or inclination for a man. Even a man with a pretty face and prettier mouth. And hotter body.

Dammit. She'd been doing so well.

Sighing, she stepped off the bottom stair and into the lobby. A fire crackled in the fireplace of the living room, its warmth reaching into the entry. On this Sunday morning, no one sat on the couches, but she caught the low murmur of voices from the direction of the kitchen. It irritated and dismayed her that she automatically listened for a particularly deep, rumbling timbre. And it also pissed her off and disappointed her when she didn't catch it. She did hear Ivy, though. Which solved the mystery of where she'd disappeared to this morning.

Nessa sighed. If Isaac's intention had been for Nessa and Ivy to bond over this vacation, then they were failing at it. The two of them had barely spent ten minutes in each other's company since arriving. Guilt pinched at her. Be-

cause if she were honest, Nessa couldn't deny her relief at
Ivy's preoccupation with pumping Moe for more information on her parents' stay at Kinsale Inn, the twins and Rose
Bend's many Christmas activities. Lying, even by omission,
twenty-four hours a day and maintaining the everything's-
fine facade around Ivy was exhausting as hell.

"Good morning, Nessa," Sinead, Wolf's middle sister,
greeted her from behind the reception desk with a smile.

"Morning." Nessa dipped her chin in the direction of
the hall that led toward the kitchen. "I'm guessing I'll find
coffee and my sister that way."

Sinead chuckled. "Yes. But wait, I have something for
you." She pulled one of the desk drawers open and withdrew an envelope. "This came for you with yesterday's
mail. I missed you in the afternoon and didn't get a chance
to give it to you."

"Oh thanks." Nessa accepted the piece of mail.

Bemused, she flipped it over and studied the front of the
envelope. Definitely addressed to her. But why would she
be receiving mail here of all places? She'd asked a neighbor
to gather her mail at home, but all the important things like
bills and her paycheck were handled or deposited online.
She scanned the top left corner. And frowned, recognizing
the name. Isaac's attorney's firm.

Her stomach executed a six-foot free fall toward her
boots. Letters from attorneys were like phone calls in the
middle of the night—they never brought anything but bad
news.

"If you'll excuse me," she murmured, turning and re-
tracing her steps back up the staircase, coffee forgotten.

The brew wouldn't sit well on the twisting mass of knots
that tightened her stomach anyway. Deliberately and quietly closing the door behind her, she crossed the room and

perched on the far edge of the bed next to the windows. The winter sun streaming through the open curtains provided more than enough light to read whatever the envelope contained.

She brushed a fingertip across the sealed flap, procrastinating, the unease in her belly building to an almost unbearable pitch.

"Screw this," she whispered. Then tore open the seam across the top and removed the letter inside. Correction. Letters.

The first, a thicker sheet, bore the attorney's official letterhead and explained how Isaac had instructed him to hold on to the letter until she and Ivy had arrived at Kinsale Inn. Just that, no further information. And it did nothing to lessen the cloying dread filling her throat.

Hands trembling, she tucked the paper behind the second sheet. A typed, single-spaced letter that contained Isaac's familiar signature down at the bottom.

Stalling again. Closing her eyes, she blew out a heavy breath. Opened her eyes.

Then read.

Dear Nessa,

First, let me apologize for being so dramatic with this letter. Then follow that up with, if you're reading this, then I'm dead. I'd apologize again for being morbid, but you get your humor from me, so I'm not afraid of shocking you.

Nessa put down the letter, pinching her nose and loosing a sound between a snort and a moan. Yeah, he was right; that joke was dark as hell, and yet, funny. But she didn't get *anything* from him. He wasn't her father. But Isaac hadn't known that.

Lifting the papers again, she continued reading.

Second, I've failed you as a father. And for that, I do need to say I'm sorry. I know this comes under the heading of "too little, too late," but your dad was a bit of a coward. I was too scared of saying this to you when I was alive. Too afraid you wouldn't forgive me for not being the father you needed, deserved. For not being as present for you as I should've. Being able to count the end of my life in months and days grants a man a certain clarity he can ordinarily cloud with "someday." I thought I had time, but even now when my hours are short and so vital, I can't bring myself to look you in your beautiful, precious face and say, I'm so sorry. Instead, I'm writing it in a letter. Again, I'm failing you. Failing us.

Nessa sank her teeth into her lip to trap a sob. Choking her. Anger. Grief. Oh God, such sorrow it punched at her chest, struggling to break out of her like a wild, desperate thing.

He hadn't failed her.

He'd *robbed* her.

Blinking furiously at the tears that stung her eyes, she refocused on the letter, her breath loud and harsh in the room.

I know what you must think of me, and I have no excuse. And as trite as it sounds, it's still the truth. My failure as a father had nothing to do with you. I need you to understand that. It was my inadequacies, my insecurities. The more time I allowed to pass without

*us seeing each other, without us speaking, the more
I convinced myself that maybe you didn't need me as
much as Ivy. That you were fine without me except
for the occasional phone call. I was the adult. It was
my responsibility to reach out. You'll never know
how much regret I own when it comes to you, Nessa.
So much. And one of them is dying, knowing you believe I didn't cherish you—love you—as much as Ivy.*

Tears slipped down her face, and she wiped at them.

"You didn't," she rasped at the ghost of the man who, if
she closed her eyes, she could still see so clearly. And not
as he'd been on his hospital death bed. But as she remembered from her childhood. Tall, robust with a big smile and
even bigger laugh. "I don't believe you."

Old sayings were old for a reason. Because they possessed a relevancy that surpassed the constraints of time.
Sayings like, "Actions speak louder than words."

*I want to try to make up for some of the hurt I've in-
flicted. It's why I've sent you and Ivy to Rose Bend.
Yes, you two are all you have left of family, and I
hope the beauty and sense of community there will
foster a bond between you and her that I'm responsible for not being there in the first place. But that's
not the only reason. Nessa, I'm your father. But I'm
not your biological father. Your mother and I spoke
before she died, and she let me know she would be
telling you the truth.*

Shock battered her, slamming into her with frigid, mer-
ciless fists.

He knew? Isaac had known the whole time that he hadn't

been her father? And neither he nor her mother had told her? Every day for twenty-eight years they'd both decided to wake up and lie to her about the most essential part of her—her very identity.

Betrayal scorched a path through her, leaving ashes in its wake. Fisted hands gripped the letter tight, threatening to rip it in two.

When I met your mother, she was seven months pregnant with you. To me, you've always been my daughter, regardless of whether or not my blood ran through your veins. Now, though, with both of us gone, I realize the best gift I can give you is the choice of finding your birth father. I don't know much about him—I couldn't glean too many details from your mother. But early in our relationship, she did share that she and your father fell in love in a place called Rose Bend, Massachusetts, a small town in the southern Berkshires. She didn't go into detail about what happened between them, but I sensed that whatever had separated them hurt her very much. She only mentioned his name once during that conversation. Paul Summers. I'm sorry that's all I have for you, but hopefully it will be a place for you to start to find him. I love you, Nessa. And it's only the wishful thinking of a dying man to hope this in some way can make up for—

"What's that?" Ivy appeared in front of Nessa, the envelope Isaac's letter arrived in clutched in her hand. "Is it something about Dad?"

Nessa shot to her feet, bowing her head as she hurriedly folded the papers and swiped at the tears dampening her face. *Shit*. She hadn't even heard the door open or Ivy enter the room.

"Nothing." Clearing her throat of the thick rasp, she grabbed for the envelope, but Ivy backpedaled, hiding it behind her. "Ivy, let me have it."

"No." She glared up at Nessa. "And you're lying. Don't tell me it's nothing. I saw the name on the address. It's from Dad's attorney. So it has to be about him. What's going on?"

"Ivy."

Nessa rubbed her forehead with the heel of her palm. Helplessness and grief swirled inside her. She couldn't tell Ivy the truth. *Couldn't*. It would mean confessing that they weren't sisters. That the only family she had left wasn't hers. That she was as alone in this world as Nessa.

That the father she adored had lied to her just as both of Nessa's parents had deceived her.

As much as they circled each other like wary, snarling dogs most of the time, Nessa refused to do that to this little girl who had already lost her world.

She'd rather Ivy hate her than Isaac.

"Tell me," Ivy insisted, tears glistening in her eyes. Tears she blinked against. "He's my father. You have no right to keep anything about him from me."

"Ivy, there's nothing to tell. It just has to do with more instructions about the will," Nessa murmured.

"Liar." Ivy charged forward the scant inches that separated them, her face screwed up in rage. In a sorrow that tore into Nessa with greedy claws and left her raw. "You're lying. You don't want to tell me what's in the letter. And you're doing it on purpose because you hate Dad, and you hate me. You're jealous that he loved me and didn't like you, so you won't tell me what's in that letter."

A harsh, heart-wrenching sob ripped free of her, and in

spite of the words that stabbed into Nessa with unerring accuracy, she moved toward Ivy, arms outstretched. But the girl smacked at her hands, tears running unchecked down her face.

"Don't touch me. And don't pretend you care about me. You never have. I hate you, Nessa. I hate you."

Ivy ran past her and out of the room, the door slamming so hard, the reverberation echoed in her body. For several long seconds, Nessa stood there, frozen by Ivy's outburst, her accusation hundreds of bee stings burrowing into her skin, leaving welts behind. Her breath, heavy and serrated, filled the room, her chest, her head.

Suddenly on fire, she rubbed at her arms as if she could put out the pain, but the movement only worsened the terrible prickling. Unable to remain still—unable to drag clean, unrestricted air into her lungs—she tunneled her fingers into her hair, tipping her head back until she furiously blinked at the ceiling.

I can't... I can't do this.

The wail caught her by surprise. And for a second, she wasn't sure it actually came from her. But the scalding path along her throat muscles assured her it had. Panic scraped her, and not for one more second could she remain in this room where the walls seemed to be shrinking, closing in on her, threatening to squeeze her until she disappeared.

And the scariest part? The part that sent her barreling from the room?

Disappearing didn't sound like an altogether bad idea.

WOLF PICKED UP the mechanical carpenter's pencil and, bending over the piece of wood centered on his workbench, marked his next cut just above the tape measure. Straightening, he studied it for a moment. Satisfied, he allowed the tape measure to snap home and set it and the pencil aside. If he could devote today and tomorrow to this table, he'd have it finished by the deadline he'd given the customer. Tuesday, he'd ask Trevor to sand and stain it while Wolf worked on the gazebo. Friday and Saturday afternoons, he'd use to complete the engraving and detail work. Then Monday, he'd have Dad ship it off.

Nodding, he reached for his safety goggles, but a flash out of the corner of his eye had his hand hovering over the pair. He frowned and turned fully toward the window of his workshop. Maybe it'd been one of the twins or Ivy or another of the guests that had arrived yesterday. When he didn't glimpse any more movement, he started to return to the workbench, but a niggling sense of…something stopped him. Striding toward the door, he pulled it open and stepped outside the workshop, glancing toward the trees and the pond beyond.

He squinted. Yeah, there was someone on the path, but… Wait… Nessa?

Shoving off the doorframe, he charged down the trail, his long strides eating up the distance.

"Nessa." She didn't slow. Was she ignoring him? Could be she wanted to be alone. That had to be it because she didn't strike him as the hiking type. He faltered, then stopped. But then narrowed his gaze on her. She wasn't wearing a damn coat. Only a long-sleeved, ribbed shirt. In December. Even as he studied her, a shiver worked through her body. What the fuck was going on? He moved forward again and grasped her upper arm. "Nessa. What's going on?"

She whipped around, jerking against his grip, and he let her go, holding his hands up, palms out.

Until he got a good look at her face.

Red-rimmed, wild eyes. Wet cheeks. Hair that appeared as if her fingers had been tunneled through it several times.

His heart seized and his hands physically ached with the need to cup her face. Erase those tears. Hold her to him.

But she hadn't invited him to do any of that. Unlike the Santa Run when they'd been tied together and they'd been required to touch, he hadn't crossed that boundary again since the morning at the gazebo.

Still…fuck. He curled his fingers into his palms and pressed his knuckles to the outside of his thighs.

For a moment, he almost spun around and stalked away from her. Away from the suffocating sense of already letting her down before he even opened his mouth. It strangled him. Yet, it warred with the need to fix what had placed those broken shards in her eyes. Had sent her tearing out of the inn as if pursued by demons.

He knew about that pursuit.

Knew even more about the futility of trying to outrun them.

And that, more than his fear of eventually failing her, of not being enough for her, kept him standing there when a part of him—a part of him he hated—longed to run.

"Nessie, talk to me. What's wrong?"

"I'm tired." Her whisper was soft, but it struck him as a shout, grating his eardrums. "I'm so tired. Tired of being the mature one. Tired of being understanding. Tired of being lied to. Tired of being expendable. Tired of being the secret keeper."

By the time she said that last, enigmatic statement, her voice had risen to a note that he could only describe as frantic. She confirmed his earlier suspicion when she burrowed her fingers in her hair, dragging the thick strands back from her face. With a horrible sound that was too damn close to a strangled sob, she paced across the path, her arms wrapped around herself. Not out of cold, though he didn't know how she couldn't be. But more out of self-protection. As if the only thing that stood between her and whatever had chased her out of the inn was the defense of her arms.

Without removing his gaze from her, he pulled his sweater over his head and covered the small distance separating them, barely feeling the chilly air through his white Henley. Employing the skill of a brother who'd had to wrangle younger siblings, he tugged the clothing over her in seconds and stepped back, letting her thread her arms through the sleeves.

She didn't break stride, didn't thank him. Hell, she might have been only half-aware of her actions.

"They lied to me. For years, my whole fucking life, they lied to me, and now I'm left holding the bag, facing the consequences of their actions. My mother kept me, but was it as a reminder of a man she couldn't have? Was that all I ever was to her? And Isaac didn't want me. Didn't love me. He says he did, but—" she loosed a jagged, terrible laugh "—how can I believe him? For sixteen years his actions told me he didn't. And Ivy? She doesn't know me, but is stuck with me. And now she hates me when all I've ever done is try and protect her. But in protecting her, now I'm a liar."

"Nessie."

"I'm mad. So damn mad. Why am I not allowed to be mad? To say, 'You fucked me over'? So what you apologized. But it makes me a monster to tell a dying man— now a dead man—that he sucked as a father. It makes me a bitch to look a little girl in the face and tell her that the man who treated her like a princess couldn't give two shits about me. I hate him, dammit. I hate him. I hate him for not being my father. For not needing me like I needed him. For not loving me. Why couldn't *he love me*?"

Jesus Christ.

His chest rose and fell on the labored breaths that soughed in and out of him. Every protective instinct howled and raged at him to claim those few steps that would bring him to her.

Pleaded with him to save himself now.

"Baby." Desperation roughened his voice until it neared a growl. "Ask me." He shifted forward before forcibly drawing up short. "Ask me. Please."

She jerked to a halt and looked at him, her hair wild, eyes wilder, trembling like a leaf battered by a winter wind. For a long moment, they stared at one another, both of them shaking. Her with the emotion that had driven her from the inn. Him with the tremendous restraint it required to respect her boundaries.

"Touch me." Her arms tightened around her chest. "Hold me."

Before the words finished leaving her mouth, he practically leaped across the short distance between them and hauled her into his arms. He whispered nonsensical things into her hair. She didn't cry, but God, he wished she would. The deep, almost unnatural quiet paired with the violent shivers that racked her body seemed worse.

How long they stood there—him embracing her, her burrowed against him—he didn't know. Didn't count the minutes. Because they didn't matter. As long as she needed to borrow his strength, his warmth, he'd let her. Later, when he was alone, he'd analyze why his heart was in danger of cracking a rib or two at just the thought of *why* she had to borrow it.

Only when the shuddering in her body eased and her

breathing quieted did he loosen his hold and slide a hand
to the back of her neck to lightly squeeze.

"You good?"

She nodded against his chest. "I'm good." Then, "I'm
sorry."

He leaned back, lifted his other hand to cradle the other
side of her neck and shifted both until his thumbs nudged
her chin up. Even with pink eyes and lids puffy from a previous crying jag and dried tear tracks on her cheeks, she
was beautiful. More so because of it. Because of this vulnerability he suspected she hid from most people.

Sweeping his thumbs over her cheekbones, he murmured, "You have nothing to apologize for. Not with me."
Her gaze dropped from his, and he dipped his head, catching it again. "Look at me, baby." Surprise flashed in her
dark eyes. Whether at the endearment, although it wasn't
the first time he'd called her that, or the order. Maybe both.
Hell, it echoed through him, too. "This." He brushed his
thumb over her cheek. "This." He trailed his fingertips
over her eyelids. "This." He caressed the soft cushion of
her bottom lip. "Isn't a weakness. And I'll never use it
against you."

She stared at him, silent, and he didn't speak again.
Didn't try to convince her. And after a moment, she nodded.

So did he.

Then, even though the most primal part of him snarled
a protest, he dropped his arms and stepped back. If she'd
been any other woman, he would've continued holding her,
but she wasn't. And he was beginning to understand that
there wasn't another like Nessa Hunt. She might've had
that moment where she'd allowed him to glimpse behind
that impenetrable wall, but even as they stood there, the
structure slid back into place, brick by brick. Her shoul-

ders straightened. Her breathing evened. Her chin tilted to an angle that dared him to comment on anything he'd witnessed in the last twenty minutes.

Yet…she couldn't do a damn thing about her eyes. The damp lashes couldn't conceal the hurt lingering there. The confusion.

God, he had to look anywhere else but those beautiful brown eyes. They were going to be the end of him. Of his resolve to keep a distance. A resolve he'd already violated. Again.

Deliberately, he conjured an image, a memory of himself sitting in his darkened living room the day after Olivia drove out of Rose Bend. Alone. Broken. Wondering what he could've done differently. What he could've said to change her mind.

Why he hadn't been enough to make her stay.

Complications. Hadn't he thought that the first day he'd met Nessa? Nothing in their interactions had altered his impression. And today set it in wet concrete with the word etched in capital letters.

Getting tangled in Nessa would be a mistake of colossal proportions. And yet…he didn't move.

Dammit.

"I guess I owe you an explanation," Nessa said, and he managed not to wince from the hoarseness of her voice.

"You don't owe me anything."

"Thank you." She paused, turned her head and stared off at the thick line of trees. And without meeting his gaze, she talked. And talked. About her parents' deaths. About finding out her father wasn't her biological father. About the estranged relationship with Isaac Hunt, only to find out he'd named her guardian of a sister she barely knew. Having to keep the secret of her paternity from Ivy. About this trip, and finally the letter she received this morning and her sister's hurtful words.

By the time Nessa finished, Wolf struggled not to commit the monumental misstep that most men—sorry, to males everywhere—did. Make this about him and his need to fix this for her. That's who he was—a fixer. But he couldn't. Logically, he acknowledged that. And it wasn't for him to do it, and that's not why she'd shared this with him. Still...

He inhaled, ordered his caveman instinct to stand down and exhaled.

"What do you want to do?"

She jerked her head up, brown eyes intent on him. Again, surprise flickered in them.

"Whatever it is—whatever you decide—I'll help, if you'd like me to," he offered.

His savior complex in full fucking effect. But this time... This time, he acknowledged it, and could control it. He was offering to help a friend. A beautiful, sexy friend who hardened his dick, but she was leaving Rose Bend. She was as meant for this town as Olivia had been. As long as he kept that utmost in mind, he wouldn't allow himself to reach for more. Imagine more.

And inevitably fuck it all up.

"I haven't had time to think about it." She tilted her head back, peering up at the sky. A moment later, she shook her head, huffing out a short, humorless chuckle. "I haven't let myself think about who my biological father is since finding out the truth. I think it's like wishing for a pony for your birthday, knowing it's never going to happen. I didn't allow myself to want that because I didn't believe I could have it."

"And now?" he pressed when she fell silent.

"And now—" she briefly closed her eyes before her

lashes lifted "——now I want to know. I want to find out the truth."

"Then we will."

He held out his hand. After a moment's hesitation where she stared at his upturned palm, she accepted it.

And if that same primal instinct that'd urged him to protect her now screamed he needed to protect himself, well, he had it under control.

He could help a guest—a friend—with an important mission and still maintain an emotional distance.

Damn right he could.

CHAPTER TEN

WOLF SWITCHED OFF the lathe and set down the paring tool, studying the piece of walnut that had started out as a blank, but was now a beautiful table leg with wide, perfect grooves. All he needed to do now was round the grooves over with the chisel, and the last one would be done.

A sense of accomplishment swelled within him. When he'd returned home from the service, there'd been a year when he'd floundered in darkness. Between coping with Raylon's death, PTSD and not knowing what the fuck he was going to do with his life, he hadn't been in a good place. It hadn't been until Cole's first wife, Tonia, had asked him if he could take a look at her armoire and see if he could fix the door that he'd rediscovered his love of working with wood and with his hands. He'd never forget her and would always love her for that reason alone.

Carpentry had saved him. For a while, it'd been the only *real* thing in his life. The wood, the dirt, the dust, the creating—they'd grounded him in a way even the service hadn't managed. Gradually, the peace carpentry and finding his purpose granted him—the solace, the space to be himself—reconnected him to his family, his community. No, maybe woodwork wouldn't land him a promotion or make him rich. But he could be a part of people's lives, could bring them joy, memories. That far exceeded seeing his name on an office door or having twenty employees under him.

Olivia hadn't been able to understand that.

And he had a feeling Nessa, with her life in Boston, her expensive clothes and faint derision of small-town life, was cut from the same cloth.

A knock reverberated on the door of his workshop, and he looked up from the table leg and lathe in time to see his father enter. Wolf smiled, tugging off his safety glasses.

"Hey, Dad. Tell me you brought—" His father held up a steel thermos. "Yeah, you did. Don't tell Moe. But you're my favorite parent."

Ian Seamus Dennison snorted. "If you believe I don't hear you tell your mother that every time she bakes oatmeal-raisin cookies, then there are two fools in this room."

Wolf laughed, accepting the thermos his father extended toward him. He twisted off the cap and retrieved a mug from the built-in cabinet on the far wall. Pouring his dad a cup and handing it to him and then filling the cap up to the brim, he pulled up stools for both of them.

The next couple of minutes were spent sipping his mother's delicious freshly brewed coffee in comfortable silence with one of his favorite people in the world. This was familiar territory for them. Several times a week, Ian ambled down to Wolf's workshop and spent the morning with him, either sitting and talking while Wolf worked, or even helping him with a few odd things. Wolf loved this time with his father.

Hell, he just loved his father.

In his early fifties, Ian Dennison still maintained the tall, powerful frame that he'd passed down to Wolf. And unless you messed with his wife or kids, his gray-blue eyes usually sparkled with good humor. Where Moe was gregarious and outgoing, his father tended to be quieter and more of a homebody. They balanced each other perfectly. Where Moe had been the framework always sheltering this family, Ian had been the rock-steady, never-failing foundation it'd been built on.

"This for that North Carolina job?" His father leaned over and ran blunt fingertips over the table leg. "Beautiful work, son."

Pride danced over his senses. "Thanks, Dad. And yeah. I'm not finished yet." He studied the leg with a critical eye, too, but not as it was on the lathe. As it would be by Monday, when it was completely finished and ready to ship. "After Trevor sands and stains it, I plan to add the roses to the corners of the tabletop. I already ordered the glass, and Alvin will have it here Thursday."

Ian nodded and sipped from his cup, gaze narrowed. "Your reputation is really growing, huh? This is the fourth out-of-state commission in a month, isn't it?"

Wolf lifted a shoulder in a half shrug. "Word of mouth sells. The good part is I get to decide which jobs I take or turn down. The last thing I want is to become so overwhelmed with orders that I can't deliver on time. Or at all."

"I've been watching Trevor, and the boy seems to really enjoy working with you, no matter how he came to be here. Maybe he'll want to join you full-time after school."

"Maybe," Wolf said. It wasn't like he hadn't thought of that himself. "But he needs to find his own way. Like I did."

"True."

Ian took another sip of coffee, studying him over the rim, and Wolf straightened, recognizing that particular look in his father's gaze. The I-have-something-to-say-and-you're-going-to-hear-me-out look. Wolf smothered a groan. But he might as well not have bothered because his father arched a dark eyebrow as if Wolf had released it anyway.

"What?" Wolf asked, resigned. "What have I done now? And how much does Moe know?"

Ian mock glared, jabbing a finger at him. "Y'know, you, your brothers and sisters better be glad I don't have much of an ego. Because if I did, it would be beat to hell that you are all way more terrified of your mother than you are me."

"Aw, don't be insulted, Dad." Wolf smirked, patting his father's denim-covered leg. "Let's not pretend we haven't seen you get scarce when she's on the war path."

"Boy, that's utter bullshit and you know it," he growled, but in the next instant, grinned. "Besides, I know how to get her out of her snit. All I have to do is grab her, take her upstairs and—"

"Holy shit, stop!" Wolf coughed, choking on his coffee and spraying droplets over his workbench. "Don't say another word," he wheezed.

"Are you okay?" Laughing, Ian stood and pounded Wolf on the back. Hard. "Need some water? You're looking a little peaked there."

"What I need—" Wolf waved his father away and dragged in air through his constricted lungs. When he could finally speak without sounding like he was suffering an asthma attack, he snapped, "What I need, old man, is for you not to traumatize me with that kind of talk."

Still chuckling, his father settled back on his stool and picked up his mug again. But peering down into it, he sobered. "I ran into Carol Brandt this morning while I was downtown." He glanced up. "She mentioned receiving a money order in the mail. There wasn't a return address, but there didn't need to be one for her to know who it was from. Especially since she's been receiving them every month for the past six years."

Wolf didn't answer.

Ian sighed, and sadness darkened his eyes, making them appear more blue than gray. From one second to the next, he appeared older than his fifty-four years, and guilt sat heavy in Wolf's gut like a boulder.

"Wolf." His father dragged a hand down his face and the abrasion of his scruff grazing his palm rasped in the silence. "I didn't know you still did that, son. You didn't say…" He trailed off. "How long are you going to punish yourself for something that wasn't your fault? She lost a son in the war. Carol would rather have you than your money."

"That's not true."

"Wolf…"

"No, Dad." He shook his head. His father didn't know that when he'd returned home without Raylon, Carol had blamed him for not protecting her son. For letting her baby die out there. And she'd been right. "Raylon was my best friend besides Cole. And when I didn't know what I wanted to do after graduating high school, Raylon followed me down to that recruiter's office just because he didn't want me to go alone. That's the kind of loyal friend he was."

And Wolf had failed him and his mother in the worst and most final way.

No, Carol would not rather have Wolf. And maybe she didn't want his money either. But Wolf *couldn't* take that money. He didn't deserve it or her forgiveness, if she even offered it. But in lieu of bringing back her son, it's all he had to give her.

His father softly cursed. "Wolf, I want more for you than an existence of guilt and loneliness. Any parent measures their success in life by how happy their children are. We aren't whole, settled, unless you are. Especially these last couple of years. When Cole lost Tonia and afterward…" Ian bowed his head and stared into his coffee with a faint frown. "I feel like you were—you weren't forgotten, but you got lost. Which wasn't fair because you were grieving the loss of a woman, of love, too."

Wolf waved off his father's words. "It wasn't the same. A broken heart doesn't compare to the death of a wife, a son."

What kind of selfish asshole complained about his girl-friend leaving him when his brother had to bury his family? No, he didn't have the right then to intrude on Cole's grief and he didn't now.

"I'm sorry," his father murmured.

"For what?"

"For whatever I did or didn't do that led you to believe that's true. Your circumstances are different from Cole's—that's true. But it was still the death of a relationship. Of a future you planned with the woman you loved. In a way, it was still the death of a woman—the woman you thought you'd spend the rest of your life with. And if we did any-thing to minimize your pain, then I'm so sorry, son."

Wolf stared at his father and attempted a chuckle, but the sound lodged itself behind the tangled ball of love, gratitude and sadness in his throat. "Is this why you came out here this morning? Next time bring whiskey instead of coffee if we're going to be doing male bonding. It'll at least give me a heads-up."

But his father didn't crack a smile. "Just because one of my sons seemed to take all of my focus didn't mean I worried any less about the other. Since Olivia left, you've closed off a part of yourself."

Wolf scoffed. "That's not true. I'm the same person I've always b—"

"You can't pick and choose which areas of your life to open your heart to, son. Shut yourself off to love and it leaks over into how open you are with family, friends. It affects how you trust yourself and your judgment. And that heart—" Ian leaned over and tapped Wolf's chest "—is too big not to gift to someone. But more importantly, the man you are—you weren't meant to do anything half measure. And that includes love."

"Dad, you don't need to worry. I promise." Wolf gripped his father's hand, squeezing it. "I'm fine."

"You sure about that?" Ian pressed, not letting up, and he flipped their hands so he held Wolf's in his still-strong grasp. "Not only is Olivia back in town, but I saw you with our guest yesterday. Nessa Hunt? You two looked...close." His gaze roamed Wolf's face as if searching for some clue into his thoughts. When Wolf didn't offer up an explanation, Ian softly sighed, his grip on Wolf tightening. "She's not staying, son. Yes, you're thirty-one and probably telling me to mind my own business, but you're never too old for me to be concerned about you. And I am concerned. I don't want to see you hurt again like with—"

"I'm not." Wolf shot to his feet but gently extricated his hand from his father's hold. "Like I said, Dad, you're worried over nothing. What you saw yesterday was a friend comforting another friend. There's nothing more between us."

Not necessarily a lie, but not the whole truth either. He had comforted her yesterday—but he didn't have too many friends who he fantasized about tasting his name on their lips while they came apart around his cock. As a matter of fact, he could count the number of those friends.

Zero.

"If you say so," Ian said, uncertainty coloring his voice.

"I love you, Dad." Wolf cupped his father's shoulder, then bent and kissed him on top of his head. "And thank you for loving me enough to be concerned. But I'm good, okay? With everything." He clapped Ian on the back and moved toward the table. "Now, are you going to sip on coffee all day like a gossiping old man, or are you going to help me finish up?"

Grunting, Ian pushed off the stool. "Gossiping old man." He removed the table leg from the lathe and handed it to Wolf. "I guess that means you don't want to hear about how Donald Harrison caught the missus sending pictures of her, uh, treasure over that Facebook?"

"Shut. Up." Wolf gaped at his father. "Talk."

And while his father told him about the seventy-six-year-old Mrs. Harrison getting caught up in the latest online love scam, Wolf couldn't help but run their conversation over in his head. And steel his resolve.

He might've downplayed his attraction to Nessa, but he hadn't been misleading his father about getting involved with her. Nessa Hunt had no intention of staying in Rose Bend beyond her checkout date, and unlike with Olivia, he wouldn't pretend otherwise. He'd played himself for a fool once and opened his heart up to that kind of pain. He'd literally watched a woman drive out of his life once.

Damn if he would do it again.

CHAPTER ELEVEN

NESSA STARED AT the laptop screen, scanning the email for what seemed like the tenth time. Stalling. She was most definitely stalling.

Just do it.

Her mind fired off the order and yet the cursor still hovered over the send button. For the *eleventh* time, she read the email to Gayle, her mother's best friend. Just one paragraph asking her to please use the key Nessa had left her for mail and emergencies to grab a box from her closet and mail Nessa the contents. That's it. Simple. Nothing explaining that the contents contained her mother's personal effects such as letters, photos and other memorabilia that Nessa hadn't been able to bring herself to go through yet.

She could've called. But that would've meant questions. And since Gayle was also an attorney, Nessa didn't feel up to fielding what would undoubtedly be an Annalise Keating–level interrogation. So email it was. But first, she had to send the damn thing.

Why the hesitation? It's just a message. A request.

Because this makes it real. There's no turning back. There's no denying that you're going to search for your biological father.

The answer blared in her mind, quick and painfully bright. She could no longer blame her mother and Isaac for not knowing the identity of her biological father; she'd have to claim some of the fault, too.

She hit Send.

And exhaled a hard breath, her pulse a dull, heavy beat in her head.

She glanced over her shoulder and out the kitchen window toward the workshop where Wolf had disappeared after he'd found her Sunday. He'd probably like to know that she'd—

No. Don't even think about going there.

Sunday had been...emotional. And in the heat of the moment—a very weak moment—she'd let her guard down and had agreed to his help. Among other things. She tipped her head back, staring at the ceiling, a memory of him asking—no, *demanding*—she ask him to hold her flashing in her head. Followed by images of him holding her close, stroking her face...

Look at me, baby.

That endearment had caught her by surprise. Had sent a shock of unexpected and terrifying pleasure jolting through her. She hadn't wanted to like that on his lips. Hadn't wanted to hear him call her "baby" again in a deeper, rougher growl as those forest green eyes blazed with a dark hunger.

Oh damn, she was such a liar. Yes, she did. She wanted it all.

And that scared her the most.

Distance. She needed distance from this wholly inconvenient and stupid-as-hell desire for Wolf Dennison. This search for her bio dad didn't require a team effort. She could do it on her own. As she'd done most things in her life. Why should this be any different? Besides, another lesson she'd learned.

If you didn't depend on people for help, then they couldn't disappoint you when they didn't come through.

"Hey, Nessa." Sydney, with Patience strapped to her chest, strolled into the kitchen, Leo behind her.

Nessa closed the laptop and mentally grimaced as the two women glanced at one another, eyebrows raised. Yeah, in hindsight the action appeared completely sketchy.

"Hey," she said, smiling and trying to play off her suspicious behavior. "What's going on?"

"Nothing much." Sydney released the catches on the carrier and gently pulled her baby free. The love on the other woman's face as she cuddled the little girl in her arms shone brighter than the winter light pouring into the kitchen, and Nessa shifted her gaze away from it. The power and beauty of that adoration was almost like peering directly into sunlight—blinding and too much. "Well, that's not true. I'm trying to convince Leo to take a break and come with me to the Christmas tree decorating contest at the high school."

"And like I've told her, I can't. This inn won't run itself. Especially with Moe taking off for her book club tonight." Leo leaned down and pressed a kiss to her niece's head.

Sydney snorted. "Is that what they're calling it now? Wine club would be more accurate." Smiling at Nessa, Sydney slid an arm around Leo. "Nessa, my best friend here is preparing to take over the inn when her parents eventually retire. Too bad she's becoming a fuddy-duddy workaholic in the process."

Leo rolled her eyes. "'Scuse me for wanting to make sure Kinsale Inn is *the* premiere destination spot in the Berkshires. I'll have plenty of time to play, just not during one of our busiest seasons. But," she said, turning to Nessa, lips pursed, "since you're not busy—definitely not surfing

Pornhub or anything—why don't you join her? Ivy rode over with Sinead to help her take cookies and brownies… Wait." Leo frowned. "You did know about that, right?"

Nessa nodded. Ivy had texted and let her know she would be with Sinead since the preteen still wasn't talking to her.

"Good, didn't want to narc her out, although if she left without telling you, she totally deserved it." Leo scooped Patience out of Sydney's arms, apparently not satisfied with just smooching the baby. Cradling her close, she peeked at Nessa from under her thick fringe of lashes. "It'll be fun. Get you out of the inn. Apparently, I'm the only one married to this place and all too happy with it."

"Actually, I'm fine. I have some things I need to finish up." Nessa waved a hand toward the laptop although it was a lie. Truth be told, between Ivy's silent treatment, the constant wondering about the next step in finding her father and avoiding Wolf, Christmas festival activities numbered somewhere below scraping ice off her windshield on her to-do list. Alcohol and anything starring Jason Momoa on Netflix numbered very high.

No, scratch that. Not Jason. Because that would only remind her of Wolf. And *that* she didn't need.

"Aw, c'mon, Nessa." Sydney plopped down in the chair across from her, propping her hands under her chin and batting surprisingly long lashes. The cynical part of her wondered if they were mink. "What else would you do here? You know what?" She held up a hand, palm out, and shook her head. "Don't answer that. Because if it involves alcohol or cookie-dough ice cream, I might lose this argument. So just put your shit on and get in the car with me."

Leo snickered. "Listen, Nessa, a Christmas tree decorating contest might not sound like a rousing good time on its face. But let me tell you. A couple of years ago, some enterprising soul replaced the ex-mayor's box of decorations with penis-and-ball-shaped ornaments. Hilarious! We've all been secretly waiting for Penisgate to happen again. You can't make this up, my friend. What if it goes down and you miss it? No." She shot Nessa a furious glare. "Not on my watch. Get yourself up, throw on layers and go on down to that high school just in case the bandit strikes again."

Nessa stared at both of them, not sure if she should laugh or back away slowly without losing eye contact.

In the end she just got in the car.

"This is going to be great—you'll see," Sydney crowed, hooking an arm through Nessa's as she led her across the high school parking lot toward the gym entrance ten minutes later. "It was one of my favorite contests, although Cole told me it's become a lot bigger since I was last in Rose Bend. Before, we decorated table-sized trees. Now..."

She slid her arm free of Nessa's and pulled open one of the doors, cradling Patience close with the other.

Good Lord.

A forest. She'd stepped into a forest. Oh sure, it was smack-dab in the middle of a huge high school gym with bleachers on either side and banners on the walls from years past, proclaiming the Rose Bend Panthers champions of basketball, wrestling or cheerleading. Tables littered with brown boxes and clear crates dotted the floor and stepladders played hide-and-seek with the many chairs but still... A Christmas tree forest.

Oh my God, Mom. Did you ever spend a Christmas here with my father? Did you see anything like this?

The thought slipped into her mind like a ghost, and Nessa shivered in its wake. Sorrow rippled through her because she might never have those answers. Because if she'd had just a little more time, another year, a few more months and a little more truth, she could've at least shared this with her mother.

"Yep. A huge step up from the table-sized trees." Sydney chuckled, tugging Nessa farther into the building, and thankfully jerking her from the spiral of her thoughts. "The town motto is All Are Welcome Where None Are Strangers. It should be Go Big or Go Home." She laughed again. "Believe it or not, we get people who not only travel from neighboring towns but as far away as Boston to attend the festival activities. And that was before I left Rose Bend. I can't even imagine how it is now."

"My mother would've loved this."

The words tumbled out of Nessa without her permission. As soon as they hit her ears, she wished she could retract them. Especially when Sydney glanced at her, sympathy in her smile and eyes. The other woman smoothed a tender hand down her baby's back, quiet for a moment.

"Since I can see how uncomfortable that admission makes you, I would ordinarily let it pass and pretend you didn't say it. But I also remember being you a year ago. Then, I would've said I didn't want anyone to acknowledge my feelings, but I did. Because a simple acknowledgment would've meant I was heard. So, I hear you, Nessa. What you said, and what you didn't say." Sydney found Nessa's hand, encircled her fingers and squeezed. "And so you know, anytime you want to share what you can't right now, I'm here. Or even if all you want to do is just sit, not talk and drink wine. I can't do the wine part because I'm breastfeeding, but I can still sit, not talk and glare at you in envy."

Nessa snorted in spite of the emotion that resembled a snarled ball of yarn in her belly. Swallowing hard, she parted her lips, and her throat contracted around the words. As if her self-preservation instincts fought the urge to share.

Clearing her throat, she tried again. "My mom, she loved Christmas. It was only us, and a lot of the time she worked most of the season, only having the actual day off. But she still loved it. She used to joke that I got my indifference toward it from my father."

Nessa used to believe she'd meant Isaac. Had her mother meant the unknown man who'd given her half his DNA?

Not that it mattered then and didn't now. Her apathy toward Christmas hadn't had anything to do with genetics and everything to do with an aversion to watching holiday movies, decorating trees and eating meals alone because her mom worked such long hours.

But telling Evelyn that would've been like stabbing her in the heart. And Nessa would've never hurt her like that. Not when she'd sacrificed so much.

"Oh isn't this nice. I didn't know you two were going to be here this afternoon." Jenna Landon appeared next to them, and Nessa stifled a curse.

She'd only met the tall, beautiful redhead once, at the tree lighting, but that one time had been enough. The mean-girl aura tended to leave a lasting impression. And nothing about the other woman's red-painted smile or the slightly narrowed eyes changed Nessa's mind.

"Neecy, was it?" Jenna asked.

Nope. Still bitchy.

"Nessa," she corrected, calling on visuals of unicorns, puppies and Jack Black TikTok videos to maintain a politeness in her voice. "Nice to see you again." She turned to the woman standing next to Jenna. "You, too, Olivia."

"Hi, Nessa." The woman who had turned Wolf into a living statue returned Nessa's greeting with a smile that radiated genuine warmth. Damn. How did you dislike a woman who seemed so nice?

Well, she *could* but it made her a wench.

"Sydney, is this your baby?" Olivia cooed, shifting closer and peering down inside the carrier. "She's gorgeous."

"She is," Jenna murmured, her mouth softening, as did her gaze. "She's really beautiful."

Nessa stared at the redhead, shocked at both the compliment and the unexpected display of gentleness. Jenna's arms flinched, and her fingers curled then straightened, almost as if she were about to reach for the baby, perhaps touch her, but then caught herself. Nessa arched her eyebrows, peered at Jenna, whose gaze remained locked on the child. Did anyone else see the yearning in her eyes? Or was it only Nessa's imagination?

"Um, thanks," Sydney said, astonishment coloring her voice.

"She must take after her father," Jenna purred, her smirk firmly back in place.

And there it was. The return of the bitch.

"Careful, Jenna." Sydney arched an eyebrow, her tone pleasant, her brown eyes...not. "You wouldn't want to end up with a tree full of dicks like your father this year."

Nessa tried to hold in her snicker. Tried and failed. Jenna's glare swung toward her, and her lips curled into a snarl that promised retribution, but the door to the gym swung open and Wolf entered, preempting her cutting remark.

"Wolf," Jenna called, waving him over. "Over here."

Well, damn.

There went her avoid-Wolf plan. It seemed she couldn't escape him, no matter how hard she tried. And she had.

Maybe her effort would be a little more convincing if she could stop staring at him.

But God... Did that man know how to fill a doorway.

Sunday, she'd rested her head on that wide chest as he'd offered her those powerful shoulders to lean on. That big body had provided a buffer against her grief—against the world. And as she peeked at Olivia, she noted the same hunger on her lovely face. Olivia didn't try to hide the desire that darkened her violet eyes.

The difference between her and Nessa? Olivia knew how it felt to be possessed by Wolf. She didn't need him to confirm it. No one reacted to a person like he had—or no one watched another person as she watched him—without having been intimate. This woman had been branded by his strength, his passion. She'd been underneath his naked body, covered by it. She knew what it meant to be burned by his need, his pleasure.

Jealousy twisted so hard in Nessa's belly she clenched her jaw against the wrenching tug of it. In that moment, she resented the hell out of Olivia for having that knowledge. A knowledge Nessa craved. But couldn't claim for herself.

What the hell? Jealousy? Was she a glutton for misery? She had no business feeling anything close to that emotion. He wasn't hers. Not even remotely. She didn't *want* him to be. She didn't want anyone.

More accurately, she didn't *need* anyone.

Least of all a man who had a woman staring at him as if he were every teenage-vampire and billionaire-fetish fantasy rolled into one.

No, even if she hadn't already had enough on her plate with figuring out how not to have a panic attack on the job, uncovering a paternity secret and handling a sister-who-wasn't-a-sister who hated her, the way Olivia looked at him was enough reason not to go there.

Dragging her gaze away from Wolf, away from the bare hunger in Olivia's gaze, Nessa scanned the gym, desperate for a distraction. From them. From herself.

She spotted Ivy in the middle of the chaos at one of the tables with the twins and a couple of other kids. As if sensing her attention on her, Ivy looked up and for the first time in a couple of days, she didn't ignore Nessa. Even across the distance that separated them, Nessa glimpsed the sadness that shadowed Ivy's eyes. Her breath snagged like a sweater caught on a nail. For an instant, her body swayed in the direction of her sister, the threat of rejection paling in the face of that sorrow.

But then Ivy turned away, giving Nessa her back. She'd been halfway prepared for the rebuff. And yet, she still sucked in a shallow gasp of air, hurt shimmering in her like steam over a hot sidewalk.

His scent hit her first. Wintergreen wrapped in the clean, biting fresh air that still clung to him. She inhaled it, hating that the scent calmed the storm inside her. Hating even more that she wanted to close her eyes and sink into it, let it welcome her, embrace her.

She tilted her head back, already knowing she'd meet a pair of densely lashed emerald eyes. Although she was forearmed with that knowledge, the impact of his gaze still reverberated through her. Lust, hot and fierce, sizzled a path that left her fighting not to tremble in front of witnesses. Maybe if he hadn't introduced her to the strength of his arms and the powerful shelter of his body… Maybe then the need wouldn't be as intense. Wouldn't have her envisioning that hooded stare raking over her as he stroked those big hands with the nicked fingers down her shivering body…

Enough.

She dipped her head on the pretense of—hell, staring at the floor. Unless she enjoyed eye-fucking a man in a gym full of people and Christmas trees, any distraction would have to suffice.

"Hi, Wolf." Sydney hugged her brother-in-law with the arm not cupped under her napping daughter. "Let me guess. Cole recruited you."

He snorted. "If that's what you want to call it. He had me over here earlier hauling in and setting up trees. Something about me owing him. I think your husband is still bitter about the Santa Run ass-kicking." Leaning down, he brushed a kiss over Patience's curls, a smile curving his lips before he straightened. Nodding at Jenna and Olivia, he said, "Hey, Jenna, Olivia. Good to see you."

Jenna beamed at him while Olivia practically glowed, her eyes lighting up at his greeting. "You, too, Wolf."

And no, Nessa's belly did *not* tighten at that look of obvious affection.

"Nessa." A nudge to her shoulder, and she couldn't avoid glancing at him any longer. "You good?" he murmured.

"All good." She rummaged up a smile, but when he arched an eyebrow, she abandoned the effort. Apparently, it'd been a fail.

"All right, people, we're about to get started," a melodic yet authoritative voice boomed. Nessa glanced toward the front of the gymnasium and spotted a lean, older Black woman with a cap of gray curls. Though clothed in a lilac sweater set and black slacks, she carried the same don't-mess-with-me air in her slender frame that vibrated in her voice. "Let's hop to, people. We're starting this contest on time. You have five minutes to grab your partners and get to your tables. You have two hours to decorate your trees.

At seven o'clock sharp, back away from the trees and judging starts."

"I don't know her, but she reminds me of my charge nurse in the ER. And I have the urge to say, 'Yes, ma'am,' and not backtalk or fear getting my ass handed to me."

"You're not far off." Sydney laughed. "And I'm not getting on her bad side. I'm going to find Cole so we don't get Ms. Eva's side-eye."

"I promised my father I'd be his partner since Mother couldn't make it this year," Jenna announced. Then with a sly smile, she turned to Wolf. "You and Olivia should team up. Just like old times. It'll be so much fun." As if remembering Nessa stood there, the redhead waved a dismissive hand in the direction of the tables. "I'm sure there will be others here without partners. Didn't you have a sister here? You should grab her."

Olivia smiled at Nessa, and she had to give it to the other woman. Olivia had the grace to appear apologetic on behalf of her rude-ass friend. Yet she still turned to Wolf, with what Nessa could only describe as hopeful delight glistening in her pretty eyes.

"What do you say, Wolf? I'd love to partner with you again."

Was "partner with you" a euphemism for "do the nasty beast with two backs"?

Oh, girl, you got to stop. Nessa mentally face-palmed herself. Somebody had to. She was officially getting out of hand.

"Awesome." Jenna grinned and clapped her hands together. "That's settled—"

"Actually," Wolf said, gently clasping Nessa's hand, sending a current of electricity zipping from her fingers, up her arm and arcing to all points north...and south, "Nessa is my partner. We can't have our guests to Rose Bend feeling unwelcome. Since you know more people here than Nessa, I'm sure you can find someone to pair up with much more easily than she can, Olivia," he said, his tone gentle, but the underlying thread of steel running through it brooking no argument.

Olivia's lips parted, her gaze dropping to their linked hands before lifting to his face. Nessa barely managed to smother her flinch at the hurt glinting in the other woman's eyes, because no woman wanted to be pitied or to have her pain witnessed by someone she considered the competition—even if she wasn't. And Olivia deserved that respect from her.

Jenna, on the other hand...

The redhead glared at Nessa. "I'm sure Neecy doesn't mind finding someone else. That's how a person meets new people, after all. And she should understand two...friends wanting to get reacquainted."

"Her name is Nessa. And, Jenna?" Wolf murmured, his voice almost pleasant. Almost. "Mind your business."

He didn't wait for Jenna's reply and ignored her outraged gasp. Nessa couldn't do anything but stare at the middle of his wide shoulders as he led her over to a table that hadn't been claimed yet. Two clear containers filled with an assortment of decorations and lights sat on top, and other bows, garland and tape lay scattered across the rest of the surface. A stepladder and two folding chairs rounded out their supplies, and Nessa examined each and every item as if the success of this tree depended on her careful analysis.

"Are the teams ready?" Eva Wright asked into the mic, arm raised in the air. When a chorus of cheers met her question, she lowered her arm and ordered, "Commence decorating!"

Nessa peeled off her coat and dropped it on the back of one of the chairs and propped her fists on her hips. Tilting her head back, she squinted up into the dark green branches of the six-foot tree. Could she get through this without looking him directly in the eye? Because each time she did, things happened.

She entered Santa Runs.

She cried.

She admitted secrets.

She imagined him naked.

No, for her sanity she had to avoid his face.

"Lights first, right? Isn't that a rule? The lights are supposed to go on first?"

"I don't know about a rule, but Moe would argue you down that it's true." Behind her, he rustled through the box and moments later appeared next to her with a coil in each hand. "Okay, here's the first and most important decision. What's the theme?"

"Theme?" She frowned, still staring at the lights and managing not to look at his face. But even his hands were distracting. Because they were just so damn...big. And sexy.

So, eyes back on the tree, since apparently she couldn't look at his hands either without her thoughts going to bad, bad places.

"Oh yeah," he continued, oblivious to her carnal dilemma. "Theme is key. Look around you." He waited until she shifted her gaze to the rest of the gym. "Some people are going with all gold. Or all white. Someone will undoubtedly choose the classic icicles and stars. Then there's bows. This is a contest, after all. Theme determines the winner."

She blinked. "Um. Okay." Risking glancing at him, she shrugged. "What do you suggest?"

"Me? I would go with an oldie but goodie."

"And that is?"

"Throw shit on it until it starts to lean, then stop."

The bark of laughter exploded from her before she could trap it inside. Clapping her hands over her mouth, she snickered, drawing amused glances from people at surrounding tables.

"Okay." She bit the inside of her cheek to contain her grin. "That sounds like a winner to me." She took the first rope of lights from him and studied it. "Let's do the white first, then follow up with the blinking lights."

"Gaudy." Wolf grinned. "I like it."

They worked in companionable silence for the first few minutes, winding the chain of bulbs and connecting them. Next, they threaded the red tinsel through the branches, and when Wolf paused, shoving the sleeves of his black sweater up his forearms, she briefly closed her eyes. But it didn't help. She could still see the strong tendons and thin veins in those muscular arms. God, a man shoving up his sleeves notched just below chest porn.

Once they were finished, she stared up at the dark branches and the lights, seeing other trees. Hearing distant laughter. Smelling the faded memories of popcorn.

"Where are you?" The question rumbled against her back, and his fresh, skin-warmed scent wrapped around her.

She continued to study the tree for another few moments, gathering her thoughts before answering. "You know how when you're angry, it overshadows everything? Makes the bad overshadow the good and you forget that there ever was any good?"

"Yeah."

Just that word, but God, such a wealth of emotion in it. What did Wolf hide? And how deep did it go?

"Well, I was just remembering Christmases with me, Mom and Isaac before they divorced. We were…happy. He used to pop popcorn and string it for the tree. She'd play all her Motown Christmas CDs, especially the Jackson 5, because they were her favorites. She'd bake cookies and we would spend all night decorating the tree. Those were some of my favorite times. My best memories of us as a family. I guess I blocked them out. Until now."

His hands slid over her waist and down to cradle her hips. She inhaled, briefly closing her eyes at the strength in those big palms. Heat melted in her veins, pooling between her thighs, and she struggled not to shift, not to betray the effect he had on her.

"When we were kids, we would all lie down, crowd under the Christmas tree and stare up at the branches when it was all decorated and lit up. It seemed like an alternate world from under there. That's one of my happiest memories. And it's why I love this event so much." He squeezed her hips, and his lips grazed the top of her ear. A shiver raced down her spine, but she didn't move away. No, she savored the sensation. "Embrace those memories, Nessie. Don't feel any guilt for having forgotten them for a time or enjoying them now. They're gifts from two people who loved you."

Oh damn. She couldn't do this. Not here. Not now.

"So—" she cleared her throat "—what do you do with all these trees once they've been decorated and judged?"

He squeezed her hips in understanding, then stepped back and released her.

"Not everyone in Rose Bend lives in a certain tax bracket," he said quietly, taking the garland from her, his fingertips brushing hers. The tingle that trekked up her arm took a back seat to his tone and words. She paused, mid-decorating, and looked at him. "I know how blessed my family and I are, but that's a privilege everyone doesn't have. Some people can't afford the shopping, the gifts and even the trees that others can. Ms. Eva makes it her mission to ensure that every family that wants a tree has one. I don't know how she does it. I don't know how she finds the families. But by this time tomorrow when the kids pile into this gym for class, every tree will be gone and delivered to a home."

"Wow." She shook her head, huffing out a disbelieving chuckle. She searched the gym for the woman under discussion, finding her near the front of the gym, talking to a small group of people. "It's almost like the people here are unreal. Working in an ER, where I always see not just people's pain but also the suffering they can inflict on each other, I can forget how…kind the world can be, too."

"Which makes me wonder if you haven't had enough people in your world being kind to you. Or maybe it's you who hasn't been gentle with yourself."

Nessa jerked her head back to him. What the hell did that mean? Anger flared inside her, a quick burst that flickered out as quickly as it appeared, leaving her oddly vulnerable. Naked.

How did he see inside her as if she were a black-and-white X-ray when the man she'd been with for two years hadn't been able to—or hadn't bothered to?

It was true; she'd faced abandonment, rejection and hurt in her life from Isaac, men she'd dated as recently as Jeremy. But if she were brutally, deep down, dirty honest—the kind of honesty that only came in the darkest hours of the morning when sleep eluded a person—she blamed herself for their defection.

If the man who was supposed to love her unconditionally

could leave her so easily, there must be something innately wrong with her. It was her fault. She was too independent. Too mouthy. Too closed off. Too…too…

Just too.

And never enough.

"You're finally looking at me." He cocked his head. "Are you through avoiding me now?"

The protest was poised on her tongue, but when she spoke, "Yes" came out.

A smile flirted with his full lips. "Good. Your profile is beautiful, but so is the rest of your face." He paused, his gaze dropping from her eyes to her mouth, lingering, then lifting. "And I like looking at it."

Silence pulsed between them, a molten heartbeat that heated the air and throbbed with the desire that darkened his eyes and pounded in her veins.

She wasn't a stranger to lust and didn't pretend to be one of those women who denied her body's needs. Sex was a pleasure, a release, and one she enjoyed sharing with a man who wanted her. And Wolf… Damn, she wanted him to want her. Was it her own desire or did she really see hunger shadowing those green depths? A fine tension coiling his muscular body? A faint flush staining his sharp cheekbones…?

A spasm wrenched inside her. Deep inside where she needed to be filled, branded by him, his fingers, his cock. She'd take whatever part of him she could…

Sucking in a breath, she blinked. Took a step back.

"What's next?" she whispered, voice hoarse.

From unsatisfied lust. From the effort of imprisoning the demand that he walk her out of this gym and defile her in the back seat of his truck.

Damn, the part of her that cried out to be touched, held,

fucked, insisted she grab him by the hand and carry this through. But the other, logical, *sane* side of her acknowledged her reasons for being here in Rose Bend might have shifted, but her priorities hadn't.

Emotional entanglements had only left her battered and alone.

She needed the truth about her father and to get back to Boston and her job, hopefully with her and Ivy's relationship not damaged more than when they'd left home. Hopefully, she'd return capable of not breaking down while in the middle of tending to her patients. She'd already lost her identity, it seemed, when she'd discovered Isaac wasn't her father. She couldn't lose being a nurse, too. Not *who* she was.

What she *didn't* need was a fling with a hot carpenter whose body was a religious experience and whose eyes could make her heart weep.

And could apparently turn her into a poet.

"Next, you stop being awkward and pass me those ornaments that look like homicidal elves."

God, she *was* making this awkward. So what if he found her attractive or even desired her. He hadn't made a move on her. Other than hugging her when she'd basically come apart in front of him, he hadn't given her any indication that he wanted anything other than friendship with the guest visiting his family's inn.

Projecting much, Nessa?

Before she had a chance to slap it down, disappointment swarmed inside her like angry bees. But slap it down she did. Yes, just glancing at the masculine perfection of his face caused an empty ache to yawn low in her belly, but she didn't need to have sex with Wolf Dennison to know it would be a huge mistake.

Because it wouldn't just be great sex. Call it a sixth sense or woman's intuition or ESP—whatever. She didn't need the gift of premonition to guess that he would leave her wide open and more emotionally tangled than five-o'clock traffic on I-95.

Not to mention changed. And not in a good way.

She couldn't afford to leave any pieces of herself behind when she left Rose Bend at the end of the month.

"Right," she finally said, turning to the table. "Homicidal elves. Coming up."

She pushed aside more garland and dug around in the crate until she came across a cardboard box of eight ornaments of... Shit. With those maniacal grins, crossed eyes and really sharp candy canes in their hands, they *did* look bloodthirsty. Hopefully, Santa left these little motherfuckers at the North Pole. Locked up.

She opened the box and passed it to him, then grabbed another carton of angels slightly less deranged looking.

"Any progress with your search?" Wolf glanced at her, hanging the ornaments on the top branches.

"I really just started today." She shrugged a shoulder. "I emailed my mom's best friend and asked her to send a box of Mom's things to me that I haven't had a chance to go through since the funeral. Wait, that's a lie." She loosed a short, dry laugh. "It's been eight months. I've had plenty of time. I haven't been able to bring myself to do it. But now..." She shrugged again.

"Now when you open it, you'll have a whole inn of Dennisons to be with you if that's what you need. Things happen for a reason, when they're supposed to happen, Nessie."

She paused, briefly closing her eyes. A moment later, she opened them and continued hanging the ornament, focusing on the task and not the beautiful man next to her.

"I wish you wouldn't do that," she murmured.

He arched an eyebrow. "You're going to have to be a little more specific."

I wish you didn't offer me your support like it's the simplest thing in the world instead of everything.

I wish you didn't offer your family to a woman who has none left.

I wish you weren't...you.

"Do that wise-old-man, Yoda thing." She waved a hand at him and frowned, summoning a nonchalance she far from felt. "It's disconcerting. Especially when you're wearing a man bun."

Wolf tsked. "Bun shaming. I thought you were better than that, Nessie."

"You thought wrong."

She teased him, but damn how she wished that thick, dark brown hair pulled back into a knot at the nape of his neck was a turnoff. On other men, it could come across as pretentious and a bit douchey. But not on him. On Wolf, it was simply him—practical, simple and sexy as hell.

"Is Ivy still angry with you?"

His low murmur pulled her from her introspection on his grooming style, and she sighed. Flicking a glance across the room, she watched Ivy talk and laugh at Cher's antics as the twin teetered on the stepladder to loop an ornament on a high branch. As Ivy turned to grab another decoration from the table, her smile suddenly dropped and sadness crossed her expression.

An answering sorrow gripped Nessa, and her fingers tightened around the tiny angel in her hand, the wings pinching her palm. This was Ivy's first Christmas without her father, and it had to be tough on her. A wild helplessness welled inside Nessa. The need to go to her, comfort her, tell her she understood because this would be her first without her mom—it almost propelled her forward.

But Ivy didn't want comfort from her.

Didn't want her, period.

Tearing her gaze away, she turned back to the tree and deliberately placed the ornament, as if it were the most important task in the world.

"Yes," she belatedly answered Wolf's question. "She still believes I'm a jealous bitch keeping information about her dad from her."

"You're not jealous or a bitch, but you are keeping information from her."

She jerked her head up. "But you know why. You're the only one who knows why." Please, Lord, don't let the hurt flaring inside her be reflected in her voice. But he was the only one she'd shared the truth with, and now he threw that back in her face?

"I do get why, Nessie," he said. "You're trying to protect her, but she's twelve, and she's observant. She senses something is wrong, that you're not being honest with her. And as long as she believes that, Ivy isn't going to completely trust you."

"What's the alternative? Ruining the sainted image she has in her head of her father?" There went that bitterness again. Dammit. She swallowed down the rancid taste of it. This wasn't about her and her complicated feelings and relationship with Isaac; it was about Ivy. "I'd rather have her mad at me than take that away from her when she's lost so much already."

"And I think you're underestimating her." Long, nicked fingers gently freed her strong hold on the angel and then wrapped around her hand. Wolf tugged her closer and, pinching her chin, tilted her head up. "That girl is more like you than either one of you like to admit. She might throw attitude, but her heart is huge. And it's hurting. Ivy loves you, Nessa—she's just afraid to show you. Probably afraid the moment she becomes attached to you, that'll be the moment you disappear from her life like her parents."

Nessa blinked, speechless. Her lips parted, but no words emerged. Wolf shook his head, the corner of his mouth quirking before he stroked his thumb over the curve of her cheek.

"I know. My man bun and my Yoda-like tendencies annoy you. But just consider being honest with her. You can never build anything strong with her unless the foundation is truth. Besides, I think she would surprise you. Yes, she adores her father, and most of us put our parents on pedestals. But she's also a great, smart kid. And, Nessie? Are you more afraid of hurting her or of losing her when she finds out you're not related by blood?"

Leaving her with that gem, he stepped back and returned to decorating the tree. Was he right? Did she fear Ivy would reject her when she found out they weren't sisters? Was that another reason she didn't want to reveal the truth to her?

Yes.

She didn't move for several seconds, that answer and his advice echoing in her head. Unbidden, her gaze drifted to Ivy again, and this time, her sister stared back at her, frowning. She glanced at Wolf then back at Nessa.

You okay?

Nessa easily read the mouthed words, and Jesus, her heart squeezed so tight she questioned the possibility of a coronary. She nodded, and Ivy hesitated before dipping her chin in response, then turning back to her tree. Inhaling, Nessa blinked back the burn of tears. Okay, so Wolf might be right. Maybe Ivy didn't hate her.

Needing a moment, she crossed to the box of decorations and rummaged through it. Only after she'd patched up the cracks that Ivy's unexpected display of concern had caused did she lift her head and return to the Christmas tree, tinsel in hand.

"You have any plans after this?" Wolf asked, extending his hand for some of her tinsel.

"No, why?" She handed half of it over. "Is there a reindeer race later tonight?"

He scoffed. "Don't be silly. That's next week." When she shot him an I-could-brain-you-with-this-tree-and-lose-no-sleep look, he chuckled. "No, there's a place I'd like to take you."

She studied him. Where? Why? For how long? What for? The questions crowded onto her tongue, and with anyone else, she would've let them fly. And she should ask, because hello, she'd only known this guy a handful of days. So, yep, he needed an inquisition—

"Okay."

Shit.

The fact that she didn't question him should've scared her more than her body's unprecedented reaction to him. And it did send alarm careening through her.

Yet, who was she fooling?

She was going with him. Because he was Wolf.

And she had apparently lost all sense of self-preservation when it came to him.

Oh this was going to end badly.

CHAPTER TWELVE

"I'M NOT SAYING the contest was rigged. But I am saying having Patience there all cute and snuggly didn't hurt Cole and Sydney's chances," Nessa muttered, pushing open the passenger door of Wolf's truck and climbing out of the vehicle.

Wolf snorted as he exited behind her and rounded the hood. For someone who claimed not to get into all the Christmas festivities, Nessa possessed a competitive streak as long and as wide as the Berkshires.

"Careful there, Nessie." He tsked. "You're starting to sound like Jenna."

"Take it back," she growled. "Take it back right now."

He laughed. "No can do. I overheard her complaining to her father that Cole and Sydney only won because he's the mayor."

Nessa groaned, tipping her head back on her shoulders. "Okay, fine. I'm sorry. I'm a sore loser. Their tree was gorgeous and all color coordinated and worthy of *Woman's World* magazine. But our tree should've won something for the sheer gaudiness factor," she added with a pout.

A pout that, frankly, delighted and aroused the hell out of him. What would she do if he leaned over and sank his teeth into that plump bottom lip and tugged? Sucked? Slid his tongue over the damp curve before thrusting inside?

Would she back away, turn away from him?

Or would she open wider for him, grant him deeper access? Moan for him...

Jesus, he dragged his gaze from her face and swung his attention to the elegant yellow-and-white Victorian sitting several feet back from the curb.

He was doing this. What he'd promised himself he wouldn't do. Getting entangled. Getting...complicated. A very real fear slicked his skin, coated his tongue. Boundaries. As long as he maintained boundaries, he could help her solve this mystery and not get involved.

Not forget.

"Ready?" He settled a hand on the small of her back and guided her up the walk and steps to the wide front porch.

Dropping his hand, he curled his fingers into his palm, trapping the heat from her body, while raising the other arm to knock on the front door. They waited several moments, and then the door opened, and Eva Wright stood in the entrance.

"Hi, Wolf. And you must be Nessa. Wolf told me he might bring you by after the tree contest." The older woman stepped back and waved them inside. "Come on in out of the cold, you two. And let me get those coats."

They entered Eva's home, peeling off their outerwear and handing them to her. Once the coats were in her closet, they followed her to a cozy living room with a huge bank of windows that encompassed nearly one wall, a cavernous fireplace with dancing flames, an overstuffed couch and love seat, a coffee table and inviting armchairs that appeared large enough to comfortably fit his frame. If he remembered correctly, Eva's husband had been a big guy, too. Though he'd passed more than ten years ago, she'd obviously kept the furniture that must remind her of him.

"Have a seat. Can I offer you some coffee or tea?" she

offered. "I just arrived home not too long ago and put a pot of coffee on for myself."

"If you're having some, then I'll take a cup, too. I don't want to put you to any trouble." Wolf settled in one of the armchairs while Nessa sat at the end of the couch.

"None at all. Nessa?"

"Yes, ma'am, thank you. I'll have a cup." Nessa half rose from the couch again. "Do you need my help bringing everything in?"

"No, no. Sit. I have hands and a tray." Eva sniffed, pointing at Wolf. "'Ma'am.' She has manners. What's she doing hanging around you?" She softened the tart question with a wink and a teasing pat on his shoulder before disappearing down the hall.

"She still intimidates me," Nessa murmured as soon as Eva was out of earshot. "But I like her."

Wolf snorted. "You would." They both had that no-tolerance-for-bullshit thing going on. He leaned back in the armchair, stretching his legs out in front of him. "Ms. Eva has lived in Rose Bend all her life. She runs the local day care center and has served on the town council forever. She's an institution here. If anyone might know about the Summers family or a member named Paul, she would be the person."

Nessa nodded. "You told her about…"

Wolf didn't need for her to finish. "No, I haven't," he said softly. "It's your story, and your decision to tell however much of it you feel comfortable sharing."

She nodded again, and he gripped the arm of the chair. Otherwise, he might reach across and grab the slender fingers that nervously plucked at the denim of her jeans. He'd been pushing his luck with how much he'd been touching her today. Each time their fingertips brushed…each time he stroked her cheekbone…each time he pressed a hand to her back… He tested the limits of his self-control when it came to her.

He enjoyed sex. Loved everything about it from the scents and sounds to that exquisite moment when he first pushed inside a woman. And in sex, he could shove back the emptiness, the loneliness. He hadn't been a monk since Olivia had left; his heart might have atrophied but his dick hadn't. But he controlled his cock, not vice versa. He'd never been one of those men who'd needed to fuck at least once a week or die of some disease as a result of blue balls.

But with Nessa?

With Nessa, one glance at that thick fall of hair, and he couldn't help imagining wrapping the dark brown strands around his fist while skimming his lips over the shaved side of her head.

One glimpse at her gorgeous, thick body with its dangerous curves, tempting dips and beautiful brown skin, and his knees trembled with the urge to buckle, taking him to the floor so he could worship her with his hands and mouth.

One look into those lovely, troubled eyes and the man in him that dated back to living in caves and swinging clubs roared with the need to fuck those shadows away.

None of those other women over the last three years had created a sense of urgency in him, but this one? This one with the prickly-as-a-damn-porcupine attitude, goddess face and wounded warrior eyes? Every second it seemed as if he battled himself not to stroke, kiss, take…possess.

In the time she'd been in Rose Bend, Nessa Hunt had become his personal delight…and hell.

And come Christmas, she would be kicking the snow from her expensive boots as soon as the sun set and leaving town.

"Why're you looking at me like that?"

Wolf blinked, jerking out of his thoughts with the painful snap of a popped rubber band. "I'm sorry. Looking at you like what?"

She tilted her head, her fingers stilling on her thighs. "Like I'm a *Where's Waldo* book."

"I can't stand those books."

"Exactly."

His head jerked back, surprise clipping him in the chin. He stared at her for a long moment, then huffed out a dry laugh saturated with disbelief. "Baby, 'can't stand' doesn't come anywhere near to describing how I feel about you."

She stiffened, shock flaring in her eyes, but he didn't laugh or tack on anything teasing to play off his words. They stared at one another, tension rising between them, so dense, so alive, it breathed like another entity in the room. Her lush mouth parted, and he zeroed in on the telltale sign of her agitation. Whether it was nerves, irritation or arousal—*oh arousal*.

Lust pooled molten and thick in his cock.

One swift glance up into her dark, glazed eyes confirmed the answer.

"Here we go." Eva entered the living room, bearing a tray laden with coffee cups.

Her presence should've been like a dousing of frigid water on his balls, but as long as Nessa was in the room—hell, breathing—he doubted that was possible. Still, he shot to his feet, thankful for the length of his black sweater that hid most of his pounding erection. Liberating the tray from the older woman, he carried it to the table he'd made himself for her several years ago as an anniversary gift. Though her husband had been gone for six years by then, Wolf had still given it to her to honor him and their marriage.

"Thank you, Wolf." Eva settled on the same couch as Nessa, leaving a little space between them. After handing them their cups and letting them doctor their coffee with creamer and sugar, the older woman settled back against the cushion with her own drink and sipped. "So, Nessa, Wolf didn't tell me much about why he brought you here. Only that he thought I might be able to assist with a situation you have. I'll admit, I'm curious. And if there's anything I can do to help you, I'm more than willing."

"Thank you." Nessa glanced at Wolf, and he nodded his encouragement. Although she didn't need it. He sensed she might doubt it, but she was courage wrapped in beauty. "My mom died earlier this year—"

"Oh, honey, I'm sorry." Eva leaned forward and covered Nessa's hand.

"It's okay, thank you."

"No, it's really not okay. I lost my husband ten years ago and it's not. But it eventually does get easier to breathe and then live without expecting them to call or walk through the door, and then not break down when they don't." She patted Nessa's hand then reclined back against the couch again, taking another sip from her coffee. "I'm sorry. I didn't mean to interrupt. But you don't have to use platitudes with me. Death is shitty and there's no point in pretending otherwise."

And this was why Wolf adored Eva Wright.

A small smile played around the edges of Nessa's mouth, and he suspected she might be halfway there herself.

"Okay, yes, you're right." She chuckled. "Death is shitty, and it still hurts. But I'm getting through it." Nessa paused, staring down into her cup for a long moment, then began speaking, head bowed as if the script for her story lay in the coffee. "Before my mom died, she told me that the man I believed was my father all my life wasn't…"

She relayed the same story she'd told him several days ago behind the inn, adding on about the email she'd sent out today and the box of things she hoped would contain a clue about her biological father. When she finished, Eva leaned forward again and pinched Nessa's chin, lifting her head until she looked the older woman in the eye.

"There. That's better. Do me a favor and never again tell that story with your head down. Our history is a part of us, but it doesn't define us. You have nothing to be ashamed of. So stop acting like it." Eva delivered that admonishment with her telltale no-nonsense tone, then rose from the couch and set her cup on the table. "Be right back."

She left the room and Nessa looked at Wolf. He shrugged, struggling to hold back a smile.

"You should see her at town council meetings. I love Cole and would do anything for him—that half-done gazebo is proof of that—but I attend to see Eva in action." He smirked, propping his elbows on his thighs. "Jenna's father is on the council, too, and the man's an asshole. But one person he won't throw any shit to is her." He jerked his head in the direction Eva had disappeared. "She can throw a verbal smackdown that would leave a person crying and sucking his thumb. But if she respects and loves you? She'll protect you like the fiercest lion."

"I didn't realize I had my head down," she murmured.

"You did the same thing with me." When she frowned, he set his cup on the table and clasped his hands together between his thighs. "You wouldn't look at me when you told me the truth."

"But I'm not ashamed. I—" She pinched her forehead then rubbed it, quiet for several seconds. "I guess I'd rather not see other people's reactions when I tell it. Like I'm some Maury Povich guest or reality TV show plot. Or even the pity. That might be worse than the curiosity."

"Nessie?" He waited until he had her full attention, then continued, "Why do you give a fuck?"

She gaped at him, but before she could answer, Eva swept back into the room, a book in her arms. "Wolf Dennison, watch your mouth in my house," she scolded. Although the twinkle in her dark eyes belied her reprimand. "But he's right, Nessa," she said, sinking onto the couch once more, setting what was a photo album, not a book, on her lap. "It's all a case of mind over matter. You shouldn't mind because they don't matter."

The woman was just dropping all the wisdom tonight.

"Now, it just so happens I'm familiar with the Summers family," Eva announced, opening the album.

Satisfaction whipped through him at the surprise that flashed across Nessa's face. She touched fingertips to her throat as she stared at Eva's bent gray head. But it was the flicker of hope in her eyes that had Wolf inching forward in his chair. Had the breath stalling in his lungs.

"Y-you do?" Nessa whispered. Then, clearing her throat, repeated, "You do?"

Eva nodded, flipping the album's stiff pages. "I'm sure of it."

Nessa glanced at him, and he smiled at her. Jesus, this had been a long shot, but he couldn't believe it had panned out. It took everything in him to remain in his seat instead of striding over to Nessa, scooping her off that couch and hugging her. And not just because he was delighted for her. Delighted because he could have a hand in giving this to her.

Yeah, it was thoughts like that he had no business thinking.

A friend. He was helping a friend.

A friend whose moan of pleasure he wanted to swallow whole.

Shit.

He raked a hand down his face and beard. *Focus, dammit.*

"Here." Eva stopped flipping and pointed at a picture.

Curious, Wolf rose and circled the back of the couch. He stared down at a color picture that, judging from the people's feathered bangs and big shoulder pads, had to have been taken sometime in the eighties. The setting—a huge fireplace set into a stone wall with floor-to-ceiling windows on either side of it—seemed familiar, but he couldn't immediately place it.

He did recognize a younger Eva and her husband, Joe, among the small group of people who smiled into the camera with their arms circled around each other's waists.

"That's Martha Summers and her husband, Roy." Eva tapped the image of the statuesque, beautiful Black woman with long hair and the tall man next to her who could've been a double for the actor Telly Savalas. "They used to own what's now Little Bird Ski Lodge."

"That's why it looks familiar," Wolf said.

Eva nodded. "Yes. The ski lodge used to be their chalet and vacation home here before Garrett Adams bought it. Anyway, Joe and I were friends of friends of the Summerses." She smiled wryly. "I ran a day care for almost thirty-five years and Joe, when he retired, was the principal of the local high school. We didn't run in the same circles as the Summerses. Roy was a Wall Street wizard from New York and Martha a socialite. Still, they were nice, down-to-earth people. Well, as down-to-earth as millionaires can be." She chuckled. "Anyway, they vacationed in Rose

Bend for the week of and after Christmas and for a couple of months in the summer."

"So you knew them well?" Nessa pressed, her gaze glued to the picture of the people who could potentially be her relatives.

Eva shrugged a shoulder. "Pretty well. I mean, we were cordial when they were in town. But definitely close enough that I can tell you they didn't have a son. Two daughters, yes, but not a son."

Disappointment speared him, and a glance at Nessa revealed the same distress. Her eyes closed, and the spasm that flickered across her face relayed just how much hope she'd held that they'd obtain information about her biological father.

"But like I said," Eva continued, "we were friendly when they were in town on vacation. I didn't know all the details of their life, including extended family. Maybe they had a nephew named Paul that visited with them, and he met your mother here. It's possible."

Wolf slid a hand over Nessa's shoulder and cupped the nape of her neck, rubbing his thumb back and forth. A surge of protectiveness swelled within him when she leaned back into his hold. That show of trust shouldn't send satisfaction and lust bolting through him.

Shouldn't.

But fuck if it didn't.

"Are you still in contact with them, Ms. Eva?" he asked. "Is there any way to get in touch with them and find out for sure?"

The older woman tapped her bottom lip. "Actually, they did return here for Joe's funeral and sent a card. I saved everything. I could definitely try." She closed the photo album and patted Nessa's knee. "I have you, Nessa."

"Thank you, Ms. Eva. I appreciate any help you can give me."

"Of course. I'm glad to help." Eva smiled, her eyes soft. "And call me old-fashioned or a silly old woman, but I believe Christmas is a time for miracles. And who knows, Nessa Hunt? Maybe there's one for you. Or..." She picked up the photo album and set it on the coffee table with a smirk. "I'm just nosy as hell and can't resist a mystery. Either way, we're going to try and find you answers."

Nessa laughed. "You know what? I'm a little bit closer to believing it."

Minutes later, Wolf kissed Eva on the cheek and Nessa waved goodbye to her as they stepped out onto the porch. She didn't speak as they climbed into his truck and he started the engine. He didn't immediately shift the gear into Drive, but instead gripped the steering wheel with both hands and stared out his windshield.

"Did I make a mistake bringing you here?" he murmured.

He felt her gaze on him. And normally, he wouldn't have a problem meeting those espresso eyes, but not at this moment. Not while he feared he'd caused more harm with this visit than good.

"Why would you say that?"

"Hope can be a dangerous thing, can't it? Sweet and beautiful one moment, cruel and ugly the next." He should know. He'd been on the receiving end of both. And the thought of taking her to that high and low tonight had nerves and regret curdling in his stomach. "I saw the disappointment on your face. And I'm sorry if this brought you pain instead of hope, Nessa."

He'd almost spoken with Eva on his own, to prevent this very thing from happening. But as he'd told Nessa earlier, it hadn't been his right to share her story. But this need to protect her—her and Ivy—to make things *okay* for her...

He'd failed with Raylon. He'd failed with Olivia.

Though Nessa would only be in Rose Bend for a few more weeks, he didn't want to fail her.

And tonight, he couldn't escape the feeling that he had.

"Wolf." A hand settled on his thigh, and warmth flared beneath the small weight. Before he could control his reaction, the muscle beneath her palm locked tight, and a sweet flare flamed, brief and bright. "I didn't get a chance to say it yet, but thank you. I appreciate what you did here tonight. I'm not used to asking for help—to accepting help. But not being alone in this...journey, I guess I can call it...is a relief. It's not as overwhelming, and I have you to thank. So...thank you."

The knots inside him slowly unraveled, and he exhaled. His grip on the steering wheel loosened.

"You're welcome."

He shifted his gaze from the windshield, finally looking at her. Looking into those beautiful eyes that he knew would follow him into his sleep tonight. The heat from her palm damn near seared a hole through his jeans and branded his skin. That, too, he wouldn't be able to escape.

Exhaling a deliberate low breath, he shifted the truck into gear and pulled away from the curb. Silence thickened between them, humming with a tension that had him aware of every breath that escaped her. Every shift of her body in the seat. Every drum of her fingers on her leg.

How it soothed and had him so on edge any sudden movement might crack him right down the middle, he couldn't explain. Just...no sudden movements.

"I'd forgotten this," Nessa said.

He glanced at her, but she stared out the window, offering him a view of the dark waves that tumbled over her shoulder.

"Forgotten what?"

"This."

She waved a hand toward the window and the scenery beyond just as he slowed to a halt at a stop sign. He took in the scenery outside the glass. At the array of houses lit up with lights and decorations.

"Like at the Christmas tree decorating contest. Memories I haven't allowed myself to think of are returning," Nessa continued in a soft voice as if she were lost in one of those memories at the moment. "Like, how at Christmas, my mom and Isaac would bundle me up in the car and we'd go riding through neighborhoods just looking at all the lights on houses. To me, it was like a winter fairyland. And even after Isaac left, she still did it until…" She trailed off. When she spoke again, her voice had lowered even further. "Until I told her I didn't want to anymore, that I was too old for it. The truth was, it reminded me too much of Isaac. Of what I'd lost when he left. I think that's when Christmas became something to tolerate or avoid instead of a holiday to celebrate for me. But this—" she dipped her head "—this reminds me of how it used to be. Of how…magical it could be."

This woman.

Wolf swallowed hard, and unable not to touch her, he slid a hand underneath her hair and cupped the nape of her neck. He eased off the brake and drove forward, his thumb lightly stroking the tender skin beneath her hairline.

"What? No words of wisdom, O wise one?" she asked a couple of minutes later.

"'Never scald your lips with another man's porridge.'"

Her head whipped around, nearly dislodging his hold on her.

"What the hell does that mean?"

He shrugged, a smile tugging at his lips. "No clue. On the rare occasions my father gets in his cups, he becomes an Irish Tyrion Lannister. He drinks and knows stuff, but he doesn't tell me what it means. I could Google it, but where would be the fun in that?"

She snorted. "You say Tyrion Lannister like it's supposed to mean something to me."

"What?" He gasped, abruptly releasing her to slap a hand over his heart. *"Game of Thrones?"* He shook his head and whispered mournfully, "Oh you sweet summer child."

"Okay, that's it. Let me out at the next corner," she muttered.

Wolf laughed, and quickly taking his eyes off the road, he caught the hint of a smile on her mouth before she turned back to the window.

"At the risk of you telling me to mind my own business, can I ask you a question?"

Unease spiraled through him, but after a beat of hesitation, he squelched his immediate deflection. If he looked up *Nessa* in any thesaurus, one of the synonyms would be *locked box*. And for her to grant him access into her thoughts, into her world... No, only an asshole would deny her the same. And he might be guarded and gun-shy, but Moe hadn't raised assholes.

"If you don't—"

"No," he interrupted, his fingers tightening around the steering wheel as if it could anchor him. "Ask me."

He heard rather than saw her shift in her seat. Felt the weight of her gaze on him. "Are you still in love with Olivia?"

His whole body jerked, his foot reflexively slamming on the brake.

"Fuck," he growled, shooting a look into his rearview mirror.

Relief coursed through him. No cars behind him, thank God. Easing his foot off the pedal, he pressed the accelerator, his clutch on the steering wheel becoming a stranglehold. Jesus Christ, he didn't want to talk about Olivia. Not with anyone. But especially not with Nessa.

"Nessa," he said.

"Because she's in love with you."

He ground his teeth together, trapping his derisive snort. Love? Olivia's "love" had almost destroyed him. Damn if he'd allow her—or anyone—to have that kind of power again.

"What we had is in the past." Three years ago this Christmas to be exact. She'd ended them two days after.

"That doesn't answer my question," Nessa pressed.

He didn't answer. Not immediately. He couldn't as he turned onto the road that led to Kinsale Inn. No way in hell he could have this conversation and drive. But Nessa took his silence as refusal, and as soon as he parked alongside the building in one of the spaces designated for family, she unbuckled her seat belt and reached for the door handle.

"Forget it," she said, voice tight. With anger. With hurt. "I shouldn't have asked."

"Nessa." His hand shot out, wrapping around her wrist. Light from the inn's side windows reached into the truck's interior, providing enough illumination for him to glimpse the taut line of her jaw. "Wait. I—" He slid his hold down until his palm pressed to hers. Until his fingers entwined with hers. "Give me a minute, okay?"

Her hand fell away from the handle, and she shifted, settling back into the passenger seat. She didn't look at him, though, her gaze fixed on their interlocked fingers. As if she couldn't believe he held on to her so tightly.

As if she couldn't believe she held on to him, too.

He should've extricated himself; he could relay this sad story without clutching her like she was his life raft in the raging waters of his past.

But he didn't.

Because, fuck it, he needed this. Needed *her*. He could admit that, even if only to himself. Even if only for tonight.

"To answer your question, no. I'm not in love with Olivia." He studied her fingertips with their short nails and black polish. Slowly, he lifted his head, met her steady, unflinching gaze. "But I used to be. Ever been in love, Nessa?"

She hesitated but nodded. "Yes," she whispered.

The hot flare of jealousy caught him by surprise, but in the next instant, he extinguished it. He had no business, no right, feeling that. A woman as beautiful, as sexy, as successful as Nessa? Of course she would've had relationships. And that Wolf battled the urge to seek out this nameless and faceless man who'd owned her heart and slap him around was his issue not hers.

"Well, then you know what it is to give your heart to someone, to plan a future with them, and then to lose it all." *Because you're deemed not good enough. Or not enough.* "That's what happened between me and Olivia."

Nessa shook her head. "There's more," she insisted.

"What was his name?" he shot back.

The echo of their breaths filled the dense silence. He'd demanded she look at him several times since she'd arrived in Rose Bend. But now, with that incisive stare slicing into him, trying to dive into his memories, into the pain, into the man he longed to keep hidden, he wanted to beg her to glance away.

"Jeremy." She leaned forward until only inches and a bucket seat separated them. "And you're deflecting. Tell me," she whispered.

"She broke me."

The admission tore from him without his permission, and as he stared at her, he prayed the horror that yawned wide inside of him didn't reflect in his expression. He didn't so much lean back from her as fall against his seat.

Allowing someone to peer at the jagged pieces of his past—left him both hollow and filled with too many emotions to dissect.

She'd asked him if he still loved Olivia. The simple answer was no. But there was nothing simple about why. Nothing straightforward about how he could never open himself to another person as he'd done with her. Never risk that kind of pain again. Never risk witnessing that kind of disappointment in another person's eyes when he let them down.

He'd seen it in Carol Brandt's eyes when he returned home from Iraq without her son.

He'd seen it in Raylon's eyes for months, years, in his dreams.

He'd seen it in Olivia's eyes when he told her he couldn't leave Rose Bend, his family and be that nine-to-five, suit-and-tie man she needed.

His heart, his soul, couldn't take seeing it again in another person's eyes.

An espresso gaze with long lashes in a warrior queen's face flickered in his mind. All he had to do was glance to his right and take in that face.

A surge of panic flared bright and hot in his chest, and he tugged at their still-clasped hands, but she tightened her grip, refusing to let go.

"Jeremy was the first person I let in," Nessa said, almost conversationally. But that tense hold on his hand, that taut set of her shoulders, the hurt swirling in her dark eyes... No, this cost her. And she was willing to pay the price. For him. "He wasn't my first relationship, but he was the first man who I believed wouldn't let me down. Jeremy made me hope that maybe, just maybe, I could have that happily-ever-after we all hear and dream about. Made me believe I might not be so damn easy to walk away from."

Wolf couldn't speak, spikes of anger piercing him with every inhale. Nessa didn't say his name, but she didn't have to—Isaac. Isaac had been the first man to walk away from her, and this Jeremy had given her hope that her father, the man who was supposed to love her unconditionally, had been at fault. Not her.

If Wolf had either man, or both, in front of him right now, he'd inflict damage for causing this beautiful, strong woman a second of insecurity and doubt.

"He left me," Nessa continued. "He claimed for a job on the other side of the country, but he didn't go without telling me it was my fault we didn't work out. Because he didn't want to spend his life trying to reach someone who would always keep him at an emotional distance. And he was right. Yes, I let him in more than any other man. But not all the way. Because Isaac crushed me. But Jeremy? He shattered what was left. So, Wolf, I understand about being broken."

"I lost myself when I fell in love with her," he rasped, the confession propelled from him by the stark honesty of hers. "I'd just...come out of a dark space." No, he couldn't talk about Raylon yet. About losing him in that desert and returning home to face his mother's devastation on top of his debilitating guilt. "Olivia had been three years behind me in school, so we hadn't really been friendly. But falling in love with her was like finding myself again. Carpentry returned part of that to me, and she was the other half. Everything made sense, and I…"

Was good enough.

Saw a chance for redemption.

Saw a chance to prove he wasn't a failure.

He clenched his jaw, not allowing those words to slip free. Only when he was certain they would remain locked down deep did he continue. He rubbed his free hand down his beard, narrowing his gaze on his windshield and the shadow of his workshop in the distance.

"I gave her my everything, but in the end, it couldn't keep her here. I didn't know she'd been discontent with her life in Rose Bend. It'd become too small for her, too stifling. She'd applied for jobs in Boston, and when she received an offer, she accepted without telling me."

Over time, the sting of that betrayal had lessened, but as he spoke of it, the echo of his helplessness scraped over him.

"Yes, she invited me to come with her, but not as a carpenter. Olivia didn't want that for me, for herself. Her vision of the future included a life in a bigger city, with access to more opportunities and entertainment than Rose Bend could offer. A husband who wore a suit and tie to the office and could provide a showpiece of a house or a high-rise condominium with a view of the city skyline. In other words, everything I couldn't give her and everything I wasn't. She chose the new job and life over me, and there was nothing I could do to keep her here."

"Did you beg her to stay?" Nessa whispered.

Wolf jerked his head back to her, shame burning behind his rib cage. "Yes," he rasped. "Did you beg Jeremy?"

"No," she said. "But sometimes I wish I had."

The quiet in the truck trembled with all they'd said and left unsaid.

"Do you still love him?" The air shouldn't snag in his lungs while he waited for her answer. His gut shouldn't tighten as he watched her lips part, desperate to see which word they would shape.

"No, I don't—"

His mouth was on hers before she could finish the sentence. He didn't need to hear the rest. He tasted it on his tongue. Feasted on it.

Later he would try and convince himself he'd been gentle with her. But he cupped her head between his palms, holding her steady for what could only be labeled a taking, a claiming. He was greedy, wild, desperate. Anything but gentle.

But thank God she didn't seem to mind. Hell no, Nessa fisted his hair, tugged him closer even as she strained toward him. Her groan emptied into his mouth as she angled her head, opened wider for him.

Maybe the emotional rawness of their conversation fueled the flames of this voracious need, stoking them higher, hotter. Maybe he just used it as an excuse to finally get his mouth on her, to justify tossing aside the many reasons why he shouldn't be indulging in this.

Maybe…

Maybe…

Right now, with his tongue thrusting hard between her lips, tangling and twisting in a dirty dance that had his cock pounding against his zipper in envy, he didn't give a fuck about maybes.

Over and over he returned to that beautiful, sinful mouth. Even when he pulled away to scatter hard kisses over her elegant cheekbones, the slope of her nose, the stubborn but delicate jaw, he came back to that lush mouth. One hit, just one taste of it, and already he was an addict.

A whisper of self-preservation urged him to slow down, to pull back. But then she sucked on his bottom lip, grazed it with her teeth. He groaned, feeling the phantom rake of that caress over his dick. Wishful thinking but wanting it with the passion of a thousand suns.

"Fuck." He tore himself away from her only to bury his face in the hollow between her neck and throat. Her scent, that sultry combination of jasmine, cedar and *her*, filled his nose, his lungs. "Baby, I'm sorry."

She stiffened against him, her hands dropping from his hair.

Shit.

Sorry he'd been so rough. Sorry he hadn't asked permission to kiss her. Sorry he'd lost control with her.

But to her, it must've sounded as if he regretted touching her. Regretted *her*.

Sometimes the old saying about men's brains being in their dicks was true.

"Nessa, I did—"

"I should go in."

She pushed away from him, and though everything in him roared not to let her out without clearing up this misunderstanding, he couldn't detain her. Even though she had moaned into his mouth and clenched his hair so hard his scalp still tingled, he hadn't asked. He wouldn't usurp that choice again. As someone intimately familiar with having no voice, no choice in someone else's decisions, he hated inflicting that on another person.

"Nessa," he said again. "You misunderstood. Just give me a couple of minutes—"

"I understand that this shouldn't have happened." She

gripped the door handle and pushed it down. "For either one of us. And no worries, it won't again." Her voice, as cold as the air rushing into the truck from the open door, cooled the lust simmering in his veins.

She slipped out of the vehicle and only then turned to look at him. And he almost broke his promise of not going after her, of not keeping her there and making her listen. Anything to wipe that inscrutable, aloof mask from her face.

"Thank you for tonight." She shut the door, the quiet click louder than if she'd slammed it. More final.

His hands flew to his seat belt, but just as he pressed the button to unbuckle it, he hesitated. He could follow her and say what? That she was wrong? That it should've happened? No, he didn't regret finding out how she tasted, but that didn't make her wrong.

The first day she'd arrived at the inn, he'd known she would be a complication. And sex would only muddy an already murky situation. That kiss hadn't changed anything. She was still leaving. She was still big-city and made no bones about it. And tonight had revealed another reason why becoming involved would be foolish as hell. She'd been leveled by a relationship just as he had and left in pieces.

What was the adage?

"Hurt people hurt people."

That's what they would do to each other. Was there really any other outcome?

No, she'd done the smart thing by retreating. And he'd follow her lead.

Shifting the car into Reverse, he backed out of the driveway, watching Nessa climb the stairs. She didn't look back as she crossed the porch and let herself into the inn. And he didn't pull off until he made sure she was safe inside.

Once he was at the cabin he called home, he would grab a beer, watch some TV. Put off going to bed. Because when his eyes were closed and his body was relaxed, convincing himself that he could stay away from Nessa now that he'd tangled with her would be a hell of a lot harder.

CHAPTER THIRTEEN

"I'M POSITIVE THERE are coffee shops and cafés in Boston that are just as good as this one, but under threat of eternal caffeine deprivation, I can't recall any." Nessa studied the chalkboard menu with the day's specials along with the permanent board beside it with the everyday offerings. "Why do I sound like a crackhead right now?"

Ivy snorted. "Well, *I* didn't want to say it."

Nessa arched an eyebrow. "Is this where I pretend I don't know you had Flo stop by here and bring you home a doughnut and hot chocolate yesterday after her shift at the ice cream shop?"

"Is this where I pretend I didn't notice you sitting in the car with Wolf last night?" Ivy shot back, raising her own eyebrow.

Well, shit. "Yeah, it is."

The preteen smirked. "Thought so."

"You know for a tiny person you are extraordinarily annoying."

Ivy's smirk grew into a full-fledged grin, surprise and pleasure flashing in her eyes. "It's a gift."

Shaking her head, Nessa returned to scanning the menu even though she'd already decided on her order. Less chance of embarrassing herself and Ivy if she pretended to peruse the coffee offerings rather than stare at the younger girl in confusion and hope.

Ivy had shocked Nessa into near speechlessness when she'd asked to tag along on Nessa's daily trip to Mimi's Café. Other than that small show of concern yesterday evening at the Christmas tree decorating contest, they'd been engaged in their own version of a cold war. But Nessa had quickly shoved past her surprise and agreed. Though she'd been trying in vain to forget that mind-fuck of a kiss with Wolf last night, she couldn't evict his question about her motivation behind not telling Ivy the truth about Isaac.

Was she afraid of losing the girl who she'd considered her sister for twelve years? Scared Ivy would reject her?

Yes. Yes, she was. Because, though genetics didn't connect them, Ivy was the only family Nessa had left. And she didn't want to lose her.

Did that mean she'd decided to reveal everything?

God, she didn't know.

She had the feeling that no matter what she did, whatever decision she made, they would both be hurt and irrevocably changed.

And sue her for wanting to avoid that for as long as possible.

"You have plans for today?" Nessa shifted forward, daring to nudge Ivy's shoulder.

"Not until later. The twins were telling me about movie night at the theater this evening, and I'd like to go. But first, I wanted to ask you if I could go with Cher to the pageant auditions. She's trying out for it and would like me to come with her for moral support. You'd never guess it, but she's shy about singing in front of people."

"You're right. I'd never have guessed it." Nessa chuckled, shaking her head. "Sure. What time?"

"After school lets out for them. Three thirty at the high school auditorium. Would you mind dropping me off?"

"Not at all." Not wanting this nice truce to end, Nessa said, "You seem to really like the twins."

Weak but, shoot, she didn't have much practice at this calm, peaceful conversation thing with Ivy that didn't contain any shut-up-talking-to-me vibes.

Ivy nodded. "They're so cool. And nice. They don't treat me—"

Nessa stiffened, staring down at Ivy, unease creeping through her. An unease that bordered on *Whose ass do I need to kick?* "They don't treat you like what, Ivy?"

She shrugged, staring down at the toes of the sneakers where she'd drawn stars and small cartoon figures. But after a moment, she said, "The kids at school…after Dad died, they acted weird toward me. They were either supernice that it was so fake. Or they acted like him dying was contagious and ignored me and stayed away from me. It sucked. I hated it."

Ivy whispered the last three words, and Nessa damn near vibrated with the effort it cost her not to wrap an arm around Ivy. Why could she offer comfort to her patients but not to this hurting little girl?

Because those people depended on her, looked to her for assurance, for answers. The chances of being rebuffed by them were slim. And if they did, Nessa never took it personally. That wasn't the case with Ivy. Her rejection would be a blow right to her heart. And after all she'd taken in the last few months, she didn't know if she could survive one more.

"But the twins aren't like that?" she asked instead, even though her palms tingled with the need to at least stroke a hand over Ivy's thick curls.

"No." Ivy gave an emphatic shake of her head, lifting her gaze back to Nessa's. "Did you know their bio parents are dead, too? That's how they came to be with Moe and Mr.

Dennison. It was a long time ago, but they still get it, and they've never treated me any differently." She scrunched up her nose. "It's like that in Rose Bend. Do you think that's another reason Dad sent us here?"

Nessa's heart stuttered, stopped. Then started again with a clang against her rib cage. For the first time since their blowup, Ivy had mentioned Isaac and her voice hadn't held any pain or resentment. Just curiosity.

Still, Nessa hesitated. Answered the question as if tiptoeing around a land mine. "I don't know what you mean."

"When Dad and Mom visited here with me, he must've found something special about it, right? Otherwise, why would he have sent us here out of all the places in the country, in the world? It's a pretty town, but there are a bunch of pretty places." She drew in a breath. "I think it's the people. Everyone's so nice. I'm not stupid. I'm sure there are mean people just like there are everywhere, but for the most part, the people I've met—strangers—are so kind. Dad must've found that, too. And he wanted that for me. To maybe connect with him through this town, through the people even though he—he's…gone." She crossed her arms over her chest and huffed out a rough laugh rimmed in embarrassment. "Anyway. I know it sounds stupid."

"No, it doesn't sound stupid. I think…" *You're so damn smart. Your father sent us both here to find connections to our fathers.* "I think that makes perfect sense, and you knew your father very well."

Ivy stared at Nessa, blinked, then glanced away. Silence fell between them as they shifted forward in line, both of them returning their attention to the menu. But then Ivy whispered, "Thank you."

"You're welcome," Nessa said just as softly. After a couple of seconds, she hesitated, nerves attacking her stomach. *Screw it.* "I know you have plans with Cher later, but until then, do you want to do a little shopping? I thought we could pick up some gifts for the Dennisons since we're spending Christmas here with them..."

Jesus, a twelve-year-old had her anxiety level about to go through the roof.

Ivy shrugged a shoulder, still giving the menu the same hard stare. "Sure. Sounds good."

"Good."

Awkward but... A smile tugged at the corner of Nessa's mouth as relief coursed through her. Awkward but good.

The customer in front of them finished up and stepped away and they moved forward. Nessa placed her order for a caramel macchiato and Ivy's peppermint mocha with two glazed doughnuts for both of them.

"Hi, Nessa." The familiar voice greeted her, and Nessa stiffened.

Slowly, she turned, facing Olivia.

She broke me.

Wolf's pained admission echoed in her head, haunting her now as it'd done all last night. This woman had been the source of that pain. She'd once owned his heart. And she'd shattered it. Rationally, Nessa grasped that Olivia had every right to decide her own future.

But the part of her that listened to Wolf talk about finding himself after being lost... The part that heard the shame in his voice as he admitted to begging Olivia to stay... The part that could still feel the brand of his lips, his tongue as he *mated* with her mouth...

That part blamed Olivia.

But that had everything to do with Nessa and her wayward and wholly unwise feelings toward Wolf, and nothing to do with Olivia, who had been only kind to Nessa. So she would return that kindness. Even if thoughts of Wolf touching Olivia as he'd done to Nessa last night in his truck had her itching to bleach her brain.

"Hey, Olivia." She smiled, then reached into her purse and removed her wallet and several bills. "I don't think you've met my sister, Ivy." Nessa cupped Ivy's shoulder. "Hey, Ivy. I'd like you to meet Olivia Allen, a friend of Wolf's and Leo's. Olivia, this is my sister, Ivy."

Ivy waved at her. "Hi, Ms. Allen. Nice to meet you."

"You, too, Ivy."

"Here you go, Ivy." Nessa handed the preteen the dollar bills. "Could you pay for our order?"

"Got it."

"She's beautiful," Olivia said, smiling. "How're you doing, Nessa? We didn't really get a chance to talk yesterday at the contest. I tried to find you afterward."

The "but you left with Wolf" went unsaid. It screamed between them, nonetheless. Leaving Nessa battling the inane urge to explain—or worse—apologize. For what? Olivia and Wolf were no longer together. Yet, Nessa hadn't missed the flash of hurt in Olivia's eyes last night. Just as she hadn't failed to notice the longing. In spite of being cast as pseudorivals, they shared a solidarity in need for the same man.

"I'm sorry," Nessa evaded. "Did you want something?"

"Yes, I—" Olivia hiked her chin toward the display window of the café. "Do you mind if we grab a table while we wait for your sister?"

"Sure." Quickly scanning, she spotted one near the front door and led the way there. Once seated, she shifted so she could keep an eye on Ivy, who stood at the pick-up end of the counter. "What's up?"

"I wanted to apologize for Jenna's behavior yesterday. She…" Olivia tilted her head, a rueful twist curving her lips. "Her heart's in the right place, but she can come across…"

"Rude. Overbearing. A bully," Nessa supplied.

Huffing out a strained chuckle, Olivia nodded. "Yes. Those. And I'm sorry you were the target of it. Especially since it was on my behalf."

Nessa held up a hand, palm out. "You don't have to apologize. It's nice of you, but it's not your place. Although, I appreciate the thought." She paused. She really shouldn't go there. Should just leave it alone. But, with a mental shrug, she powered ahead. What the hell? Olivia had brought it up. "I'm just going to put this out there, and I don't mean to offend you. But your friend is a…" *bitch* "…piece of work. And let's face it. I'm not the only person she's directed that attitude at. Sydney, for example. I don't get it. You two are so different. Why do you put up with someone who is so nasty to other people?"

Olivia blinked, then a grin quirked the corner of her mouth. "Wow, you just put it out there."

"Believe me, I held back."

The other woman laughed, genuine humor lacing the sound and warming her eyes. God, why couldn't she be a bitch like her friend? She was gorgeous, sweet and the bully whisperer. Made it impossible to dislike Wolf's ex when knowing she'd seen him naked should be enough of a reason.

No, it shouldn't, she sharply reprimanded herself. Not my business. Not my man.

It didn't bode well for her that she had to keep reminding her subconscious of that fact.

"I understand if you don't know Jenna well, she can come across as off-putting. But that's just it—I'm one of

the few people who know her well. She has a softer side not
many people see. Well, let's be honest. She doesn't allow
many people to see, and she has her reasons that are her
own and not for me to share." Olivia's lashes lowered as
she wrapped both of her hands around her to-go coffee cup.
"And when I really need a friend, she's never let me down.
She's always been there for me. Even after I left town. And
believe me, leaving the only home you've known can be
extremely lonely. But she's stuck by me. I know she can
be abrasive and that outer shell can be pricklier than the
offspring of a porcupine and fire ant." Olivia grinned at
Nessa's snort. "But if you have her as a friend, you're the
hill she will die on."

No matter how hard she tried, Nessa couldn't match up
the picture Olivia painted with the woman who'd run the
gamut from dismissive to petty and rude. But Nessa wasn't
in a friendship with her.

"I'll take your word for it. Either way, she's lucky to
have you for a friend, too." Nessa glanced from Wolf's ex
toward Ivy. The barista handed the girl their drinks, and
she would be arriving at the table in the next few moments.
Switching her attention back to Olivia, Nessa met the other
woman's lilac gaze. "But you didn't want to just talk to me
about Jenna, did you?"

Surprise flickered in her eyes, then she let out a short
bark of laughter. Almost under her breath, she murmured,
"I didn't want to like you, Nessa, but I just can't help myself." She dipped her chin, as if silently making a decision.
"Okay. Are you and Wolf involved? Is there something between you?"

All right, so Olivia had definitely gone for it, too.

Even though Nessa had suspected this question lay behind Olivia's impromptu conversation, her eyebrows still

winged upward. But right on the heels of her astonishment nipped an irritation and need to…to…what? Protect what she and Wolf shared? Which totaled a few conversations, an offer of help in the search of her father and a kiss.

An ark-of-the-covenant, melt-your-face-off kiss, but still, just a kiss.

But she was discovering when it came to anything having to do with Wolf, rationale took an extended smoke break while waving a middle-finger salute. Emotion captained the helm, and right now the instructions were to give up nothing.

Sigh. Apparently, Rose Bend was turning her into a drama queen.

"We're friends," Nessa said.

Not a lie. Not the complete truth either. At least, not on her part. Because she'd never fogged up the windows of any of her *friends'* trucks with them before. But hadn't Wolf made it abundantly clear that he didn't desire a repeat? He'd apologized for kissing her like she was oxygen and he suffered from a collapsed lung. Apologized for holding her like she was the only thing anchoring him to that truck. Apologized for making her hot and wet and hungrier than she'd ever been for any man—even the one she'd loved.

Apologized.

God, that continued to sting.

So yes, friends it was.

She caught the relief that flashed in Olivia's eyes, and that twisted the knife deeper in her chest. And it didn't matter how many times or how often she reminded herself that Wolf wasn't hers and that he didn't want her—it still hurt.

"Truth?" Nessa asked.

Olivia nodded. "Yes."

"If I'd said yes, that we were involved, would it have made a difference to you?"

This time Olivia's smile carried a hint of sadness. "No."

"Why did you leave him?" Nessa asked quietly. "I get it's none of my business, and you don't have to answer, but you obviously still have feelings for him. If he's so important to you, why did you leave?"

Olivia sighed and shifted her gaze to the café's window. "I don't know all of what you've heard about my relationship with Wolf, but I loved him. God, so much. But his whole life was here—family, friends, career. Maybe if I had a family like the Dennisons, my view of Rose Bend would've been different, but I didn't. My home life growing up was vastly…different. And as a result, this town…" She dropped her head, studying her fingers on the tabletop. "It was suffocating. I stayed as long as I did because of Wolf. I hoped, prayed, he could change things for me, make me see it the way he did. Love it the way he did. But every day, every year that passed, I felt like I was strangling. That if I didn't leave, I would die. No, not physically. But my soul, my spirit. And one day, the man I loved with all my heart would be the man I resented with all of it."

Whoa. She hadn't expected *that*. An impossible decision—decide between the man you loved and yourself. Live for him or for you. How devastating that choice must've been for her.

"I begged Wolf to come with me, even knowing he wouldn't. No, he couldn't. He would've never been happy in a city like Boston. Away from family. Still, part of me hoped he would choose me. That I would be enough for him. But…" Olivia drew her arms, tucking her hands under the table, her lips turned up into another sad smile. "Here we are. Both of us living with our decisions and regrets."

Before Nessa could reply—if she could say anything—Ivy appeared at their table, setting their drinks on the table. "Here you go, Nessa. Do you want your change?"

Nessa tore her gaze from Olivia, deliberately shoving down the surge of sympathy for the other woman into the hollow pit her stomach had become. Sympathy for a woman who'd admitted she wouldn't let a hypothetical budding relationship prevent her from pursuing Wolf? Nessa should be hypothetically putting hands on her and instead she possessed the insane urge to…hug her.

She was losing her damn mind.

"Keep the change," Nessa said to Ivy, forcing a dry humor into her voice that must be one of those Christmas miracles everyone in this town went on and on about. "Although, I already see a dollar bill sticking out of your pocket."

Ivy shrugged, sipping her drink. "I'm an incurable optimist."

Nessa snickered, then shifted her attention back to Olivia as she slid from her chair. "Olivia, it was nice seeing you again. We're about to head out and get some Christmas shopping done." Relief cascaded through her, and she eyed the front door of the café like a prisoner about to be released after a five-year stint. "See you later."

"Have a great day shopping. It was nice to meet you, Ivy."

"You, too." Ivy waved the hand not wrapped around her peppermint mocha, and they made their way to the exit. "She was nice."

"Yeah, she is," Nessa muttered.

Ivy eyed her. "You don't sound happy about it."

Lord, the girl was too smart—and observant—for her own good. Just like Wolf had warned her. Damn, she had to stop. Thinking. About. Him.

Grinding her teeth, she reached for the entrance handle, but the door flew open before she could touch it. Both Nessa and Ivy drew up short, and she swallowed an undignified squeak.

Sydney appeared in the doorway, her gaze locking on Nessa. The other woman pressed a hand to her chest, and her lips moved in what might've been a silent prayer.

"Oh thank God," Sydney mumbled, moving forward and shifting Nessa and Ivy back into the café. "I've found you. Moe told me you come here for coffee every morning, but I was afraid I'd miss you."

"Why didn't you just call?" Nessa patted her coat pocket. Found it empty. "Oops. I must've left it in the car. My bad." She sipped her caramel macchiato. "What's going on? You look…frazzled."

"That's one word for it," Sydney muttered, running a hand over her curls. "I'm sorry, this is not your emergency, but I have a huge favor to ask you. My father owns the clinic here in town and one of his nurses called in today. Her mother-in-law had a stroke and they had to rush her to the hospital in the next town over. This wouldn't be a hardship for the clinic if another of the nurses wasn't already out on maternity leave." She heaved a sigh. "Again, I know this is a big ask. But Leo mentioned right after we met that you are an ER nurse back in Boston. Would you be willing to help my dad and his partner out for today while they're shorthanded? They have a packed schedule and that doesn't even account for the walk-ins they're bound to receive."

Razor-edged panic flared in Nessa's chest. The last time she'd been in the ER, she'd had a full-blown panic attack. It was the main reason her charge nurse had "encouraged" Nessa to take time off. It was one of the justifications she'd given herself for spending a month in a small town she'd never heard of.

But she hadn't told anyone about the panic attack or being forced to take vacation from the hospital.

Nessa glanced down at Ivy, already shaking her head. "Listen, Sydney, I'd love to help, but—"

"I get it. You're on vacation, and I feel like a complete jerk even coming to you. And I wouldn't if my dad hadn't specifically sent me to see if you would help him out today. That's how I knew they were in trouble. Because him asking for help is right up there with Jesus turning water into wine. A miracle."

"I really wish I could, but Ivy and I were just about to—"

"It's okay, Nessa," Ivy interrupted. "You can go help out Sydney's dad."

Nerves jangled in her stomach, twisting and clenching so hard she set her palm over her belly. "No, we had plans. I'm not going to flake on you."

Yes, anxiety filled her at the thought of attempting to try anything work related. What if she froze again? What if... what if her issue had been less about her unresolved grief and more about her job? Here in Rose Bend, she'd been able to avoid analyzing those questions, those what-ifs, but she wouldn't if she headed over to the clinic. So yeah, panic was twisting her into knots.

But also, she didn't want to abandon Ivy. Just when they'd formed a truce, she'd be leaving the girl again. Shopping would be the first time they were spending together, just the two of them, since they'd arrived in town. She didn't want to disappoint Ivy—or herself. Nessa couldn't believe it—and even a week ago, she wouldn't have—but she wanted to spend the day with her sister.

"Seriously, it's okay," Ivy insisted, tipping her head back

and meeting Nessa's gaze. "Sydney's dad sounds like he really needs you, and we can shop tomorrow. Honestly, Nessa, I'm fine."

Sincerity rang in the girl's voice, and it loosened at least one of the knots inside Nessa. Still...

"What about the pageant auditions? I thought you needed me to drop you off there?"

"I can take her," Sydney volunteered. "As a matter of fact, Ivy, if you want to hang with me until then, I'd love the company. Somehow, I let my husband convince me to help set up the theater for movie night. I'd love your help, and I'll even pay you so you'll have more money to shop with tomorrow."

Ivy grinned at the words "pay you." Barely managing not to roll her eyes, Nessa caved. It was either agree or explain why she couldn't. And though she liked Sydney and even considered her a new friend, she wasn't prepared to share about her meltdown in the ER.

"Okay, then. I'll head over to the clinic now. It's down the street, right? Next door to a dentist's office?" Nessa pulled her car keys from her pocket.

"Yes, that's it, and thank you." Sydney slung an arm around her shoulders and tugged Nessa into a half hug. "I owe you one."

"No problem." Oh but there might be one. Especially if her chest started to feel like it was collapsing, and she couldn't breathe. Foraging for a smile, she found one and pasted it on her face. "Ivy, I'll come over to the middle school after I leave the clinic this evening to pick you up. If you want, we can do dinner at Sunnyside Grille and then head over to the movie theater."

"Cool. If it's okay with Moe, can the twins come?"

"Sure." Nodding at Sydney, Nessa asked, "Since my

phone is in my car, can you call your dad and let him know I'm on my way?"

"Sure thing."

For a moment, Nessa hesitated, unsure whether or not to hug Ivy or squeeze her shoulder or wave. God, they all seemed incredibly awkward. Her arms—and heart—ached to be free to hug her without reservation as Leo and Flo did with Cher. But that wasn't who Nessa and Ivy were—who they might not ever be. Fear crept beneath the yearning. Fear of Ivy stiffening or, worse, pushing her away.

Nope. Nessa wasn't *that* brave. Not today when she already faced one potential hurdle in returning to work and possibly ending up a patient herself when the doctor had to treat her for a panic attack.

"All right. I'll see you in a little bit." Giving Ivy's shoulder a nudge, she exited the café and exhaled.

She'd dodged the should-I-show-affection? bullet but now she had another one she couldn't evade.

Part of her longed to drive back to the inn, run up that beautifully decorated porch and not stop until she burst through the door to her room and had the covers pulled over her head. She wanted to hide. But she couldn't.

That other half that even now yelled *I'm Evelyn Reed's daughter!* wouldn't allow her to curl up in a fetal position and pretend the world didn't exist. She *had* to know. And maybe starting at a slower pace at the clinic rather than at a much busier and hectic emergency room would be a way of dipping her toe back into work.

Her hand dropped to her coat pocket as if reaching for her absentee cell phone.

"Dammit," she muttered, palming her keys and glaring at her car.

She didn't bemoan her forgetfulness over the phone.

No, she bemoaned who she wanted to call. Wolf. To confide in him about her insecurities and worries. He would listen without judgment and offer unconditional support.

And it was why she couldn't call him.

She'd already allowed herself to lean on him too much, to become too close to him.

Time to start placing distance between them before it became too late.

Oh, that ship has not only sailed but is just a hazy shadow on the horizon.

Shaddup.

Yes. Yes, she was standing on a public sidewalk arguing with herself. This was what lust did to a person.

Mumbling under her breath, she opened her SUV and slipped inside. Moments later, she pulled out into morning traffic and headed toward the clinic.

She had this. She could do this.

Please, Lord, let her be able to do this.

SHE DID IT.

Relief and pride flooded Nessa as she changed out of her borrowed scrubs in the employees' bathroom. And underneath those two emotions? A quiet but powerful joy.

Relief because she hadn't crumbled. There'd been a frightening moment when she'd first arrived and another nurse named Jackie had handed her the scrubs. Nessa had frozen, her breath whistled in her head, edges of black and gold encroaching onto her peripheral vision. But after a few moments of dragging in deep, deliberate breaths, she'd beaten back the beginnings of anxiety and pushed through. And the rest of the day had been like slipping into familiar, comfortable pajamas. It'd been...fun.

Pride because she hadn't allowed fear to conquer her.

And joy because she hadn't lost her purpose. That had been another unspoken worry of hers. That maybe the reason for her panic attacks hadn't been grief but an ambivalence toward nursing. Because after Evelyn's death, she hadn't enjoyed going to work; she hadn't enjoyed anything. But no. Today showed her she hadn't lost that happiness in helping and serving other people, the satisfaction in determining a diagnosis and seeing another person on their way to being healthy again.

Today showed her *she* wasn't lost.

Unable to hold back her smile, she folded up her scrubs, slipped her purse strap over her shoulder and exited the bathroom.

"There you are, Nessa." Dr. Luke Collins stepped out of his office, his partner, Dr. Kelly Prioleau, right behind him. Nessa had worked with the distinguished older man today, but had crossed paths often with the other stylish doctor, who rocked beautiful twists and gorgeous leopard-print shoes. "We were hoping to catch you before you left. Thank you, again, for pitching in today. You were wonderful and a perfect fit."

"I heard so much about how kind and professional you were from patients," Dr. Prioleau added. "You were amazing today for stepping in, Nessa. We have a check waiting for you at the front desk with a bit of a Christmas bonus added in."

"Oh you didn't have to do that—"

"Yes, we did," Dr. Collins objected. "You rescued us today, and we appreciate you. Especially since it's your vacation." He offered his hand toward her. "Thank you."

"You're welcome. It was my pleasure. Really. I'm not saying I'm a workaholic, but I will say I missed this environment, being with patients, even charting." Nessa laughed. "I *never* thought I'd say that."

Dr. Prioleau chuckled. "Luke, if you ever hear me say that, call the cops. Someone has taken over my body, and I need to be saved."

When Dr. Collins smiled, Nessa clearly glimpsed where Sydney inherited her lovely smile.

"I need to head out and meet my sister at the middle school if you don't need me for anything else," Nessa said, holding up the scrubs. "I can drop these off in the hamper on my way out."

"Keep them." Dr. Collins waved. "Consider them another gift from us."

Nessa grinned. "I love gifts. Thank you both for a great day. This being Rose Bend, I'm guessing I'll see you around. Good night."

Waving goodbye, she collected her check for a day's work from the front desk and left the clinic. Glided was more like it. And any moment, she would stop smiling like a loon. It just felt so *good*.

After weeks—hell, *months*—of life being this cold, unfamiliar stranger, it was wonderful that it had finally decided to give her this gift. A small gift, but one that offered her hope that maybe things might start to look up for her.

Maybe Ivy would stop viewing her as the enemy.

Maybe she would discover the truth about her biological father.

Maybe when they returned to Boston, they would do so as a family.

Maybe she would now have a reason to stop working so much during Christmas.

Maybe.

Suddenly, that word didn't seem like a profane curse.

Ten minutes later, Nessa parked in the middle school parking lot. After asking directions from a couple of kids who loitered outside, she located the auditorium entrance and pulled open one of the double doors. Shadows clung to the back of the cavernous room, crowded with rows of red upholstered chairs. Slipping into one of the seats, she removed her hat and unwrapped her scarf, her gaze trained on the front of the auditorium where about twenty or thirty people gathered. Heavy ruby-red curtains framed either side of the stage, and a piano occupied one corner. And in front of the microphone stood Cher...and Ivy.

Nessa slowly straightened, leaning forward, shock an electrical current running through her. The two girls—one taller with butterscotch corkscrew curls and the other a little shorter with dark, looser curls—held hands, and instead of looking out into the audience and at the guy standing in front of the stage with the clipboard, they stared at each other.

"I didn't know Ivy was auditioning for the pageant."

She didn't have to turn around to identify the person behind her. Didn't need his fresh wintergreen scent to tease her nose or her memory of how it sharpened when thicker with desire. Didn't need to hear the low, dark rumble of his voice that seemed to delight in rolling around in that wide chest before taking its time in climbing up his throat and sliding off his tongue.

No, she didn't need any of those to recognize him. Not when every nerve in her body erupted like sparklers on July Fourth, sizzling through her, leaving her singed and... marked.

So...no. She didn't need to look behind her to identify Wolf.

"I didn't either," she murmured.

As they watched, Ivy leaned toward Cher and whispered to her, and the other girl nodded, her gaze not moving from Ivy.

"Maybe she isn't," Wolf said. "I think your sister is helping mine."

"Ready, Cher?" the man with the clipboard called out.

"She's ready," Ivy answered instead of Cher, confirming Wolf's hunch.

Nodding at the pianist, Ivy took Cher's other hand in hers, and as the first notes of a song echoed in the auditorium, the two girls didn't move. Didn't sing. The pianist trailed off, peeking over her shoulder. Even from the distance of the huge room, Cher's fear was clear in the stiff set of her shoulders and the unnatural stillness of her body.

"You got this, sweetheart." Wolf propped a forearm on the chair beside Nessa, his blunt fingertips grazing her shoulder. "You can do this."

Once more, Ivy whispered something to Cher, and the twin briefly closed her eyes, nodded. And Ivy glanced at the pianist, who turned around and played again.

This time, Ivy started singing. "O Holy Night." The purity of her voice. So mature. So clear. Almost painful in its beauty. It filled the auditorium and reached into Nessa's heart, gripping it, squeezing it.

"Jesus." Wolf shifted, dropping into the seat next to hers. "Mozart has one hell of a voice on her."

Yes, she did. And Nessa hadn't known. Her sister could sing like a freaking angel, and she'd had no idea.

At the second verse, Cher joined in, her perfect, sweet soprano harmonizing with Ivy's alto. Their rendition of the Christmas carol held her spellbound, the girls' voices joyous and celebratory and…honest. That honesty had Nessa blinking back the tears pricking her eyes.

The last note rang clear and high, and for an instant, an expectant and reverent hush rested on the auditorium, almost as if it'd transformed into a church. Then applause rang out, as thunderous as thirty people could manage. Nessa rose to her feet, Wolf beside her, and they clapped along with everyone else. Wolf popped two fingers in his mouth and whistled, yelling his sister's and Ivy's names.

Stunned, Nessa clasped her hands to her chest, staring as Ivy and Cher grinned at one another, then turned to their audience and sank into sassy curtsies. Wolf chuckled, and Nessa tried. The humor bubbled up inside her chest but all that left her was a tight wheeze.

"I didn't know," she rasped. "I didn't know she could sing. How did I not...?"

A huge hand slid across the back of her neck in a caress that, with a hard thump of her heart, she was coming to recognize as their thing.

They shouldn't—couldn't—have *a thing*.

"Nessie, let it go." He squeezed her neck, and she looked at him, caught up in the warmth of his beautiful emerald gaze. In the warmth that swept through her like a swollen stream after a violent rain. Yet the understanding there... That threatened to strengthen *and* undo her. "You can't change what was. But you do have now. And here, this moment and what you do with it is what matters."

"Nessa." Ivy skipped up the aisle to her and Wolf, Cher right next to her. "I didn't know you were here. Did you see us sing?"

Nessa cleared her throat. "I did. You two were great."

"Yeah." Wolf dragged Cher into a hug that swallowed the girl until only several of her curls sprung over his arms.

Envy crept into her heart as he smacked a loud kiss on the top of Cher's head. It must be nice to have that kind of easy affection with her. To know that it wouldn't be rebuffed, but would be returned. Be welcomed.

"I knew you could sing since I've been hearing you blow around the house forever, but wow, you were awesome. And you, Mozart—" he flashed a grin at Ivy "—you're a regular Celine Dion."

Ivy blinked at him.

He sighed, rolling his eyes. "Billie Eilish."

She smiled. "Thanks, Wolf."

"You were…" Nessa cleared her throat again. She shouldn't be this nervous. Waiting in the bay for an incoming ambulance from a three-car pileup didn't have her stomach twisting this hard. "You were…God, Ivy, amazing. Simply amazing."

The girl's face blanked, and she stared up at Nessa, her lips parted, dark eyes wide.

"Really?" Ivy whispered.

"Damn amazing," Nessa whispered back.

"Language."

They smiled at one another, and when Nessa reached for Ivy's hand, she met her halfway.

It wasn't a hug.

But it was a start.

CHAPTER FOURTEEN

"THE WOMAN THINKS of everything," Nessa muttered, shaking her head and staring down at the line of Christmas-themed mugs set out on the counter and the boxes of tea bags or K-Cups behind them.

And were those…?

Yep. On the other side of the farm sink sat a covered platter of muffins.

Moe Dennison had the hospitality game down on lock. Even at eleven o'clock at night, when her guests should be in bed instead of wandering her inn, she found a way to take care of them.

The Four Seasons might have top-notch room service and amenities, but did they serve tea at almost midnight in cups with Santa Claus faces? She thought not.

Picking up a mug, she set it on the base and hit the button for hot water.

"Couldn't sleep?"

Trapping a scream behind her closed teeth, she whirled around, snatching up another cup, arm wound back and ready to hurl it at the intruder.

"Whoa. Stand down." Wolf held his hands up in front of his chest, palms out. His eyes narrowed on the mug in her hand. "And if you crack Moe's elf mug and break up the set, she's going to be pissed."

"Dammit, Wolf. You scared me." Huffing out a breath

as her heart slowly started to ease its pounding beat, she cautiously replaced the cup and focused on the steaming water pouring into her mug.

Better than staring at him like he'd transformed into one of his mother's chocolate chip muffins.

God, standing there in his bare feet, a long-sleeved shirt thin enough that she could grab a pencil and outline those hard, powerful muscles, and all that thick, brown hair tumbling around his face and hooded eyes... She blew out a breath that did nothing for the heated squirming low in her belly. He appeared as if he could've just climbed from bed. Fresh from satisfying some woman who Nessa instinctively resented.

"What're you even doing here?" she demanded, tone sharper than she intended. Unfounded and irrational jealousy tended to do that to a person.

"I stopped by after the drive-in to see how your day at the clinic went but you were already upstairs. So I ended up staying and talking with my dad. He just went up about five minutes ago."

His feet barely made any sound across the floor as he moved next to her and chose a cup for himself. She shifted out of his way, careful not to allow any part of her—not even a wayward elbow—to brush against him. It was self-preservation at this point. In a middle school auditorium surrounded by people, she could permit the occasional touch. But here? In this kitchen with only shadows and memories of what happened the last time they were alone?

No.

She couldn't tempt fate. Or herself.

"How did you know about my working at the clinic?" She removed a tea bag from the box and slipped it in the hot water.

Wolf prepped the machine with a coffee pod. "Sydney mentioned it when she and Ivy dropped by the town square earlier today to check out our progress on the gazebo. Which is coming along, by the way. You should visit and I'll give you the tour. Short as it is."

"I did. See the gazebo," she amended, fiddling with the tea bag and avoiding his gaze. "I'm starting to believe you might actually finish it by Christmas Eve."

"You saw it? Then why didn't you come over and speak?"

Of course he would latch on to that part.

"I was on my way to the clinic."

"Nessa." His big hand covered hers, halting her incessant dunking of the bag.

"I was," she insisted.

And she'd been in a hurry. Yet, she'd still taken a moment to study Wolf at work. To remember how those hands that so skillfully set beams had cupped her head, held her steady and stroked her face. To recall the strength he so easily tempered.

"Nessa," he repeated her name, gentler this time but no less firm. "Your tea is shitty."

She jerked her gaze to him, scowling. "I happen to like it this—"

"There it is." Cocking his head, he grasped a thick strand of her hair, winding it around his finger. "I get tired of ordering you to look at me. If insulting your tea-making abilities does the trick, I'm not above it. Because, Nessie, I enjoy your eyes on me."

The air in her lungs evaporated, and she struggled not to allow the shiver that trembled in her knees to work its way through her body.

"Your coffee is finished."

"Fuck the coffee."

She blinked, the vehemence of the words not matching with the almost pleasant tone of his voice.

"I gave you a chance to talk to me after the audition. And then again at the movie—"

"It was Alastair Sim's *A Christmas Carol*. I wasn't missing that," she grumbled.

"But you're avoiding me. Nessie." He lifted his hand from hers and raised it toward her face, but it hovered next to her jaw before he dropped it to his side, as did his other hand, releasing her hair. "Did I push too hard last night?"

She tried—and failed—to hide her flinch. The reference to that kiss, the kiss he apologized for, scraped over her raw nerves. A jagged chuckle that revealed too much escaped her.

"Shouldn't you be asking yourself that question? But to answer yours, I'm fine."

"If you were fine, you wouldn't have used Ivy and the twins like human shields tonight. Or you would've been able to look at me for longer than two seconds. Or you would've said more than two consecutive sentences to me. Baby…"

"Don't." She pinched the bridge of her nose. Dammit. So much for convincing him she was *fine*. "Don't call me that."

"Why not?"

She wasn't a violent woman; as a nurse, she was a healer, had promised to do no harm. But right now, with Wolf deliberately playing obtuse, she could easily envision herself swinging on him. With her luck, though, she'd most likely break her hand on the perfect line of his jaw.

"Because I don't like it," she lied between gritted teeth. Wolf edged closer, lowering his head until his breath brushed her skin. Until she could taste the tease of his kiss on her mouth.

"We both know that's a lie."

Silence throbbed between them, loud and hard like a heartbeat. Instead of blood, it pulsed with heat, with desire. *Step away. Leave the kitchen. Return upstairs.* The orders marched through her head, but her feet remained glued to the floor. She stayed there, trapped by his gaze, by his heady scent, by the magnetic essence of *him*.

"I have a theory, Nessa. Do you want to hear it?"

The "no" trembled on her tongue, but she couldn't shove it off. Wolf nodded as if he heard it anyway.

"Last night I apologized, and you misunderstood the reason why. But after a lot of thought, my theory is I think you *chose* to take it the wrong way."

Nessa's chin jerked back as if clipped, and she scowled at him. That was bullshit, and she parted her lips to tell him so, but his pressed to hers, quieting her. Shock rippled through her, the kiss-that-wasn't-a-kiss locking her down. He lifted his head, taking his mouth away, and she swallowed the groan that clawed at her throat. Yes, he'd effectively shut her up with the equivalent of placing a finger over her lips, but she didn't care. She just wanted that delicious, heavy pressure back.

Wanted to taste him.

Dammit. After this, she and her pride were going to have a serious talking-to.

"When I said I was sorry last night, I meant for being too rough. For not asking if my mouth on you was what you wanted. And even if you didn't know those specific reasons, you suspected I didn't mean I was sorry for kissing you. But you grabbed on to that so you could get out of the truck and away from me. So you could put distance between us and have time to put that wall of yours back up."

For being too rough. For not asking if my mouth on you was what you wanted.

His words tossed kindling on an already simmering fire, and the flames shimmered and danced inside her. Was he kidding? She'd loved how he'd handled her. How he'd just…claimed her. As if she weren't fragile. Or…damaged. Just desired.

"See, take away the beard, your stunning beauty, my height and your wicked curves and we're the same," he murmured, bending his head so his lips grazed her ear and his hair tickled her nose, her cheek. Closing her eyes, she inhaled him into her lungs, held him there. "We're two people finding ways to push others away, so we're not hurt. So they don't dig below the surface and glimpse who we try so fucking hard to hide, afraid they might not like who they see. We're dirty street fighters, you and me. And last night, you slung mud."

Nessa shivered. But this time, not from lust.

From a murky jumble of fear, joy and…excitement. There was terror in being seen so clearly, but in that same vein existed a joy at not having to hide.

And underneath? Underneath crackled an excitement that this man called her on a truth she hadn't acknowledged before this moment. Pushed her on it. Because no, she hadn't been able to read his mind and ascertain the reasons behind his apology, but Wolf wasn't wrong about her reaction. If she were bone-deep, dirty honest, she had jumped to that conclusion out of self-preservation. It'd been the safest assumption—for her.

If he regretted kissing her, then it made keeping her physical and emotional distance easier. Then she wouldn't make the mistake of touching him again…of becoming involved with him.

Of falling for him.

She fisted her hands next to her thighs. What the hell was in Moe's tea bags? There existed zero chance of her developing feelings for Wolf Dennison. A kiss—or anything more—didn't equate affection. Or, lo— Hell, she couldn't even utter the word in her head.

She didn't subscribe to the antiquated belief that women couldn't separate sex from emotion. She could definitely enjoy one without losing herself in the other.

And why was she standing here, arguing with herself over this?

"I don't know what you want me to say?" she whispered, haltingly. For the first time with him, uncertain. About what he would say next. Do next.

What she would do next.

As someone who valued control, who needed it especially when everything in her life had tripped and fallen on its head, not having it terrified her.

"I want you to tell me that for tonight, at least, you're not going to deny us what we both need. I want you to tell me to kiss you again and make it all go away. I may not be able to offer you much, but that I can give you."

She didn't need to ask what he meant by "it." The grief of her loss. The secrets of her paternity. The uncertainty of her relationship with her sister. The pain of her past.

She could hand it over, and he would make it disappear under passion.

Oh God, he was temptation and seduction rolled into sinful flesh.

I may not be able to offer you much…

Like that unspecified "it," she didn't need to ask him to

clarify what he meant by that either. More than tonight. A promise of commitment. A future. His heart.

He didn't have that to give her because as he'd told her—warned her the night before—he was broken. If she possessed the sense God gave a gnat, she'd make her excuses and exit right now.

Instead, like Eve before her, Nessa was going to fall.

She didn't reply. Didn't want to risk it. Instead, she turned her head, captured his mouth and sank into him. Deep. Sank so deep into him that she didn't care about breathing, about existing. All she needed, wanted, was him. On her tongue. Under her hands.

Inside her.

Tunneling her fingers through his thick hair, she fisted the strands, tugging him impossibly closer. Opening impossibly wider. Tumbling impossibly further.

Like last night, he clasped those big hands to her face, holding her steady for his taking. Tilting her head at an angle he desired, an angle that provided them both with the greatest pleasure. Because with every greedy stroke of his tongue, each dark, rumbling growl, each luxurious lick, he gave her so much, *so much* pleasure.

It'd been a long while since she'd felt desired. No. *Craved.* As if she were sustenance to a dying man. It filled her with a headiness that had her feet lifting off the floor...

Oh wait. Her feet were literally off the floor.

Tearing her mouth away from his, she glanced down, blinking. What the hell?

"Can't do this in my mom's kitchen," Wolf muttered, cradling her in his arms and sweeping her across the room.

His lips grazed a path along her jaw even as he stalked toward a door off the kitchen. Setting her down in front of it, he twisted the knob and, with a palm to her lower back, ushered her inside. A flick of a switch revealed a mudroom with several hooks, coats, hats and boots along one of the walls. A bench lined another, and Wolf guided her there, gently pushing her down, and then lowering to his knees in front of her.

Cool air whispered over her, but she barely noticed as he cupped her knees and nudged them apart, wedging his big body between her thighs. He sent her free-falling even as he anchored her in this erotic storm. Digging her fingernails into his wide shoulders, she tipped her head back, clinging to him and pressing her aching, wet core to his ridged abdomen. Shameless, she bucked against him, seeking that delicious friction that had her trembling like a wind-tossed leaf. Abandoning a shoulder and leaning a hand behind her, she sought and found leverage to roll and grind, pursuing a release that should've been far away but loomed much too close.

Wolf gripped the back of her neck, his favorite hold with her, and tugged her closer, but not stopping her from working him. He nipped her bottom lip, then sucked the kiss-swollen flesh, flicking his tongue over it.

"Are you going to use me to get there, baby?" he breathed against her lips. "I want you to." Another small bite. Another long suck. "Do it."

He cradled her hip, pulling her closer to the edge of the bench. Granting her a better angle to writhe against him. Her cotton pajama bottoms and his thin shirt didn't present any kind of barrier. And she chose not to dwell on what kind of mess she could possibly leave behind on him. Not when she trembled on the very edge of orgasm. So close. So close.

Wolf shifted again, moving closer, tipping her lower. And oh God. A whimper clawed its way free of her throat. His cock pressed against her sex, the long thick column a hot brand even through denim. The breath punched from her lungs, and before she could identify that short, animalistic cry as her own, pleasure swelled harder, higher, and broke over her. The pleasure had a tight, almost too tight, quality to it that hovered in an odd space between ecstasy and pain. But it didn't stop her from chasing it.

Of their own volition, her hips continued to work, to rub her cotton-covered sex over his dick, until the last wave eased, and she collapsed. Or she would've if not for that hand at the nape of her neck.

"That better?" Wolf took her mouth, his tongue plunging inside, tangling, dueling, leaving her scorched and panting. "Now that you have the edge off…"

He dipped his head, and before she could demand he return and kiss her or guess his intentions, he sucked her nipple between his lips. Right through her T-shirt. Shock and lust snapped and sizzled through her veins, lighting her up, seizing her body.

Oh God. *Ohhhh God.*

His rumble of pleasure vibrated through her, connecting them. She trembled, the shock wearing off to leave her a conduit for the sharp-edged ecstasy that gripped her in its teeth and shook her like a boneless, weightless thing. And as he grazed the peak with his teeth, then pulled her deeper, drawing harder, swirling and flicking, torturing her, she lost all rational thought. Just became this carnal creature that growled and pleaded for more.

As he switched to the other breast, she clutched his head, holding him to her, nonsensical words tumbling from her lips amid whimpers. Pleasure had her in its hold as surely as Wolf did. She brushed her lips over his damp forehead, urging him to suck harder, to please don't stop.

And he didn't.

Cupping both breasts in his big palms, he lifted her to him like a fine feast that he had no intention of missing out on. Hungry. No, *ravenous*.

She couldn't have trapped her cry inside any more than she could've pushed him away. Like that first kiss, he didn't ease her into passion. He consumed her, damn near threatening her with it. He didn't treat her as if she were breakable.

Take it, I'm not holding back.

Wolf didn't utter those words, but they were there. Along with his silent insistence that she *could* take it.

A fever raged through her, born of lust. Desperate to feel him skin to skin, she dropped her arms to his waist, her hands skimming around his back and burrowing under his shirt. She'd never keened before—didn't think she'd actually even heard one—but was pretty sure she did it when her palms slid over his taut, hot flesh. The contact burned through her, and she dug her nails into him. Needing to hold tight? Needing to mark him?

Maybe both.

Right now, with his mouth on her, with him arching into her touch, she didn't dwell too long on the why. It didn't matter. Nothing mattered but the pleasure he gifted her with and that he didn't stop.

Wolf lifted his head, crushing his lips to hers, his thumbs whisking around and around her wet, beaded nipples. Her belly clenched, pulling so hard, the ache reverberated in her sex, in her clit. She squirmed, hurting with the lust that swirled and churned within her as if she'd come years ago instead of minutes.

"Wolf," she breathed, gripping the dense muscles of his shoulder blades underneath his shirt. "Please."

Please make it better. Please give me what only you can. Please fuck me.

She twisted her head away from Wolf, burying her face into the crook of his neck, pressing her mouth to the base of his throat to trap those words inside her.

But it didn't make a difference. Wolf understood—as he always did.

In a swift and seamless motion, he stood, picked her up, switched places with her and set her on his lap. His hands arranged her legs so she straddled his thighs, her back pressed to his chest. Circling her wrists, he lifted her arms, linking them behind his neck. She obeyed the silent command, and kept them there, her fingers sinking into the thick, cool strands of his hair.

His hands stroked down her arms and the sides of her torso, one molding to her breast and the other trailing lower, over her belly, and lower still...until his fingertips slipped beneath the waistband of her pajama bottoms.

Anticipation and desire raced through her, and her breath soughed in and out of her lungs, echoing in her ears. Had she ever wanted, needed anything this much? Possibly. But at this moment, with his fingers only inches from her wet and aching sex, she couldn't think of anything. Hell, she just couldn't *think*.

"Wolf." She tried to squeeze her thighs but couldn't. Not spread over him as she was.

"Tell me I can, baby." He feathered a caress over the tender, sensitive skin below her navel. "Give me permission to go here."

Because this touch would be different, more intimate than his tongue dancing with hers or his mouth on her breasts. They would cross a line here, and it was one they couldn't come back from. Couldn't deny.

She didn't want to deny it.

"Touch me."

He didn't make her wait. With one stroke, those long, beautiful fingers swept through her folds, parting her, stoking the flames inside her from hot to incineration. Groaning, she turned her face into her arm, biting the soft skin as if the hint of pain could counteract the fiery pleasure he hurled her in like a virgin sacrifice. It didn't; it only served to heighten it.

"Fuck, how do you feel so good?" He punctuated the question with a firm rub of the bundle of nerves cresting her sex. Sizzling bolts slammed into her, and her hips jerked into his touch, demanding more. Demanding he not ever stop or else she'd lose what little mind she clung to. "Kiss me."

She surrendered to that command, offering him her mouth. And as his tongue plunged between her lips, two fingers speared low and thrust inside her. He swallowed her small, high scream, giving her back his hum of approval. Gifting her with a roll of her nipple.

So full. She was so full. Tearing her mouth free, she tipped her head back on his shoulder, blinking and staring blindly at the blurred ceiling. She'd known pleasure before. Believed she had. But this... What Wolf stirred within her with his fingers driving in and out of her, the heel of his palm grinding over her clit and the erotic play on her breast... This detonated and shattered that idea. He'd set a new precedent and she hadn't even had his cock yet.

Fear spiked within her fast and furious.

Wolf could change her. Irrevocably. Irreversibly. In ways her mother's announcement and Isaac's letter hadn't.

For a second, she stiffened in his arms. And beneath her, inside her, Wolf stilled.

"Where'd you go, Nessie?" he murmured, planting a soft kiss to her temple. "Your pace. Your choice. Do we stop?"

Jesus. This man. His fingers were buried in her vagina, and he offered to stop. God, yes, he was going to change her. But she couldn't bring a halt to this. That chance had come and gone about the time he'd called her a street fighter. About the time he called her out and claimed to see her as no one else did.

That kind of careful observation in a man was an aphrodisiac to the body and soul.

"I'm right here." She lowered an arm and slid a palm beneath her pajamas to cover his hand with hers. Pressed it. "Don't stop."

Slowly, he withdrew his fingers then, twisting his wrist, drove back inside her. She arched against him, thrusting her breast into his palm, grinding the back of her head to his shoulder. Over and over, he propelled her closer to the crumbling edge of release. With his fingers inside her, his palm on that pulsing, aching nub of her sex, his hoarse whispers of praise at her ear. She writhed on his lap, danced for him, shook for him, cried for him.

And when he curled his fingers over a spot high inside her, firmly petting it, she broke for him.

She came hard, flying into pieces. A tiny part of her shouted in worry, in fear. But the larger part... The larger part exulted in the freedom, the abandon of pleasure, of soaring with no strings even for these few seconds. Wolf held her through it, anchoring her, even as he continued to drive into her, ensuring she wrung dry every ounce of ecstasy.

Finally, moments—a millennium—later, she slumped against him, air whistling from her lungs. Pleasure flickered and sparked in her veins, aftershocks of a cataclysmic orgasm that left her pleasantly empty of thought. Of sorrow. Of anxiety.

Just at peace.

Yet, as exhausted as she might be, she couldn't ignore the thick, hard length of his cock underneath her. Unable to stop herself, she undulated against it, earning a dark growl that vibrated against her back. Gooseflesh erupted over her skin, and her breath hitched. Damn, she'd just had a brain-melting orgasm, and her sex quivered at that sound, spasming.

She hadn't even realized she'd reached behind her until his fingers cuffed her wrist, preventing her from wrapping her fingers around his erection.

"No, Nessa."

She twisted around so she could fully look at him. "What? Why? You don't want me—"

He shut her up with an almost bruising crush of his lips to hers. "Does this—" he pressed her palm to his cock "—feel like I don't want you? Want your hands on me?" He huffed out a serrated laugh. "If I were only thinking with my dick, I'd already have you turned around, on your knees and sinking down on my cock, giving me what you just had."

As if he couldn't say those words and *not* kiss her, he took her mouth again, stroking his tongue inside her, licking and sucking. But in the next instant, she stood on her feet, his hands cradling her hips, his forehead nestled against her belly.

They didn't move for several moments, the only sound in the mudroom their sharp, staccato breaths. Finally, he stood, towering over her.

Those beautiful green eyes studied her, touching her as surely as his hands and his lips had only moments ago.

Lifting his hand from her hip, he traced the curve of her cheekbone, trailing a path down to her jaw. He cradled it, brushing the pad of his thumb back and forth just under her bottom lip.

"If I didn't suspect you'd resent both me and yourself in the morning, I'd finish what we started."

She frowned. "No, I wouldn't." Irritated, she pushed his hand away from her face. "And it might surprise you, but I know my own mind and am fully capable of owning my decisions."

He did that Wolf thing where he didn't immediately respond, but scrutinized her, analyzed her to the point where she barely resisted fidgeting. And protesting.

"I'm not being condescending or trying to tell you what you're feeling or thinking, Nessa. But I also know last night you jumped out of my car like you were on fire after a kiss."

He shook his head, turning away from her. A muscle ticked along his jawline, his beard not hiding the telltale sign of agitation. If she'd had any doubts about this conversation affecting him as it did her, that relieved her of them. His voice might be gentle, but Wolf was most definitely... affected.

"I'm going to walk out of here, and with each step, I will call myself all kinds of idiots for letting you go back up those stairs. But that regret is nothing to what I would feel if after the orgasms fade and the sweat dries, you looked at me like you did last night. Or worse, you *don't* look at me, like you haven't been able to all day."

He sighed, dragging a hand through his hair, the muscles in his arms flexing in a sensual dance that shouldn't have held her spellbound. But did.

"Nessa." He cupped her cheek, stared down at her, those mesmerizing eyes entrapping her. Enthralling her. "Tomorrow, or the day after that. Or the day after that. Whenever you decide you're exhausted of hiding and want to let the walls down for just a little while without fear of judgment, drive past the inn to the first corner and make a right. My cottage is at the end of the road. Or just take the path past my workshop and follow it until you come to my house. Either way, you need me, come to me."

Dropping his hand from her, he stepped back but didn't release her from his gaze.

"We can be each other's comfort while you're here in Rose Bend. No questions. No expectations. No tomorrows. No disappointments. Nothing but comfort and pleasure. I want to give you so much pleasure, Nessa. And yeah, take some for myself. Your choice."

After throwing down that sensual gauntlet, he brushed a kiss over her cheek and walked past her, leaving her in the mudroom. Without his presence, the cool air rushed in, prickling her skin. The muted warmth of the kitchen beckoned her, but she didn't move, Wolf's words swirling around her head like the snowflakes that fell beyond the inn's walls.

He'd bounced the ball in her court and challenged her to make the next move.

A move that required her to trust in him.

In herself.

She shook her head, turning on her heel and returning to the kitchen.

That might be the line she couldn't cross.

CHAPTER FIFTEEN

WOLF STARED DOWN into his cup of coffee, but he didn't see the dark brew. With Eva Wright's voice in his ear through the cell phone, an image of a beautiful face replaced it.

"I'm sorry, Wolf," Eva said, her regret clear. "I spoke with both Martha and Roy. And like I remembered, they don't have a son. And Roy is an only child so no nephew on his side. Martha has a brother, but he also only has daughters. So she has nieces, no nephews that would've visited with the last name Summers."

Shit.

He pinched the bridge of his nose, then tunneled his fingers through his hair, fisting the strands. Nessa was going to be so damn disappointed.

"Thank you, Ms. Eva. I really appreciate you calling the Summerses and checking on this. I'll let Nessa know what you found out."

"It wasn't a problem at all. I just wish I had better news for her." Eva sighed. "If there's anything else I can do, please don't hesitate to ask, okay?"

"I promise. Thanks again, Ms. Eva."

Wolf ended the call, setting the cell on the table, coffee forgotten. How did he tell Nessa this? Regardless of what she'd said after they'd left Eva's house three nights ago, he knew she'd set her hopes on this lead. Hell, he had, too. But now…

"Damn," he growled, knocking his fist on the small dining room table.

Wheeling around on his heel, he stalked to the hall closet and snatched his coat off the hanger. After locating his keys on the bar separating the kitchen from the living room, he headed toward the front door.

It'd been two days since he'd left the inn and Nessa. Two days since she'd shattered in his arms, his name the sweetest cry on her lips. Two days since he'd offered her...him.

Two days since he'd heard a word from her.

This was what he got for being so damn noble. For once, for just fucking once, he really should've thought with his dick.

That was a lie. He couldn't have dealt with seeing remorse in her eyes when she looked at him. Couldn't bear being one more regret for Nessa. But that didn't change the fact that his body had been in a perpetual state of hardness for the last couple of days.

In hindsight, touching her had probably been a mistake. Because that kiss had shown him once he started, stopping would be like accomplishing a Herculean labor. But he had. Yeah, it'd been after he'd had his tongue and mouth wrapped around her nipple and his fingers buried inside the liquid heat of her sex, but he had.

Shit. Chivalry shouldn't just die; it should be impaled, set on fire and the ashes scattered on barren ground.

But could it really be called selfish when his motives for calling a halt to what would've ended up in them fucking in his mother's mudroom weren't exactly pure? He hadn't let her unzip him, stroke his cock, take him inside her, because he wanted more. Maybe it made him a selfish, greedy bastard but there it was. He wanted more than a quick screw on a bench.

Because once wouldn't be enough.

Not with her.

Yeah, it could be called selfish. He fisted the keys, the ridges biting into the flesh of his fingers. Because if he was really fucking chivalrous, he wouldn't touch her at all. Doing so was setting them both up for something that had the potential for an epic fallout. Where was that fucking savior complex now when he should be saving them from each other? Saving them from themselves?

Jaw clenched, he grabbed the knob and wrenched the front door open, then drew up short. It was either that or barrel into the woman standing on his welcome mat.

Nessa rocked back on her heels, and he shot his hand out, grabbing her arm and steadying her.

"Nessa? What're you doing here?"

Reluctantly, he released her and glanced over her shoulder. Frowning, he returned his gaze back to her. "Where's your car?"

"I walked. You told me to follow the path past the workshop..." Her voice trailed off as she looked behind her.

His heart clutched at the hint of nerves in her tone and dark eyes when she turned back to him. The urge to take her in his arms and assure her that it was okay to be there welled in him so hard, he had to steel himself against it. He fought his own nature in not physically comforting her, because touching her in any way would be like setting a match to dry kindling. And she'd obviously walked over here to talk to him.

So he had to keep his hands off her. At all costs.

"Yeah," he said, rubbing a hand down his beard. "Is everything okay?"

"Yes. Can I come in for a minute? To talk to you?"

"Oh sure, yes." Damn. He mentally winced as he stepped

back inside his cabin. One look at her, and some of his brain cells had suffered. "Come on in."

She moved inside, passing by him. Pausing in the small foyer, she scanned his home, and he did the same, peering at it through her eyes. The cabin had originally been his parents' when they'd bought Kinsale Inn all those years ago. They'd lived here while they completed renovations. When he'd returned home from Iraq, as much as he loved his family, he hadn't been able to live with them in the family wing of the inn. When his parents had suggested the cabin, it'd been perfect—close to his family, but a quiet space of his own.

The spacious log cabin possessed an open layout with a living room, dining room and kitchen that all flowed into one another. Large windows allowed the sun to bathe the room in natural light and the requisite bachelor furniture occupied the space—couch, recliner, huge mounted television, dining table. A hallway led to the two bedrooms and bathroom.

Simple. Ordinary. The fanciest piece of furniture was the coffee table he'd built himself. Probably a far cry from what she was used to in Boston. What she was returning to.

"Would you like some coffee?" he offered, stepping toward the kitchen.

"No, I'm fine," she said, and he halted. "Since it's Saturday, Ivy is going with the twins and their friends to a reindeer rally, whatever that is. Then they have pageant practice. Did I tell you she's in the show, too? Her and Cher are going to sing together. While she's busy, I thought I'd just… Well, I needed to talk to…" She laughed softly, shaking her head. "And I'm honest-to-God babbling. Dammit, I feel like I'm making this awkward as hell."

"Even when you had a wreath on your head, you weren't

awkward. You wore it like a crown," he murmured. *Like the queen you are.* Somehow he managed to trap those too-revealing words inside, but to prevent anything else from slipping, he shrugged out of his coat and gestured for hers. "Let me have your coat, and you can start talking."

She removed the outerwear, revealing a cream-colored V-neck sweater that clung to every curve and dip and dark blue jeans that highlighted the feminine swell of her hips and tightness of her thick thighs.

He almost handed her back the coat.

Because he had no idea how he could carry on a conversation without picturing his mouth on those breasts, his hands cradling that waist, or his legs squeezed by those thighs.

Exhaling a low, deliberate breath, he turned toward the closet, using those moments to get his throbbing body and rebellious thoughts under control.

Yeah, good luck with that.

"Sure you don't want any coffee?" he asked, returning to the living room. *Please, give me something to do other than stare at you.*

"I'm sure." She rubbed her palms down the sides of her jeans, and the nervous gesture snapped him out of his own head.

"I'm sorry. Moe would kill me over what she'd call my barnyard manners. Have a seat." He waved toward the couch, taking a step in that direction. "I'm actually glad you stopped by. I was on my—"

"I don't mean to be rude, and I want to hear what you have to say, but please, can I get this out first? If I don't…" She shrugged, lifting her hands, palms up. "I don't know if I will be able to later."

Wolf pivoted and peered at her. Noticing the sinking of

her teeth into her bottom lip. The slight fidgeting. The restless drumming of her finger against her legs.

The obvious signs of unease triggered a dread that coiled in his gut. Crossing his arms over his chest, he leaned against the back of the couch. And waited.

Nessa Hunt did ballsy. Snarky. Even aloof.

But Nessa Hunt did not do nervous.

He braced himself for whatever she had to say, even knowing the effort would be pointless, fruitless. He didn't like it, hadn't been prepared for it—even on some level resented it—but this woman had the power to fell him with a word, a glance, a touch.

And he suspected she was about to prove it.

Shit. If this wasn't proof that he'd failed to protect himself—hell, failed to protect her from him—then he didn't know what was.

Nessa blew out a hard breath, running a hand over the shaved side of her head. "For the past day, I've been thinking over what to say. How to say this without it being offensive or even selfish."

"Just say it," Wolf said, his tone even, though inside... Inside, his heart pounded like an anvil striking iron. "You're responsible for the heart and intention behind the words, not for how the other person hears them."

"You're doing the wise-old-man thing again." The corner of her mouth quirked up in a faint smile, but after an instant, it disappeared. "Wolf, I haven't been honest with you. That seems to be a theme with me, lately. I haven't been honest with Ivy, you, myself."

She shook her head, glancing away from him and shoving her hair behind her shoulder. Her chest rose and fell on a deep breath, then she returned her gaze to him.

"You asked me the other night about how my day at the

clinic went. I avoided the question then, but I'll answer now. It went amazing."

"I'm glad for that," he murmured, a little confused about where this was going, but something inside him stilled. Waited.

"I was scared, Wolf. So damn scared when I pulled up to that clinic." Nessa pressed a fist to her chest, over her heart. "Because bringing Ivy to Rose Bend at Isaac's request wasn't the only reason I came. Before..." She hesitated, slicked the tip of her tongue over her lips. Wolf locked his muscles, physically restraining himself from going to her. "Before I left Boston, I collapsed in the emergency room. A panic attack. It was the first time it'd happened to me, much less occurring at work. My supervisor insisted I take time off. She believes I haven't truly dealt with my mom's and Isaac's deaths and suddenly becoming the guardian to a twelve-year-old who's cast me as the evil stepsister in her own fairy tale."

"Do you need me to hold you?"

She blinked at his offer, her lips parting. Then, she closed her eyes, her soft hitch of air almost deafening in the silent room. Jesus, she was killing him. The pressure to ease that pain, that sorrow, shoved at him until he damn near shook with the urge to go to her. In his twisted head, was he more addicted to being the rescuer, no matter the person being rescued? Was that what he found so irresistible and...and consuming about her?

Like a flailing man hanging over the side of a mountain from a threadbare rope, he grasped at some kind of explanation.

Some reason why he should usher her out of here right now before he took them past the point of no return.

But she looked at him again. A glimmer of warmth had

banished some of the shadows in those espresso depths, and he knew he wouldn't. He couldn't.

"How do you *do* that?" She didn't wait for him to answer but continued, "No, I'm okay. I need to do this." She paused and inhaled a breath. Let it go. "So after being forced to take vacation, I headed here with Ivy, hoping to, I don't know, fix myself. Fearing I was too broken for that to happen. Then I was asked to fill in at the clinic. And I survived. Not only that, I realized I hadn't lost the career I love, the path I'd chosen. Because I had been scared, Wolf. That seems to be the theme of my life for the last eight months since Mom died. Fear. I'm tired of that. The clinic was one step out of it. This is another."

She took that step toward him. Then one more. And one more until she stood in front of him, the toes of her boots nudging his.

"I've always played by the rules. Toed the line. Made the correct and expected decisions. And walking out your front door and letting the other night be the farthest we go would be the wisest decision right now. But I don't want to."

She inched closer until her toes bumped the heels of his boots. Until her legs brushed the insides of his thighs. Until her sultry jasmine-and-cedar scent taunted and teased him. He unfolded his arms and curled his fingers around the back of the couch. Holding on so he didn't grab her.

"Even though I've followed the rules, I've been lied to, walked away from, abandoned. So now I'm going to throw all that out the window and see what happens. I owe it to myself to take what I want…and I want you. Even if it's just for the next few weeks before I return home. But, Wolf—" she held up a hand and slowly shook her head "—that's all it can be. You offered me a temporary arrangement, no questions, no strings. And if that's what is still on the table, then I'll accept it. Otherwise, I don't have it in me to give more than that. Not right now. Maybe not for a long time. I'll be the first to admit, I'm an untrusting, suspicious, emotional bad bet. I'm being up-front with you about that because you've been hurt, and I won't lie to you. There's nothing happily-ever-after about me."

"Can I touch you now?"

The question emerged rougher, harsher, than he'd intended but all he heard in the last part of her speech was a yes. Though a phantom vise squeezed his chest at her "before I return home," it didn't compare to the acceptance. And that she'd set important boundaries that allowed him to have her without risking his own pain. He was going in, eyes wide open, knowing she would leave. Knowing he couldn't disappoint or fail where there were no expectations.

He wanted her. And he could have her.

She wanted him. And she wasn't turning him away.

That's all he cared about.

Well, that and getting her naked as quickly as possible.

A smile—a small but true one, not that nervous facsimile—curved her mouth. "Yes."

Before the consent completely passed her lips, he shoved off the couch, already reaching for her. But at the last moment, he abruptly drew up short.

"Are you sure you're okay?"

"What?"

"The panic attack. The day at the clinic. Are you sure you—?"

She threw herself at him, crushing her mouth to his. Her arms wrapped around his neck, fingers tunneling through his hair and tugging. Prickles of pain darted across his scalp, and he rumbled his pleasure into her mouth. Opening wide for her, he thrilled in the possessive thrust of her tongue, the hungry growl that preceded the wet, raw tangle. No foreplay for them. Their mouths got straight to fucking with hard, demanding strokes, greedy sucks and lush licks.

The woman could kiss like nobody's business.

Could willingly bring him to his knees with one of those needy whimpers.

Dropping his hands to her prayer-inspiring ass, he hiked her up, and her legs immediately wound around his waist. With long strides, he stalked around the couch and set her on the dark brown cushions whose only sellable factor until now had been the color that hid all manner of food and drink stains. Now it would forever remind him of the beautiful color of her eyes.

His lips tingled, swollen from the delicious carnal abuse they'd just suffered, as he trailed them over her cheek, over her temple to the closely shaved side of her head. Fingers sliding up her arm, shoulder and neck to burrow into the long, thick strands on the other side, he fisted them, tilting her head.

"I promised myself when I finally got you here, I'd go slow, take my time and worship you and this body like you deserve. But reality is a different animal, and I don't know if I can follow through on that wish."

He brushed his mouth back and forth along her scalp, dipping his head to graze the top of her ear with his teeth. She trembled, her grip on his hair tightening.

"Wing it."

He laughed, amazed that he could when lust gripped him in its razor-sharp teeth. But as he pressed his lips to her temple, his humor softened then evaporated. Fuck, he wanted this woman. Wanted her with a fierceness that should terrify him. And later, later when her powerful, toned thighs weren't cradling his waist, when her intoxicating, rich scent didn't have his head thick and his cock even thicker, he'd have the sense to be scared.

But not now.

Now he just needed to be balls deep inside her.

Bowing his head, he captured her mouth again, delving deep. He couldn't get enough. Of her taste. Of those sexy sounds. But they weren't enough. Not nearly. He craved more. And then more. And even more.

Gripping the bottom of her sweater, he jerked the top up, barely granting her a moment to lift her arms before tearing it over her head and dropping it to the floor. In seconds, he'd returned the favor to his own sweater. He stared at her, hair tousled and spilling over a shoulder, brown skin gleaming against the light blue of a silk-and-lace bra. Last time, he hadn't touched her bare flesh, and now his fingers almost cramped with the need to be on her.

"You're stunning." Lust and something more tender— that he wasn't ready to acknowledge, especially here, when softer emotions could be mistaken for more—pulsed and beat within him. Alive and hungry.

She stroked a hand down his face, her fingers tracing his cheekbone, the arch of his nose, the top curve of his lip, painting the bottom one with a damp fingertip. Her hand dropped to his chest. He stiffened, the air stalling in his lungs as she followed the lines of his tattoo on his chest.

"Sometimes it's hard to look at you," she murmured, lifting her hand from his chest to join the one mapping his face. Brushing his chin, jaw. He exhaled the breath he held. "No person should be as beautiful as you."

This mating of their mouths was gentle, slower but no less erotic, no less hot and full of intent. As he curled his tongue around hers, he demonstrated what he intended for her nipples, her clit. What he promised with his touch.

Sliding his hands down her shoulders, he didn't hesitate in cupping and squeezing her breasts, slightly less than a handful and utterly perfect. Didn't waver in popping the front clasp and stripping the bra from her, leaving her naked from the waist up.

Didn't pause in pulling free of their kiss and taking a dark brown, tightly furled nipple in his mouth.

Nessa's soft cry was a symphony he longed to record and play over and over. He'd settle for drawing it from her as often as possible. Pinching the other tip, he licked and sucked, tonguing it until her hips writhed like an untamed thing. Then, he switched to the other nipple and started over.

By the time he lifted his mouth, she clutched his head, holding him to her, arching so hard, her swollen flesh trembled. He should feel a little sympathy; after all, his cock throbbed. But only pride swept through him as he studied his handiwork. As heavy, loud pants and pained whimpers broke on her lips.

"Are you with me?" His hands dropped to her thin belt, but his gaze found hers, searching. For the slightest hint of hesitancy, for doubt.

"Yes," she breathed, backing her answer up with a jerk of her head. "Yes."

He unbuckled the belt and released the top button of her jeans, then skipped to her knee-high boots, quickly removing them.

"Wait," she ordered.

She batted his hands out of the way when they returned to her zipper and she reached for his jeans. Within moments, she had the button loosened, the zipper down and her hand inside his boxer briefs. Their twin groans saturated the room as her fingers closed around his cock and squeezed.

Jesus. His head fell back on his shoulders and his ass hit his heels. He punched his hips up into that first tight stroke, and maybe he swore, maybe he groaned again. Hell, maybe he cried. He didn't know because his ability to form rational thought vanished under her pumping hand.

And then she pushed off the couch, bowed over him and sank her mouth over his cock.

"Fuck." He thrust his hands in her hair, holding her... trying to pull her away...

Goddamn, he'd lost his mind. To the pleasure that attacked his spine and balls. To her. His dick, though. His dick understood which side it wanted. More. More of her tongue flicking over its head. More of that greedy suckle. More of that hard squeezing.

"Baby," he grated. Shifting, he sat, raising his knees so she knelt between his thighs, working him over as if he were the most delicious treat she'd ever had in her mouth.

He couldn't tear his gaze away. Not from the sight of himself disappearing between her lush lips, of her flushed cheeks, of the pleasure that glazed her dark eyes when her lashes lifted and she looked at him. He ground his teeth together, trying to trap the orders to *suck harder, open wider, take all of him.* But when she dipped her head lower, hollowed her cheeks and twisted her fist, they spilled from him anyway.

A jagged telltale electrical pulse sizzled up his legs and down his back, culminating in his cock. Swearing, he gently but firmly tugged her away from him and covered her mouth with his. Not here. The first time he came wouldn't be in this perfect, wicked mouth.

But the first time she did today would be in his.

Before she could form a protest, he flipped her on her back, stripped her of her jeans, panties and socks. If she hadn't damn near stopped his mind with that impromptu blow job, he could've taken a moment to admire her nakedness. But she had. And now, he took in the stunning beauty that was the dip of her waist, the flare of her hips, the toned muscle of her legs, but it was the bare, soaked flesh that demanded all of his attention.

Throwing her thighs over his shoulders, he wedged himself tight in that thickly scented V and feasted.

He licked her folds, following the path his fingers had enjoyed a day ago, and moaned as her sultry flavor hit his tongue. That jasmine-and-cedar scent was richer, stronger here. More delicious here. Fuck, he could survive on this for the rest of his life.

Flicking a caress over the nub of engorged flesh hidden in the top of her folds, he returned to circle it, softly suck it. With a raw cry, Nessa went wild beneath him. Unhooking an arm from beneath her leg, he laid it low across her hips, anchoring her, holding her still so he could continue to explore the sweetest flesh he'd ever had the privilege and pleasure to indulge in.

Over and over he licked, nibbled, kissed, losing himself in those swollen feminine lips, that pearl of flesh. She bucked into his mouth, clawed at his shoulders, pleaded with him to stop, don't stop. And when he thrust two fingers into her slick, tight sex, she came with an abandon that sent pride streaking through him. That humbled him.

He pressed kisses to the curve of her hip, and on a whimper, she pushed his head away, curling into herself. Not removing his gaze from her, he finished removing his jeans and boots, pausing to grab his wallet and the condom he had stashed there. In seconds, he had the foil package ripped open and the protection rolled down his hard, throbbing cock.

Crawling to Nessa, he crouched over her, pressing his forehead to hers. Though it seemed his whole body had turned into one giant ache, he waited until her lashes fluttered open, and he lifted his head to meet her orgasm-glazed eyes.

"Kiss me." It sounded exactly as it was meant—a request. An entreaty.

He needed her to center him, to leash the beast that threatened to fall on her in a ravenous haze. She could do that for him.

But more than that. He just wanted the quiet, intimate connection of their mouths. Of trading breath for breath. Of looking into those beautiful eyes and knowing she was right there with him.

Some of the fog cleared from her gaze, and she cupped his face, tipping his head down. Then she kissed him. Tenderly. Softly. Slipping one hand between them, she grasped his cock and guided him into her.

She gasped into his mouth. And he might've gasped into hers.

Such warmth. Such wet.

Such bliss.

He couldn't keep his eyes open. Not when he fought the sensation of drowning with every inch of her too-tight, too-perfect sex. Like a victim going under for the final time, he battled the sense of panic that he would never emerge from this—from her—whole again. Hiding his face in the crook of her neck, he thrust forward, burying himself so deep inside her it propelled the breath from his lungs in a hot burst of air.

They stilled, the only movement in both of their bodies the rapid rise and fall of their chests. Her nails dug into the back of his neck and the space between his shoulder blades. Twin urges raged within him—never move again and for godsake, *move*.

But the flutter of her feminine flesh around his cock glued together his steadily fracturing control like nothing else could. He gritted his teeth, granting her time so she could become accustomed to him. No matter how long it took—no matter if it killed him—he'd wait.

"You with me?" He lifted his head and uncurled his fist to brush tangled, damp strands of hair away from her face. Later, he would be embarrassed that those fingers trembled. "Nessie?"

She nodded, shifting underneath him. A soft cry escaped her, teeth sinking into her bottom lip as she arched and twisted. "Please. Wolf, move."

It's all he needed to hear. Entwining their fingers together and pressing their linked hands to the floor on either side of her head, he withdrew, slowly dragging his cock over slick, quivering flesh. Then, when cool air brushed every inch of his damp length except for the head still lodged within her, he paused, opened his mouth over her jaw and surged back in.

He shuddered, the pleasure racing over him—his skin, through muscle and bone—and almost ending it for him right there. But fuck, never. He never wanted this to end. Never wanted to leave this place.

Inside Nessa.

With Nessa.

Shutting his eyes, as if that would block out any more similar traitorous thoughts, Wolf powered into her, losing himself in her liquid heat. Nessa eagerly lifted her hips, bucking up to meet every thrust, every stroke, riding him even as he rode her. She took him with no inhibition, vulnerable and unreserved here in a way she wasn't outside his cabin door. As he gazed down into her beautiful face, she allowed him to see every emotion, whether she intended to or not.

He accepted it as a gift, one he treasured just as much as her body and her pleasure.

Close to the edge, his pace stumbled, quickened. Not that Nessa seemed to mind. She damn near threw her body against his, their hips meeting in a clash, a supplication. Gripping the back of her neck, he hauled her closer, covering her mouth, thrusting his tongue between her lips in a mimicry of how he took her body.

Slipping a hand between them, he traced and firmly caressed that sweet nub of flesh at the top of her sex.

"Give it to me, baby." He pistoned into her, rubbed her. Needing her to come first because he refused to go without her. "Get there for me."

With a cry that echoed in the room, she shattered. Her sex clamped down on him, drawing a pleasure-pained grunt at the almost bruising grip on his cock. Fuck, he loved it. Gathering her impossibly closer, he drove harder, faster, between her spasming walls, ensuring she received every measure of the orgasm racking her body.

And only when those shivers started to ease did he let go. He pounded into her, but after only a few strokes, he cracked, following her into that blazing fire that both consumed and rebirthed him. Leaving him powerful and weak.

Leaving him unfettered, at peace.

Leaving him scared as hell.

CHAPTER SIXTEEN

"I'M EITHER GOING to look like I had an allergic reaction to something or that I rolled around on a rug naked," Nessa grumbled, holding open the sides of the plaid shirt Wolf had given her. "I don't know which one I'd rather have people think—that a nurse can't remember to monitor her own allergies. Or that I'm a pervert who enjoys one-on-one time with carpet."

Wolf snorted from the stove, and she eyed his naked back. If he wasn't so damn sexy in only jeans that valiantly clung to his lean hips, she might be offended at his lack of sympathy. Especially when he was the reason behind her beard rash.

Who was she kidding? She liked glancing down and seeing his marks on her body. Did that take away her feminist card? Maybe. Yeah, sitting here on his breakfast bar stool, body pleasantly loose and a little tender from earth-moving sex and watching him competently cooking breakfast in his kitchen, she didn't care.

Part of her still had its mouth open in shock that she'd actually gotten up the nerve to come over to Wolf's house, lay out her terms and climb him like a horny howler monkey. She'd never considered herself *brave*. The last time she'd taken a risk, she'd moved in with a man who'd ended up leaving her for a job. Not even another woman—a job. So no, she would never be one of those people who jumped out of planes. But coming to Wolf, being honest, baring her body and entrusting it to him, had been like leaping out of the sky with only a hinky parachute strapped to her back.

She'd been terrified, hoping and trusting he would be there to protect her. To keep her from crashing.

And he had.

He'd been...perfect.

And just *thinking* that word had her belly twisting with unease. *Pull back*, every self-protective instinct in her whispered. *Pull back before you're a casualty. Again.*

She should heed that warning; she hadn't with Jeremy.

Yet, she continued sitting on the stool, waiting on scrambled eggs and bacon.

In which camp did this put her? Team risk taker or team glutton for punishment?

Yeah, she wasn't analyzing that right now. Especially not without bacon.

"I'm voting for the rug love." Wolf smirked, turning toward the refrigerator. He pulled open the door and, good goddess of all arm porn, she clutched the edge of the bar to keep herself from falling off the seat. She would demand he put a shirt on, but she was no hypocrite. "The idea of you rolling around butt naked on my mother's rug is a little creepy...but kinda hot, too. I feel so conflicted."

She laughed, picking up her coffee and sipping. Minutes later, he slid a plate piled with fluffy eggs, crispy bacon and buttered toast in front of her. He sat across from her with his own breakfast, and they tucked into it with all the hungry enthusiasm of two people who hadn't eaten in weeks. Or two people who'd just indulged in hot, dirty, calorie-burning sex on a floor.

To-may-to, to-mah-to.

As she ate, her gaze drifted to the tattoo on his left

pectoral muscle. When he'd first torn his sweater over his head, revealing the ink, she'd been stunned...and turned on. Then, she'd gotten a good look at it. Had traced the pair of combat boots with dog tags and the name Raylon Brandt with a date of birth and death. Eight years ago.

Her heart had twisted in her chest, constricting so hard she'd found it hard to breathe and not because of the lust that'd been racing through her veins.

Wolf...beautiful, sensitive, funny Wolf...had lost someone in war. And it'd been someone he'd cared enough about to ink a memorial to him permanently on his body. Over his heart. Who was Raylon? Had he been another Dennison? A brother? A friend?

The questions sprinted through her mind. She should leave it alone. Wolf had stiffened up when she'd touched the tattoo; that revealed everything she needed to know about the soreness of the subject. Not to mention, she'd set the parameters of their relationship—fuck buddies. They had screwed. They didn't deep dive into each other's heads and souls for treasure better off left buried.

Yet...she wanted to know him. This man who could create beauty out of wood, dispense wisdom with quiet humor and make her come hard enough to confirm the truth of alien life-forms in other galaxies.

Pretty sure she'd glimpsed their home planet during that last orgasm.

"You finished?" Wolf stood, picking up his empty plate. "Need more coffee?"

"No, I'm good." She forked the last of her eggs into her mouth and handed him her plate and silverware. "Thank you. That was great."

"You're welcome." He crossed the small kitchen to the

sink and rinsed off the dishes before setting them in the dishwasher. "What're your plans for the day?"

"Well, Moe and Leo were telling us about a sled relay tonight. Not exactly sure what that is, but Ivy's excited about going. I said I'd go."

Wolf glanced at her over his shoulder, smiling. "Okay, I know for a fact Boston has holiday events. Maybe not sled relays but Santa runs and candlelight walks, and yet you claim to not know about any of them. Where exactly do you go during the Christmas season? A bunker?"

She shrugged a shoulder. "My mom was the big Christmas person, but she was an attorney, so she didn't have much time off to celebrate it. We used to spend the day together for dinner, but once I became a nurse, I volunteered to work so people with children could have it off. Except for when I was younger, it's been pretty much another day to me." She traced the edge of the coffee cup, staring at a chip on the handle. "Isaac left mom and me the week before Christmas when I was twelve. For most people it's a holiday for family, but for me it's a constant reminder of when mine broke up."

Pressure built behind her ribs, and she focused on the mug as if it would spring fangs and go for her throat if she dared glance away.

"Damn." She loosed a hard, self-deprecating chuckle. "I've never told anyone that. Especially not Mom. I think in my head I've called Isaac the grinch all these years 'cause he stole all my fucking Christmases." She laughed again, and surprisingly, it carried a trace of humor. "I really need to let that go."

"For yourself."

Soft and firm lips brushed the shaved side of her head, sending sparks cascading down her spine even as warmth stole through her veins. Wolf pressed his wide chest to her back, his powerful arms enveloping her in a hug she hadn't known she needed until that moment. His wintergreen scent, mixed with the musk of them, wrapped around her, as well, and she inhaled, turning around on the stool to return the embrace. She burrowed against him, seeking his heat, his strength.

It was okay to lean on him. Just for a minute.

"Just from his letter, I believe your father was a man who lived with a lot of regrets. His relationship with you being the biggest one. His *relationship* with you, Nessa. Not *you*. He made mistakes, and he knew that. Divorcing your mother most likely wasn't one of them, because as sad as it is, people break up all the time. But letting that divorce come between the two of you? Yes, it was a mistake I think he went to his grave grieving. And that saddens me. Because instead of peace, he only wanted time. Time with Ivy. Time with you to repair the damage he'd caused."

Wolf leaned back, linking his large hands behind her neck, his thumbs tilting her chin up so she had no choice but to meet his gaze.

"Christmas isn't just about family and love and celebrating both. It's also about birth, new beginnings. Letting go of what was and welcoming the new. You might not be in the place to completely forgive Isaac yet, but I can't think of a better gift to give yourself than letting go of what he cost you and looking at what—who—he gave you. Ivy. Maybe another chance with a father. Accept the gift of forgiveness not for him, but for yourself so you aren't so imprisoned in the past that you can't see the future, see what's ahead of you if only you're brave enough to grab it." He stroked the line of her jaw. "I might be the worst hypocrite to talk to you about forgiveness, but I know it takes courage. That's the thing, Nessie. Of the two of us, I'd place my bet on you any day as the bravest."

He pressed his lips to her forehead, and she closed her eyes. His words echoed in her head, sinking into her heart, her soul. Part of her ached to scratch them out, to deny them. Evict them. But they resonated. And that little girl who rode through neighborhoods lit up with Christmas lights, singing carols—the little girl who'd loved her father with only the passion that a daughter could have for the man who was her first hero—clung to his words. Clung to the seeds of hope buried in them.

She inhaled, easing back and loosening her hold on him. As she opened her eyes, her gaze fell on the tattoo on his chest. Without conscious thought, she touched her fingertips to the inked dog tag. To the name Raylon Brandt.

"Who's Raylon?" she whispered.

Like earlier, he went rigid. One moment, she caressed a flesh-and-blood man, and in the next a statue.

And in the next, thin air.

In several long strides, he crossed the living room and stood in front of a large window, his back to her. For the first time since he'd given her his shirt to put on after they'd peeled themselves off his floor, the cold swept over her bare legs, crept under the hem that hit her midthigh. She rubbed her arms to ward off the cool air, but she could do nothing to combat the chilliness of his rejection.

The age-old, primal sense of self-preservation needled at her to get dressed, walk out that door and leave before he could rebuff her again. She'd shared her thoughts about Isaac with him, and the first personal question she asked, he shut her down? The sting of that hurt more than her pride. It wounded the most vulnerable side of her, which didn't often allow people past the barrier she'd long ago erected.

Yet… She slid off the stool and instead of crossing to the couch where Wolf had tossed her sweater and jeans, she continued past them to the big, silent, leave-it-alone zone he'd formed around himself.

And she crossed that, too.

Heart pounding against her sternum, she swallowed the acid at the back of her throat. He'd called her brave. She didn't feel it as she approached him, pressed her cheek to his back and encircled him with her arms.

He didn't relax against her, and she didn't relax either. The metallic taste of fear poured into her mouth as she waited for him to break her hold and walk away from her again. To reject her offer of comfort. To reject her.

But she held on.

And minutes—hours—passed. Her breathing evened, her heartbeat slowed, and when the rushing in her ears faded, she noticed Wolf had become flesh and bone again. One hand braced against the window, but the other…the other covered both of hers.

She sighed.

And continued to hold on.

"Raylon Brandt was my best friend. And he died because of me."

His low, bald statement fell into the silence of the room like a crash of thunder. But if he expected her to let go, to be disgusted, he'd underestimated her. She knew the man Wolf was; there had to be more to the story. So she waited. And held on.

"After I graduated high school, I didn't know what I wanted to do with my life. I worked at the inn for a year, but when I was nineteen, I decided to enlist in the army. Besides Cole, Raylon had been my best friend since second grade when he and his mother moved to Rose Bend.

Cole had already left for college, and Raylon refused to let me go into the service by myself. That's the kind of friend he was. He didn't think about himself. His concern was all for me. And I didn't try and dissuade him from joining me. I wanted my best friend with me. Because that was the kind of friend I was."

He trailed off, and she didn't need to see his eyes to tell Wolf had traveled back into the past. That even though he stared out his window, in his mind's eye, he was seeing his best friend again. Seeing that time when they'd been young and innocent. Invincible.

"Carol, Raylon's mother, didn't want him to go. He was all she had—his father had died when he was three. But I promised her I'd watch out for him as I'd been doing since we met on the playground and Bobby Lutrell tried to steal Raylon's Batman Pez dispenser." His faint chuckle quickly faded, and his grip on her hands tightened. "I swore I'd protect her son and bring him home to her. I didn't keep that promise."

Tension coiled so tight in him she could imagine his muscles turning like cogs in a machine, grinding, pulling. She curled her body around him, willing the strength that he'd offered her so many times into him. Something bad was coming. Something that had left that hollow note in his voice. That brokenness in his spirit. That memorial tattoo over his heart.

Never mind, part of her silently begged him. *I should've minded my own business. You don't have to do this.*

But the other half, which understood the nature of wounds and their care, remained quiet and let him continue. Let him purge this festering sore that she suspected he hadn't shared with many people—if anyone.

Flipping their hands, she covered one of his with both of hers, clasping it, telling him without words that she had him.

He didn't glance down, didn't remove his gaze from that window. But he did clutch her hands.

"We were both sent to Iraq and stationed together in Karbala. I enjoyed serving. It gave me purpose, direction, what I didn't have at home. And I met some of the best men and women, who became brothers and sisters to me. Plus, I had my best friend beside me. Four years. Four years we were together. Then, one day, my unit was in a convoy moving from FOB Spiker to FOB Duke. As we traveled through one of the smaller villages, we were pinned down by insurgents. Because we were in the first Humvee, we were hit along with the last one. I'll never forget the sound of bullets hitting the metal frame. We couldn't move. We couldn't... move. The firefight lasted for...hours," he rasped. "That's how long it seemed, but in truth, it was only about fifteen minutes. But a fight that takes the life of three of my friends—my brothers—including Raylon, should've lasted hours. It should've been so much goddamned longer than fucking minutes to snatch their laughter, their dreams, their futures, away."

He dragged in a serrated breath that hurt her own throat. Shaking his other hand loose, he flattened that palm against the window, too, leaning all his weight onto his arms. Head bowed, his big body trembled, but he didn't utter a sound.

But that jagged inhalation and the tremors shaking his frame told their own tales.

"We immediately sent out chatter about being pinned down, but because of how far away we were from the FOB, it took a couple of hours for air and then ground support to reach us. The parajumper medics carried me and the other injured away, but ground support retrieved the..." He swallowed, cleared his throat. But when he spoke again, his voice was just as hoarse. Maybe more so. "The dead— Raylon. For the first time since we'd enlisted, we weren't together. And we'd never be again."

Nessa gasped, shifting away from him, her gaze running over him in a frantic search. *Carried me and the other injured away...* With only his jeans on, most of him was revealed to her. But she saw no scars, no raised skin, no lighter or shiny patches.

"You were hurt?" She circled him, slipping between him and the glass. "Where? What happened?"

Terror spiked within her as if the injury had happened eight hours ago instead of years. The thought of him lying there, in pain, bleeding. Dying... Not this vibrant, larger-than-life man. She couldn't imagine a world where he wasn't in it. She patted his shoulders, sliding her palms down his chest, his torso, gripping his waist.

He emitted a harsh, almost ugly chuckle, slowly straightening and lowering his arms to his sides. "I was shot in the knee. A bullet can go through metal like butter and the shrapnel is a bitch." He shook his head, the caustic tone like sandpaper over her skin. But he didn't shift away from her touch. No, he leaned into it, into her. "I had to get a knee replacement and then I was shipped home. Without an army career. And without my best friend."

"I'm so sorry, Wolf. Jesus, I'm so sorry."

"But just as bad as losing Raylon," he continued, as if she hadn't spoken. "Just as bad was facing Carol Brandt, looking her in the eye and telling her that I'd failed. I'd failed to protect her son. I'd failed to keep my promise. I'd failed both her and Raylon."

"That's not true." She grasped the waistband of his jeans,

jerked it. "That's just not true, Wolf. And no one would ever believe that or blame you."

"See, now *that's* not true." A faint, mocking smile curved his mouth. "Carol told me herself after I returned home that it was my fault that her son died out there in that desert, for not bringing him home to her. And even though I've been giving her every one of my combat disability checks for the last six years, trying to make up for what I took from her, it'll never be enough. I'll never be enough."

"Grief and pain," Nessa said, letting go of him and wrapping an arm around her waist. "She lashed out because of grief and pain, and you can't place any stock in anything she said in that time. And you also can't hold that against her."

She stumbled back a step, her back hitting the window.

"Nessa," he murmured, reaching for her, but she shook her head, holding up a hand.

"No, people say mean, ugly things when they're hurt. When Mom told me about Isaac not being my real father, I—I accused her of being selfish, a liar, of not loving me. I threw a fucking temper tantrum and hurled some very hurtful words at her, a dying woman who had given me everything, sacrificed everything. But in that moment, all I could think about was my pain, my confusion, my grief over her news combined with losing her to cancer. I left her hospital room with that hanging between us. When I returned a couple of hours later, she was gone."

"Baby," Wolf breathed.

"We say things…" Her breath shoved in and out of her chest in sharp pants. "We say things we don't mean when we're hurt," she reiterated. "And you can't hold it against us."

"No one holds it against you," he whispered.

"Because I didn't mean it."

"I know you didn't, baby."

Nessa blinked. "We're not talking about me."

Wolf closed in on her and cupped her face. She cuffed his wrists with her fingers but didn't push him away. No, she hung on.

"No, we're talking about me," he softly agreed.

"Yes, and I'm telling you, Carol didn't mean it when she blamed you. You need to forgive her, and most importantly, you have to forgive yourself. War is…hell. On the men and women who serve and put their lives on the line for us, for our country. On their families, who sacrifice and have to wait at home not knowing if they will ever see their husbands, wives, daughters, sons, mothers or fathers again. They're heroes, too, and it's unfair that those soldiers are sometimes the martyrs, as well."

She shook her head despite his hold on her, her grip on him tightening.

"But the truth is, just as you knew there was a chance you might die, so did Raylon. It's the horrible nature of war, and there was nothing you could've done to prevent it. You're not God, Wolf. You're not all-knowing, all-powerful. And since you're not, there's no way you could've divined the future to throw yourself in front of that bullet for Raylon. Although I believe without any doubt that if you could've, you would've."

She turned her head into his palm. Kissed it. And released one of his wrists to place her hand over his tattoo, over his heart.

"You said the best gift I could give myself this Christmas would be forgiveness. I think the best gift you could give Carol Brandt—and yourself—this Christmas would be releasing her from those rash, grief-stricken words. And releasing yourself from the burden of them." She lightly traced the dog tag and the name of the man who'd been Wolf's best friend. And whose death was the source of such great guilt and pain. "I'll try if you try. Deal?"

"Deal."

He tilted her head farther back, his emerald gaze dark with shadows but warm. So warm she could trick herself into imagining something more than affection swam there. She lowered her lashes, not willing to trick herself. He stroked his thumbs over her cheekbones, the slightly abraded skin sending a shiver through her.

"Look at me, Nessie." The order, though gentle, carried a thin vein of steel underneath it, and she met his eyes again. "She knew you loved her."

He skimmed his lips over tears she hadn't realized had tracked down her face. Brushed a kiss that tasted of those tears over her mouth.

"Just like Raylon knew you loved him."

He didn't say anything. But he nodded.

For now, it was a start.

For both of them.

She parted her lips under his, accepting the slow, tender thrust of his tongue. Giving her own in return. This kiss, unlike their others, was a quiet storm. Furious but gentle. Carnal but warm. Rising on her tiptoes, she opened wider for him. Angled her head and took him deeper. Surrendered to him even as she demanded he do the same for her.

And he did.

He tangled with her, plunging over and over. But then acquiescing to her questing flicks and sucks. His hands roamed over her. Touched everywhere. Her hair. Her neck and shoulders. Her breasts. Her hips. Her ass and thighs.

In between her thighs.

Oh God. Her head tipped back, breaking that lush kiss. She whimpered as those blunt-tipped fingers dipped and stroked. Rubbed and circled. Pressed and penetrated.

Gripping his arms, she dug her fingernails into his skin, holding on.

"Wolf, please."

But he seemed to be past hearing her pleas. He fell to his knees before her, his hands grasping the front of his shirt, and with one twist, wrenched open the front. Buttons scattered, and excitement screamed through her. He hovered on the edge, their emotional conversation having shoved him there. He needed this outlet, this physical release.

And she would be that vessel for him.

In the mudroom, he'd offered her his body for her use.

Here, in his living room, with shadows and lust darkening his eyes, she'd offer him the same.

Tunneling her fingers through his hair, she hummed low in her throat at the sensation of all that thick, cool silk on her skin as she held him to her. His mouth skimmed between her breasts, pausing to draw on each nipple until she twisted against him. Harsh pants escaped her as he traced a damp path lower down her belly, over her hip until he tongued the crease where her thigh and torso met.

Fuck. She almost didn't survive this the first time. She might pass over into glory and meet her ancestors this time. But *oh God.* She sank her teeth into her bottom lip as he nuzzled her soaked folds. She was willing to make the sacrifice.

Using his thumbs, Wolf parted her, exposed her. And then devoured her. Her back thumped against the wall, and she gave herself over to his lips, his tongue, his fingers. He held nothing back, and neither did she. For every lick, she gave him a whimper. For every suck, she offered up a cry. For every thrust of his fingers, she gifted him with a buck of her hips.

And for an orgasm, she gave him part of her soul. Or at least it felt like it.

Rising to his feet, Wolf grasped the back of her thighs and lifted her in his arms. The rest of his cabin flew by in a blur as he strode from the living room, down the hall and into a bedroom. In moments, he gently deposited her on his bed, grabbed a condom from a bedside drawer and shed his jeans.

He climbed onto the mattress and, with her as a rapt audience, quickly sheathed himself.

She held her arms out to him.

And he fell into them.

Burying his face into her neck, he slammed inside her, filling her, stretching her. God, branding her. Arms wound tight around him, she breathed deep, holding still, letting her body become accustomed to this delicious invasion all over again.

Fisting his thick hair, she pulled his head up. Eyes so dark with passion they appeared almost black, she waited until he focused on her, wanting his attention. Needing him to hear her. Understand her.

"Don't hold back with me. Use me. Take what you need from me." She leaned forward, kissed him. Hard. Nipped his bottom lip even harder. "I don't want gentle."

Something shifted in his expression, and a tingle of feminine apprehension flashed through her, followed quickly by lust so bright it rivaled the sun.

Dragging his head down, she whispered in his ear, "I can take it, Wolf."

Maybe he needed that permission from her. Maybe he'd been waiting on it. Or maybe he'd already been on a tattered, crumbling edge. Didn't matter. Because he let go. He let go all over her.

His hips drew back, torturing her with a slow, heavy glide over sensitive muscles. Then he snapped forward, plunging inside her and nearly nailing her into the mattress. Over and over, he rode her, his big hands cupping her ass, holding her aloft at the angle he deemed perfect. Which, *God yes*, was absolutely perfect.

Just as she'd promised him, she took it. Gladly. Willingly. He pounded into her, showing her body no mercy, and she didn't want any. She craved this special brand of hurt. Of sensual torture. And when he reached between them and pinched her clit, sending her shattering, she held nothing back, embracing the pleasure. Embracing the dark.

Trusting him to soften her fall.

Promising she would do the same for him.

Even if only for now. Because that's all they could be for each other.

Right now.

CHAPTER SEVENTEEN

WOLF FROWNED DOWN into his cup of hot cider. He didn't really care for hot cider.

But either they'd added something special this year—and by *special* he meant something with proof after it—or he was really thirsty, because this was actually good.

He sipped the drink again, turning around and surveying The Glen. Instead of multicolored Christmas lights, bulbs in the shape of candles adorned the posts and booths of the market. The switch in decoration created an almost ethereal effect of a world lit up by candlelight. Perfect for Rose Bend's annual Candlelight Walk.

In honor of Christmases past when there were only candles to light houses and the town, Rose Bend's citizens gathered together with lit candles and walked a mile from the top of Barrow Road to The Glen, the high school and middle school choirs leading the way, singing carols. Once the procession reached the field at the end of Main Street and Barrow Road, a Christmas market with booths selling everything from cider to stockings to ornaments and other crafts dotted the area. The aroma of roasting chestnuts and freshly baked cookies filled the air, along with laughter, chatter and more singing from carolers.

It was one of Wolf's favorite Yulefest events.

"Do I want to know what you're over here scowling

about?" Cole snorted, strolling up to him, Patience cradled to his chest in her carrier.

Wolf smiled down at his niece, rubbing his knuckle over her soft, chubby cheek. She blinked her brown eyes, yawned, then went back to sucking her tiny fist. And it was adorable. Hell, everything his niece did was adorable.

"This cider. I swear it's spiked. Otherwise, I see no reason for it to be this good."

Cole laughed. "Wilma Long was in charge of it this year, so there's no telling."

Wilma Long, owner of the Book Nook, was one of the kindest women in town and had run the town's bookstore for as long as Wolf could remember. She was also rumored to have the largest stash of moonshine in three counties.

"That explains a lot." Wolf grinned, taking another long sip. "I might have to get another two or three cups to go." He nodded at Patience. "You on baby duty tonight?"

"Yeah, Sydney's hanging with Leo since she's actually taking a night off from the inn. I think Moe threatened her with the spoon if she didn't 'get the hell out from under her feet.' Her words, not mine. Not that I mind."

Cole smiled down at the baby, a look of such love on his face, Wolf cleared his throat of the emotion suddenly clogging it. Patience might technically be Cole's stepdaughter, but he didn't treat her that way. He loved her as if he'd fathered her.

"Sydney mentioned that Daniel and his wife are arriving next week for Christmas," Wolf said, cocking his head with a smirk. "Careful. Last time he was here I actually heard him compliment Rose Bend's cleanliness." Wolf snickered. Sydney's ex-husband and Patience's father, though a pretty good guy, had a bit of a stick up his ass. "He might fall for Rose Bend during Christmas and decide to move here."

Cole grinned. "If that happens, I would be happy for Patience that her father is even closer to her. But I might have to join that yoga class Cher has been bugging me about to learn deep-breathing techniques. And meditation. And I might secretly take up day drinking."

"C'mon, man." Wolf clapped him on the shoulder. "I'm your brother. I'd never let you drink alone."

They laughed, and as Patience let out a soft coo and Cole tended to her, Wolf surveyed The Glen once more.

"You did good, Cole," he murmured. "Real good."

Cole glanced up from his daughter, scanning the booths and crowd in the pseudocandlelight, a satisfied smile curling his mouth.

"Not just me, but yeah. It is all good. I'm proud of what we've accomplished."

"You should be. Between the motorcycle rally, the building of the new elder and children center and this bigger Yulefest, you're already one of the better mayors this town has had. And I'm not just saying that because you're my brother."

Cole nodded. "Thanks, man. That means a lot. Thank you."

Wolf sipped more cider, eyeing his brother over the rim of the cup. "Should we hug now?"

His brother's loud bark of laughter elicited a surprised squeal from the baby, which he immediately smoothed. Lightly bouncing the baby, Cole chuckled. "I'm going to pass. But what about Nessa?" He hiked his chin in the direction over Wolf's shoulder, a smirk riding his mouth. "You been…hugging it out with her?"

"Really?" Wolf scoffed. "As mayor, aren't you above gossip?"

"Have you met our family? No," Cole said, arching an

eyebrow. "And nice job trying to deflect. Not that it's going to work. Is there something going on between you two?"

Wolf searched the crowds of people, and as if she were a beacon drawing his attention, located Nessa among them. She stood with Sydney, Leo, Cecille Lapuz, the owner of the ice cream shop, and Flo. Nessa had her head thrown back, laughing at something. The sight of that amusement and her uninhibited freedom in showing it had his throat tightening. Just a couple of weeks ago, she hadn't been capable of displaying that carefree display of emotion.

No, he corrected himself. She hadn't been willing to display it. Hadn't felt safe enough to. But now, in this town, surrounded by his family and friends, she did. And it…it…

Fuck, he was scared to admit what it did to him.

It'd been a little over a week since she'd come to his cabin and they'd agreed to the terms of their temporary friends-with-benefits arrangement. Since they'd had sex. Since he'd told her about Raylon, and she'd comforted him.

And the last eight days had been—amazing. Not just the sex, which, God yes, was better than any he'd had. But it was more than that. She'd become his friend. He hadn't been able to talk to his parents or his brother and sisters about Raylon and Carol. Yet he'd opened up to Nessa. About what happened with Olivia. About Raylon and his death. Maybe because she understood pain and loss. Maybe because of her no-nonsense manner, which invited honesty and didn't allow him to lie.

Maybe because he trusted her in a way he'd found difficult since returning home from Iraq.

This woman called to his protective nature, his sexual side and his brokenness.

She made him want to…heal.

And she scared him more than Olivia ever had.

That fear of disappointing her, of failing her, haunted him like that proverbial shoe just dangling by the laces, waiting to drop.

Because the last decade had taught him that loving someone meant failing them.

And watching them walk away.

It was as inevitable as the sun rising in the east and sinking in the west.

"Wolf?"

Wolf jerked his head back toward his brother, who studied him with a small frown.

"Yeah?"

"You okay?" Cole glanced in the direction Wolf had been staring, catching sight of the small group of women. "I guess that answers my question."

"What question?" he hedged.

Cole snorted. "You're such a shit liar. You damn well know what question. How deep are you?"

Wolf sighed. "She's not staying, Cole. She's leaving after Christmas."

"That's not what I asked you."

"That's my answer," he snapped, then dragged a hand down his face and beard. "Shit, sorry. We're... We're friends. Are we...involved? Yeah. But we both know it can't go anywhere. She's going back to Boston, and I'm—"

"And you're too afraid to risk your heart again."

Anger flashed through Wolf, lightning quick and hot. Before he could say anything, though, Cole chuckled.

"Yeah, I know. I'm a smug bastard and really don't deserve to preach to you. But I'm the most qualified because I've been where you are. And it's only fair since you tried to do the same for me. Payback is a bitch." His smile faded, and his gaze searched Wolf's. And try as he might, Wolf couldn't avoid the concern in Cole's eyes. Neither could he begrudge his brother that concern. Not when it came from a place of love. "I almost let Sydney go because of fear. Fear of what I could lose again instead of focusing on all that she could bring me. Love. Joy. A second chance. A family."

Cole stroked a hand down Patience's head, and Wolf didn't need to be a mind reader to guess that his brother's thoughts dwelled on another baby. One who'd died in childbirth along with his first wife. Yes, Cole had been blessed with another child to love, another opportunity to be a father.

"I don't want to even think about where I'd be if I'd let her go. If I hadn't decided loving her and Patience was worth the risk of being hurt again. Wolf, I remember how Olivia's leaving hurt you. And I also remember how that was kind of swept under the rug by me, the family and you when Tonia and Mateo died. I'm sorry for that. All of these years, I never did get the chance to apologize for that. I'm sorry, because even though Olivia didn't die, that pain…" Cole shook his head. "But I've watched you and Nessa these last few weeks. For the first time in years, I've seen something in you. You're happy. And it's because of her. I don't want you to lose that shot at a future with her, at love instead of fear."

Love.

Inside, Wolf shrank from that word like it hissed and rattled at him. No.

No.

"I appreciate the advice. No, I'm serious, Cole, I do," he said when Cole frowned. "But you're mistaken. That's not the kind of—" *arrangement* "—relationship we have. It's temporary. We went into this with an expiration date, so there wouldn't be any misunderstandings or hurt feelings when she leaves after Christmas. Neither of us want more than that."

"Wolf, I don't—"

"Excuse me. I'm sorry to interrupt," a gruff voice said.

Both Wolf and Cole turned and met the serious light brown gaze belonging to Garrett Adams. Surprise jolted through Wolf. The handsome older man wasn't exactly a recluse, as he owned Little Bird Ski Lodge and enjoyed a brisk business, but he didn't come down off his mountain into town that often. Especially to events like the festival, although the lodge hosted the Noel Dance every year. But even then, Garrett only made an appearance and then disappeared, letting his staff run it.

Cole extended his hand toward the older man. "Hello, Garrett. Good to see you."

"Yes, you, too." Garrett shook it, then repeated the gesture with Wolf. "Wolf."

"Garrett. How're you doing?"

"Fine." The older man nodded, then looked at Cole. "Can I borrow you for a couple of minutes? I dropped by your office but forgot there was an event tonight, so stopped by here on the off chance we could speak. I promise not to take up too much of your time."

"Sure," Cole said. "Let me just hand off the baby to my wife and I'll be right back. We can go grab a coffee and talk. Be right back."

He strode off, and Wolf and Garrett watched as he approached Sydney and her group.

"Well, I'll let you two handle your—"

"Who is that?" Garrett interrupted. Wolf glanced at him, a little taken aback at the abrupt tone. But Garrett's attention remained focused on where Cole stood with the small circle of women. "The woman with Cole's wife, your sisters and Mrs. Lapuz. Is she new in town?"

"Nessa?" Confusion swarmed Wolf at not just the question, but the intensity radiating off the other man. Why would Garrett Adams, of all people, care? "She's a guest at Kinsale Inn. Her and her sister. Why? Do you know her?"

"What?" Garrett jerked his gaze back to Wolf and blinked. "No. How could I?" He shook his head as if trying to clear it. "She just didn't look familiar."

Wolf studied Garrett's face, but the man turned away to meet Cole, who strode over toward them.

"Ready?" Cole asked. "Wolf, we'll talk later, okay?"

"Yeah, sure," Wolf murmured, still unable to shake the unnerving sensation that he'd missed something here with Garrett.

Before he could figure it out or analyze it further, the two men walked off, leaving him alone. He stared after them for several more seconds before heading off toward the middle of The Glen and the Christmas Wishing Well, another Rose Bend tradition. From this night until Christmas Eve, people could throw their Christmas wishes into the well, and town legend had it that the wish would come true. When he'd been a kid, there hadn't been one Christmas season where he'd missed tossing a folded piece of paper with a written wish into the well. A new bike one year. His own room the next. A kiss from Laura Haddock another. Some years he'd received his wish, and some he hadn't.

The last time he tossed a note into that well had been the Christmas before he enlisted in the army.

Before he could question what the hell he was doing, he reached into his back jeans pocket for his wallet and drew out a scrap of paper and pulled a pen from his coat pocket. Quickly, he scribbled down a note, folded the paper and tossed it into the well.

How old am I again?

"I don't think I've seen you do that since high school."

Olivia appeared next to him, peering down into the well before tipping her head to the side and smiling at him. "Feeling a bit of Christmas nostalgia?"

Wolf returned her smile, and for the first time since Olivia returned, it didn't feel forced or stiff. Inside, he stilled, and waited for the familiar tightness that seized him when he encountered Olivia. That suffocating sense of failure. That grimy stain of unworthiness.

Yes, something deep within him twinged, like an echo, but mostly…nothing.

The curious sensation left him a little disoriented. But when a person existed with the heavy load of shame and resentment for so long, being free of the burden would leave him off balance.

"Maybe a little." He shrugged a shoulder. "How're you, Olivia?"

"Good, Wolf. Thank you for asking," she murmured. "Do you have another piece of paper, by chance?"

He pulled out his wallet again, found an old drugstore receipt and handed it to her along with a pen. She accepted both and, turning her body just enough to shield what she wrote, jotted something down, folded the slip of paper and threw it in the well.

"Thanks," she said, passing him the pen. He stuffed it back in his coat pocket. "I'll tell you mine if you tell me yours," she offered with a small grin.

"Isn't that supposed to make the wish null and void?"

"I think that only pertains to wishes on stars and birthday cakes."

"Too many rules to keep straight."

She laughed. "I missed this," she softly admitted. "Us laughing together. Teasing each other. The easiness between us. I missed *you*, Wolf."

"Olivia…" He needed to stop this before it went any further.

"No, Wolf, please." She held up a hand. "Please let me finish. I've tried to respect your space and not press anything, because God knows I'm the one who broke us. I owed you that time. But the last few weeks, I have to be honest, I've been getting more and more scared that I've waited too long."

Christ, he *really* needed to stop this. "Olivia," he tried again. "You don't want to do this."

"I have to try," she insisted. "Because I returned home for you. And I feel like you're slipping through my fingers."

She held her hands out, palms up, fingers spread wide. Even though alarm at her words crept through him, sympathy swirled inside him, as well. Because pain drenched her eyes, her voice. While she'd broken his heart years ago, seeing her hurt didn't bring him any joy.

"Wolf, I left Rose Bend chasing a life I believed I wanted. And yes, Boston revealed some things to me. Mostly about myself. And I did enjoy my job and the city. In the end, I think I did need to experience it. But without the person I loved, it all seemed like shades of gray instead of living in full color. I convinced myself I'd get over you, that I could let you go. But I was fooling myself. It took me three years to gather my courage, to get rid of my pride and ask you to forgive me."

Shock rippled through him, and he turned away from her, swearing under his breath. Three years ago, hell, maybe a year ago, he would've given anything to hear these words from her. To somehow grant him redemption and prove that he hadn't failed in being enough for her. In being who she needed—a provider, a protector.

Yet, now… Now, he didn't need that validation from her.

If he ever did.

A different, deeper level of shock ricocheted inside him, leaving him bracing his body before he stumbled backward, and his ass hit the ground.

He'd *never* needed her validation.

You're not God, Wolf. You're not all-knowing, all-powerful.

Why those particular words from his conversation with Nessa echoed in his head at this moment, he didn't know, but they resonated in his chest, his soul. Who was he kidding? He knew why. Because all this time, when he'd been taking on the guilt of Raylon's death, the blame for not protecting him and failing to bring him home to Carol, the shame of not being enough to keep Olivia here—all this time he'd been playing God. As if he, Wolf Dennison, sat on some celestial throne and determined life and death and free will. For all these years, he'd had a savior complex, when he was no one's savior. Just a man. A fallible man who did the best he could.

He thrust his hand over his hair, knocking his hat off. He barely noticed it falling to the ground and didn't bother picking it up. One couldn't be concerned with such inconsequential things when one was having an existential crisis. The "one" being him.

The air he dragged into his lungs tasted clean, fresh... free.

For the first time in eight long years. And that scrap of paper he'd thrown in the well on a whim? It suddenly veered further from the realm of foolish wishful thinking into—possibilities.

"Wolf, are you okay?"

His head jerked, and he snapped out of his thoughts. Hell. He'd forgotten all about Olivia.

"Yeah, I'm good. And look, you don't need to ask my

forgiveness. You made a decision that was best for your life. Did it hurt? Yeah, but I couldn't ask you to put aside your dreams for me. It wouldn't have been fair. And you shouldn't beat yourself up over it now."

"You mean that?" she whispered, eyes glistening.

"I do. Not going to lie. It took me a minute to get there, but I do. Now, if you'll excuse me…"

He took a step backward, the urge to see Nessa as soon as possible riding him hard. There was something he needed to tell her. To ask her.

Starting with *I love you.*

Yeah, that word he'd been afraid to think even minutes ago when Cole had mentioned it. The same word that had brought him so much heartache and pain, he'd shied away from it. But his brother had been right. He'd rather risk the pain for what they could have, for who they could be, than watch her walk away from him because he was too afraid to try.

Oh fuck.

He loved her.

"I love you."

Shit, did I say that aloud? But staring down into Olivia's expectant face, catching the nervous twisting of her gloved hands, he had his answer. Not him. Her.

His gut twisted. And sorrow punched him in the chest. Because he was going to hurt her. There was no avoiding this. At one time, he'd been on the receiving end of this rejection, and he took no pleasure on inflicting that pain.

"I love you, Wolf," she repeated, shifting closer to him and setting a hand on his forearm. "I'll tell you my wish that I threw in. Part of it has already come true. You forgave me. But I want us to be happy again. Together. In love. With that family we always talked about. I want the happily-ever-after. With you."

Before he could gently inform her that what she desired couldn't be, that he loved another woman, Olivia gripped his arms, surged up on her toes and kissed him.

Icy wave after wave of surprise crashed over him.

Wrong.

It was *so wrong*.

It wasn't Nessa's mouth on him.

Precious seconds passed as the frigid talons of shock gripped him, paralyzing him, and Olivia softly moaned, pressing her lips harder to his. Parting hers…

"No." Voice harsher than he intended, he grabbed her shoulders and set her away from him. "Olivia, no."

"I—" She blinked, her fingertips lifting to her mouth, confusion and arousal gleaming in her eyes. "I thought you—"

"Wolf."

He turned away from Olivia at the low murmur of his name, meeting his sister's wide, solemn gaze. Leo shifted slightly, and Wolf glanced away from her, noticing the silent woman standing beside her.

Nessa.

Nessa had seen Olivia kissing him.

Fear clawed at him.

"Nessa, it's not…" *…what it looks like.* Fuck. He cringed as the words of every busted guilty man reverberated in the air. He took a step toward her, his hand outstretched. "Nessa."

That shuttered, cold expression had terror and sorrow slicing through him, damn near cleaving him in half. He'd fucked up. It didn't matter that he hadn't kissed Olivia first or invited it. In his mind, he could picture what it had

looked like. What those few moments of him being stunned
had cost him.

And for a woman who didn't trust easily, had been
let down, hurt and abandoned by the men in her life, she
wouldn't grant him the benefit of the doubt.

She would just break off their arrangement early and
cut her losses.

Cut him off.

But dammit. *Dammit*, he had to try. He had to…try.

"Baby, give me a minute, please? Talk to me," he whispered, his fingers tingling, aching with the need to touch
her. Hold her.

"Later," she said, her voice even. No, flat. "I should go
find Ivy and check on her." Giving Leo a nod, she pivoted
on her heel and walked away.

Damn that. She had to listen—

"Let her go, Wolf," Leo murmured, her hand encircling
his upper arm, stopping him from following Nessa. "Just
give her some time. As someone who's been on the receiving end of—" she glanced behind him to Olivia, then returned her gaze to him "—this before, I can promise you,
going after her and pushing a confrontation is only going
to make things worse, not better."

"There isn't any *this*," he insisted. "Shit." He scrubbed
both palms down his face. But he heeded his sister's advice
and didn't go after Nessa. Whirling around, he linked both
his fingers behind his neck, staring down at the ground. "I
know what it looked like. But I didn't kiss Olivia. I would
never do that to Nessa. I—"

He broke off. Damn if he would tell his sister he loved
Nessa when he hadn't even told her yet.

"Yeah, I know," Leo said, and he shot her a sharp look.
She shrugged, a wry smile lifting a corner of her mouth.

"I've had twenty-seven years to make a study of you, Wolf. I know when my brother is in love with someone."

"Wolf." Olivia touched his arm, and this time he flinched, pulling away from her. "I didn't think…"

"No, you didn't," Leo snapped, moving next to Wolf and clasping his hand in hers. "I'm not going to accuse you of staging that whole thing and sabotaging him and Nessa. I'll give you credit for that, although considering who you're friends with, maybe I shouldn't. But you, especially as a woman, know better than to take what isn't given without permission."

"You're right." Olivia shook her head. "Wolf, I'm sorry. And I didn't know you and Nessa were… Or I didn't want to think you were… I can find her. Talk to her. Tell her what happened."

"No." He rubbed at his chest, but nothing alleviated the constriction, the constant flare of pain. Part of him wanted to tell her she'd done more than enough, but what would it serve? "I appreciate the offer, but no." Gently extricating his hand from Leo's, he pulled her closer and kissed her forehead. "I'm going to head back to the inn. Maybe…"

What? Wait for Nessa there? Ambush her? Yeah, everything inside Wolf roared at him to do just that. But just as Leo had said to Olivia, he couldn't take what Nessa wasn't offering. Whether that was conversation, her touch…

Her heart.

Just like he couldn't make her love him, he couldn't force her to stay either.

CHAPTER EIGHTEEN

NESSA HIT THE "end call" button on her cell, concluding her conversation with Beverly, her mom's best friend. Tossing the phone to the mattress behind her, she cursed under her breath and paced the space between the window and the bed.

"Where is it?" she muttered, rubbing her hands up and down her arms. "Where could it be?"

The box her mom's friend had promised to send should've been here a week ago. After Wolf shared the disappointing info he'd received from Eva Wright, that box had become more important than ever. Beverly promised she'd mailed it out last week, and she'd also tracked the package. The postal service website showed a delivery date of four days ago here at the inn. A couple of days ago, she'd checked with Sinead and Moe, and neither of them had accepted a package. Nessa had even gone to the post office yesterday, and all they could tell her was it'd been delivered.

Where. Was. It?

She came to a halt, threading her fingers through her hair and whimpered. She needed the box. It was her last connection to her mother. It might have the answers she needed. Dimly, she acknowledged that part of her urgency could be attributed to the need to distract herself from Wolf and the memory of Olivia's mouth on him. From the devastation that had streaked through her like a forest fire, leaving her in ashes right there in The Glen.

From the shattering knowledge that she'd opened herself again.

That she'd let her guard down and let Wolf in like she'd never even allowed Jeremy. She'd known—*she'd known*—Wolf would be far more destructive. That he was an atomic bomb that would change the very landscape of her life, leaving her nothing like who she'd been. Unrecognizable. And still, she hadn't stopped, hadn't heeded.

She'd lied to herself, had broken the promise to herself, and was now paying the price.

A sob welled up in her chest, scrabbling for her throat, but she swallowed it back down. Tears hadn't stopped Isaac from walking out on their family. Tears hadn't kept her mother from dying. Tears hadn't changed the fact of Jeremy leaving.

They wouldn't change anything now.

"Nessa?"

Swiping at the tears she'd already deemed useless, she turned to find her sister standing on the other side of the bed.

"Hey, Ivy." She tried to inject a cheer into her voice, but when the preteen narrowed her eyes on her, Nessa assumed she failed. Miserably.

"Are you okay?"

"I'm fine." When Ivy's mouth flattened and she glanced away from her, Nessa sank to the wide window seat, suddenly exhausted. Of the pretense. Of the lies. *Fuck it.* "No, Ivy, I'm not okay. I'm actually kind of sad."

Surprise flashed through Ivy's dark eyes, the same surprise that echoed inside of Nessa. Well, that had popped out. Her lips forming a little "o," Ivy rounded the bed and perched on the end of the mattress, across from Nessa.

"Is this about Wolf?" she asked.

Nessa tried and failed to contain a flinch at the sound of his name. Hadn't she always said Ivy was too perceptive? But then again, since they'd arrived in Rose Bend, Nessa had spent time with him. Even more so in the last two weeks. So it would probably be obvious to Ivy when Nessa hadn't gone near him.

"Yes," she admitted. No point in lying to her. "But it's nothing you need to worry about, okay? Friends argue, just like you do with yours. We'll be fine."

Well, so much for lying to Ivy.

"True." Ivy shrugged a shoulder. "Except I don't kiss Sonny or Cher."

Nessa stared at her. Then snorted. "Okay, you got that one. But I'm serious, I don't want you to think about me or Wolf. You're here in Rose Bend to enjoy Christmas. And in spite of all that's happened lately, you're still a kid. A kid who should enjoy this holiday and not think about adult issues. Just like your father wanted."

"Our father," Ivy whispered. "And you, too. He wanted you to enjoy Christmas here, too."

"Yeah, me, too." Isaac had his own reasons for sending her here, but yes, it'd been a gift he'd hoped she find and hopefully love. "But honestly, I'm a little upset about a package my mom's friend mailed out to me. It was supposed to have arrived here at the inn. I can't find it."

"A package? What was in it?"

"It was a bunch of my mother's personal items. After she, uh," she paused, swallowed. "After she died, I couldn't bring myself to go through them yet, so I brought them with me to your house when I moved in. But now, the box seems to have disappeared. No one can find it. Not the post office. Moe. I don't know where it could've gone, and I'm worried I've lost— Ivy? What…?"

But her sister wasn't listening. She'd climbed down off the bed and hunkered down at the bottom. Lifting the long bedskirt, she pulled out a white postal box with Nessa's name printed on the label.

"Ivy?" Stunned, and still a little disbelieving, Nessa shifted her gaze from the box to her sister. "How did you…?"

"I'm sorry," Ivy whispered, picking up the package and placing it on the window seat beside Nessa. "I didn't know it was your mom's things. I wouldn't have kept it from you if I'd known. I found it on the porch a few days ago and brought it upstairs and hid it under the bed. I know I should've told you, but I thought it might be from work since the return address had Boston on it. I didn't want to go back home yet. And I didn't want you to leave."

Nessa should be pissed. After all, the girl had lied to her. And maybe if the *I didn't want you to leave* would stop echoing in her head over and over, she would be. But it did, and love for her sister—because yes, regardless of blood, this girl was her sister—filled her chest to the point of bursting.

Clearing her throat, she jabbed her a finger at Ivy. "Federal offenses of taking someone's mail aside, you're forgiven. Next time, though—but you promise me there won't be a next time?—I'm pressing charges."

Ivy grinned. "I promise. Besides, they don't allow You-Tube in jail." Hopping off the bed, she grabbed Nessa's car keys off the bedside table and handed them to her. "Here you go."

"Thanks, Ivy."

She accepted the keys, but as eager as she was, she didn't tear into the box. Instead, she splayed her fingers wide on the top. Procrastinating. Yes, she was definitely procrastinating, even though the rapid thudding of her pulse insisted she *hurry, hurry.* And not just because for the first time in eight months, she would touch her mother's belongings. But because some intuition whispered that the key to her search lay in this box.

"Nessa?" Ivy whispered.

But Nessa couldn't tear her focus from the box, from the certainty that as soon as she opened it, everything would change for her.

How long she sat there, hands flattened to the top of the package, staring at it, she didn't know. She didn't even tear her gaze from it when Ivy left the room, the door closing shut behind her. Or when she returned minutes later.

But when a large hand settled on her back, Nessa wasn't shocked. Part of her—that stupid, glutton for punishment part—was perhaps waiting for Wolf to arrive. It didn't surprise her that Ivy had sought him out and brought him up to their room. Regardless of what happened between them the night before—and if she were honest, at some point during the early hours of the sleepless morning, she'd already started questioning the optics of that—he was her friend. He'd been on this journey with her in Rose Bend. It seemed only right that he be here for her when she dived into her past.

And if she were even more honest… She needed him, his strength, in this moment.

Inhaling, she held the breath, then slowly exhaled it. She could do this.

"Here, Nessa." Ivy tucked a tissue in her hand, and wow. When had she started crying? Wiping away the damp

tracks, she picked up the keys, and with her sister and her...
well, Wolf, beside her, she opened the postal package. And
then the carboard box within.

Ivy's thin body pressed against the outside of Nessa's
thigh as she pulled open the flaps. A waterlogged chuckle
escaped her as she removed a program for the one and only
school talent show Nessa entered in the fourth grade. Her
mom had even circled Nessa's name under the group per-
formance of *Annie*'s "It's the Hard-Knock Life." She'd been
one of the nameless orphans.

Setting it aside, she waded through more of her childhood.
Report cards, arts 'n' crafts Mother's Day cards and Christmas ornaments, awards and certifications. Hands shaking,
Nessa stroked a hand over her mother's jewelry box. It'd sat
on her mother's dresser for as long as she could remember.
Lifting the lid, she sifted through the various pieces—some
costume, some not—coming to one she recognized.

She gasped, removing the thin gold chain with the ring.
For as long as Nessa could remember, Evelyn had worn this
necklace and beautiful ring with the setting in the shape
of a rose with a diamond in the middle. Evelyn had only
removed it when she'd gone into the hospital for the last
time. Nessa released the clasp and raised it to her neck.

"Here." Wolf gently took it from her and within moments
it hung around her neck. "It's beautiful."

"Thank you," Nessa whispered. "It was my mom's favorite."

Picking up a lovely charm bracelet, Nessa turned to Ivy.
"This was also one of her favorites. I think she would've
loved for you to have it."

"You don't..." Ivy's gaze jerked from the bracelet to
Nessa. "Really? You don't think she would've minded?
I'm not her daughter."

"You're my sister. She would've insisted," she said, knowing it was the truth in her heart, her spirit. "If you want it, that is. You don't have to—"

"I do." Ivy thrust her arm out. "I'd love it. It's so pretty." She held still as Nessa attached it around her wrist. "I'll never take it off, I promise."

Squeezing her hand, Nessa turned back to the jewelry box and carefully closing the lid, set it aside. Breathing deeply, she brushed her fingertips over a small photo album beneath. It wasn't the one that had occupied her mother's entertainment center. Nessa had packed that, and others, away in storage. This one, with its cream jacket and spiderweb of cracks, was older.

Nessa removed it and opened the cover.

The air whistled from her lungs as if punctured. An old, faded picture of her mother. Young. Early twenties, maybe. And happy. So happy. Her hair in two long braids that fell over her shoulders, she grinned at the camera.

And whoever was behind it.

"Isn't that…" She pointed at the white church with its distinctive steeple in the background.

"St. John's Catholic Church? Yeah." Wolf leaned over her shoulder, his scent a comfort and torment. "This picture was taken in Rose Bend."

"Rose Bend?" Ivy peered at the picture. "Your mom visited here, too?"

"A long time ago," Nessa murmured, touching a fingertip to her mom's smile, forever captured in the image.

"You look like her," Wolf commented.

Nessa nodded. "I got that a lot from people."

A murky jumble of anxiety, excitement and sorrow tangled in her belly. She wanted to continue flipping the pages, but God…she didn't. A little afraid of what she would find.

But she couldn't stop. Not when she had this glimpse into a side of her mother she'd never known.

The next picture was of her mother again, with the mountains in the background, looking more carefree than Nessa had ever seen her. In the next, her mother posed in front of what Nessa recognized as the ice cream shop, though it didn't look the same as it did today. Only this time, she stood with a man. He didn't appear to be that much older than her. Tall, Black, lean but built, handsome. And as he stared down at her mother instead of into the camera, he seemed completely enamored.

She stiffened, shock striking her like a bolt of lightning. Could this be him? Her father? What were the odds that Isaac sent her here on a search for him because her mother had mentioned this was where she'd met him? And then in a photo album that she'd hidden away were pictures of her and a mysterious man in this very town?

She didn't believe in coincidences.

"You think this could be him?" Wolf asked, and it felt eerily like he'd read her mind.

She tipped her head back to find him frowning down at the image. Before she could answer, Ivy jerked her attention from the photo to Nessa.

"Who's 'him'?" she demanded. "Are you talking about your biological father? Is that him?" She pointed at the picture.

The photo album tumbled from Nessa's suddenly numb fingers to her lap as she gaped at the preteen. Dimly, Wolf's low, muttered curse reached her ears.

"You knew?" Nessa rasped, unable to tear her gaze from Ivy. Unable to comprehend the words that Ivy had just stated. White noise roared in Nessa's head, and she shook it in a vain attempt to clear it. "How could you…?

How long…?" Yeah, finishing a complete sentence was beyond her.

Ivy swallowed, uncertainty crossing her expression. Her lashes lowered and her bottom lip trembled. Crossing her thin arms over her chest, she murmured, "I've known for a long time. I overheard Daddy talking to Ben, his lawyer, one night a couple of years ago. Daddy thought I was in bed, but I'd gotten up for water. I kind of—" she squirmed, still not looking at Nessa "—eavesdropped. Daddy was telling Ben that your mom wanted to tell you he wasn't your real father years ago, but Daddy wouldn't let her. Because you were his."

Nessa's lips parted on a soundless gasp. Isaac had been the one against telling her? Because she was…his? He'd loved her. Isaac really had loved her.

She blinked against the fresh sting of tears. Shit. At the rate she was going, she'd be able to water Moe's huge Christmas tree downstairs.

"Why haven't you said anything, Mozart?" Wolf asked gently.

Ivy glanced at Wolf, and a tear rolled down her cheek before she hurriedly brushed it away with the back of her hand.

"Because I didn't want Nessa to leave me, too, if she found out. She's all I have left." Ivy dragged in a shuddering breath and switched her gaze to Nessa. Sorrow drenched her dark, glistening eyes, and her face crumbled. "I know I've been mean to you, Nessa. And I'm sorry. I've just been so mad at Dad for dying. And I'm scared, too. You didn't like me before Dad died and you didn't want to be my guardian. I thought if you knew that Dad wasn't your real father, then you might go and not come back."

"I didn't like you? God, Ivy," Nessa said, cupping the

girl's elbows, tugging her closer, "why in the world would you think that?"

"You didn't come see me," she said in a small voice. A small voice carrying a lot of hurt in it. "Why else would you not come see me?"

"Oh, sweetheart." Nessa stood, setting the photo album aside and pulling her sister into her arms. With a sob, Ivy wrapped her arms around Nessa, and they clung to one another. "Me not coming around had nothing to do with you and everything to do with my stupid stubbornness and pride. Your dad's and my relationship—it was complicated. That's a discussion for another time, but I need you to understand one very important thing, okay?" She drew back and cupped Ivy's damp face, tilting it up so she had no choice but to meet her gaze and see the truth in her eyes. "You were not to blame in any of that. At all. And I'm sorry. I'm so, so sorry if I made you believe for even a second that you were the reason I didn't come around. I love you, Ivy. You might be a know-it-all little shit sometimes, but you're my know-it-all little shit and I love you."

"Language," Ivy whispered, then laughed.

Nessa joined her, the sound light, if more than a little watery. Unable to help herself, Nessa glanced at Wolf, who leaned against the window, watching them, a small smile curving his sensual lips. Catching her eyes on him, he nodded.

"I need to apologize, too, for not telling you the truth, Ivy," Nessa continued. "The mail from the attorney? It was from…Dad." God, it felt so odd calling Isaac that when she'd been referring to him by his first name for the last eight months. "He'd left me a letter containing some information about my biological father. I should've trusted you with the truth, but I was scared of losing you, too, so I convinced myself I was protecting you and didn't tell you. I'm sorry about that. I should've been honest with you."

Ivy hugged her again, pressing her cheek to Nessa's stomach. "It's okay. And I don't care who your real father is. You're my sister."

"You're mine, too. Always."

"I knew I wasn't wrong about why Dad sent us here. Family. Not just so we could both find our fathers, but so we could find us. You and me. Sisters forever."

"See? A know-it-all." Eyes stinging with a fresh wave of tears, Nessa gave her another squeeze and dropped a kiss on top of Ivy's head. Then she pulled Ivy down beside her on the window seat. "Let's keep looking through this album and see what we can find."

She flipped through several more pages, all with more pictures of her mom, some with the man and some without. When they came to the second-to-last picture, Wolf's hand shot out over her shoulder, pinching the corner of the page and preventing her from turning it.

"Wait. I know this place," he said, voice a little strained.

She studied the image. Her mom and the same guy again, their arms around each other. It was the first picture where he either wasn't looking down at her mom or wasn't wearing sunglasses but smiled fully into the camera. She immediately noticed his striking light brown eyes. The couple stood in front of a stone wall that boasted a mantel and large windows. It appeared vaguely familiar.

"Why does it feel like I've seen this place before?" she murmured.

"Because you have." Wolf tapped the stone wall in the background. "The Summerses' place. Or what used to be the Summerses' place but is now Little Bird Ski Lodge. It's the same house that was in Eva's picture. Your mother was there with him... And oh my God, it can't be," he breathed.

"What?" Nessa twisted around to stare up at him, heart thudding against her rib cage. That same sense of the world shifting under her feet when she'd been about to open the box returned. "Wolf, what is it?"

"All this time, in these photos, he seemed familiar to me, but I couldn't place him. But now I can. I know that face." He lifted his attention from the photo to her. "I know who Paul Summers is."

"THIS PLACE IS GORGEOUS." Nessa surveyed the foyer of Little Bird Ski Lodge with more than a little awe. Like a hell of a lot.

And why was she whispering like the place was a church?

Probably because she felt like she'd stepped into one. With its vaulted, beamed ceilings, walls of glass and mounted sconces, it didn't seem far off. And though it was Saturday morning and people gathered in small groups near the two roaring fires or in the sitting areas, the chatter was low, almost respectful. Little Bird Ski Lodge wasn't a party hot spot for winter-break partiers on the make. No, it was an elegant resort for those looking to relax and ski.

"Easy, Nessa." Wolf settled a hand on her lower back, and though she wore her coat, the weight of it burned through the layers to the skin beneath.

She should've moved away from it. After all, she was weaning herself away from becoming dependent on it. Regardless of what happened here at this lodge, she was leaving for Boston in a little over a week.

And even though part of her didn't believe Wolf had instigated that kiss, the sight of it had devastated her. Left her the equivalent of an emotionally demolished building. It'd showed her that in spite of her resolve to not become attached, to keep her heart out of it, she'd screwed up. She'd become entangled, and the longer she remained in Rose Bend, the longer she remained around him, the tighter, the more suffocating, those strings would become.

So yes, she should've moved away from that hand. From him.

But she didn't.

Because, call her weak, but it wasn't every day a person potentially came face-to-face with their long-lost father. So she could be forgiven for leaning on his strength one more time before she cut herself off cold turkey.

A small hand slid over hers, slim fingers enclosing hers. Nessa glanced down at Ivy, and her sister gave her an encouraging smile. Ivy had refused to be left behind at the inn, insisting she be by Nessa's side for whatever she found out.

In spite of the anxiety whirling inside her like a storm, gratefulness for this unexpected turn—this blessing— glowed within her like a warm, welcoming light in the midst of this chaos. When she'd driven across that covered bridge weeks ago, heading into Rose Bend, she'd never imagined she'd be here. And not in a ski lodge about to possibly meet her biological father. Well, yes, that, too. But *here*. In this lovely, special place of sisterhood with Ivy. Even if she never found her father, finding this with Ivy would be worth the trip.

"Let's go see if Garrett is available," Wolf said, guiding them toward the front desk, which ironically, sat at the back of the room.

Nerves strangling her vocal cords, Nessa nodded and followed.

When they neared the desk, the young man behind it

smiled at their trio. It warmed with recognition as his gaze landed on Wolf. "Hey, Wolf. Good morning. You're checking in?"

"Morning, Laurence," he greeted. "No, I wanted to see if Garrett Adams was available. Cole sent me to speak with him about a few details regarding the Noel Dance. It shouldn't take up too much of his time."

"Uh, okay. Let me check." The young man picked up the phone, and a few moments later, replaced the receiver. "He said sure, go on back to his office. You know where it is?"

"I do. Thanks."

With a nod, Wolf led Nessa and Ivy away from the desk and down a hall that branched off the lobby. Though it had obviously been heavily renovated to make the home a commercial building, she could still easily envision it as it had been. The corridor they walked down, with its pretty, cream wallpaper, might have once led to bedrooms or even a den. The graceful sideboard and the polished mirror above it could've been leftover pieces from that time.

What if her mother had slept behind one of these closed doors? What if she'd relaxed or watched TV there?

Sorrow injected its presence on top of her nervousness, and she had to find a way to distract herself before she aborted the mission and bolted for the door.

"I hope this Garrett Adams doesn't think we're nuts for approaching him like this," she said.

"It's a possibility," Wolf conceded, and she shot him a glare. "But I doubt it. His face when he saw you the other night at The Glen? At first, I couldn't pinpoint it, but now I can. Like he'd seen a ghost. I'm certain he recognized you. And after seeing your mother's pictures, I'm sure it's because you look like her."

They paused in front of the last door at the end of the

hall, and with a perfunctory knock on the panel, Wolf twisted the knob and pushed the door open.

Nessa's heart raced a hundred-yard dash for the back of her throat, and she stumbled to a halt right at the threshold. Her feet suddenly refused to work, her knees the consistency of Jell-O.

I can't. I can't do this.

"Nessie, you got this," Wolf murmured, pinching her chin and tilting her head up to meet his eyes. His big body blocked out everything behind him, so all she saw was him, his beautiful eyes and his belief in her.

It tore her heart in half to look into his face, to see her heartbreak written all over the sharp angles, the soft and hard curve of his mouth. And yet, she couldn't tear her gaze away.

"*We* got this," Ivy corrected, squeezing the hand she hadn't let go of the entire time. "Together."

Borrowing strength from both of them, Nessa again nodded, briefly closing her eyes. When she lifted her lashes, she whispered, "I'm ready."

Wolf didn't move for a long moment, continuing to peer at her with the scrutiny of a surgery scalpel. But whatever he glimpsed must've convinced him, because he stepped aside, and with a palm pressed to the middle of her shoulder blades, moved forward.

And she caught her first look of Garrett Adams, aka Paul Summers.

Because there was no mistaking that Garrett Adams, owner of Little Bird Ski Lodge, was the man from the photograph with her mother.

Yes, he was older, gray sprinkled his hair and a neatly cropped beard surrounded his jaw and mouth. Lines fanned out from the corners of his eyes and deepened the grooves under his striking cheekbones. But the facial structure remained the same. The strong brow and jaw? The same. The tall, lean but powerful build? The same. And the stunning light brown eyes? The same.

All moisture in her mouth dried up, and try as she might, she couldn't swallow. Could barely breathe. Sweat prickled her underarms, her palms and dotted her forehead. Gooseflesh executed a break along her spine and her arms. And not because of maybes or suspicions.

Because of how he looked at her.

Slowly, Garrett Adams rose from behind her desk.

Shock widened his eyes and bled the color from his face, leaving him pale. Even from the distance of his office, she noted the fine tremble that shook his frame.

He knew her.

Or the woman who'd borne her.

"Who are you?" he asked, voice hoarse, the sorrow, the hope in it, almost painful to her ears.

"Nessa Hunt," she said, her tone just as low, just as serrated. "But I think you knew my mother. Evelyn Reed."

"Evelyn."

That hope Nessa had detected in his voice leaped to his gaze, and he even glanced behind her as if her mother would walk through the office door. Oh God, if only she would.

"I'm sorry, but she died earlier this year. Cancer." Even eight months later, still saying those words caused her to bleed inside. And as this man flinched, and seemed to bow in on himself, his fists bracing on the desktop, that wound ripped open a little more. She waited a couple of minutes, trying to grant him time to absorb that news before hitting him with another punch. "I hate to tell you this right on the heels of that, but I don't know another way of doing it. I—I think you're my father."

Garrett jolted as if struck by a bolt of electricity. His face, still pale, and seemingly even more lined than when they'd entered his office, hardened and went blank. Except for his eyes. They burned like golden fire.

"Tell me everything," he quietly demanded.

So she did.

Starting with her mother's deathbed confession, Isaac's death, her and Ivy's trip to Rose Bend and the letter from Isaac she received with information about Paul Summers. She talked about Eva Wright's hunt for information with the Summers family, and finally receiving the box of Evelyn's belongings that included the photo album with pictures of him and her mother that led them here.

By the time she finished talking, she, Wolf and Ivy had settled on the couch in the office's sitting area and Garrett stood at the floor-to-ceiling window next to it, staring out the glass at the view beyond.

A silence descended on the room, and for long moments, he didn't speak, but his tense shoulders and rigid, unmoving frame shouted.

"Your mom and I met in New York City the summer of my junior year at Columbia University. She was visiting the city for a weekend from Boston, where she was attending Boston University. If you'd have asked me before she entered that bar on that Friday night if I believed in love at first sight, I would've said an emphatic no. But I hadn't met your mother yet. We were inseparable from the moment I approached her and said hello. She was..." He gave a gruff but humorous chuckle. "Well, you know how your mother was. Funny, brilliant, charismatic, beautiful. And when Monday morning arrived, I begged her not to return to Boston."

He sighed, and the sound bore a lifetime of memories,

grief and yet, joy. Nessa understood that spectrum of emotion only too well.

"She had a waitressing job to go back to at a restaurant, but somehow I convinced her to give it up and spend the summer with me. I had just ended a two-year relationship with Cara Summers. It was on amicable terms, though, and Cara agreed to still let me stay at her family's summer home in Rose Bend, Massachusetts. We'd planned to go together, but with the breakup, she was going to summer in Paris before we both entered our senior year of college and then the 'real world.' So, I asked your mother to spend the summer with me there. It took some doing, but she agreed. And that was huge for her, to do something as spontaneous as quit her job and vacation for months with a guy she barely knew. But she did it. Because she'd fallen in love with me, too."

Garrett turned away from the window and strode over to the sitting area, sinking down to the chair. He propped his elbows on his thighs, his clasped hands dangling between. Nessa stared at him, enraptured by his story. By the flashes of emotion that whispered across his stoic face. By the glimpses into a past her mother had kept completely hidden from her.

"When we arrived in Rose Bend, I told everyone my name was Paul Summers so they would assume I was a member of the family. Paul is my middle name, and therefore easy to remember. It was also the name most of my friends and family called me by since my father was Garrett, Sr.... It was the name I gave your mother. I told Evelyn the home belonged to a friend, but I didn't tell her exactly who—didn't think she would like that we were staying in the family home of my ex-girlfriend. So I lied. For two and half magical months, we lived together. Explored the town, the surrounding mountains and country together. Loved together. She was my everything, and we planned how we could stay together. Since it was my senior year, and she was in her freshman year, she would transfer to a college in New York, I'd find an apartment for us and we'd live together there in the city. Yes, we'd struggle for a little while until I graduated and found a good job, but none of that would matter because we'd have each other." He laughed, and it was harder, sharper. "We were young, naive."

Garrett fell silent, and nothing but the crackle of the fire in the office fireplace and their breaths punctuated the room. Well, not her breath. Because she held hers. Because she could guess what came next. The ending of this fairy tale he'd spun.

"One day in August, near the end of vacation, I went downtown for…something. I can't even remember now. It seems I should remember every detail about the day that changed my life so irrevocably. But the sharpest memory is when I returned to the house, Evelyn was gone. But Cara stood there, waiting for me." His mouth twisted into an ugly parody of a smile. "My ex had surprised me with an impromptu visit because she'd missed me while in Paris. When she'd arrived at the house and found Evelyn there, she'd told your mother it was her house, we were still together and I was using her while Cara was out of the country. Evelyn left, without even waiting to hear my side of the story. I looked for her. But she'd withdrawn from Boston University and disappeared. And later on, when I was able to scrape the money together to hire a private investigator, he couldn't locate an Evelyn Reed. But I guess that's because she'd become Evelyn Hunt by then."

He smiled, but like his laughter, it carried no humor. His gaze roamed Nessa's face, as if searching for himself in her. She didn't take offense, because she did the same. And found it. While she had her mother's eye color and bone structure, the shape of her mouth, nose and eyes were his. She had a feeling, maybe she'd inherited his "sunny" disposition, too.

"I had no idea she was pregnant," Garrett rasped. "No idea. If I had, I would've never stopped looking until I found you. Found both of you. As it is, I never forgot your mother. Sometimes, I wish I could've. I graduated, started my own wealth management business, moved on. And yet, when this place came up for sale, I bought it because it was where Evelyn and I spent the happiest moments of my life. I even named the lodge after her. Evelyn means *little bird* in French. I never could explain to myself why I did it, other than masochism. Other than falling in love at first sight all those years ago, I've never been a man given to sentiment. But now, with you sitting here, maybe I finally understand why. You were meant to find me. We were meant to find each other."

"You don't even know me," Nessa whispered. "How can you just accept at face value that I'm your daughter?"

He chuckled, and it sounded rusty, as if he didn't do it too often. "Besides you looking just like her? If I had any doubts, that skepticism right there would've erased the last of them." He shook his head. "We can get a DNA test done, if you'd like. I'm sure my lawyers will insist on it. But I don't need it. I know. Here." He thumped his chest with a fist. "You're mine. Mine and Evelyn's. It always struck me as inconceivable how something so powerful as my love for your mother could just…end. But now, I know it didn't. You're proof of that, Nessa. I'd love a chance to get to know you. As a daughter. And if that's too much too soon, as a friend."

Fear gripped her. Squeezed as tight as the hope, as the joy trying to sneak in between its suffocating grip. Though she'd forgiven Isaac, the scars of one father walking away after claiming to want her, to love her, still remained. She didn't know Garrett Adams, and yet, her heart yearned to get to know him. To claim this second chance at having a father in her life.

But she was scared.

When she'd driven up here with Wolf and Ivy, she'd expected Garrett Adams to hear them out, and on the off chance that he ended up being her father, to say, *Okay, thank you for the info, let's keep in touch.* That had been the best-case scenario. She hadn't expected him to share this grand love story worthy of movie credits, stare at her in wonder and basically call her a gift he wanted in his life.

As someone who people found it easy to leave, she didn't understand how to react to this man desiring her presence. Desiring to stay.

"I—" she splayed her fingers over her thighs, staring down at her upturned palms as if they contained the answers "—I honestly wasn't expecting this. I'm not sure how to answer right now. I just wanted to let you know the truth. And to find out the truth."

"Thank you for coming here. It's been a long time since I've had a reason to celebrate Christmas but believe me when I say that you are the best gift I could have ever received." Garrett cleared his throat, glancing away from her, and her own throat tightened at the show of emotion in this man she sensed didn't show affection easily or often. "I won't push. But whenever you're ready to talk, my door is always open to you. So much time has been wasted, and I'm just going to be honest. I hate the thought of any more passing between us. On that note, my home is yours. And yours." He shifted his attention to Ivy. "I'm sorry for the loss of your father, Ivy. And in no way would I presume to try and replace him. But family of my daughter's is family of mine. So this is your home also."

"Thank you, Mr. Adams." Ivy glanced at Nessa, then Garrett.

"Garrett, please." He stood, holding his hand out to Nessa. "Thank you for coming to me. I know that couldn't have been an easy decision. But I'm so grateful you did. I, uh…" He trailed off, paused. He briefly closed his eyes, then started again. "Your mother was the love of my life. There's been an emptiness since she left, and meeting you, knowing I have a daughter with her, well… Let's just say there's more to life than business. You can call me Garrett, too, Nessa. Although, one day, I hope…" He cleared his throat again. "I hope to talk to you soon."

Nessa accepted his hand in hers, shaking it. Then, on a whim, she stepped into him. Hugging him. His arms closed around her, and he returned the embrace.

"Thank you, Nessa," he rasped. "Thank you so much."

For another moment, they stood there, holding one another, and Nessa choked back a sob. She'd found her father. Against all odds, she'd actually found her father.

Thank you, Isaac.

Reluctantly, she let him go, and he shifted away, offering his hand to Wolf and then to Ivy. Surreal. This was all so surreal.

She'd come to Rose Bend without a father, a mother or a sister.

Now she had a sister of the heart, a father by blood and a whole new perception of the mother she'd thought she'd known.

Of course, her heart had been a little bruised but perfectly intact then, too.

Now... She glanced at Wolf from under her lashes—and couldn't prevent the frisson of pain that crackled through her. Last night, she'd had a premonition, a preview of the hurt he could inflict on her heart. Without even trying. Was she afraid? God, yes. Fucking terrified. Because she wouldn't survive Wolf Dennison. Where Jeremy wounded her, she now understood that had been all it'd been—a wounding. An injury. If Wolf were to hurt her, abandon her... That blow would be lethal. And she couldn't do it. He'd once called her brave, but she wasn't. Because she couldn't scrounge up the courage to take a risk on him as she'd done with Ivy and Garrett.

Him, she wouldn't survive.

Garrett and her mother's love story had taught her one lesson. Her heart couldn't be broken if she didn't put it on the line.

So, she might be returning to Boston with a found family, but her heart?

That was a different story.

CHAPTER NINETEEN

WOLF GATHERED THE last of the tools he'd need before heading out to the town square to finish the gazebo. Just a few days before Christmas Eve, and it finally seemed like they were going to be done in time. The beams for the roof had already been cut to length; they just needed to be attached in place. Then he and Trevor would have to add the rest, including the fascia boards and shingles. The aesthetic designs wouldn't take long at all, while another committee would be in charge of decorating it for the ceremony and concert that would take place on Christmas Eve evening.

That full sense of accomplishment wouldn't fill him until he stared at a completed job, but curls of it slid through his chest, winding around his rib cage. Satisfaction and pride that he could do this for his town, his brother. Maybe he was being too deep, but this gazebo didn't just symbolize a structure from a time past for Rose Bend; it stood as a monument to family. To the fact that whenever the Dennisons called on one another for help, they always answered. And not out of obligation. Always out of love and loyalty.

Take *that*, Jasper Landon.

He smirked, mentally flipping off Rose Bend's ex-mayor and Cole's nemesis as he placed his tool belt on the table behind him. Grabbing his coat, he slipped it on just as the door to the workshop opened and Nessa stepped in. His fingers paused over the zipper. And he stared.

Yeah, this was where he should play it cool. Politely inquire how she was doing. Pretend his heart hadn't become a hammer striking against anvil.

But let's face it. He'd blown that cover yesterday when Ivy had found him in this very place and told him Nessa was crying over a box. He'd damn near broken the sound barrier racing to the inn, charging up the stairs and getting to her room. It hadn't mattered then that she'd avoided him since seeing Olivia kiss him. Didn't matter now that another afternoon and night had gone by since they'd returned from Little Bird Ski Lodge and her reunion with her father.

The truth couldn't be plainer.

When it came to Nessa Hunt, he had no sense of self-preservation. He was like an animal with his head leaned back, throat exposed. Vulnerable, trusting, hoping the one on the other end would either show mercy or make it quick.

"Nessa." He leaned a hip against his worktable and crossed his arms over his chest. At the moment, he didn't trust himself to keep his hands off her. The other day, she hadn't minded, but those had been extraordinary circumstances. Today was, well...today. And the sense of dread curdling his gut didn't strike him as an auspicious omen. "How're you doing?"

"Good," she said, closing the door behind her and surveying his workshop. Her gaze landed on his tool cabinets, his projects in progress, pieces of wood, his table—landing everywhere but on him. Then, finally, she had nowhere else to look but at him. And the shadows in her dark eyes had him tightening his arms, battling the urge to push off the table and go to her, unease be damned. "I wanted to thank you for going with me to the ski lodge. For everything you did for me."

"You don't need to thank me. I promised you I'd help in any way I could."

She nodded. "Yes, you did. After we returned from the lodge, Ivy told me she came here looking for you. And considering…everything, you didn't have to come for me. Not everyone would have, Wolf. So I do need to thank you."

"By everything, you mean Olivia kissing me and you believing I wanted it. Or at the very least, believing I let it happen." He arched an eyebrow, not letting her off the hook.

Nessa moved farther into the room, stopping at the end of the table. She didn't flinch from his direct gaze, met it head-on.

"I don't believe you kissed her or that you let it happen. Yes, I was stunned and needed space and time. But at some point that night, I admitted to myself that you wouldn't have kissed her. We might have met weeks ago and been lovers less than that, but I know you, Wolf. You have too much integrity to have done something like that. Especially in front of most of the town. You're not a stupid man either."

Relief poured through him so strong, it left him a little light-headed.

"Then what the hell, Nessa?" he asked, dropping his arms and approaching her. "For days you've avoided me, treating me like I was the damn villain in that scenario, when you're telling me you don't believe I was at fault?"

"I had to get there, Wolf. Because that wasn't my first thought. With the choice of believing you or my eyes? I believed my eyes. But later, after a sleepless night, I knew the truth. I don't know why I was surprised, though." She laughed, the sound dry. "Olivia warned me she had every intention of getting you back."

"I have a choice in that, and I don't want her. I haven't in a long time."

Nessa cocked her head to the side, studied him, and he allowed it. Let her see what he'd said—and what he hadn't. A corner of her mouth quirked, but the half smile didn't hold humor. "Do you remember the night of the Christmas tree lighting? The first night you saw her? You could barely speak to her. As a matter of fact, I don't think you did. The tension between you was so thick, I didn't need anyone to tell me you two had a past—you relayed that info all by yourself with your actions. No, Wolf." She slowly shook her head. "In my experience, if you still have that much emotion connected to someone, then that door isn't closed. You haven't truly let go of that person."

"I can't decide if you truly believe that or if you're digging to find something to put between us so you can justify walking away."

"Wolf," she murmured.

"No, Nessa. I'm not making it easy for you. That's what you want. To hide behind that wall that's a shield for you. I should know. I have my own. Had. I *had* my own until you came into my life and I didn't need it anymore. Not with you." He flattened his hands on the table, leaning forward. "But let's play this your way. That night of the lighting. Do you want to know what my reaction was about, or does it matter? Because your mind is already made up, isn't it? You already have one foot out of this shop. Out of Rose Bend."

"Our arrangement was temporary. You promised me no strings, no attachments." A note of desperation crept into her voice.

His heart—his foolish, foolish heart—tried to soften, but he deliberately hardened it. They needed to do this. To get all of this out there and said.

"If that were true, baby, you wouldn't be in here so desperately trying to cut those strings," he said, gently. Firmly.

"I told you I wasn't a good bet. That there wasn't anything happily-ever-after about me." She slashed a hand through the air. "You don't get to change the terms now because they don't suit you."

"Go ahead, Nessie. Fight," he whispered. "Fight hard for that wall. To protect your heart. To keep from being hurt anymore."

She reeled back, her chin jerking as if his words were physical blows. "Is that what you're lowering yourself to? Mocking me? Does that make you feel better?"

"Making fun of you? Baby." He shook his head, closing in on her, erasing the distance separating them. He cupped her cheeks. "Never. I'm refusing to let you go. This is me fighting for you. Why is it that you don't recognize it when you see it?" He stroked his thumb over her silken skin. "I'll throw down for you even if it means battling against that part of you that doesn't believe you're worthy of happily-ever-afters."

Her eyes glistened, and her sharp catch of breath brushed his palm. She wrenched out of his hold, spinning around and giving him her back.

Go to her. Hold her.

The urge kicked at him, but he resisted. This had to be her choice. And she had to choose them.

She had to choose herself.

Just as he had. Fighting that part of him that whispered he wasn't enough, that he was two steps from driving her away, was hell. But he did it. Because she was worth it. *They* were worth it.

"At that lighting, you saw my shame. My guilt. Not my love for Olivia. I couldn't look at her without remembering how I'd failed in being a provider, a protector—again. How I hadn't been enough. Again. She was a reminder of my failure. That's why I couldn't look at her, couldn't speak. I felt choked by that. But here's the truth, Nessa. Even if there had been any feelings left in me for Olivia, it wouldn't have happened. Because just hours earlier, I'd bumped into you. The moment I picked that wreath off your hair, the possibility of you became better than the absolute of anyone."

She slowly turned around and stared at him.

"I love you."

He saw the moment panic flashed in her eyes. Noted the moment he made a mistake.

Saw the moment she would run.

"You can't—you don't mean that. It's only been… No. Take it back." The terror in her eyes edged into her voice, sharpened it. "That's not what we are. You promised."

"I'm not taking it back," he softly said. Even though pain streaked through him like fire, branding him, tenderness for this woman beat within him. "Everyone who has said they loved you has left you, abandoned you. Your mom. Isaac. Your ex. And now you're afraid to trust in me, in my love for you. I understand that fear, Nessa. And I can't take it away for you. I can't make you believe me. You said you knew me. Well, then you should know that I would never willingly leave you or hurt you. I wouldn't betray the gift of your heart."

"You don't know that," she whispered. "You can't possibly promise that. No one can promise me that…"

"I can, and I do. But what I can't do is be brave for you. I can catch you if you fall, but, baby, you have to be willing to take the leap. You'll never know if I'll follow through if you never try me. I'm begging you to try me."

Please. Please, Nessa. Take a chance.

But even as the plea ran through his head, he knew she wouldn't. Some scars ran too deep. Same with fears.

She couldn't trust him, because when it came down to it, Nessa didn't trust herself.

"I can't be who you need, Wolf. I'm sorry. I'm so sorry."

She turned and exited the workshop, the air redolent with the remorse and grief in her voice.

It was all he had left of her.

CHAPTER TWENTY

"THANK YOU FOR coming with me, Dad." Wolf shut off his truck and stared out the windshield at the ranch-style house that had once been as familiar to him as his own home.

He hadn't been to the Brandt home since the last time he'd been here with Raylon, when they'd both been on leave more than eight years ago. It'd been at least that long because he hadn't felt like he'd been welcome in this house. Hell, he still didn't know. But it was long past time he found out.

"Of course, son." Ian patted Wolf's knee. "I'm always here for you. Always."

Wolf nodded. But he didn't move out of the truck.

"Wolf, it's going to be okay," his father murmured. "Now get your ass out of this truck."

With a snort, Wolf grabbed the door handle and pushed. "Thanks for the pep talk."

"Like I said, I'm always here for you."

Chuckling, Wolf stepped out of his truck and joined his father on the sidewalk outside the Brandt home. His pulse was a dull roar inside his head, his heart a bass drum. He moved forward up the walk strictly by muscle memory, and as he and his father climbed the porch stairs, the front door opened. Carol Brandt stepped outside.

Wolf froze.

Carol didn't.

Strong arms enveloped him first. A warm vanilla-and-cinnamon scent the next.

A sob welled up inside him, and he enfolded the woman who'd once been a second mother to him in a tight embrace. He held back his tears, but he didn't let her go. Which was okay, because she didn't seem inclined to release him just yet either.

"It's about time you got here," she finally said, gripping his arms. "I've been waiting a long time for you to get your head on straight. And good God, I thought my Raylon was stubborn."

He tried to smile, but his lips failed to curve. Instead, he searched her face for any sign of regret, of anger...of accusation. "I thought you blamed me. I didn't want to cause you any more pain than I already had."

"No, Wolf. If anyone is to blame for all of this, it's me. I said some very ugly things to you when you first came home. By the time I came out of my own grief and remembered all that I hurt you with, I was so ashamed. And it's guilt that's kept me from approaching you and apologizing, fearful that you wouldn't be able to forgive me. Please forgive me."

"No," he insisted. "God, no, there's nothing to forgive."

"Well, I don't know about that, but thank you. C'mon in. You, too, Ian. I just took cookies out of the oven. I'll put a pot of coffee on and we can have a long-overdue talk about what you've been up to. And checks. Lots of checks." She arched a graying eyebrow.

Wolf grinned, and though his heart had patches and cracks in it, God, it was lighter. "Yes, ma'am."

NESSA STARED AT THE—okay, there was no other word for it—feast laid out before her on the table in the ski lodge's private dining room. She lifted her head from the smorgasbord of ham, green beans, brown rice, chicken, greens, corn, asparagus and gravy to look at Garrett.

"Is someone else joining us?"

He smiled, sheepish. "Since I wasn't sure what you like, I might have gone a little overboard."

Nessa chuckled. "Just a wee bit." She pinched her fingers together, squinting, and laughed again. "But thank you. For the invitation to lunch and the food. It's really nice of you."

"Thank *you* for accepting. Like I said a couple of days ago, I don't want to push you." He picked up his red cloth napkin, flicked it open and spread it over his lap. "So tell me, Nessa. What *is* your favorite food?"

"Chicken and dumplings, hands down. Mom and I had a tradition. She used to make it the first time it snowed. After she got sick, I made it for her."

Surprise winged through her. She'd been able to mention her mother without a wave of grief rolling through her. Yes, it was there—it probably always would be—but it had dulled to where she could talk about a favorite meal of theirs without wanting to shut down.

"I remember your mom's chicken and dumplings. She made it for us while we were here. And you're right. It was an amazing dish. I'm stealing your answer. Next. Favorite movie?"

And so an hour went with them eating a delicious meal and swapping favorite colors, books, TV shows, music, actors, anything they could think of to share. Even when she couldn't eat another bite, they continued to talk, moving to one of the sitting areas in front of a huge fireplace.

"Your necklace," Garrett murmured. "Where did you get it? The ring?"

Holding her cup of coffee in one hand, she touched the

piece of jewelry. "This? It was Mom's. She wore it for as long as I can remember."

"I gave it to her."

"Did you really?"

"Yes." He lowered his head, and for a moment, silence claimed them. When he spoke, his voice had thickened. "I gave it to her days before she left Rose Bend as a promise ring. I can't believe she kept it all these years."

"She never took it off. Not until...the end."

"I'm glad."

Garrett peered into the fire, and she allowed him several minutes of peace. She needed them, too. Wow. All those years, her mother had held a piece of the man she'd loved, the father of her daughter, close. She'd loved him to the end. Nessa now believed that.

"Why haven't I seen you at any of the Christmas events, Garrett?" Nessa sipped from her perfectly brewed coffee. She didn't know how much it cost to stay at the resort, but a good part of that fee must go to food and beverage. Because they were top-notch. "I thought most of the town turned out for them."

"I host the annual dance for Yulefest here at the lodge, but I haven't been one who celebrates Christmas much. My parents are gone—they both died before I left for college—and I never married. So I don't have a family, and Christmas is a family holiday. I've worked for most of it."

"Wow." Nessa laughed. "You and I are more alike than I originally thought."

He arched an eyebrow. "A workaholic? Why? You had your mother, Isaac Hunt and Ivy, right? Why would you be apathetic toward Christmas?"

"Long story," she murmured. "But Mom was pretty much a single parent after I turned twelve, and she worked a lot to support us. Ivy and I weren't that close. Until we came here to Rose Bend, we were more of the evil-stepsister variety. But that's changing, and I'm really thankful for her. Still, Christmases weren't a big deal for me. And since I wasn't married or a mother, I preferred to work and let people with either or both have it off."

"I guess we are alike, then." He paused. "But I'd like to change that."

"What do you mean?"

"I don't know about you, but being me is lonely. I'm never more aware of that than at Christmas when the lodge is packed with families and couples. Or when the town celebrates with Yulefest. Losing your mom, it left me bitter, I guess. Bitter and gun-shy to ever open myself to people again. And while that definitely keeps your heart safe, it also means you're alone. And I'm tired of that. Especially now. I don't want to be alone anymore. I want to change that."

Nessa tore her gaze away from him and stared into the dancing flames of the fireplace.

"Aren't you…?" She swallowed. Tried again. "Aren't you afraid? What if it's been so long you don't know how?"

"Don't know how to what, Nessa? Love? Trust?"

Yes. Yes. "Be happy."

"God, yes."

Stunned, she turned back to him. "Really?"

"Yes. When you lock down your emotions for so long, it becomes a habit. More than that, it's comfortable. And at some point, it's all we know. So yes, opening up is scary. But as a businessman, I've learned one thing. It's more of a risk to do nothing than to try, take a risk and perhaps fail. Because even if I fail, I learn something. But if I don't try, I learn nothing. And I definitely don't gain anything. If I can apply that logic and courage to business decisions and profit, then I'm willing to do it with people who are a more worthy investment. I'm willing to try with you, Nessa. You and Ivy. If you are."

Was she brave enough?

In that workshop with Wolf, she hadn't been. All she could think of was how he would eventually leave, just as everyone she loved did. How she would shatter if she had to watch him do it. Shatter into so many pieces, she would never be the same.

No, she hadn't been brave.

But sitting here with her father, she wanted to be. Even knowing that Garrett could possibly disappoint her like Isaac. Even knowing this risk might cost her more tears, more pain.

So if she could be brave for Garrett, who she'd just met, why couldn't she be brave for Wolf, who she...loved?

Because God, she loved him.

So desperately, she'd run hard and fast.

He'd been right about her. She longed for the strings, for the attachments. That's why she'd been like a wild animal trying to chew off its own foot, attempting to slice them off before he could. Let him go before he left first.

She just couldn't bear to watch another person she loved walk away from her. So she'd chosen loneliness over pain. Pride over grief.

The certainty of depending on herself over the risk of trusting in another person. In Wolf.

She didn't want to be alone anymore.

She wanted not just a future, but a future with him. With her father. With Ivy.

She wanted family.

"I'm willing to try." A resolve, buoyed by a freedom of

spirit she hadn't felt in eight long months, resonated within her. "No, I'm going to do it."

Garrett smiled. Then arched an eyebrow. "Are you going to do the same with Wolf Dennison?"

She blinked. Snorted. "Yes. *Dad*," she drawled.

Shock and laughter flared in his eyes. He picked up his coffee and sipped.

"That's my girl."

CHAPTER TWENTY-ONE

FINISHED.

Wolf stood several feet away and studied the gazebo, Trevor next to him. They'd finished the gazebo ahead of schedule. Two days ahead of schedule, to be exact. Amazing what a person could accomplish when he used work to keep his mind off other things.

Like a woman he loved.

Her leaving town in less than a week.

Losing his heart.

Yeah, he'd been working *a lot* over these last few days.

"It looks great, Wolf. Really great."

Wolf grinned at the teen. "That's some great praise coming from you, Trevor." He clapped him on the shoulder. "And it looks amazing, thanks to you and your help. It looks simply amazing."

Again, they studied the building in silence. With the domed roof, the large, octagonal open sides and shallow sets of steps on three sides, it followed the blueprint of the original town gazebo down to the weather vane at the top. Wolf had added his own touches with carvings of vines and roses in the side beams.

He was proud.

And when Cole had come by just a few minutes ago, and Wolf had glimpsed the joy on his brother's face, he'd barely managed not to pump his fist in the air.

All right, so after Cole left, he'd pumped his fist a little.

"Let's clear out of here so they can start decorating it for the ceremony and concert. I'll treat you to lunch over at Sunnyside Grille. You deserve it for all the hard work." Wolf held out his fist and Trevor bumped it.

"Bet."

They worked quickly and gathered the last of their tools and stowed them in the back of his truck. On the last trip, to make sure they'd grabbed everything, he stopped once more in front of the gazebo, head tilted back. He couldn't wait to see it draped with bows, wreaths and garland, and lit up with white lights...

"It's beautiful, Wolf."

He didn't immediately turn around. Partly, because he didn't want to. Didn't want to risk turning and her being a figment of his ravenous imagination. But denial had never been his thing. As eager as he might be to avoid...this.

Pivoting, he faced Nessa.

And hoped like hell he did a decent job of concealing the hunger that flared hot and bright within him at the sight of her. Three days since he'd seen her. Three long days, and now, he was like a junkie jonesing for a hit of her. Dark hair streamed over one shoulder, and a vibrant red slouch hat covered the shaved side of her head. Her puffy black coat covered her from neck to waist, and dark blue jeans encased her thick, beautiful legs, brown ankle boots performing the impossible and making those legs look even more beautiful.

Roaming back up her curvy length, he met her lovely espresso eyes, and tried to ignore the kick to his chest that they elicited. How many times had he dreamed of those eyes? Gleaming with quiet, wicked humor. Heavy with solemnity. Glazed with passion.

Glistening with tears as she told him she was sorry she couldn't be who he needed her to be. Which was in love with him.

Too many to count.

Shit. He needed to wrap this up.

"Yeah, thanks," he said. "We were able to finish it on time." God, this was awkward. Now he was stating the obvious. "Did you need something? Trevor and I were getting ready to go…"

"Yes, I do actually need something." She reached into the gift bag she carried and pulled out a small green box with a bright red bow, then set the bag on the ground. "I wanted to give this to you."

He frowned at the present, shifting his gaze back to her. "What?"

She moved forward, her step hesitant. "It's not Christmas yet but I wanted to give this to you."

"Nessa." He sighed, not sure what the hell was going on. But he didn't have the time or desire to play games—or whatever this was. Last time they'd talked, she'd rejected his love, and now here she stood, offering him a gift like some hot Mrs. Claus. *Confused* didn't begin to cover what he felt. "I don't—"

"Wolf," she interrupted. "Please."

She held the present out to him.

Swallowing another sigh, he took the gift out of her hands, undid the bow and lifted the lid. He moved the tissue paper out of the way and nestled inside he found a glass Christmas ornament in the shape of a wreath.

It was gorgeous.

But he was still confused.

"Mom, Isaac and I had a Christmas tradition. We bought an ornament at the beginning of every season that had special significance for that year. When I was born, they bought one with a baby's bottle. The year Mom graduated from college, we had one in the shape of a graduation cap. When I started first grade, we had a little red schoolhouse. Mom and I continued it for a couple of years after Isaac left, but eventually we stopped."

His fingers tightened around the box, just as a phantom fist squeezed his heart. When would this woman ever stop having this effect on him? When would he ever stop wanting to protect her? Love her?

"I hadn't thought about that in a long time. Just another thing I chose to forget about, I guess. Until coming here to Rose Bend. Until you." She studied him, and his overactive, too-damn-desperate-for-its-own-good imagination allowed him to think for just a couple of moments that she might be trying to memorize his face. Soak him in even as he did the same with her. "When I arrived here, I had one goal. Get through the month of December and Christmas and get home. Back to my job, to my life. Preferably without strangling Ivy." A smile ghosted over her lips. "But no sooner was I knocked on my ass by a giant with a stack of wreaths than that goal was flipped on its ass, too. Being here suddenly wasn't about getting through, but about living for the first time, not just existing. About learning who I was, who I could be. Learning who my sister was. Who I came from. Being here was about learning to love."

About loving.

His heart stalled. Stuttered. Then slammed against his rib cage. He didn't ask her to explain. Couldn't. This step she would have to take. To him. To them. He had no problem with chasing her. He'd do it to the end of the earth. But only if she wanted him to. Only if she was willing to pursue him back.

"I say 'learning to love' because before I did it with reservations. Waiting for someone to snatch it away, so I didn't let them have all of me. Because if I did, and they left, what would I have? Who would I be? You scared me, Wolf. More than anyone, you scared me, because no matter how hard I fought it, whether I admitted it to myself or not, you had all of me. I gave everything to you the day you held me while I cried, wiped my tears and told me they weren't a weakness. I've loved you from that moment, Wolf Dennison."

He closed his eyes. Clenching his jaw, he held back the punch of emotion that swelled so huge inside him he almost buckled underneath the power of it. Joy, hope, love. So much love he didn't know how it was possible for a person to feel it, contain it for another.

When he looked at her again, she'd moved closer and had lifted the ornament out of the box, holding it between them.

"With this ornament, I want to take a tradition that started with my family and continue it with my new family. Let this be the first for you, Ivy and me, for our new life here in Rose Bend."

"You're staying?" he rasped.

She nodded, a glint of doubt flashing in her eyes. "Dr. Collins and Dr. Prioleau asked me to work for them at the clinic after the New Year. One of their nurses decided to stay at home with her new baby instead of returning to work, so they offered me her job. I accepted. Ivy's excited about staying. I hope you are—"

He didn't let her finish that foolish sentence. Covering his mouth with hers, he kissed her. And kissed her. She opened for him, meeting him thrust for thrust, stroke for stroke. He'd missed this. Missed her taste. Missed *her*. God, he'd missed her.

"I wished for you," he breathed against her damp lips.

Cupping her face, he pressed another kiss to her mouth, unable to resist sampling her once more. "For the first time since I returned home from Iraq, I threw a note in the Christmas wishing well. Do you know what I wrote?"

"No, tell me."

"I wished that you would stay in Rose Bend. That you would stay with me."

This time when he kissed her, he took his time, telling her without words how much he loved her, cherished her. Thanked her for choosing him. Cradling the back of her neck with his hand, he scattered kisses over her face, grinning at her laughter and promising he would hear that every day for the rest of their lives.

"Can I have that ornament?" When Nessa gave it to him, he held it high. "I have just the place for it." Cocking his head, he arched an eyebrow. "How do you feel about Victorians as far as houses?"

"Um, good?"

He laughed, pulling her close and smacking a kiss on the top of her head. Winding his arm around her shoulders, he led her toward his parked truck.

"Remind me to tell you over lunch about the savings account Carol Brandt set up with six years' worth of my checks deposited in it. And how, after I donate half to Purple Heart Homes to help build homes for disabled vets and their families, I'll still have more than enough to buy you, Ivy and me a home."

"Holy sh—" Nessa's mouth dropped open. "Wolf Dennison, are you really telling me you're buying me and my sister a whole *house* for Christmas?"

"Merry Christmas, baby."

EPILOGUE

"OH MY LAMB." Nessa opened the front door and stepped into the foyer, stomping the freshly fallen snow off her boots. "It's colder than a witch's tit out there."

"Language." Ivy appeared in the kitchen doorway down the hall, eyebrow arched high.

Nessa snorted, peeling off all her outerwear and hanging her scarf, coat and sweater on the coatrack. Toeing off her boots, she glanced over her shoulder at her younger sister in her hoodie, skinny jeans and socks with frolicking candy canes all over them.

"I'd like to argue that 'tit' isn't a curse but since that would be setting myself up to hear it come out of your mouth with every third word, I'll concede." She stretched her hands out toward Ivy, wiggling her fingers. "Tell me one of those is for me."

Ivy shook her head, but grinned wide as she headed toward Nessa, holding out a cup topped by a mountain of marshmallows.

"Thank you." She groaned as her palms cupped the warm mug. Wrapping one arm around her sister, she squeezed and smacked a kiss on top of Ivy's curls. "Just for this, I won't auction you off at that charity thing Leo is organizing."

"All heart, Nessa. All heart."

Nessa laughed, and the joy in her heart swelled, nearly

swamping her as a pair of strong arms wrapped around her from behind. Instinctively, she leaned back into that embrace, rested on that wide chest.

Yep. *Now* she was officially home.

"How was work?" Wolf asked, his voice a sensual rumble against her back.

"Oh, don't ask."

She tilted her head back, and he took the opportunity to steal a kiss. Well, actually, how could he steal what she so freely gave? She melted into him, parting her lips and savoring his taste after a long day without him.

"Oh God." Ivy pretended to gag. "Get a room. You have several of them to choose from in this house."

Wolf snickered, planting another quick kiss on the lips.

"Why did I think that just because I moved to Rose Bend from Boston that the Christmas medical lunacy would be any different?" She winced, sipping her hot chocolate. "Another Christmas-lights back injury. What's wrong with you men? Stay off damn roofs."

"Language," Wolf and Ivy singsonged together.

Whatever. They better be glad both her hands were wrapped around the cup or the bearded one would get a finger.

"Well, I have something for you. Hopefully, it'll make your day better." Stepping to the side, he slid a hand down her arm and enclosed her fingers in his.

"A surprise?"

She followed him into the huge living room with its cavernous fireplace, bay windows, hardwood floors, cathedral ceiling and an eight-foot Christmas tree in the corner. As it always did, a sense of awe and peace stirred in her heart. This man, this house, this life. Part of her still metaphorically pinched herself because she couldn't believe it was hers. Only a year ago, she'd been lost, grieving and alone. Now, she had a husband, her little sister, a father, a huge, boisterous family, a gorgeous home and a beautiful new town.

She had home.

Her gaze shifted to the fireplace and the mantel above the dancing flames. So many framed pictures crowded it, and she cherished every one of them. Her and Wolf on their wedding day. Wolf, her and Ivy during the motorcycle rally. Her and Garrett on the slopes at Little Bird Ski Lodge. Her on her first day of work at the clinic. The whole Dennison family—including her, Ivy and Garrett—at Thanksgiving.

And one of her absolute favorites. Her, Wolf and Ivy at Loch Ness last summer. Wolf had surprised Nessa with the trip in honor of her mother because Evelyn never made it. It'd been so special, and she swore she felt her mom there with them.

So, yes, when Wolf said he had a surprise, she got excited because they were the best.

"Here you go." He plucked a small gift bag off the coffee table. "This is from Mozart and me."

Nessa glanced at her sister, then back at Wolf. Something cheesy like *I have the best gifts ever with you two* welled up in her, but she wasn't going out like that. She could damn well think it, though...

Setting down her mug, she accepted the bag and didn't even hesitate to tear into it. What could she say? She had zero shame.

Pushing aside the tissue paper, she pulled free a gorgeous crystal ornament in the shape of a star.

"Wolf."

She didn't get much else out because the emotion lodged

in her throat wouldn't allow her. He'd remembered their tradition. And he'd added to it.

God, this man. Was it any wonder why she adored every hair on his head? And in his beard?

Wolf leaned forward and pushed a switch at the bottom, and the middle flickered to life. Images appeared, fading in, then fading out. Some were the same that were on the mantel. But there were new ones. Pictures from her mother's box of Evelyn and Garrett when they were younger. One of Isaac and Ivy's mom.

"I hope you don't mind," Ivy said softly.

"Oh, not at all." Nessa wrapped an arm around her sister's shoulders. "We're all family. They belong there, too."

More images passed, and Nessa stared, enraptured by all of them. And the last one...

The very last one to appear in the ornament was the black-and-white image of the sonogram they'd received just last week.

The image of their baby.

Tears stung her eyes.

"It's beautiful. It's so damn beautiful, and I love it."

This time no one called her on her language. Wolf drew her into his arms and held her, scattering gentle kisses on her temple and the top of her head. Ivy gently took the ornament from her, and Nessa wound her arms around her husband, holding him tight.

"I love you. So much," she whispered.

"I love you, too, baby." He lowered a hand and covered her still-flat stomach. "And baby."

She chuckled, brushing a kiss over his heart. Her heart.

"You know what, Wolfgang? You were right. It does look like a whole 'nother world from down here."

Both of them turned and looked down to find Ivy lying

down on her back, head under the tree. Wolf laughed, and smacking one last kiss on Nessa's lips, took her hand and guided her down beside Ivy. The three of them gazed up into the tree's glistening branches.

Fingers linked with Wolf's, Nessa wrapped her other hand around Ivy's.

This was her family.

Forever.

* * * * *

Look for Leo's story!
With Love from Rose Bend
Available April 2022
From HQN Books

A Kiss to Remember

CHAPTER ONE

"EXCUSE ME. Can I kiss you?"

Remi Donovan blinked at the tall, ridiculously gorgeous man standing at the library's circulation desk.

Impossible. He couldn't have just said what she thought he said. It was Declan Howard in front of her, after all.

"I'm sorry?"

His eyes briefly slid away before landing back on her in their lilac—yes, lilac—glory. "I know this is...unorthodox. And I wouldn't ask if it wasn't an emergency. But can I kiss you? Please?"

An emergency kiss?

Well, *okay*. She'd heard a lot of bullshit in her years—one couldn't have a high school teacher as a best friend, who regularly regaled her with students' excuses about homework and not be well versed in bullshit—but this? It definitely landed in the top ten.

But again. Declan Howard. Recent transplant to Rose Bend, Massachusetts, Declan Howard. Successful businessman Declan Howard.

Secret crush Declan Howard.

She blinked again.

Nope, the face of sharp angles, dramatic slants and masculine beauty didn't still disappear. A proud, clear brow that could rock a Mr. Rochester–worthy scowl. An arrogant blade of a nose that somehow appeared haughty *and* like it'd taken a punch and come out the winner. The slopes of his cheekbones and jaw could've received awards for their melodrama, and that mouth… Well, the less said about that sinful creation the better.

As a matter of fact…

She glanced over her shoulder just to make sure he wasn't talking to someone behind her.

When no one appeared, she turned back to him. Swallowed and forced a nonchalant shrug. He was still standing there wanting to kiss her?

"Um. Sure."

Relief flashed in his eyes. Then they grew hooded, lashes lowering, but not fast enough to hide another flicker of emotion. Something darker, more intense. Something that had her belly clenching in a hard, heavy tug…

His arm stretched across the circulation desk and a big hand curled around the nape of her neck, drawing her forward.

Oh God…

That mouth. She would be a liar if she claimed not to have stared at the wide, sensual curves that were somehow both firm and soft. Both inviting and intimidating. She'd often wondered how the contrast of that slightly thinner top lip would compare to the fuller bottom one.

Now she knew.

In complete, exacting detail.

Perfection.

Giving and demanding. Indulgent and hard. Sharp as the drop in temperature on an October night in the southern Berkshires. And as sweet as the candied apples the middle school PTA sold for their annual fall fundraiser.

His lips molded to hers, sliding, pressing… Parting. First his breath, carrying his earthy cloves-and-cinnamon scent, invaded her. Then his tongue followed, gliding over hers, greeting her before engaging in a sensual dance that teetered on the edge of erotic. And as he sucked on her tongue, then licked the sensitive roof of her mouth, she tipped closer to that edge.

A whimper escaped her, one that she would no doubt be completely mortified over later, and holy hell, he licked that up, too. And gave her a groan in return as if her pleasure tasted good to him.

She released another whimper, this one of disappointment as he withdrew from her. That whimper, too, she'd cringe over later. But now, as the library's recycled air brushed her damp, swollen lips and her lashes lifted, all she cared about was that beautiful mouth making its way back to her and—

Oh God.

She stiffened.

The library. She was in the middle of the library. During lunch hour. Right before the kindergartners from the grade school arrived for Friday Story Circle.

"Um..."

Say something.

You've got your kiss and rocked my proverbial world, now move along unless you'd like to check out a book. Can I suggest Crave *by Tracy Wolff?*

Because of course she'd noticed his preference for YA paranormal fiction. Jesus be a fence, one lip-lock with Declan Howard had rendered her befuddled. She—logical, reasonable, sometimes too plainspoken for her own good Remi—didn't do *befuddled*.

Until now.

"Thank you for that," Declan murmured. His eyes dipped to her mouth, and her breath caught in her throat.

If he tried to kiss her again, she would have to...to... *stop him*. Yes, yes. That's what she was thinking. Stop him.

Didn't matter that heat, smoky and thick, flickered inside her. She pressed her fingertips into the top of the desk, the solidity of the wood grounding her. And if she touched it, she wouldn't lift her hand to her tingling mouth.

"You're welcome. I—" She hadn't been sure what she'd been about to say, but the rest of it evaporated as Tara Merrick appeared behind Declan.

Remi knew the beautiful blonde who worked at The Bath Barn, the shop Tara's mother owned that sold bath products, lotions, perfumes and candles. This was Rose Bend, so of course everyone knew everyone. But Remi had never given the other woman cause to glare at her as she was doing now.

"Declan, I've been looking for you." Tara wrapped a proprietary hand around Declan's forearm, the sugary sweet tone belying the dark fire in her eyes.

"There was no need," Declan said, gently but firmly extricating himself from her grasp.

His purple gaze returned to Remi and, though she resented herself for it, electricity crackled over her skin. She resented it because the pleasure that had fizzed inside her chest like a shaken soda can over *Declan Howard* kissing *her* had fallen flat.

She might've sucked at calculus in college, but she didn't need to know infinitesimals to add one plus one: Declan had only kissed her for Tara's benefit. To make her jealous? To play hard to get? Remi didn't know. What she knew for certain?

It hadn't been because he so desperately needed to get his mouth on her.

It hadn't been because he wanted *her*, Remi Donovan.

And damn if that didn't just slice through her like a fierce winter wind?

"Remi, if you have a moment, I'd—"

She shook her head, cutting off Declan, not allowing her poor heart to flutter over him knowing her name. "I'm sorry but I don't. I really need to get back to work. Do either of you need to check out or return books?"

Her voice didn't waver, and thank God for the smallest of favors. Declan studied her for a long, tense moment. She forced herself to meet his gaze and not back down.

For years, she'd fought the good fight—learning to love herself and to deep-six her people-pleasing tendencies. Right now, she waged an epic inner war against the whisper-soft voice pleading with her to just *Listen to what he has to say.*

Gifting him with an opportunity to apologize for using her? No thanks. She'd had her share of Pride Smackdown XII. The pay-per-view event would air next week.

"No, all good here. Thank you, again." With a nod, he pivoted on his heel and strode toward the exit.

With one last narrow-eyed stare, Tara hurried after him.

Only after the door closed behind both of them, did Remi heave a sigh.

And as a hushed smattering of whispers broke out behind her, she closed her eyes, pinching the bridge of her nose.

Weirdest. Friday. Ever.

CHAPTER TWO

IT WAS OFFICIAL.

Declan had hit rock bottom.

How else could he describe the desperation that had him sitting in his car with an anxious stomach and a numb ass?

Damn, this was humiliating.

Yet, he didn't drive away from his parking space outside the Rose Bend Public Library, where he waited for Remi Donovan to emerge after locking up for the day. Maybe he'd missed his calling. He should've become a private investigator instead of a wealth manager. Uncovering Remi's work schedule had been ridiculously easy. All he'd had to do was sit in one of the library's reading nooks on one of the Thursday and Friday afternoons he visited Rose Bend. Soon enough, he'd overheard Remi, a coworker—a tall, lanky Black man who seemed to own an amazing number of DC shirts and Converse—and their supervisor discuss work schedules.

He shifted in the driver's seat of his Mercedes-Benz S-Class, fingers drumming restlessly on his thigh. If his colleagues in Boston could see him now, their laughter would threaten the buttons on their three-hundred-dollar shirts. After the humor passed, they'd just stare at him, bemused, and offer to escort him to the nearest high-end gentleman's club.

As if staring at another woman's body could possibly

substitute for a certain five-foot-nine frame with gorgeous, natural breasts that would fill his big hands. And a wide flare of hips that never failed to draw his gaze when she strode around the library. And an ass that, by all rights, deserved its own religion.

Fine. He might be a little preoccupied with Rose Bend's beloved librarian.

The librarian whose mouth he claimed for all to see in the middle of the day for his own selfish reasons.

And try as he might—and he did try because he wasn't a prick—he could only rummage up the barest threads of remorse.

Because even though desperation had driven him to that circulation desk with the request of a kiss, desire had chosen her. The need to finally discover if that lush, ripe mouth would taste as good as it promised had won out. And at that first press of lips to lips...

His fingers fisted on his thigh, and he slowly exhaled. Lust tightened inside him... One move and he would snap. As if even now, he dined on that sweet, butterscotch-flavored breath. Licked into the giving depths of her mouth. Twined around that eager tongue. Swallowed that little, needy sound.

"Shit." He shook his head.

Reminiscing about this afternoon wasn't what he'd come here for. Wasn't why he'd set up a stakeout in front of the library. That kiss had been *cataclysmic*, but, in the end, it'd only been the impetus for a plan he needed one Remi Donovan to agree to.

That's all she could be to him—a coconspirator.

He'd learned his lesson the hard way with Tara. If he wanted to do casual friends-with-benefits relationships, he'd have to keep that in Boston, not here in Rose Bend,

where the town was too small and everyone knew everyone's business.

Especially when the woman was the daughter of his
mother's neighbor and friend.

Yeah, not his brightest moment.

The door to the library opened, spilling a golden slice
of light onto the steps before it winked out. He opened his
car door, stepping out to watch as Remi appeared, closing
the large oak door and locking it.

He stared. Openly. Even though she wore a cream-
colored wool coat against the night air, he could easily
envision the dark green dress beneath that caressed every
wicked curve. Another thing he liked about her. She didn't
try to conceal or downplay the gorgeous body God had
blessed her with—she worked it. And damn if that confidence wasn't sexy as hell.

Not here for her sexiness, he sternly reminded himself.
Get on with it.

Firmly closing his car door, he rounded the hood.

Remi's head jerked up, her eyes widening as she spotted him on the curb, near the bottom of the library steps.

She didn't move down the stairs. A tight, almost-tangible
tension sprang between them. It vibrated with the memory
of that conflagration of a kiss. Of the need for *more* that
sang in his veins.

A more he had to deny.

Christ. He tunneled his fingers through his hair. She'd
been a beautiful distraction before he'd touched her, before
he'd learned the butterscotch-and-sunshine taste of her.
But now? Now that he knew? He was finding it difficult
to focus on anything else.

He'd graduated from Boston University with a bachelor's degree in business administration and he'd gone on

to acquire his dual degree, an Executive MBA in Asset Management. But at this moment, he'd become a student of Remi Donovan. And he wouldn't be satisfied until he earned a PhD.

"I'm sorry for just showing up like this," he said. "But I didn't have your phone number. And showing up during your workday again didn't seem like a good idea."

"No." She finally spoke in a husky tone more appropriate for a sultry siren in an old black-and-white film noir than a small-town librarian. "That definitely wouldn't have been a good idea. As it is, my supervisor is contemplating tacking your picture to the bulletin board with Not Allowed scrawled across the top. I'm not sure if I've successfully convinced her you didn't accost me."

He winced, only half exaggerating. "God, I hope she doesn't resort to that. The library is one of the few places I can actually find some privacy and quiet." He frowned, thinking of Tara hunting him down earlier. "Well, it used to be."

She arched a delicate eyebrow, descending a step. A spiral of gratification whistled through him at that small movement toward him.

"Last I heard, you have a very nice home at the edge of town with plenty of space and, I would imagine, privacy."

The corner of his mouth curled. "Yes, I do have a nice home with a lot of space. But I also have a mother with boundary issues and a key to said nice house, which impedes my privacy." He shook his head, holding out an arm toward his car. "Can I give you a ride home?"

She studied his hand for a moment before lifting her gaze to him. "No, thank you. I drove to work this morning. Besides, I intended to walk down to Sunnyside Grille for dinner."

"In the dark?"

Declan glanced down the street. It was a little after six and the sun had just settled beyond the horizon in a spectacular display of purple, dark blue and tangerine. If he were a sentimental man, he would remove his cell and capture the beauty of it over the small Berkshires town.

But he wasn't sentimental; he was logical, factual. A man who dealt with numbers, figures and statistics—and data that assured him a woman walking by herself after dark wasn't a good idea.

A rueful smile flirted with her pretty mouth. "This is Rose Bend, not Boston. And the diner is just a few blocks away, not a long walk at all."

"So you're telling me crime doesn't happen in this town?"

"Of course it does. We wouldn't need a police department if it didn't. And if it eases your mind..." She held up her key ring. Showing him the small canister of pepper spray dangling from it. "I'm not an idiot."

"Never thought you were," he murmured, though that coil of concern for her loosened. Silly, when he barely knew her. When today had been the first time he'd really talked to her other than a murmured greeting or nod of acknowledgment. "Would you mind if I joined you?"

She hesitated, and he caught shadows flickering in her hazel gaze. "Why?"

He blinked. "I'm sorry?"

Remi crossed her arms over her chest, but a second later lowered them to her sides. The aborted gesture struck him as curiously vulnerable—and from the trace of irritation that flashed across her face, she obviously regretted that he witnessed it.

Curiosity and protectiveness surged within him. He

wanted no part of either. Both were dangerous to him. Curiosity about this woman was a slippery slope into fascination. And from there, captivation, affection. Then... *No.* Been there. Had three years of hell and the divorce papers to prove it.

And this protectiveness. It hinted at a deeper connection, a possession that wasn't possible. A connection he'd avoided in his brief attachments since his ill-fated marriage six years ago. As stunning as Remi was, he wasn't looking for a relationship, a commitment.

At least, not a *real* one.

"Why do you want to join me? And let me help you out. I appreciate the chivalrous offer, but I'm a big girl—" a humorless twist of her lips had an unconscious growl rumbling at the base of his throat "—and I can take care of myself. So what's this really about?"

He parted his lips to... What? Take her to task for that subtle self-directed dig? For cutting him off at the knees by snatching away his excuse for escorting her to the diner? Admiration danced in his chest like a flame, mating with annoyance.

"I do have something to talk about with you. Can I walk you to the diner?"

After another almost-imperceptible hesitation, she nodded. "Okay."

She turned, and he fell into step beside her. Silence reigned between them, and he used the moment to survey the picturesque town that had so completely charmed his mother three years ago that she'd moved here. Elegant, quaint shops, trees heavy with gold, red and orange leaves, lampposts and cute benches lined Main Street. A well-manicured town square, with a colonial-style building housing the Town Hall, and a white, clapboard church with a long steeple soaring toward the sky completed a picture that wouldn't have been out of place on a glossy postcard.

Walking down this sidewalk with people strolling hand in hand or as families, their chatter and laughter floating in the night air, it was easy to forget that heavily populated, traffic-choked Boston lay three hours away.

He tucked his hands in the front pockets of his pants, pushing his coat open. The night air, though cool, felt good on his skin. Inhaling, he held the breath for several seconds, then released it, slowly, deliberately.

"Remi, I apologize if my kissing you earlier today caused you any problems. Sometimes I forget how small towns can be. Especially since I'm only here every other weekend, which isn't the case for you. I'm sorry I didn't take that into account." He paused. "Has anyone…said anything to you?"

"You mean besides my supervisor, who wanted to quarter and draw you, then lectured me on professional decorum? Or do you mean Mrs. Harrison, my hair stylist's grandmother, who'd been standing in the reference section and offered me her advice on how to handle a beast like you? Her words, not mine. Or do you mean Rhonda Hammond, the kindergarten teacher there for Friday Story Circle, who gave me a thumbs-up because she'd heard about it from a friend?"

He grimaced, nodding at a person passing by. "The grapevine is alive and well, I see."

"Thriving."

"Are you in trouble at work?" he gently asked. He'd never forgive himself if his impulsive—and yes, selfish—actions cost her job. "I know you already spoke to your supervisor, but I can, as well. I'll call first thing Monday—"

"That's not necessary." She stopped next to a bench

across from the shadowed windows of a closed clothing boutique. "Declan, could you get to the reason why you showed up at the library?"

He stared down into her upturned face. Dark auburn waves framed her hazel eyes, the graceful slope of her cheekbones, the upturned nose and the wicked sinner's mouth. And that shallow, tempting dent in the center of her chin. It never failed that, whenever his gaze dropped to it, he had to resist the compulsion to dip his finger there. Or his tongue.

Madonna and Delilah. That's what she was. Saint and temptress. An irresistible lure that he had to resist.

"I need your help, Remi," he said, resenting like hell the roughened quality to his voice. Clearing his throat, he continued, "This is going to sound...odd, but... Will you be my woman?"

Her face went blank. "Excuse me?" she whispered.

His words played through his head, and he slashed a hand through the air between them. "Hold on, let me re-phrase. Will you *pretend* to be my woman? *Pretend*."

Relief and another, more complicated, murkier emotion wavered in her expression. He peered at her. The need to delve deeper prickled at his scalp.

But that damn curiosity. That protectiveness.

He backpedaled away from her secrets like they had detonators and a steadily ticking clock attached to them.

"Maybe you should start at the beginning." She leveled an inscrutable glance on him, then turned and continued walking down the sidewalk.

Resuming his pace next to her, he huffed out a dry chuckle. "I don't know how to relay this without looking like a dick." Stuffing his hands into the pockets of his coat, he continued, "I don't think it's a secret around here that I…took Tara Merrick out a few times."

"I believe the word you're struggling to find is *date*," she drawled.

He arched an eyebrow. "And I believe *date* is too strong a word," he shot back. "I took her to the movies, dinners— a few of those were at my mom's house so they really don't count, since she and her mother are my mom's neighbors— coffee. Nothing serious."

Remi stopped in the middle of the sidewalk and whipped out her phone. Seconds later, she started tapping on the screen.

"What are you doing?" Frowning, he nudged her to the side, out of the flow of pedestrian traffic.

"I'm pulling up my online dictionary. I mean, I'm just a librarian with a whole reference desk at my disposal, but I'm pretty sure you gave me the very definition of a *date*. But I want to double-check before I call you out. I so hate being wrong."

"Smart-ass," he growled, snatching the cell from her hand and tucking it back in her coat pocket.

His cock perked up at the mere mention of her fantas- tic ass even as he hungered to press his thumb to the plush bottom curve of her mouth and come away smeared with her deep red lipstick.

"And for your information," he said, voice lower, heavier, unable to scrub that image of her smeared lips from his mind. "It isn't a date when I'm up-front from the begin- ning that I'm not looking for any kind of attachment, and I warn her not to expect anything to come out of it. We were just two people enjoying each other's company while I was in town for the weekend. Nothing more. I was very clear about that."

I always am. I always will be.

She tilted her head to the side, her long dark red waves spilling over her shoulder. "Then why bother?"

"Because…" Declan turned, strode off, and the sweet scent of butterscotch and the aroma of almonds assured him she followed. "It made my mother happy. And after years of rarely seeing her smile after my father died, giving her a reason to didn't seem like much of a sacrifice on my part."

Silence beat between them, filled by the chatter of passersby and the low hum of Rose Bend's version of Friday-night traffic.

"That kind of detracts from your dick status," she finally murmured.

He glanced at her, a smile tugging at his mouth. "Thank you…I think."

"That's why you bought a house here, too, isn't it?" She slid him a look, and the too-knowing gleam trickled down his spine like an ice cube. "Mrs. Howard moved to Rose Bend three years ago, but you didn't buy a house here until last year. You're only in town every other weekend—really you could stay with her. There was no need for you to buy a house. But you did it so she would feel like she had family here. So she had her son here."

He shrugged, not liking this feeling of… Vulnerability. Of being so easily read like one of the books at her library.

"It was nothing. Like I said earlier, I need my space. And what little privacy she allows me." He smiled, even if it was wry. "Which brings me back to why I need you." Lust struck a match against the kindling of need in his gut, flaring into flames at his choice of words. He deliberately doused them. "After our…display at the library, Tara seemed to finally back off."

"Not how I saw it," Remi muttered under her breath, but he caught it.

"True, she chased me out of there, but when I told her we were involved, and what she saw was me being dead serious about what I'd been telling her for the past two weeks—which is that there would be no more movies, no more dinners—the truth seemed to sink in. But I'm not fooling myself into believing it will stick. Not if I don't follow it up with reinforced behavior. Otherwise, she'll convince herself kissing you was a fluke, and I didn't mean it when I said she and I were over." He rubbed his hand over his jaw, his five-o'clock scruff scratching his palm. "That we were never a 'we' to begin with."

"So you want me as your beard to run her off?"

He frowned. Her bland tone didn't hint that he'd offended her. Neither did her perfunctory summation. Yet, he still got the sense he had.

"My beard?" he repeated. "No, I wouldn't put it that way—"

"What other way is there to put it?" She waved a hand, dismissing the question. "And what do I get out of this little…bargain? Well, other than the title of the latest woman you dumped when we end the charade."

Oh yes, definitely offense there. And maybe a trace of bitterness.

"Remi." He gently grasped her elbow, drawing her to a halt. "I didn't mean to insult you."

"You didn't," she argued, stepping back and removing herself from his hold. Chin hiked up, she offered him a polite smile that halted just short of her hazel eyes. "I'm sorry, but I have to turn down your proposal."

Fuck the fake girlfriend arrangement. Fuck wanting her agreement. He'd inadvertently hurt her; she didn't need to say it. The evidence drenched those eyes, drowning out the green and gold so only the brown remained, dark and shadowed.

He reached for her.

"Remi—"

"If it's okay with you, I'm going to head back to the library. I'm not hungry anymore."

She sharply pivoted on her ankle boot, but just as she started to head in the opposite direction, the door to the establishment behind them opened and two older couples and a younger one spilled out into the night.

Remi skidded to an abrupt stop, her entire body going as rigid as one of the statues that littered the Boston Public Garden. Concerned, he dragged his gaze from the small group of people to her and shifted closer. Close enough to hear her mutter...

"Shit."

CHAPTER THREE

DECLAN'S CURIOUS STARE damn near burned a hole in the side of Remi's face, but she avoided meeting that sharp lilac scrutiny. Afraid that while she stood there in the middle of the sidewalk in her own version of an O.K. Corral showdown with her parents, her younger sister, Briana, her sister's new fiancé, Darnell Maitland, and his parents, Declan might spy entirely too much.

Too much of what she didn't want him to see.

Like the hated, grimy envy that had no place alongside her happiness for her sister.

Like the uneasy mixture of love and dread for her mother.

Like the anxiety-pocked need to run, run and never stop until her lungs threatened to burst from her chest.

"Remi, honey." Her mother, voice pitched slightly higher, switched rounded eyes from her to Declan and back to her. "What a surprise."

Translation: *What's going on and what're you doing with Declan Howard?*

No. *Nononono.*

Remi smothered a groan. Why was this happening to her? Today must be cursed. First, the hottest, make-her-lady-parts-weep kiss she'd ever experienced. Then the whispers, not-so-subtle high fives and unsolicited comments and advice. Then Declan's surprising appearance after work and his, uh, unconventional proposal.

And now this.

Twenty-six years as her mother's daughter had earned Remi a W-2 and pension in all things Rochelle Donovan. And Remi recognized that particular shrewd gleam in her mother's eyes.

No way in hell could Remi have Rochelle start thinking Remi and Declan were a *thing*.

"Hi, Mom, Dad." She forced herself to move forward and brushed a kiss over her mother's cheek, then gave her big, lovable bear of a father a hug. "Hey, sis. And future in-laws." Her smile for Briana, Darnell and the Maitlands came more naturally to her lips.

After all, it wasn't Briana's fault that she was three years younger than Remi, had fallen in love and was getting married, much to the delight of their mother.

"Hi, sweetie," Sean Donovan greeted. "How's my best girl doing?"

"Hey!" Briana playfully jabbed their father in the side with an elbow. "I'm standing right here."

"Sorry, you weren't supposed to hear that. You know you're my best girl," he teased.

Remi shook her head, grinning at their father and the joke that had been running around their house as long as she'd been alive. All the Donovan girls—her, Briana and Sherri, their oldest sister—knew with 100 percent certainty that Sean loved them equally and completely.

"I was hoping you could join us for dinner tonight," Briana said, then shot her a sly smile. "But now I see why you turned down the invite. You had a better offer. I ain't mad at you," she stage-whispered.

"What?" Remi blinked, heat blasting a path up her chest and into her face. Thank God for the dark. "No, this isn't—" She waved a hand between her and Declan, silently ordering herself not to look at him. "No," she repeated. Firmly. Because that glint hadn't disappeared from either her mother's or sister's gazes. But wait. Hold up a second. "And what invitation? I didn't get..." She glanced at Rochelle.

So did Briana.

"Mom?" Briana frowned. "I asked you to tell Remi about dinner tonight. You didn't call her?"

"I'm sorry, honey. I must've forgot." She winced, lifting a shoulder in an apologetic half shrug. "You were at work anyway, Remi. And besides, you probably would've been uncomfortable as a third wheel."

Anger and hurt coalesced inside her, shimmering bright and hot.

Her mother hadn't forgotten. More like she hadn't wanted to be embarrassed by her middle daughter's perennially single status. And as Briana's gaze narrowed on Rochelle, Remi could tell her sister knew it, as well.

"But," Rochelle continued, smiling at Declan, who'd remained silent since bumping into her family, "since you're here, why don't you join us? We were heading to Mimi's Café for coffee. You, too, Declan. We'd love to have you."

Panic ripped through Remi, and she glanced at Declan. As if he'd been waiting for that moment, his eyes connected with hers, and the clash reverberated like a collision of metal against screeching metal. She *felt* him. In her chest, belly... Lower.

"Declan?" her mother asked again, breaking their visual connection like cracked glass sprinkling to the ground.

He looked at her mother. Smiled.

"I would be delighted to join you. Thank you for inviting me."

Shit.

Again.

"WHAT THE *HELL*, REMI? I heard Declan Howard kissed you in the middle of the library today, but I thought that was just gossip! But apparently not! You've been holding out on me." Briana hip-checked Remi, her mock scowl promising retribution. "How long has this been going on?"

Remi sighed, sneaking a peek in Declan's direction. He stood with her father and Darnell near the bakery case, talking. Part of her battled the urge to save him from a possible pumping of information by her father. But the other, admittedly petty, half thrilled in leaving him served up to that grilling since he agreed to this craziness.

"Bri, we're just friends," Remi hedged. Were they even that? In the years since his mother had moved to Rose Bend, she'd barely said a handful of words to him.

"Friends who tongue wrestle?" Briana nodded. "Yes, Darnell and I are the best of friends, too."

Remi snickered, then sipped her caramel macchiato. "I have no idea how he puts up with you."

"Right?" Briana beamed. She turned, scanning the café until her gaze landed on her fiancé. And her pretty face softened with such adoration that Remi cleared her throat. As if sensing her attention on him, the handsome IT analyst with dark brown eyes and beautiful almond skin, looked up and sent his fiancée the sweetest smile.

"I'd say, 'Get a room,' but you might take that literally," Remi drawled, those conflicting emotions of envy and happiness warring in her chest again.

Briana chuckled, and Remi rolled her eyes at the lasciviousness of it. *Yech.*

"Bri, I need to borrow your sister for a minute." Rochelle appeared beside Remi, slipping an arm through hers. "You should go entertain your future mother-in-law instead of flirting with your fiancé and making the rest of us blush."

Remi bit back a groan even as she allowed herself to be led away to a corner of the café. She'd been trying to avoid her mother since arriving at Mimi's. Even a cup of her favorite hot beverage couldn't make her forget that her mother had an agenda by inviting her and Declan to join a gathering she'd intentionally excluded Remi from in the first place.

And yeah, best not dwell too long on that.

"Honey, what is that you're drinking?" Rochelle scrunched up her nose.

Dread swished in her stomach like day-old swill. "Caramel macchiato."

"That's nothing but dessert in a cup. Tea is so much better for you." She shook her head, and her disappointment dented the hard-won, forged-in-fire armor of confidence Remi had built around herself—her heart. "Now, tell me about what's going on between you and Declan."

God, if she held in all these sighs, she would end up with gastric issues.

"Mom, don't get ahead of yourself," she warned.

"You know I'm not one to listen to gossip." Remi coughed, earning a narrow-eyed look from her mother. "But I heard about the kiss at the library. Really, Remi, a little more propriety would've been appreciated, but if the story is true…"

Remi didn't confirm or deny, just sipped her drink. But her mother obviously took her silence as confirmation, and a smile that could only be described as cat-ate-the-whole-flock-of-canaries spread across her face.

"If the story is true, then why haven't you brought him by the house for dinner? Do you know how embarrassing it is to hear that my daughter is dating one of the most eligible men in town from someone else? And here I've been so worried about—"

"Mom, please, stop. Declan and I— We're just friends," she interrupted, holding up her free hand, palm out.

Her mother's excited flow of words snapped off like the cracking of a brittle tree limb. She stared at Remi, the delight in her eyes dimming to frustration and… Sadness. It was that sadness that tore through Remi. As if her *mediocrity* actually pained her mother.

Rochelle's gaze dropped down to Remi's body, skimming her dress. Before her mother's scrutiny even lifted back to Remi's face, anxiety and unease churned in her belly. Tension invaded her body, drawing her shoulders back, pouring ice water into her veins.

She knew what was coming.

Braced herself for it.

"Maybe… Maybe if you would try to dress just a bit more appropriately for a woman of your—stature, you could possibly be more than friends. If you wore clothes that…concealed rather than drew attention to problematic areas, perhaps Declan would focus more on your lovely face and ignore everything else."

The gentle tone didn't soften the dagger-sharp thrust or make the wound bleed any less.

That it was her mother who twisted the knife and sought to slice her self-esteem to shreds only worsened the pain.

"I'm only telling you this because I love you, and I want you to be happy like your sisters. You know that, don't you, honey?" Rochelle covered Remi's cold hand, squeezed it, the hazel eyes that Remi had inherited, soft and pleading.

I don't know that! If you cared, if you really loved me like you do Briana and Sherri, then you would see how you're tearing me apart.

The words howled inside her head, shoved at her throat with angry fists. Only the genuine affection in her mother's gaze chained them inside. That and her unwillingness to hurt her mother, even though Rochelle didn't possess the same reluctance.

"If you'll excuse me," Remi murmured, setting her drink down on a nearby table. She couldn't stomach it anymore.

Couldn't stomach... A lot of things anymore.

Without waiting for her mother's reply, she strode over to the small group where Declan stood. He glanced down at her, and that violet gaze sharpened, seeming to bore past the smile she fixed on her face.

Several minutes later, before she had time to fully register being maneuvered, she found herself bundled in her coat on the sidewalk outside the café, Declan at her side.

She didn't speak as they strolled back in the direction of the library, and he didn't try to force her into conversation. The events of the entire day whirled through her mind like a movie reel, pausing on the kiss before speeding on fast-forward to him showing up at the library only to pause on her discussion with her mother.

I want you to be happy like your sisters.

Remi could pinpoint the last time her mother had been proud of her. Because it'd been the time of her last heartbreak, her last failure.

And the whole town had been there to bear witness.

For Rochelle Donovan, happiness meant a husband, marriage, children. And Remi desired that—she did. But if she didn't have them, she wasn't less of a woman, less worthy. Not having the whole fairy-tale wedding and family thing wouldn't be due to the size of her breasts, hips or ass. And she refused to decrease in size—whether in weight, personality or spirit—for someone else to love her.

She'd been willing to do that once. Never again.

And yet... Yet, for a moment, Remi had glimpsed that

flicker of pride in her mother's eyes again, and her heart had swelled. It'd been so long.

She was tired of being a failure in her mother's eyes. Of being a disappointment. Was it so wrong to yearn for that light in Rochelle's gaze directed toward her, the one Briana and Sherri took for granted?

Remi knew who she was. Knew her own worth. Owned herself.

But just once…

She slammed to an abrupt halt. And turned to Declan.

To his credit, he didn't appear surprised or alarmed. He just slid his hands into his pants pockets, his coat pushed back to expose that wide chest, flat abdomen and those strong thighs. A swimmer's body—tall, long and lean. And powerful. Staring at him, she combatted the need to step close and closer still, curl against the length of him and just… Rest. She'd come to rely on herself a long time ago, but in the café, she'd uncharacteristically allowed him to take charge. And it'd been a relief. To let someone else carry the burden for a few moments—yes, it'd been a relief.

But that had been an aberration.

She just needed him for one thing.

"I've changed my mind. I'll pretend to be your girlfriend."

Declan cocked his head to the side, studied her for a long moment. "Why have you changed your mind?"

"Does it matter?"

"Yes," he murmured. "I think it does."

A flutter in her belly at his too-soft, too-damn-understanding voice. "No, it doesn't," she said. "Are *you* changing *your* mind?"

Again, he didn't immediately reply. "No, Remi, I'm not. I still need you."

Dammit, he should choose his words more carefully. A greedier woman could read more into that statement.

"Well then, I accept. But I have my own counterproposal." When he dipped his chin, indicating she continue, she inhaled a breath, held it, then exhaled, attempting to quell the riot of nerves rebelling behind her navel. "You have to agree to attend Briana's engagement party with me in a month. Four weeks should be more than enough time to convince Tara that we're a legitimate couple." She stuck out her hand. "Deal?"

Declan stared at her palm as if he read all her secrets in the lines and creases. Slowly, he lifted his intense gaze to hers and, without breaking that connection, engulfed her hand in his bigger, warmer one.

Then drew her closer.

And closer.

Until his woodsy cloves-and-cinnamon scent surrounded her, warmed her. Seduced her. She sank her teeth into her bottom lip. Trapping the moan that nudged at her throat and ached to slip free.

The hand not holding her hand cupped her neck, his thumb swept the skin under her jaw. She shivered.

And held her breath.

Those beautiful, carnal lips brushed over her forehead. "Deal."

She exhaled.

These next four weeks were going to be... Killer.

CHAPTER FOUR

Declan: Hey, are you up?

Remi: It's 9:30. I'm not 80.

Declan: Is that a yes?

Remi: *sigh* Yes.

Declan: Is it ok for me to call?

Remi: Sure.

REMI STARED AT her phone screen, heart thudding in her chest, waiting on the black to light up with his name as if she were a teen and the captain of the football team had promised to call. And when the screen lit up with his name, she had to slap her traitorous heart back down with a reality check.

Fake relationship. Get it together. This isn't some chick flick starring Zendaya.

"Hello."

"Why don't I remember you being this snarky before?" he asked in lieu of greeting.

Because we've never had a real conversation past "Hi" and "Excuse me, I need to get to the creamer" at Mimi's

Café. Since saying that would reveal more than she was willing to expose, she went with, "I'm not sure I can answer that. And tell me that's not what you called to ask me."

He snorted. "No. It hit me that we didn't come up with a cover story for how we got together. If our...relationship is going to be believable, we'll have to be of one accord with that."

"Wow." Remi shook her head even though he couldn't see the gesture. "Is even saying the word *relationship* painful?"

"Oh, sweetheart, if you only knew," he drawled.

No, Remi ordered her damn heart again. You will not turn over at that endearment. *Cut the shit!*

She cleared her throat, absently picking at the thread on the couch cushion beneath her. "So do you have any ideas for how we became completely enamored of one another?"

"I'm guessing me trying to stop you from bringing disease and destruction to the earth, but we ended up falling for one another is out?"

A loud bark of laughter escaped her, and she clapped a hand over her mouth even though no one lived with her to hear it. "And what's this disease that I'm so intent on bringing to the earth? Love?"

His mock gasp echoed in her ear. "How did you know?"

She snickered. "Okay, I've read *Pestilence*, too, and Laura Thalassa is brilliant. Oh, which reminds me." She snapped her fingers. "I've been meaning to recommend *Crave* by Tracy Wolff, if you haven't read it already. I think you'll love it."

"Thank you. I'll definitely pick it up." A pause. "How do you know what books I'll love?" he murmured.

Heat surged into her face, and she closed her eyes, lightly banging her head against the back of the couch. Dammit.

"I'm a librarian. It's my job to notice what people are reading." *Nice save*, she assured herself. She hoped. *Please God, let it be a nice save.* "Besides, when a man comes into the library and I catch him unashamedly reading YA paranormal romance, my nerd heart rejoices. And I want to feed his literary addiction."

When he chuckled, she silently breathed a deep sigh of relief. And sent up another prayer of thanksgiving. And maybe a promise to attend service on Sunday. It'd been a while.

"There's our story," Declan said. "We met at the library when you noticed what I was reading and suggested a book you thought I'd like. We struck up a conversation, I asked you out, the rest is history."

"It's like our own book nerd fairy tale."

"Book nerds are the shit."

"Hell yeah we are." Remi grinned, and once more had to order her heart to stop doing dumb things. Like swooning.

"'Night, Remi. And thank you again."

"Good night, Declan."

Remi: I've arranged our first date for Friday night after you get to Rose Bend. Hayride.

Declan: Pass.

Remi: Sorry. Bought the tickets. You wanted to be visible. What's more visible than a hayride?

Declan: Dinner. Coffee. A stroll. Standing in the damn street. All don't involve hay. Or hay.

Remi: We're doing it. Suck it up, city boy.

Declan: Why am I doing this again?

Remi: Hey! You kissed me!

Declan: Oh believe me. I can't forget.

Remi: ...

Declan: Too soon?

Remi: Bundle up. It's going to be cold.

* * *

Declan: So the hayride was fun.

Remi: ...

Declan: I can hear you saying I told you so.

Remi: Me? Nooooo.

Remi: But I did.

Declan: No one likes a know-it-all. Even beautiful ones.

Remi: You don't need to do that.

Declan: Do what?

Remi: Do the compliment thing when no one's around to hear it.

Declan: I can be truthful whether I have an audience or not, Remi.

Declan: If it makes you uncomfortable, I won't say or rather type it.

Remi: No it doesn't. Just… It's not necessary.

Declan: Are we having our first argument as a couple?

Remi: I think we are… And just for the record, I win.

Declan: Of course, dear. Yes, dear.

Remi: Such a good fake boyfriend.

* * *

Remi: Heads-up. If Tara asks, my nickname for you is baby-cakes.

Declan: WTF??

Remi: She was pushing it. Had to come up with something.

Remi: Ok, kidding. Sorta. But she did corner me today and was her usual petty self.

Remi: Why didn't you tell me you used to be married?

THE PHONE RANG seconds later, and Remi sighed before swiping her thumb across the screen. She should've expected this call, but her stomach still dropped toward her bare feet. All afternoon, since Tara had approached Remi outside Sunnyside Grille after lunch, she'd gone back and forth about whether or not she would ask Declan about his previous marriage.

Over the two weeks they'd been "together," the texts and phone calls had been constant, and when he came to Rose Bend, they'd spent every day together. As couples did. But they weren't real—no matter how her pulse tripped over itself at just the sound of his voice in her ear or the sight of his name in her messages. Or how thick, hot desire twisted inside her when his hand rested on her hip or cupped the back of her neck. A shiver rippled down her spine at just the memory of the possessive touch.

No. Not possessive. She had to remember and remind herself what this was. Fake. A sham. For the benefit of another woman who'd done what Remi could not allow herself to do.

Fall for him.

She could not be that naive or stupid.

Raising the phone to her ear, she said, "Hey."

"Remi," he replied. "What did she say to you?"

"She didn't go into details," she gently reassured him. Because from the tautness of his voice, it seemed as if he needed to be reassured. "It seemed more like she wanted me to know she had information about you that I didn't have." She hesitated but couldn't hold back the question that had been plaguing her for hours. "Why didn't you mention it, Declan?"

"It's not important."

The abrupt, almost-harsh reply echoed in the silence that fell between them, mocking his adamance.

"Your mom might not have moved to town yet during my last relationship, so you may not have heard about it.

But it was the topic of conversation three years ago, for months." She inhaled a deep breath, bile pitching in her stomach at the thought of talking about Patrick and the disastrous, public ending of their relationship. But if she wanted Declan to trust her with his story, maybe she had to take that first step.

"Patrick Grey was a resident at the hospital in the next town over but lived here. We met at the annual motorcycle rally, and I fell hard, fast. Handsome, smart, and yeah, he was going to be a doctor. Not bad, right?"

She gave a soft, self-deprecating laugh. Because, yes, bad. If only she hadn't allowed those things to blind her to his other, not-so-favorable traits.

"We were together for a year and a half. And him being a resident, we didn't have a ton of time together. But I loved and enjoyed every minute when we were. So much that when he started criticizing my dinner or breakfast choices, or offering his opinion on what I wore, I didn't see his comments as negative. Just that he was concerned with my health or wanted me to look my very best. But when he started using what he called 'reward systems'—lose five pounds and he would agree to take me to the bar around his work friends—then I couldn't deny what I'd been ignoring."

"Remi," Declan breathed. "You don't have to tell me this."

"I'd like to say that I broke up with him," she continued as if he hadn't spoken, because *yes*, she did need to get this out. She hadn't spoken about it since it happened. It was time to purge herself of this festering wound. "But I can't. One Saturday morning, I walked into Sunnyside Grille to meet my sisters for breakfast since Patrick had to work a double shift. Or so he'd texted me. But that wasn't true. Because when I entered, there he was. Sitting in one of the booths near the door, sharing the Sunnyside Up Special with a slender, gorgeous brunette. Well, that's not true. They weren't sharing it because they were too busy kissing."

She swallowed hard, still seeing Patrick, the man she'd imagined building a life with, giving another woman what he should've only offered her. Three years had dulled that pain to a twinge.

"When he saw me, he didn't even apologize. Instead, he blamed me for sending him to another woman. He wasn't original. The usual. If I'd only taken care of myself, lost the weight, hadn't been so fat and lazy. In front of everyone in that diner. He didn't give a damn about humiliating me in front of my family, the people I'd grown up with. And I was so stunned, so hurt, I stood there and took it. Grace, the owner, came over and ordered him out. Told him to never bring his ass in there. And Cole and Wolf Dennison *escorted* him to the sidewalk." A faint smile curved her lips, and it went to show how she'd healed, because there was a time she'd never believed she could feel any humor with the memory. "But the damage had already been done. People get dumped all the time. But mine had been devastating, humiliating *and* public."

"What happened to the asshole?" he snapped.

She blinked. "Um, I don't know. I don't care. Last I heard, he found a position in a hospital out of state."

"That just means it's going to take me more time to track him down."

"What?" She laughed. "Declan, stop playing."

"Who's playing?" he growled. "And next time I'm in town, I'm treating Cole and Wolf to beers."

"That's...sweet." She smiled, and warmth radiated in her chest. "Thank you."

"You're perfect, Remi. I hope you know that. And fuck him if he was too much of a narcissistic, insecure bastard to realize it. Or I bet he did realize it. But to make himself feel better about himself, he tried to make you smaller. And I'm not talking about the size of your gorgeous ass or hips—which you fucking better not touch. I hope you know any real man would see the beautiful, sexy, brilliant woman you are and not ask you to change a damn thing. Hell, he would have to up his game to be worthy of you."

Her lips popped open. Thank God they were on the phone because she would've hated for him to glimpse the tears stinging her eyes or the heat streaming into her face. If he looked at her now, he would see her feelings for him. She didn't have to cross her bedroom to the mirror over the dresser and know that the need, the hunger, the... No, she backed away from labeling *that* emotion. But she knew those emotions would greet her in her reflection.

"Remi?" he murmured. "Sweetheart?"

Her fingers fluttered to the base of her throat, and she closed her eyes.

"I'm here. And thank you. I... Thank you."

"You're welcome, sweetheart. But I'm only speaking the truth." He sighed. "I get why you shared that with me. Thank you for trusting me. I know it wasn't easy." He paused, and several moments passed where his breath echoed in her ear. "Ava and I started dating in college. People said we were a 'golden couple,' whatever that means. I guess I can see it now. Similar goals—both financial majors, wanted to be entrepreneurs, desired a certain lifestyle, had the same ideals about the family we desired. She was beautiful, driven, ambitious, and I admired all of that about her. So after we graduated, we married."

A hard silence ricocheted down the line, deafening in its heaviness.

"I love my parents, especially my mother. But their marriage... It wasn't healthy. My father wasn't physically abusive, but emotionally, verbally? He cut her down with words, by withholding affection if she didn't have his dinner on the table on time or if she disappointed him in any small way. And my mother's identity was so entangled with his that when he died, she crumbled, didn't know who she was, how to carry on from one day to the next. That's why when she sold the house and moved here, I dropped everything and made it happen. She needed to escape anything that had to do with my father so she could *finally* discover herself apart from him. I think that was one of the things that attracted me to Ava. She had her own identity, her own goals. But I didn't count on that tearing us apart."

Questions pinged against her skull, but she remained quiet, letting him tell his story at his own pace. Yet her whole body ached with the need to wrap around him, hold him.

Protect him.

She shook her head, as if the motion could dislodge the silly idea. Declan didn't need her protection. Didn't need *her*.

"We both entered graduate school and took jobs in our fields. While my career seemed to rise fast, hers didn't go as smoothly. And listen, I'm a white man in a field that is set up for me to succeed. So I understood her frustration. I knew there were certain advantages for me that weren't there for her. But she turned bitter, and she took that bitterness out on the one person who unconditionally loved and supported her—me."

Remi almost asked him to stop because what was

coming… It had turned him off relationships all these years later. So it must've scarred him.

"It started with complaining about me not having enough time for her. So no matter how tired I was from work and school, I tried to give her more attention. Then she accused me of being too needy, so I pulled back. I'd arrive at work and discover that my files were missing information, or the numbers had been transposed. Or I had to make a presentation, and the PowerPoint had disappeared from my computer. When we attended my office parties, she either flirted with my colleagues or deliberately insulted them. Or as I later found out, slept with them."

"Shit," she whispered.

"Yes, shit." He chuckled, but it didn't carry any humor. "She tried to sabotage my career before it could really begin. The betrayal…" He cleared his throat. Paused. "The betrayal when you've done nothing but love a person… It destroys something in you. Your trust. In other people. In yourself. It's not something you forget—or want to repeat."

She got it. God, did she get it.

"She didn't break you, though," she whispered.

"No," he whispered back. "She didn't."

"Declan?"

"Yes."

"I'm glad."

CHAPTER FIVE

LAST HALLOWEEN, DECLAN attended a friend's party, dressed as a pirate, and ended up going home with a sexy as hell cat—or maybe she'd been a mouse.

The Halloween before that, he'd spent the evening at a business dinner. And had his dining partner for dessert.

This Halloween, he stuffed goody bags with candy, toys and small books for the fifty or so excited children that crowded into the Rose Bend Public Library for the Spooks 'n' Books Bash.

Being the town librarian's "boyfriend" definitely had its perks.

He smirked as he tossed a mini pack of M&M's into a plastic bag decorated with goofy ghosts, cats and witches. In the three weeks since he'd started dating Remi, he'd gone to a high school–sponsored haunted house, judged a pumpkin pie contest that she'd volunteered him for when the scheduled judge came down with food poisoning, and gone on his first ever hayride. He'd eaten his first s'more in nineteen years, tasted his first cup of homemade spiced cider ever and snacked on honest-to-God grapenut custard, hauling out and dusting off childhood memories he'd long forgotten.

Yes, these last three weeks had definitely been an experience. As different from his outings with Tara as the Patriots from the Lions. He'd had fun.

Damn.

When had his life stopped being fun?

Not that his life was bad. God, no. It would be the height of white privilege to cry about a challenging career he enjoyed, the luxurious lifestyle it afforded him, the doors to the elite business and social worlds it opened to him. And he indulged in it all.

But did he feel that pure excitement like a child on Christmas morning or a kid soaring down a steep hill on his bike at full speed? Like a teen discovering the bloom of his first crush?

No. That had been missing.

Until now.

Until Remi.

His pulse an uncomfortable throb at his neck, his wrists, he scanned the library, and like a lodestone, his gaze found her. Maybe it was the dark fire of her hair—or the brighter flame of her very essence—but she seemed to gleam like a ruby among the crowd of parents who stood in the outer ring surrounding the children who gathered for story time.

A smile flashed across her face at something, brief but so lovely, and the air in his chest snagged.

Jesus, the power of it.

Like a hard knee to the gut and a gentle brush of fingers across his jaw at the same time.

He blinked, dragging his much-too-fascinated scrutiny away from her and back to the task at hand. Goody bags. Candy. Toys.

"Is this my son over here in the back doing manual labor?" His mother appeared in front of the table, a wide smile stretched across her pretty face. Tiny lines fanned out from the corners of Janet Howard's blue eyes as she nabbed a small box of crayons and swung it back and forth in front of him. "If I didn't see it with my own eyes…"

He snorted, holding his hand out and curling his fingers, signaling for her to hand over the box. When she did, with an even-wider grin, he drawled, "Laugh it up now, woman. But just because I work behind a desk doesn't mean I don't know the meaning of labor." He arched an eyebrow. "I mean, who do you think mows that big yard I have?"

She mimicked the eyebrow gesture. "That reminds me. James Holland lost your number. But he wanted me to pass along the message that he would be glad to take care of your lawn like he does mine."

"Freaking blabbermouth," Declan muttered, dropping the crayons into the goody bag. No sense of male solidarity at all.

"Hi, Declan." Tara strolled up to them, smiling widely. "This is so cute." She turned, waving a hand in the direction of the larger area set up with game stations, the story circle and tables of books. "When Janet told me she was stopping by, I had to tag along. All this time I've lived here, and I can't believe I've never made it to this charming little event."

"It's only the second time the library has held it. Remi started it last year," he said, pride for Remi and the staff's hard work evident in his voice. He didn't even try to conceal it.

He'd only witnessed the tail end of their labor, helping set up and put up decorations, but more than one person had regaled him about all the time and effort she put into the event. And when his mother's gaze narrowed on him, he met it. There was nothing wrong with being proud of a friend's achievements.

Fuck, he was a terrible liar. Even to himself.

His mother and Tara glanced at one another, then Janet hooked an arm through Tara's, clearly telegraphing where her allegiance lay. "Well, that's nice. I just remembered you mentioning you were spending Halloween here, so I thought we'd come over and see if we can convince you to join us for coffee afterward."

We.

He didn't bother looking at Tara, but kept his attention focused on his mother. "I'm sorry. Remi and I already have plans after this wraps up." Technically, they didn't, and he hated fibbing to his mother, but if he had to take Remi to Sunnyside Grille for a late dinner to make the lie true, he would. "But thanks for supporting the event."

His mother's smile tightened around the edges, and she turned to Tara. "Honey, would you mind giving me a moment with Declan?"

"Not at all," Tara said. He ignored her and the smug note in her voice.

If she expected him to bow to his mother's coercion on her behalf, then neither woman really knew him.

"Son—"

"Mom, I love you, and I would never intentionally disrespect you." He interrupted her before she could get on a roll. He flattened his palms on the table and leaned forward, lowering his voice, not desiring an audience for this long-overdue conversation that he would've preferred to have in private. "But that—" he dipped his head in the direction Tara had disappeared "—is not going to happen. There has never *been* any chance of it happening. Something I made very clear to Tara even if she decided not to hear me. I only took her out those few times because it made you happy to see me with her. Or with someone."

He stretched an arm out, clasped his mother's hand in

his, squeezed. "I love you, Mom. You're the most important person in the world to me. And I would hate to see our relationship damaged in any way by you choosing this hill to die on. Tara's not for me."

"And this new woman is? A woman you haven't brought around and introduced to me, I might add?"

True. And he'd purposefully avoided doing so. His and Remi's relationship was fake; having her meet his mother smacked too much of "real." It crossed a boundary into territory he hadn't been prepared to enter. But Janet arriving here tonight might snatch that choice out of his hands.

Especially since Remi was headed their way.

He straightened, his gaze shifting from his mother and over her shoulder to the sexy, stunning woman walking toward them. How could she make a simple long-sleeved, V-necked shirt, a dark pair of high-waisted skinny jeans and ankle boots so hot?

Lust rippled through him, and he clenched his teeth against the primal pounding of it in his veins... In his cock.

Goddamn.

Kittens batting balls of yarn. Dad's old baseball mitt that smelled like Bengay and sweat. Grandma Eileen's dentures in a glass on the bathroom sink.

Thinking of anything that would prevent him from springing an erection in front of his mother and all these kids. But most of all his mother.

"Oh." His mother hummed. "That's the way of it."

Declan didn't tear his gaze from Remi. Couldn't. But if by some small miracle he could, yeah, he still wouldn't. Disquiet scurried beneath the throb of need. And he didn't want to glimpse the acknowledgment of that disquiet in his mother's eyes.

"Hey." Remi smiled, glancing down at the table packed

with goody bags. "Thank you, Declan. So much. First you saved me with the pie contest and now with this. When my volunteer called out, I thought I was going to have a bunch of screaming kids on my hands." She laughed and turned to his mother. "We've met before, Mrs. Howard, but it's nice to see you again. Thank you for coming tonight."

"Nice to see you, too, Ms. Donovan. Or is it okay to call you Remi, since rumor has it you're dating my son?"

The pointed and faintly accusatory tone wasn't lost on Declan, and apparently not on Remi either, since pink tinged the elegant slant of her cheekbones. But to her credit, she didn't back down.

"Rumors in a small town?" Her lips curled into a rueful twist. "If only we could monetize it, we could single-handedly support our economy. And yes—" she nodded "—I would be honored if you would call me Remi."

Declan smothered a bark of laughter. *Nice side step.* "Remi, my mother's not new to a library. When I was a kid, she used to take me there often and let me pick out any book I wanted, then let me participate in the scavenger hunts or watch afternoon movies. And she even volunteered at our school library sometimes. Or maybe she just wanted to keep an eye on me," he teased.

His mother snorted. "Both."

"Mrs. Howard, I don't know if you'd consider it, but the library can always use volunteers," Remi said.

"Volunteer? Me?" She scoffed, but Declan glimpsed the interest flicker in her eyes, even though her features remained guarded. "What could I possibly do?"

"Whatever you enjoy." Remi half turned, sweeping a hand toward the room. "If you like clerical duties such as helping us entering patron info into our computer system or returning books to the shelves or manning the help desk, that would be wonderful. Or since we are an interactive library, if you love working with the children, you can read to them, help with tutoring, assist us with our events or even man one of those scavenger hunts Declan mentioned."

Declan stared at her. Excitement shone in her hazel eyes, the gold like chips of sunlight, and enthusiasm lit her face so brightly, he blinked at its gleam.

She was beautiful. No—such a paltry, lazy word to describe the purity and loveliness of a spirit enhanced by a stunning face and body.

He'd met gorgeous women, dated them—fucked them.

But they all faded into an obscure corner of his past the longer he looked at Remi. His heart thudded against his sternum, a rhythm that drowned out the chatter of adults, the happy squeals of children. His world narrowed to her, to the fine angle of her cheekbones, the sweet sin of her mouth, the alluring dent in her chin. To the lush, sensual curves of her body.

Panic ripped through him, and out of pure survival, his mind scrambled back from a treacherous edge his damn heart should've known better than to go anywhere near.

"Declan?" Fingers touched the back of his hand, and just from the delicious burn, he didn't need to glance down and identify its owner. But he did anyway, because *not* looking at Remi Donovan wasn't even an option for him. A small frown creased her brow. "Everything okay?"

"Yes, fine." He flipped her hand over, rubbing his thumb over her palm, catching the small shiver that trembled up her arm. And because that vulnerability still sat on him, he repeated the caress. "I was just thinking how lucky this place is to have someone as loyal, hardworking and beautiful as you."

Her eyes widened, an emotion so tangled, so convoluted

flashing in them that he couldn't begin to decipher it. He'd surprised her. Good. Though they were engaged in this arrangement, there was something freeing about being able to touch her, to murmur compliments and neatly, *safely* categorize them under "for the charade."

Like now.

"Thank you," she murmured, giving him one last lingering look before shifting her attention back to his mother. "Do you want to get a cup of hot chocolate, and we can talk more about volunteering?"

"Yes." His mother nodded, and warmth slipped into her expression and voice. "I would like that very much."

"Wonderful. Let's go before the kids beat us to it." She laughed, leading Janet away.

"Is that her plan, then?"

Declan clenched his jaw. Hard. Until the muscles along his jaw ached in protest. Instead of replying to Tara, he walked away from the table, knowing she would follow. Pausing next to a volunteer, he asked her if she would mind watching the goody bags for a moment, and then he continued to a quieter side of the room.

Before he could speak, Tara crossed her arms over her chest, her lips forming a sulky pout that he hoped to God she didn't think was attractive.

"Is that her new plan? To ingratiate herself with your mother?"

"No," Declan said, arching an eyebrow. "That's your strategy. Hers is simply being her. Interested in other people and their needs. Being *nice*. That's who Remi is."

"Please." Tara sneered. "It's an act. No one is that nice. Not without a motive."

"You don't say," he drawled.

Red stained her cheeks, and she huffed out a breath, her chin hiking up.

"That's not what I meant," she said through gritted teeth. "And you know it."

Declan sighed, pinching the bridge of his nose. Briefly closing his eyes, he dropped his arm and met Tara's dark brown eyes, glinting with tears.

"Don't." He didn't bother blunting the sharp edge of his tone.

Maybe if he suspected the tears were authentic, he would've. But he'd witnessed this ploy before; she'd tried to use it on him with no luck, and she regularly employed those tears with his mother with much more success.

"I'm going to say this once again. And this will be the last time, Tara. I've been patient and have tried not to hurt your feelings, but you don't seem to understand kindness. Or you see it as something to take advantage of. There. Is. No. Us. There never was. There never will be. Hear me. Accept it. Move on. And if you genuinely like my mother and enjoy spending time with her, then fine. But if you're doing it only to get to me, then leave her alone, too. I won't allow you to use her, and more importantly, I won't let you hurt her."

"Where was this concern for a woman's feelings when you led me on?" she scoffed. Tears no longer moistened her eyes, but anger glittered there, and it pulled her mouth taut, turning her beauty as sharp and hard as a diamond. "You shouldn't have slept with me if you *claim* we didn't have anything."

He nodded. "You're right. I shouldn't have allowed my dick to do my thinking. But I've never lied to you, Tara. I was always up-front that we wouldn't have a relationship—that I didn't want that with you. With anyone. I convinced myself that you accepted that, when obviously you had other intentions the entire time. That's on you, not me."

Tara shook her head. "That's not true," she said, quietly, sounding a little lost.

And for a moment, he softened. Thrusting his fingers through his hair, he said, "Tara, I didn't want to hurt you. It's the one thing I actively tried to avoid. And I'm sorry if I did."

"It's just…" Tara turned from him, tightening her arms around herself, her lips rolling in on each other, thinning. When she faced him again, her shoulders lifted, and she fluttered a hand between them. "I know there is affection between us."

"Tara."

"Y'know, whatever you're doing with Remi Donovan isn't fooling me or anyone in this town."

And that quickly, any sympathy for her evaporated. He stiffened, studying her, the frustration pinching her skin tight and adding a jerkiness to her usually fluid movements.

"I don't really give a damn what other people think, including you."

He ignored the voice that pointed out that he'd proposed the bargain with Remi in the first place because of Tara.

"Obviously. Because the thought of you wanting *her*, being with *her*, of all people, is laughable. She's boring, fa—"

"Shut the hell up," he growled. "Say one more word, Tara, and I'll forget that I was raised not to disrespect women."

"Excuse me."

Declan jerked his head up and to the side just as Tara whipped around.

Fuck.

Remi stood there, perfectly composed and calm. And if

not for her eyes… His gut twisted, and he fisted his fingers, the blunt tips biting into his palms. The brown nearly swallowed the bright green and gold. If not for that darkness, he would assume she hadn't overheard Tara's ugly words.

Would assume those words hadn't landed direct, agonizing blows.

"Remi." He moved forward, Tara forgotten, his one goal to get to her. To somehow ease that hurt, make it disappear.

But she shifted backward. Away from him. And damn if a spike of pain didn't jab into his chest.

"We're about to give out the goody bags. When you're free, we could use your help passing them out." Dipping her chin, she pivoted and left, shoulders straight and without a glance back at them.

"Tara." His mother stepped forward, and for the first time, Declan noticed her. "I'm going to catch a ride home with a friend. I've known you for three years now, and you've never been anything but kind to me. But hearing you speak so horribly about someone a couple of minutes ago?" Janet shook her head. "It makes me wonder who you are when I'm not around. And if that is a person I want to know."

Janet reached for Declan, squeezed his hand and glanced in the direction Remi had disappeared.

"She's special, and you'd be a fool to let her get away." Brushing a kiss over his cheek, she left.

"She didn't mean…" Tara whispered, her voice catching.

Declan glanced over his shoulder at the other woman, spotting the moisture in her eyes, and for the first time, he believed her tears were real. But they failed to move him.

"She did. You just looked the consequences of your spite and pettiness in the face. I hope you remember them."

He walked away, leaving her alone. Like she deserved.

CHAPTER SIX

WHO KNEW A person could be completely numb inside and still smile, laugh and behave as if humiliation and pain hadn't pummeled her with meaty, bruising fists until she'd become a block of ice?

Seemed every day Remi discovered something new.

Returning to the Halloween event after overhearing Tara and Declan's conversation, then pretending nothing had occurred, had been one of the most difficult things she'd ever done. She'd been grateful for the coldness that had seeped into her veins, her chest.

But the library had emptied of parents, children, staff and volunteers forty-five minutes earlier, and now she sat in the passenger seat of Declan's car as he drove through the quiet streets. She couldn't escape the slow thawing around her heart. Couldn't escape her relentless thoughts. Couldn't escape *her*.

You wanting her, being with her, of all people, is laughable. She's boring, fa—

Remi squeezed her eyes shut, blocking out the scenery passing by her passenger window. Too bad she couldn't block out the memory of Tara's words. The other woman hadn't needed to finish the sentence for Remi to discern how it ended.

Fat.

Boring and fat.

Oh God how that hurt.

The mental door to that vault she tried so hard to keep shut creaked open and more memories crept out. Memories of her mother's and Patrick's voices.

A minute on the lips, a lifetime on the hips, Remi.

I just want you to be healthy, Remi.

Are you sure that choice of dress is wise? It's not very forgiving, is it?

The judgments, backhanded compliments and criticisms framed as concern poured into her mind. It'd taken Remi years, but she'd come to love and accept herself. But there were moments like tonight—like the other night with her mother in the café—when her hard-won confidence took enough of a hit that she wavered.

When she had to remind herself she wasn't lovable *despite* her weight or size.

She was lovable *because* of them.

Smothering a sigh, she silently urged the car to go faster. She longed to get home, drag on her favorite Wonder Woman pajamas, pop open a bottle of wine, put on *Pride and Prejudice*—the version with Keira Knightley and Matthew Macfadyen otherwise known as *the best version*—and lick her wounds.

Tomorrow. Tomorrow she would be okay, but God, she needed tonight.

"Remi, we need to talk about tonight."

The thaw inside her sped up, the red-tinged hurt throbbing. *Home. Just get me home.* It'd been years since she'd last cried in front of someone, and she didn't intend to break that record tonight. Not with him.

"I didn't get a chance to thank you for helping out with setting up and then stepping in when my volunteer didn't show. I really appreciate it. We all did," she said, switching the subject from what she suspected he really wanted to talk about.

"You're welcome. And the deflection isn't going to work," he murmured, voice gentle but firm. Too firm. "Since she would probably never apologize, I'm going to say 'I'm sorry' for Tara. What she sa—"

"Forget it. I have."

"Remi," he tried again.

"Let. It. Go."

Silence permeated the car, weighing down her shoulders, pressing on her chest. She desperately counted the minutes until she arrived home. Rose Bend wasn't that large a town, but right now it felt like the size of Boston.

Finally, he pulled up outside her house. Any other time, she would've taken a moment to admire the cute, quaint cottage that she'd saved for and bought on her own not far from the beautiful Kinsale Inn. But now, the sight of the yellow-and-white home only inspired relief. She reached for the door handle.

"Remi." Declan's hand clasped her wrist. "Wait."

She paused but didn't glance over her shoulder to look at him, instead perched on the passenger seat ready to flee.

"Please don't leave like this. Talk to me, sweetheart."

She trembled at the "sweetheart," her eyes briefly closing.

Whatever you're doing with Remi Donovan isn't fooling me or anyone in this town.

She wasn't his sweetheart, and everyone knew it. Hell, even her own mother found it hard to believe. Because a man like him couldn't desire, couldn't... *Love* a woman like her. A beautiful, charismatic, brilliant, sexy as hell man couldn't want a successful, independent, educated woman just because she happened to wear a size sixteen.

At least, that's what they believed.

Her? Well, before tonight, the last three weeks had offered her hope that Declan was attracted to her. Her mind had warned her that the heated glances, the fleeting caresses to her cheek, the holding of her hand, the jokes and laughter they shared, the phone calls and texts they exchanged—they were all part of the charade. But her heart failed to get the message. Her stupid heart took each gesture as proof that he felt *something* for her.

And she understood now why she grasped that hope so desperately.

Because in these three weeks, each caress, each glance, each compliment had worked toward transforming her long-time crush for him into love.

Yes, she so, so foolishly had fallen in love with Declan Howard.

Her head bowed, forehead pressing against the cold window.

She'd fallen for the most emotionally unavailable man in Rose Bend.

"Talk to you?" she said, leaning back in the seat and turning to him. "What is there to *talk* about? I told you I'm *fine*."

"Actually, you didn't. You just ordered me to let it go. But too many people in your life have done that, and I refuse to be another one who ignores your pain."

She stared at him, forcing her fingers to remain flat on her thighs and not to ball into fists. "Do you want me to admit that what Tara said hurt? Okay, yes. It hurt like hell. Do I want your apology on her behalf? No. I don't want it or need it. It's insulting to both of us. That should sum it up, right? Are we done here? Good."

"Hell no, we're not done. We're friends, dammit."

Oh God, didn't *that* just punch a hole in her chest?

"There. Satisfied? Now, good night."

She reached for the door handle again.

"If you get out of this car, I will follow you to that front door, Remi," he rumbled.

She threw her hands up in the air, loosing a harsh laugh that abraded her throat. "What more do you want from me? A pound of flesh? According to your ex-girlfriend, I can afford to sacrifice a few—"

His arm shot out, and his hand hooked behind her neck, hauling her forward. His mouth crushed down on hers, swallowing the words from her lips. Her moan surged up her throat, offering itself like a sacrifice to him. She was helpless at the erotic onslaught, opening herself wider and wider to this wild thing that masqueraded as a kiss. He took from her over and over, slanting his mouth, diving deep, sucking harder as if starved, as if desperate.

As if afraid she would disappear if he didn't gorge himself in this moment.

Or maybe she was projecting.

Declan lifted his other hand to her chin, swept his hand over the shallow cleft there. Once and twice. Such a simple, small caress, but it echoed in a soft flutter between her legs, and she clenched her thighs against the sweet, erotic sensation.

God, touch me there... Kiss me there.

The plea bounced inside her head, words she longed to utter aloud. She'd never believed that opportunity would be hers.

Did you want it to be?

The low, insidious whisper slid through her lust-hazed mind. And no matter how hard she pressed her lips to Declan's, how hard she thrust her tongue against his, she couldn't evict the question from her thoughts. Did she?

If she took this step with him, there was no coming back. And for her, it wouldn't be just sex. Not with him. Her heart was already involved. Giving him her body, too, would cement an epic fall that would make Icarus's look like a mere stumble.

"Invite me inside."

Declan issued the hoarse plea-wrapped-in-a-demand, and it reverberated loudly in the confines of his car. She stared at him, emotionally on a precipice. One step off could mean joy for her... Or utter heartbreak.

Was she brave enough to find out which?

He brushed his thumb under the curve of her bottom lip, the hand at her nape a gentle weight. But he waited, allowing her to make this decision, even though desire darkened his eyes to indigo and his mouth bore the damp, swollen mark of their raw kiss.

"Come inside."

Inside my house. Inside my body. My heart. My soul.

She issued the invitation, knowing he would only take her up on two of those. And even as he exited the car, rounded the hood and opened her door, she accepted it.

Moments later, she led him into her home, and as soon as they crossed the threshold, Declan closed the door behind them, twisting the lock. All without removing his hooded gaze from her.

Need dug its dark claws into her, and her thighs trembled with the force of it. How was it possible to *want* this much? To feel like if he didn't put his hands on her, his mouth on her, his cock *inside* her, she would crawl out of her skin? Lose her mind?

"Touch me."

Two words. They were all she could push past her constricted throat. They were all that were necessary.

He stalked forward, shrugging out of his coat, peeling his sweater and dark T-shirt over his head, dropping all the clothing to the floor. Her breath expelled from her lungs on a hard, long *whoosh*.

Jesus Christ.

Clothed, he was beautiful.

Bared, with golden skin stretched across taut, flexing muscle, he was magnificent.

She couldn't move, her gaze greedily bingeing on the wide breadth of his shoulders, the wall of his chest, the corded strength of his arms. That ridged ladder of abs with the dark silky line of hair that disappeared beneath the waistband of his pants.

A waistband his hands had dropped to.

"Wait." She popped her palms up in the universal sign of Stop.

"Let me," she whispered. "I want it." She clasped her hands together as if holding her passion for him between them. "I want you."

"I'm yours." He beckoned her closer, and as imperious as it seemed… Damn, it was hot, too. "Come get me."

Oh God, if only that were true, she mused, crossing the few steps toward him. If only he was really hers. To keep. She shook her head. No place for those thoughts here. Stay in the now.

"What're you telling yourself no about?" he murmured, tugging her closer, tunneling his fingers through her hair, his nails scraping over her scalp. Her lashes fluttered closed, and she turned into his big palm, sinking her teeth into the heel, giving him back a little of the pleasure/pain he'd doled out to her. A hiss escaped him, and when he fisted the strands of her hair, pulling, she nipped harder. "This is going to be over before it begins, sweetheart," he warned, dipping his head to take her mouth in a brief but thorough conquering. "Now what're you telling yourself no about?"

No way in hell could she answer that loaded question. So she didn't.

Instead, she tackled his belt and the closure on his pants. Desperation climbed high inside her, neck and neck with lust. She wanted to drown herself in pleasure. In need. In him. Forget about what awaited her tomorrow. Forget the uncertainty.

For the first time, she was taking for herself and damn the consequences.

But he covered her hands with one of his, halting her frantic actions. The other cupped her cheek, tilting her head back.

"So many times I've wondered what goes on behind these lovely hazel eyes. What secrets you're keeping. And it's those moments, I consider switching careers and becoming an archeologist whose main job is unearthing those treasures." He danced his fingertips over her cheekbone, the arch of her nose, the top bow of her lip. "You wouldn't give up those secrets easily, but they would be worth the work. *You* are worth the work."

Her chest squeezed so tight, she locked her teeth around a cry. No one had ever spoken to her like that. She closed her eyes and bowed her head on the pretense of pressing a kiss to the base of his throat. Anything to avoid having him see the love she knew was in her gaze.

Declan gripped the sides of her shirt, balling it in his fists until it untucked from her jeans and bared her stomach. She lifted her arms, stamping down the nerves in her stomach. That dark hot need in his eyes couldn't be faked. He wanted her; he liked her body just as she did. Still… When the top cleared her head and the heat in that indigo gaze flared, the lingering remnants of doubt dissolved like mist.

"Fuck, sweetheart." Lust stamped his features, pulling his skin taut over his cheekbones, his lips appearing fuller, more carnal. "Let me..."

"Please," she damn near whined.

He lifted his hands toward her, but at the last minute, lowered his arms.

"Bedroom," he ground out.

Wordlessly, she turned and led him down the hall and into her shadowed bedroom. Moonlight streamed through the large windows, providing more than enough illumination. But Declan must not have thought so because he crossed to the lamp on her bedside table and switched it on, bathing the room in a warm, golden glow. Then he crossed back to her in that sensual, almost-feline glide of his, and lust wrenched low in her belly, high in her sex. She couldn't contain her whimper. Didn't even try.

When he reached her, Declan slowly lowered to his knees, his pose worshipful, reverent. As were the hands that removed her boots and jeans. As were the lips that pressed a kiss to her hip just above the line of her black panties.

As were the words that ordered her back on the bed, heels to the edge of the mattress.

She shuddered, excitement and vulnerability dueling inside her as she lay exposed to him, evidence of her overwhelming desire for him evident in her soaked flesh, in the damp panel of her underwear.

Teeth nipped at her sensitive inner thigh, and she jerked at the sensation and the taut anticipation of his mouth giving her what she so desperately hungered for.

"Shh," he soothed, brushing a caress over the tender area. "Tell me I can have you, Remi." He grazed his fingertips over her folds, and she gasped at the featherlight touch, arching into it. Her hands fisted the covers at her hips, needing something to anchor her.

"Have me, Declan." She bit her lip, trapping anything else that would've spilled forth without her permission. "Please have me."

Without further prodding, he stripped her panties off and dived into her.

He tongued a path up her folds, swirling and licking. Sucking. No part of her remained a mystery to him. She dived her hands into his hair, clutching the strands and holding on as he lapped at her, his ravenous growl vibrating over her flesh and through her sex.

Two thick fingers pressed against her entrance then inside her, stretching her, filling her. She cried out, grinding against his hand, his mouth. Pleasure struck her, bolt after bolt streaking through her. And as his lips latched on to her clit, and his tongue flicked and circled the pulsing nub, she curled into him, breathless, *aching*.

Declan rubbed a place high inside her, and she exploded, came so hard black crept into the edges of her vision. She tumbled back to the bed, her breath a harsh rasp in her lungs, her bones liquefied. Dimly, she was aware of Declan standing at the foot of the bed and the whisper of clothes sliding over skin.

The mattress dipped, and she focused on the gorgeous sexual beast crouched above her. While she silently watched, he tore open a silver packet, removed a condom and sheathed himself. And *oh God...*

Renewed lust fluttered, then flowed inside her in a molten rush. A cock shouldn't be lovely, but then again, this was Declan. It didn't seem possible that anything about him could be less than perfect. Including his dick. And long, thick, with a flared, plum-shaped head, he was indeed *perfect*. And mouthwatering. Before her mind could send the message to her body, she was reaching for him...

"No, sweetheart." He caught her wrist, bending down to crush an openmouthed kiss to the palm. "I want to make it inside you. Sit up."

He didn't wait for her to comply but tugged on the hand he held. Quickly, he divested her of her bra and dipped his head, sucking a beaded nipple into his mouth. Cradling her, he lifted her breasts, his thumbs circling the tip he hadn't treated himself to yet. Yet.

She clawed at his shoulders, tipping her head back, those pulls of his mouth echoing in her sex. Where she needed him. Now.

"Declan," she whispered. Pleaded.

"Take me in, Remi." He took her hand, wrapped it around him. "You take me."

She did.

Raising her hips, she guided him to her, notched him at her entrance. And cupping his firm ass, welcomed him inside her.

Their twin groans saturated the air.

She'd thought his fingers had filled her. No, they'd just prepared her for this... Possession. This branding.

Never had she felt so *whole*.

Slipping his arms under her shoulders, he gathered her close, and she did the same to him. Clinging to him. He held himself still, allowing her to become accustomed to the size and width of him. And yes, she needed those few moments. But as a fine shiver rippled through his body, she nuzzled the strong line of his jaw, nipping it.

"Move," she urged, flexing her hips against him. "Your turn to take me."

Tangling his fingers in her hair, he tilted her head back and claimed her mouth just as he claimed her body.

Over and over, he tunneled deep, burying his cock inside her, marking her as his. She undulated and arched beneath him, giving even as she accepted. The slap of skin on skin, the musk of sex, the damp release of sex greeting sex punctuated the room, creating music for their bodies' erotic dance. Each thrust, each grind, each growled word of praise shoved her closer to the edge, and she flitted close, then scampered back, not wanting this to end. Needing to be in this moment, in this space with him forever, but the pleasure—the mind-bending, body-aching pleasure—wouldn't permit that.

He reached between them, rubbed a thumb over the rigid bundle of nerves cresting the top of her sex. The scream building inside her was more than a voice; it was physical. And when he pistoned into her once, twice, three times, her body gave it sound.

She flew apart.

Her body. Her mind. Her soul.

Pieces of her scattered, and she doubted she could possibly be whole again.

As he stiffened above her, his hoarse growl of pleasure rumbling against her chest and in her ear, she gave in to the darkness closing in on her.

I love you. I love you.

And as she let go, she whispered the words in her head that she could never permit herself to say aloud.

I LOVE YOU.

Remi's whisper echoed in Declan's mind, crashing against his skull like waves against the shore.

I love you.

She probably hadn't meant to let the admission slip out; she'd been halfway asleep as she uttered those three words that carved fear into his chest.

Maybe she didn't mean them. People said things like that in the heat of passion all the time, and they regretted it later. Let sex—especially such cataclysmic, hot as hell sex—get mixed up and muddled with emotion, and they were temporarily confused. Yes, that was it. Remi didn't—

That wasn't Remi. She might not have meant to say she loved him—might not have intended to let him know—but she'd meant it.

Or else Remi believed she did.

He propped his elbows on his thighs and dropped his head into his hands.

I love you.

A howl churned in his gut, surging up his throat, but at the last second, he trapped it behind clenched teeth. Pain, fear and anger—yes, anger—eddied inside him in a grimy cesspool. He wanted to lash out. To yell that he didn't ask for her love. That love wasn't part of their deal.

He wanted to curl his body behind hers and beg her to take it back, to please take it back. Before *love* crushed them both and he lost the woman he'd come to depend on, to admire, to desire, to need... God, he'd come to need her. Her texts, her calls, her smiles, her...

Everything.

Love would ruin who they were to each other.

Just as it'd diminished his mother, so she'd had to rediscover who she was as a person.

Just as it'd morphed into something ugly and destroyed his marriage.

People used that particular affection as a reason to hurt and damage one another every day, and he wanted no part of it.

Not even from Remi. Especially not from Remi. Because to witness how it would extinguish the light from those beautiful hazel eyes... How it would steal the radiance that shone from her like a beacon piercing darkness...

"I'm surprised you're still here."

Declan slowly straightened, glancing over his shoulder. Remi, with the cover tucked under her arms, sat up, her expression shuttered. Grief careened through him. It'd been weeks since he'd seen that look on her face. Since she'd closed him out.

"Remi..." he murmured, turning to her.

She shook her head. "At first, I thought it was a bad dream, but when I woke up and saw you fully dressed and sitting on the side of the bed as if you couldn't wait to bolt out of here, I knew it wasn't a dream. More of a nightmare."

"Remi, I don't want to hurt you."

She huffed out a low, dry chuckle. "This isn't about hurting me, but just the opposite—you're the one who doesn't want to be hurt."

He couldn't deny that. Hell, if he were brutally honest, he'd been running scared since he'd signed his divorce papers. But he'd been doing it so long, he didn't know how to stop. Didn't know if he had the courage to stop.

Even for her. And if anyone deserved someone to be brave on her behalf, it was Remi.

"You don't want to take the risk of falling in love and being hurt again, of being betrayed. And your greatest fear, Declan? You're afraid of loving someone so much, so deeply, that you lose yourself. That you become your mother. And there's nothing I could say... Not that I would never betray you, never do anything that would demean you rather than support you. Not that I might very well hurt you, but I would hope my love would pave the way for forgiveness, that you would see it wouldn't be intentional. True love only makes you stronger, better. You could never lose yourself in it. Because it would never allow you to become lost."

She spread her hands wide on her crossed legs, staring down at them before lifting her gaze to him. Tears didn't glisten in her eyes, but he almost wished they did. He'd rather have the tears than the bottomless, hard resolve he saw.

"But there wouldn't be any point in trying to make you believe that, because your heart is closed by fear. I'm scared, too, Declan. Scared to trust, to take a leap of faith on love when it's only disappointed me in the past. But I'm willing to take a risk on you. On us." She shook her head. "What I'm not willing to do is fake it any longer or settle."

Her shoulders straightened, and the deep breath she drew in resounded in the room. That, too, held the ring of finality.

"I love you, Declan. And you need to leave."

"Remi, I'm sorry."

"I know you are. And that makes you refusing to fight for yourself, for who we could be, sadder. Now, if you have any feelings for me, any respect at all, please go."

Stay, dammit. Don't you fucking go.

But he stood, exited the bedroom and her house as she requested.

Like the coward he was.

He drove through the dark quiet streets of Rose Bend, images of the evening bombarding him. Of them laughing and working together at the library. Of their kiss in the car. Making love in her bedroom. Of her eyes, dark with pain and pride, ordering him out.

A while later, he pulled his car to a stop and switched it off. But he didn't sit, parked outside his home.

Opening his car door, he numbly climbed out, rounded the vehicle and climbed the steps to the blue-and-white Victorian with the dark blue shutters. Even before he knocked, the front door swung open and his mother stood in the doorway.

"Declan? What on earth? What's wrong?" she asked, tying her robe belt.

"Mom," he rasped. "I messed up."

CHAPTER SEVEN

"I LOVE YOUR MOTHER," Briana growled, sailing up to Remi with a smile that appeared more like a feral baring of teeth, "but she is seriously working my last living nerve."

Remi hid her grin behind her glass of wine, sending up a prayer, not for the first time, that she'd found a safe corner out of the path of Hurricane Rochelle. The whole week before the engagement party, their mother had been driving all of them nuts with the preparations. And today, with guests crowded into their home, enjoying the hors d'oeuvres and sipping a variety of beverages and celebrating the happy couple, Rochelle hadn't calmed down yet. After being ordered twice to circle the room with the appetizers, then told she wasn't doing it right, then being barred from the kitchen, Remi had been trying to fly under the radar.

"You know she's in her element. Even if she's acting a little batty. She just wants everything to be perfect for you." Remi slipped an arm around Briana's shoulders, hugging her close. "Besides, you have to give it to her. The place looks ah-mazing. The food is great. The guests are enjoying themselves. And you're engaged to a truly great guy."

"Yeah, you're right," Briana grumbled, then chuckled. As if she couldn't help herself, her sister sought out her fiancé, locating him next to the living room fireplace, surrounded by several of his friends. "He's wonderful. And I can't wait to marry him."

"There you go. Just keep that in mind. And avoid Mom, like I'm doing."

Briana laughed, wrapping an arm around Remi's waist and squeezing. But then she sobered, wincing. "God, Remi, I'm so sorry. I wasn't thinking. Are you okay being here with all—" she twirled her hand in the direction of the party "—this? You know I wouldn't have minded if you begged off. I would've understood."

"*I* would've minded, though. And I'm fine. No way I would've missed my sister's engagement party. But thank you."

God, she loved her sister. Both of them. After Declan left her house a week ago, she'd called her sisters. Sherri and Briana had come right over and stayed with her for most of the weekend, holding her while she cried, bingeing Netflix and snacks with her when she didn't. And they'd been running interference with their mother, whose disappointment at her and Declan breaking up had seared her.

But it didn't make her change her mind or call him. She'd made the right decision for herself.

"What are we doing over here in the corner?" Sherri shoved a sun-dried tomato and basil roll-up in her mouth, following it with a healthy sip of champagne. Her older sister, barely five feet and willow thin, could eat her weight in hors d'oeuvres, run roughshod over her adorable three-year-old twins and rule her husband, who worshipped the ground she walked on. "Talking about people? Ditching Doug so he can't leave me with the kids? Avoiding Mom?"

"C," Remi said, taking her sister's glass and sipping.

"Oh, me, too." Sherri scrunched her nose. "And you know I was just kidding about the kids, right?" When Remi and Briana gave her the blandest of bland looks, she sighed.

"*Fine.* Sue me. Doug so owes me for…for sticking his penis in me."

"Wow." Briana slipped the champagne away from their sister with a snicker. "We're going to lay off these until the toast, 'kay?"

"What? No, I—" The doorbell rang, and she clapped her hands, nearly bouncing on the balls of her feet. "That should be the babysitter. She was running late so she offered to pick the twins up from here. Sooo…" She snatched her glass back and took a healthy sip.

"You'd think she didn't get out much," Remi drawled, laughing, but as her mother led the newest guest into the living room, the humor died on her lips. *"Oh God."*

Declan.

Her breath stalled in her lungs, increasing the deafening thud of her heart in her ears, her head. Adrenaline rushed through her, temporarily making her dizzy, and she pressed her palm against the wall, steadying herself.

What was he doing here?

"What is he doing here?" Sherri whispered, echoing the question in Remi's head. "I thought you said he wasn't coming."

Remi had confessed everything to her sisters—the true reason behind The Kiss, the fake relationship, Declan's agreement to be her beard at the engagement party.

"I didn't think he was, either." She couldn't remove her eyes from him. No matter how much her pride begged her to stop making a fool of herself in front of all these people.

She'd been here before, except this scene had taken place in a diner, not at an engagement party. But her romance woes being center stage for the townspeople of Rose Bend again? No. Thank. You.

She straightened, pushing off the wall, and maybe he

sensed her movement, because his gaze scanned the room before unerringly landing on her. It was like crashing into a star—hot, consuming and so close to flaming out.

She froze.

Inside, she longed to flee. Away.

Or straight to him.

"Sweet baby Jesus, Remi, that man is in love with you," Briana breathed.

Remi tore her gaze from Declan and frowned at her younger sister.

"What? What're you talking about, Bri?"

"C'mon, Remi—the man showed up at an engagement party. No man shows up at an engagement party all alone, voluntarily, unless, A, he's the groom or one of the parties involved is family, B, he's being blackmailed, or C, he has an agenda. You, big sis, are his agenda. That man is so in love with you." She leaned forward, jabbing a fingertip in her arm. "But I swear to God, if he proposes to you at my engagement party, I'm tackling him to the ground like J. J. Watt. And then I'll show up at your wedding and announce I'm pregnant. And expecting quadruplets."

Remi stared at her sister, caught between laughing hysterically and being horrified. Because she suspected Briana meant it.

"Remi, can you help me in the kitchen for a moment?" Their mother appeared in front of their trio, smiling brightly, but Remi spied the taut edges.

"Sure."

She followed her mom, pausing to smile at a few guests, putting on a good front, but her belly twisted into knots. Strain rode her shoulders, so by the time they entered the spotless kitchen, where more food platters covered the butcher-block island, her body was rigid with the strain.

"Declan showing up is certainly a surprise," her mother said, leaning back against the edge of the island.

Jumping right into it, are we?

Remi smothered a sigh, wishing she'd stolen Sherri's champagne.

"It is."

Rochelle threw her hands up, huffing out a breath. "Remi, he's here. That means something."

"It could mean a lot of things. The main thing being not wanting to be rude by not showing up." Although, she wondered, too. As of the night she'd kicked him out of her bed, her house, he didn't have an obligation to her anymore. "Mom, don't get your hopes up." She was preaching to the choir. "He's a nice guy, and that's all there is to it. We're done."

"Honey." She shook her head. "Why can't you just put in a little effort? You had a man who actually took an interest in you, and what happened? What did you do?"

Hurt slapped at her, and her head jerked back. "What did *I do*?" she whispered. "Why do you assume it's my fault?"

"Oh stop," Rochelle snapped, slicing a hand through the air. "I'm not assigning blame. I'm just saying I wish you would try harder—"

"And do what?" A calm settled over her. Almost as if she stepped out of her body and gave herself permission to speak, to no longer hold back on every hurt, every wound that she'd paved over with excuses, disregard or laughter. "Talk less, laugh softer. Wear baggier clothes. Lose fifteen pounds. Try harder for Declan or any other man? Or try harder for you, Mom?"

"Remi?" She frowned. "Whatever are you talking about?"

"Maybe at this point you've become so used to criticizing me that you don't notice. And I don't know which is worse—doing it on purpose or being so accustomed to taking my inventory that it has become habit. The problem is, with you, I always come up short. I've never been enough."

"Remi, honey," she whispered, tears glistening in her eyes. "That's not true."

"It is. I don't doubt you love me, Mom. But you have a lousy way of showing it. And if you don't change it, I won't be coming around as much. I can't accept that toxicity in my life anymore. I won't."

She crossed the space separating them, cupped her mother's arms and kissed her cheek.

"I love you, and I love myself. I need you to accept that."

Tears pricked her own eyes and her pulse pounded like a snare drum. She turned and exited the kitchen, moisture blinding her.

"Hey, I got you."

She didn't hesitate. Didn't question. She wrapped her arms around Declan, burying her face against his hard, welcoming chest. And when his arms closed around her, she sighed, relaxed into him. Feeling home.

"Come on, sweetheart," he murmured.

She didn't really pay attention to where he led her, but then the cold air brushed over her face. The backyard. Inhaling a deep breath, she pulled her hand free of his and paced several feet away. His earthy cloves-and-cinnamon scent clung to her nose, and she longed to roll in it, bathe in it. She had to move away, because yes, in a moment of weakness, she'd leaned on him, but she couldn't depend on that. Couldn't depend on him.

"What are you doing here, Declan?"

He studied her for several long moments, his lilac gaze piercing. "You did good, Remi. And I'm damn humbled by you."

She blinked. And blinked again. Stupid tears. Not now. Not in front of him.

"What?"

"I overheard what you said to your mom. That was incredibly brave, and I want to live up to you. Be worthy of that courage." He paused. "I should've never left your house last week. I should've told you no, I wasn't leaving, that I would fight for me, for you. For us."

If she could move, she would've stumbled backward.

Or run to him.

But fear, doubt—hope—kept her frozen.

"You called me out, and I was afraid. *Was*, Remi. I knew as soon as I drove away that I made the hugest mistake of my life. Over the last month you have become my friend, my confidante, my lover, my delight, my...freedom. You've helped me free myself from my past simply by being you. By showing me bravery, hope and faith. I want to take that leap with you, Remi. And I'm sorry that I hurt you, that I might've been one more person to make you doubt how beautiful, special and precious you are. If you can trust me with your heart again, I promise never to break it."

He reached into the inside pocket of his suit jacket and withdrew a folded sheet of paper and extended it to her.

As if her arm moved through water, she reached for that paper, accepted it. Her breath whistled in and out of her parted lips, and she tried to tamp down the hope that seemed determined to rise within her, but it welled too big, too huge.

She unfolded the sheet and scanned it. Once. Twice. After the third time she lifted her gaze to him. That hope she'd tried to stifle soared, and she didn't try to control it. Not when love surged with it.

"You're moving here full-time?" she rasped, the paper trembling in her hand.

"Yes." He moved closer to her, paused, but then eliminated the space between them. His hand rose, hovering next to her cheek, but he didn't touch her. "I'm leasing the building next to Cole Dennison's law firm. Of course, I'll still need to go back to Boston for some meetings, but I can run my business from anywhere. And I choose for it to be here. With you. Because I love you."

She cupped her hand over his, turned her face into it and pressed a kiss to the palm. Then rose on her toes and pressed another to his lips. On a groan, he took her mouth like a man deprived of water, of breath. And she was his oxygen.

God, she knew the feeling.

"Does this mean you're giving me your love again?" he asked, resting his forehead against hers.

She cradled his face between her palms, brushing her thumbs over his cheekbones. Smiling, she brushed a soft kiss to his mouth.

"You never lost it."

* * * * *

"Maybe you could stay." Her voice felt scratchy; she felt scratchy. Her heart was pounding so hard she could barely hear, and the steam filling up the room seemed to swallow her voice.

But she could see Jericho's face. She could see the tightness there. The intensity.

"Honey..."

"No. I just... Maybe this is the time to have a conversation, actually. The one that we decided to have later. Because I'm getting warm. I'm very warm."

"Put your robe back on."

"What if I don't want to?"

"Why not?"

"Because I want you. I already admitted to that. Why do you think I'm so upset? All the time? About all the women that you bring into the winery, about the fact that my father gave it to you. About the fact that we're stuck together, but will never actually be together. And that's why I had to leave. I'm not an idiot, Jericho. I know that you and I are never going to… We're not going to fall in love and get married. We can hardly stand to be in the same room as each other.

"But I have wanted you since I understood what that meant. And I don't know what to do about it. Short of running away and having sex with someone else. That was my game plan. My game plan was to go off and have sex with another man. And that got thwarted. You were the one that picked me up. You're the one that I'm stuck here with in the snow. And I'm not going to claim that it's fate. Because I can feel myself twisting every single element of this except for the weather. The blizzard isn't my fault. But I'm making the choice to go ahead and offer…me."

"I…"

"If you're going to reject me, just don't do it horribly."

And then suddenly she found herself being tugged into his arms, the heat from his body more intense than the heat from the sauna, the roughness of his clothes a shock against her skin. And then his mouth crashed down on hers.

Don't miss what happens next in…
Rancher's Christmas Storm
by New York Times *bestselling author Maisey Yates!*

Available October 2021 wherever
Harlequin Desire books and ebooks are sold.

Harlequin.com

Get 4 FREE REWARDS!

We'll send you 2 FREE Books plus 2 FREE Mystery Gifts.

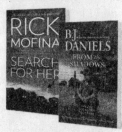

FREE
Value Over
$20

Both the **Romance** and **Suspense** collections feature compelling novels written by many of today's bestselling authors.